BLAZE

A Small Town, Nerdy Girl, Opposites Attract, Protector Romance

Ghost Ops
Book 1

LYNN RAYE HARRIS

H.O.T. Publishing, LLC

*For Joyce Webster and Elizabeth Harris
You left us too soon. My heart hurts that I won't get to talk horses
with you both or spend an afternoon at the barn in your company. We
had great times, didn't we?*

Prologue

"Got a job for you, gentlemen."

Alex "Ghost" Bishop eyed the five men he'd hand-picked for this mission.

"But you'll have to take risks you've never taken before. Get it right, nobody's going to know except those of us in this room. Get it wrong, millions of people could die."

Blaze "Shadow" Connolly, Chance "Wraith" Hughes, Seth "Phantom" King, Kane "Demon" Fox, and Ethan "Dragon" Snow didn't blink. He hadn't expected they would. They were the best of the best. Hostile Operations Team to their cores. Men he'd worked with on some of the shittiest missions imaginable.

They'd had his back and he'd had theirs. He'd been given a blank slate when selecting his team for this operation, and he'd chosen men he knew he could rely on. Men who fit the special requirements.

Patriotic. Moral. Willing to sacrifice themselves for the greater good.

That described all of HOT.

But there was more.

No strong family ties. No connections. No wives or children to worry about.

"What's the job?" Shadow asked.

"I'm getting there. But first you gotta understand something. Get caught, and you'll be cut loose. You'll proceed through the criminal justice system. If you're convicted of a felony, you'll lose any military benefits you might possess. This job isn't going to be easy, but it will be worthwhile. Nothing less than the future of this nation is at stake."

"Not hearing anything to make me say no," Wraith drawled. "What's the catch?"

The other guys laughed. Ghost grinned. He loved these guys. They'd all been on the same squad back when he'd still been leading missions. That was a few years ago, but their first time as a unit hadn't gone smoothly. They'd gone into enemy territory for a hostage rescue. Misinformation had nearly tanked the mission and gotten them killed, but they'd found the hostages and gotten them out. That was due in no small part to the well-oiled machine these guys made when operating together.

"This mission is Ghost Ops, gentlemen, and not just because I'm running it. We *are* ghosts. We're doing this job silently and secretly, without sanction or official support. Our orders come from the president, but we can't be associated with her office if anything goes wrong. If this is not for you, I need to know now. Because if you don't say anything, you're a part of this. There's no turning back, no quitting in a month or two. Once I've revealed our objective, you're locked. This is your shot to walk."

The men exchanged looks. Shadow crossed his arms. Phantom crossed his legs. Demon whistled a soft tune. Dragon and Wraith merely looked at him.

He could hear their curiosity, but none of them voiced

it yet. They understood the consequences. Stay in this room and you're in no matter what. There were no do-overs. No take-backs.

He nodded when it was clear nobody was leaving. "You were picked for a couple of reasons. First, you're my team. We know each other. We've saved each other's asses. And though our paths led in opposite directions at times, we're here now. Second, and this is a shit thing to say, but you've got no family, no wives or kids, and no messy relationships to navigate. Same for me. We don't have to explain, don't have to leave anyone behind. We're free to move, and free to suffer the consequences if things go wrong without dragging loved ones into it."

Their faces were a little harder now, but he had to say it. They had to know it was important.

It wasn't that special operators didn't have families, because they did. But this team wasn't going to be the norm. The mission, their cover; everything about it was a potential minefield.

It was simpler not to have people waiting at home for them.

No hard questions being asked. No families to worry over or explain to, especially if something went wrong.

"You said *we're* ghosts," Shadow stated, looking at the other guys. "Am I wrong, or does it sound like you're going along?"

"I am."

He let them exchange bewildered looks before he spoke again.

"If you look behind you, you'll find envelopes with your names on the table by the door. We're separating from the military, effective immediately. You're officially civilians now, friends, though if this ends well, you'll have full military benefits and the shot to go back on active duty if you want it. For now, we're just a bunch of former Army guys about to open a training facility with a range and gun store in Alabama. We'll be there for some duration, hence the cover."

"Always wanted to open a range," Shadow said. "Sounds fun."

The other guys nodded their agreement.

"Why Alabama, sir?" Demon asked, his brow wrinkled in confusion.

"It's Alex now, Kane. We'll need to get used to calling each other by our names instead of call signs. Ranks don't exist. I'm no longer a colonel."

He studied them. Blaze, Chance, Seth, Kane, and Ethan. They were wondering what they'd gotten themselves into by now.

But he knew, even if he gave them a way out, they wouldn't take it. That's not how men like these were wired.

It's not how *he* was wired.

"We're going to Alabama because that's where we've been asked to go. Huntsville is home to a top-secret project vital to our national security. Unfortunately, our nation's enemies are aware of the project and actively trying to sabotage it. Our mission is to protect it, find the spies, and make sure development stays on schedule. The president trusts HOT to get this done. Not the FBI, not Homeland Security. Us."

He eyed them. "You'll keep your identity, but your military records will be sealed, your DNA wiped from the system. Nobody will have access to anything we've done. You weren't spec ops, you weren't elite soldiers. You were regular Army grunts who served your time in a combat unit and were honorably discharged. We're friends who served together, and we've finally decided to follow our dream and open a range and training facility. We chose northern Alabama because property is cheaper than Virginia or Maryland, and we like our prospects there."

Seth slapped the envelope he'd retrieved against his leg. "Good enough for me."

"Amen," Kane said. "President Willis chose right when she chose us."

"Y'all best get to working on your Southern accents," Chance drawled with his finest Mississippi vowels. "Might stand out a bit if you don't."

"And we'll stand out even worse if we try to fake it," Ethan grumbled, New York state coming through in his words. "Do they even *have* good pizza down there?"

Blaze laughed. "Always thinking with your stomach. Man, they got barbecue. Pulled pork, chicken with white sauce. I had to go to Anniston once, and that was some of the best damned barbecue I ever had. You'll be fine, promise."

Ghost loved their banter, loved that they could fall right into the unknown without fear. That was another reason he'd picked them.

"What's the timeline?" Ethan asked.

Ethan was the planner, the one who'd always mapped out the mission down to the second.

"Four weeks until we meet up in Alabama. Details are in the envelopes."

Blaze got to his feet. "Guess I'd better get to packing then."

The rest of the guys stood too. Ghost walked over and shook their hands.

"Whatever we need to do to protect this country, we got this," Chance said.

"I know you do. So does the president and her closest advisors. It's why you're standing in this room instead of anyone else."

When the men were gone, Ghost looked around the briefing room, taking it in one last time. He'd thought he'd take command of the Hostile Operations Team one day when General John "Viper" Mendez retired.

Instead, he was hanging up his hat. The others had a shot to rejoin the military if the mission was successful, but it wasn't a possibility for him. There was a new deputy commander waiting in the wings. Ghost couldn't step out of the stream for this mission and step back in like the water hadn't moved on without him.

It was different for the team guys. They could return to operations like nothing had changed. Not so for him.

Maybe he could join Ian Black's organization, or he could start his own security firm.

Then again, he could collect his military pension, buy a small house somewhere, and go fishing all day. Forget how to spell colonel, much less salute anyone or take orders.

Decisions for another time.

For now, he was heading to Alabama.

Dead to his past. A ghost. No family and no connections. Nothing but his guys and the biggest mission of his life.

Chapter One

Blaze knew something was wrong the instant he walked into the gas station.

It was too quiet.

A woman he didn't recognize stood frozen against the wall that housed the soda machine and coffee pots, eyes wide as they darted between Blaze and a tall, thin man in a hoodie and face mask. He was leaning across the counter where patrons bought snacks and paid for gas when the pumps weren't taking credit cards.

Well, fuck.

Blaze had been in Alabama for the past month and a half, working with his team to create One Shot Tactical in warehouses on an old farm, and he stopped at this gas station at least four times a week for a pulled pork sandwich. One of the amazing things about Alabama was that some of the best 'cue in the state was found in Mom & Pop gas stations.

Clarence had a stick burner out back and kept it fed with hickory. He smoked pork, ribs, and the occasional brisket, and sold them with the sides his wife made fresh every day.

Blaze had really been hankering for some mac and cheese with his sandwich today. Looked like he wasn't getting it. Not without some effort.

He didn't see Clarence, but June made her sides at home and Clarence went to pick things up a couple times a day if she was still busy cooking and couldn't leave the kitchen. It was only a ten-minute trip, and the station was never so slammed that whoever was there couldn't handle the load.

The man pointed a weapon at Blaze. Black. Nine mil. Looked like a Taurus, maybe a G2C. A decent gun, but not the best on the market. Cheap as guns went, which might explain why this waste of skin had one.

"Hands up, asshole!"

Blaze lifted his hands slowly. "Hey, man. Just wanted a sandwich. Not looking for trouble."

The man jerked the gun in the woman's direction. "Get over there with her."

Behind the counter, the teenage clerk had a look of numb shock on her face as she took money from the register with shaking hands. Blaze recognized her as the daughter of one of their regulars at the range. Poor kid was terrified. A quiet current of rage reared inside his gut.

He fucking hated criminals. Hated anyone who terrorized innocent people. It'd been his job to take those kinds of people down for years. Still was, even if the setting was different.

"I'm going." He edged toward the woman. "You haven't committed a serious crime yet. You can fix this. Put the gun down, don't take the money. This can be over with nobody getting hurt."

"Shut the fuck up, old man."

"Aw, dude, that hurts. I'm thirty-eight. Not that old. How about you?"

"Shut up or I'll kill you." He glanced at the cashier. "Keep filling the bag and hand it over."

Blaze eased into place beside the woman. She had brown hair pulled back in a ponytail, and pretty features beneath her glasses. Her eyes were blue, which was probably why she'd chosen blue-tinted frames. Those eyes were currently wide as she stared at the gunman.

Blaze did the math. He could make it to the guy's side in three strides. Disarm him. Put the fucker on the ground.

The whole thing would take two seconds, tops. It was as simple as breathing.

He could do it with his eyes closed because it was so routine. His muscles tightened as he prepared to strike. But something banged in the back room, and Clarence called out, "Britney, can you come help me with these trays?"

The man swung the gun toward the stockroom as Clarence emerged.

Everything happened at once. The pistol boomed, Britney screamed, and Clarence dropped to the floor, food exploding all over the place. Blaze was already in motion as the man tried to turn the gun on him.

He knocked the assailant's arm up, the gun boomed again, and then Blaze was holding the weapon, pointing it at the wide-eyed man on the floor. The man wheezed as he tried to catch his breath. Blaze didn't give a fuck. He'd swept the guy's legs from beneath him and dropped him to the concrete like the sack of shit he was.

Blaze reached down to rip off the mask and toss it aside. Hell, he wasn't much more than a kid, maybe twenty years old. He had the shadowed look of a drug addict.

A look Blaze understood all too well.

"You motherfucker," he growled. "Bad day to piss me off. If you've hurt Clarence, I swear to God you're going to meet your maker in the next few seconds."

The dark-haired woman sprinted past them and around the counter to where Clarence lay on the floor. Blaze couldn't see what was going on, but he was surprised she went to help instead of sinking to the floor in relief or falling apart the way Britney was currently doing. That's what most people did.

Blaze ejected the magazine from the pistol, cleared the chamber, and dropped it on the counter. Then he flipped the kid over and zip-tied his wrists behind his back with the ties he still had in his jacket from the training course they'd given at One Shot earlier in the day. He pulled out another pair and tied the kid's legs.

"What's going on over there?" He left the kid on the floor and went over to the counter, his heart hammering in his chest. Not from dealing with the gunman, but from fear for Clarence.

The woman knelt on the floor beside the old man, feeling along his chest and arms. Clarence blinked up at her in shock. Macaroni and cheese coated the floor in yellow globs. It'd also sprayed the walls and half of Clarence's body. Blaze didn't see any blood, but that didn't mean it wasn't there.

"Let me check him." Blaze said as he dropped to the floor beside her. "I'm a trained medic."

All special operators were trained in field medicine, which meant he could patch people up long enough to get them to a real doctor if he had to.

"He's fine," she said coolly. "The bullet missed him

entirely. But he hit his head when he fell, and he'll need some tests. I'll call 911."

"I'll check anyway."

"Suit yourself." She gave Clarence a pat on the arm before she took her jacket off and pushed it beneath his head. "It's going to be fine, Clarence. Promise."

She stood to grab the phone on the counter. "Yes, hello. This is Doctor Emma Sutton. I need an ambulance at the Gas-n-Go over on Highway 127. There's been an attempted robbery, and two gunshots were fired. No one was hit, but there's a seventy-year-old male with a possible head injury. The attacker is subdued. If you could please send the police... Yes, thank you. I'll be here."

Blaze finished his examination. "You could have said you were a doctor."

She put the phone on the counter and hugged her arms around herself. He could see her fighting the shock of everything that had happened. She might be a doctor, but she probably didn't find herself on the business end of a robbery every day.

"Yes, well, you seemed determined. You okay, honey?" she asked the teenager.

Britney sniffed. "Yes. My ears are ringing though."

"I think we're all experiencing that, sweetie. Those shots were very loud. It'll be better in a few minutes."

Blaze stood and examined the area. The bullet had gone clean through the wall near the door jamb. Thank God the guy wasn't any good at hitting what he targeted, or Clarence wouldn't be alive.

Emma glanced at the gun on the counter. "How did you do that?"

"Do what?"

"You disarmed him so fast I didn't see what you did."

"I spent a few years in the Army. Learned a thing or two."

He'd been a Delta Force operator before he'd joined the Hostile Operations Team. He'd more than learned a thing or two, but it wasn't the kind of thing he talked about with most people. Even before he'd been ordered not to.

"That's where you trained as a medic?"

"Yes." He didn't say more because that would likely open up a whole new spate of questions.

"Well, thank you for your service and for what you just did. I think he would have shot us all before he was through." She still hugged herself, and he knew she was thinking about what could have happened.

"You're welcome. Emma Sutton... You related to Doc Sutton?" He hoped to pull her attention from the grim possibilities, get her thinking about something else.

She nodded. "He's my dad."

"Blaze Connolly." He held out a hand. "I'm renting one of the apartments over your dad's office."

She seemed to hesitate a second, then slipped her hand into his. Her skin was warm, soft, and a current of interest percolated inside him. Surprised him. She wasn't what he usually went for. He liked a girly girl with painted nails, long silky hair, and hips he could grab onto while he rocked deep inside her body.

Emma Sutton was pretty in a nerdy way, not a sexy way.

"Nice to meet you." She dropped his hand like it stung, then tucked hers against her side again.

Not the reaction he'd expected after the one he'd felt in response to her. Then again, maybe he didn't know shit anymore. Maybe his instincts were fucked up beyond repair. If they were better, he'd have stopped the gunman before the first shot was fired. Before Clarence walked into the middle of an ambush.

Blaze swallowed, clenching and unclenching his left fist at his side. Grounding himself.

Clarence hadn't walked into an ambush. This wasn't Afghanistan. He wasn't operating in the high desert with his team.

What happened here had nothing to do with there. The kid had been startled when Clarence walked in, and he'd fired. Wildly, thank heavens. Then Blaze did what he was trained to do and stopped the bad guy.

Nobody was bleeding out on the desert floor while he frantically called for air support. He wasn't going to lose anybody today.

"Are you okay?" Emma asked. "Did you strain yourself disarming him?"

It took him a full three seconds before indignation roared to life and drowned out the memories. Maybe thirty-eight felt like forty-eight some mornings, but damn, did he look like he was ready for the grave?

"I'm in peak physical condition. I didn't strain anything."

She dropped her gaze to his fist. "I was just wondering."

"Nothing to wonder."

Sirens shattered the air as emergency crews hurtled toward the gas station. Blaze dug into his pocket for his pistol permit and took his weapon from the holster at his back. He ejected the magazine and placed everything on the counter, added the knife from his boot, then stepped away so the cops would know he was carrying and licensed.

A line had formed on Emma's forehead as she stared at him. Before he could ask her what the problem was, cars skidded into the parking lot, sirens cut off mid-scream, and cops boiled through the door.

Chapter Two

"You okay?"

Emma dragged her gaze from the retreating ambulance to the man who'd walked up beside her. His voice was like whiskey, smooth and rough in all the right places. She didn't want to notice, but it was impossible not to.

"Fine. Thank you."

"Good. You hungry? I was after one of Clarence's sandwiches when that went down." He put a hand over his belly. His very flat belly, she noted. "Gonna have to find something else now, I guess."

She turned back to the view across the field. The sun was sinking behind the horizon, turning the sky pink and purple, and the chill in the air was more pronounced than it had been earlier. Late February in northern Alabama could go either way. Freezing cold or balmy. Today was one of the cold days. She'd retrieved another jacket from her car earlier, so she wasn't cold, but she would be if she stayed out here much longer.

Blaze Connolly watched her expectantly. She didn't have to look at him to know it was true. He was tall, broad, with muscles that were packing muscles, and he made parts of her tingle that definitely shouldn't be tingling. His dark hair was a little shaggy, and he had a couple of days' worth of scruff on his face. His eyes were blue. Not the blue of denim, but more like a cloudless Alabama sky on a hot summer day.

Emma shook herself. She had no use for men these days. She'd barely escaped the last one. He was the reason she'd tucked her tail and run away to Alabama instead of staying in Chicago and working hard to advance in the ER. Her dreams of a big city career were shattered. She could thank herself for that.

"Thank you, but no." She was still a polite Southern girl to her core. Her mama would have been bitterly disappointed if she wasn't. "It's been a long day. I just want to crash."

"Got it. You did good in there, you know." He shoved his hands in his pockets. "Maybe you don't need me to say this, but a lot of people wouldn't handle it well. You kept your head and helped Clarence."

"It's my job." She bit her lip, emotions spinning inside her belly, her heart. She'd lost everything she'd ever wanted when she'd walked away. Now she was here, planning to take over her dad's practice and be a small-town doctor for the rest of her life. The very thing she'd never intended to do. "I did ER shifts at my hospital in Chicago for four years. I've seen gunshot wounds, Mr. Connolly. I wonder if you have, or if you sat behind a desk during your time in the Army. I understand that many military jobs are like that."

And that little speech right there was something her mama would *not* approve of. He'd pretty much saved her life—all their lives—and she couldn't be nice? What was wrong with her?

His eyes were hot. "I've seen more than I cared to. I didn't sit behind a desk. And it's Blaze."

Emma dragged in a breath. Why was she being rude? He wasn't to blame for her choices any more than she was to blame for his.

"That's an interesting name. B-l-a-i-s-e?"

"Family name. And no, my mom wasn't that subtle. It's Blaze with a *z* and no *i*. Like a fire."

Like a fire. She could believe it if the heat rolling off him was any indication. Or maybe it was her embarrassment for the outburst.

"I'm sorry for being so rude, Mr.—Blaze. I've driven over twelve hours today, and when I stopped to grab some of my favorite barbecue, I found myself in the midst of a robbery. My first one, I should add."

He arched a brow. "So you *are* hungry. I love Clarence's pulled pork sandwiches. Add some slaw and a side of Miss June's mac & cheese, and life is perfect."

She couldn't help but smile. "That's true, it is. And you caught me."

He held up both hands. "It's okay. I can take a hint. No is an acceptable answer, Doc." He hitched his thumb toward the black pickup sitting beside her BMW. "I'm heading out. But I can't go until I make sure you're safe inside your car."

Her heart squeezed a fraction. In another life, she'd probably tell him she was fine. But since Simon, she didn't believe it was true. She held her hand out again, determined to end this encounter on the proper note.

"It was nice to meet you. I'm sure I'll see you around."

He took her hand in his, and a jolt shuddered through

her. She focused on the way his skin felt against hers. Smooth, warm, safe.

Safe?

That definitely couldn't be right. Men weren't safe. And a man like this who'd moved fast and sure against a gunman with nothing but his bare hands even though he'd had a gun and a knife tucked away on his body?

Definitely not safe or tame. Best to steer clear.

"I'm sure you will," he said.

She wanted to stand there with her hand in his and hold on to the safe feeling. But it was an illusion. There was no safety for her. She wasn't sure there ever would be.

He let go first, and she found herself staring at him, unable to speak.

"It's normal."

His voice was soft, and Emma jerked to attention. "I'm sorry?"

"That feeling you have. The fear of what might have happened. The shock of the violence. It's normal. It'll fade, but if it doesn't, don't wait to get help." He shook his head. "But you're a doctor. You already know that."

"Yes. But thank you." She hooked a thumb over her shoulder. "I should go."

"See you, Doc."

She didn't know what to say, so she nodded. Then she hurried over to her car and climbed inside, her heart pounding. When she drove away, Blaze was still watching her.

Chapter Three

EMMA DROVE INTO TOWN, SKIRTING THROUGH THE SQUARE where her dad's office was located—and where Blaze Connolly lived in one of the apartments above the practice. She didn't need to drive through the center of town to get to the historic district where her parents lived, but the closer she got to reaching the end of the journey, the tougher it was.

She'd stopped at the Gas-n-Go to give herself more time before she had to face her parents. Her mother would have cooked a big pot of soup or stew, but Emma had wanted pulled pork. She'd had a hankering. They didn't have real barbecue in Chicago, at least not to her. Sure, there were people all over this country who worshipped at the altar of smoked meat these days, knew how to cook low and slow, and put their own spin on the food they made.

But there was nothing in this world like a little BBQ shack tucked away in a gas station on a rural Alabama road. She'd been craving it since she'd crossed into Tennessee earlier in the day.

Last thing she'd expected was to find herself in the

center of a robbery. If Blaze Connolly hadn't shown up, she didn't know what would have happened. Maybe the robber would have succeeded in shooting them all before he took off with his bag of cash.

Emma slowed the car to a crawl as she drove past the Salty Dawg Tavern. Her bestie was part-owner these days. She and Aurora Harper had been best friends since they were in Sunday School together as three-year-olds. Maybe even earlier than that, come to think of it, but her first memory of Rory was when they were cast as shepherds in the Nativity play and Rory kept waving her shepherd's crook around like it was a sword.

The adults had howled as the play went sideways. Rory kept waving, and Emma joined her. So did Rory's brother, Theo, who was two years older and maybe should have known better.

These days, Theo owned the other half of the Dawg and ran it with Rory. They'd been close as kids and still were.

Emma's fingers tightened on the steering wheel. She'd been a bad friend the past four years. She'd tried to keep in regular touch with Rory, but the ER had been hectic. Their daily calls and texts had dwindled to monthly texts by then. The rare occasions when they talked, Rory acted like everything was fine and she was happy they were connecting, but Emma still felt remorse for not being a bigger part of her friend's life during those years.

They'd been texting again since Emma had decided to come home, and it was like they'd never stopped. Tomorrow, she'd go see Rory at the farmhouse she'd inherited from her grandparents. Theo lived over the tavern because he preferred it, and Rory had the house and worked on renovating it in her spare time.

Emma couldn't wait to see it. But first she had to face her parents. Her heart squeezed with fresh guilt.

There was nothing bad about seeing any of the people she loved. It was her.

Her guilt for staying away while she worked on her career, for wanting to. Her shame for what had happened to her.

None of them knew about Simon.

When the relationship was new, she'd wanted to keep it to herself, not get her mother's hopes up that she was going to get married and start producing grandchildren. Not until she knew if it was going somewhere first.

She hadn't told them about him when things went wrong, either. Because she was ashamed. How could she tell them what had happened? That she wasn't as smart as she'd thought she was, that she was actually a failure? That she'd let a man control her, abuse her?

"Stop putting it off," she muttered as she circled the square, looking at the buildings and shops she'd known most of her life as if they were brand new and worthy of study.

She thought of Blaze Connolly leaping into the fray, disarming the robber, and preventing him from killing anyone. He hadn't hesitated. He'd just *acted*.

Sometimes, that's what you had to do. Rip off the bandage and get it over with.

Emma pointed the car west and left the square behind. The Sutton's Creek historic district was filled with homes that'd been built pre- and post-Civil War, as well as homes from the early to mid-1900s. Designating the area a historic district had brought federal funding and tourist dollars to the town. It had also brought new residents who snapped up the homes when they went on the market.

Emma figured these days Sutton's Creek was about half longtime residents and half new folks who'd moved in to take jobs in the booming Huntsville job market.

Emma pulled into the driveway, shut off the car, and climbed out to stand on the cobblestones. The motion light over the back door had clicked on when she drove up, and the door opened to emit a furry bullet of a dog who barked her head off as she ran toward Emma.

"It's me, Coco," she said, dropping to her haunches. Coco, who was a toy poodle and not in the least bit scary, started to dance on her hind legs around Emma, waving her little front paws as she did so. It filled Emma with happiness to be greeted so enthusiastically. Coco had been a puppy when Emma went off to college, but the dog hadn't forgotten, no matter how long it had been between visits.

"She's happy you're home. So are we."

Emma scooped Coco up with one arm and stood. "Hi, Mama."

Tears pricked her eyes at the sight of the woman standing on the back steps. Ellen Sutton's blond hair was perfectly coifed and curled up at the ends where it hit her shoulders. A yellow headband perched artfully on her head, and her dress looked like something out of the 1950s. Mama loved shirt dresses and always looked fabulous in them. She didn't look like a woman who'd had a heart attack and emergency bypass a year ago.

"Hi, baby. We were starting to wonder if you'd make it home tonight. Did you run into traffic?"

"Emma Grace." John Sutton's voice boomed as he emerged from the house with his arms wide. "You're here."

"Hi, Daddy."

It felt good when she met her dad on the cobbles, and

he wrapped his arms around her and Coco both. Coco squirmed happily, and Emma's insides did the same.

She'd been running away from home for years, wanting more than small town life, but home was still here. Still waiting for her with open arms.

Her dad squeezed her, then let go and announced he'd get her suitcases while she went inside with her mother. Emma put Coco down and helped, mostly because she had all her belongings crammed in the car and she didn't want him emptying the whole thing out.

Once inside, her mother asked if she was hungry. She had to admit she was. When she perched at the kitchen island with a bowl of chicken stew and a biscuit, she told her parents about the robbery.

"Oh my goodness," her mother said, pressing her hand against her collarbone and the string of pearls she wore.

What Southerners called a pearl pressing moment, which was a little different from pearl clutching.

"Emma Grace, that's awful! Is Clarence okay? And that poor little Britney. She's just a kid! Who was it? Do you know? Probably someone who came over here from Decatur or Huntsville, thinking he could take the money and nobody would catch him."

"I didn't recognize him. Clarence fell pretty hard, but he should be fine. The ambulance was taking him to Huntsville for tests, and June was going to meet him there. Her neighbor was coming over to clean up the kitchen and put things away. Blaze and I cleaned up the mac & cheese and put the food in the walk-in."

Her dad looked stern. "I'm glad you had a man like Blaze there. He's renting one of the apartments in the building."

"He told me."

"I've had nothing but a good impression of him and the men he works with. Former military, hard workers. They opened a training facility with a range and gun store on the old Jackson farm. Converted the warehouses out there, brought in some shipping containers for ammunition storage, and created an outdoor range too. It's a top-notch facility."

Emma didn't like guns. She'd seen too much of what they did to human bodies in Chicago. And though she'd been terrified when the robber pointed the gun at her, it wasn't the first time she'd been on the wrong end of a weapon. A shiver rolled through her. "Do we need another range around here? And what kind of training facility are they running?"

Her dad laughed. "You'd think not, but the closest one before One Shot Tactical opened was over on County Line Road in Madison. I think they're doing courses for corporate groups. Security training, that kind of thing. They also offer self-defense classes."

"I'm thinking of signing up for one," her mother said primly.

Emma's jaw dropped. She tried to picture her mother in her swingy skirts and heels with her pearls and headband, taking self-defense lessons. It did not compute. Not that she thought it was a bad idea, though. She didn't personally approve of guns, but she approved of self-defense.

"It's a good idea," her dad said. "For everyone."

Emma spooned up some stew. "If the rest of them know how to do what Blaze did today, then you'll be well-equipped to protect yourself. He moved so fast I still don't know what he did. But one second the guy was pointing the gun and the next he was on the floor and Blaze had it."

Her dad blew out a steady breath. "I can't tell you how glad I am he was there."

"Me too."

Her mother slid a look toward her dad before reaching across to grip Emma's wrist.

"Honey, I know you just got here, but I want you to know that your father and I realize you don't want to live with us, though you are more than welcome to. Nothing would make me happier than to have my baby girl home with me. But we've been talking about it, and we thought maybe you'd like to take the other apartment in the building. The previous tenant moved out last month, and we haven't asked Phil to advertise it yet. We were waiting until the third-floor apartments were finished."

"But if you don't want to live above the practice," her dad said, shooting a look at her mother, "we understand that too. It might be hard to feel like you've left work behind if you're just upstairs."

Emma's gaze bounced between them. Her mother looked hopeful, and her dad frowned, though he didn't look upset. "Are you trying to set me up with Blaze Connolly, Mother?"

Ellen pressed her pearls again. "What? Child, no. I just thought you'd want to be in your own place, near your friends, with Sutton's Creek nightlife so close by. And when you mentioned Blaze again, I thought of it. That's all. But you have to admit he's very attractive."

Her dad snorted.

"Not my type, Mama. Also, the nightlife in town consists of the Dawg, and that's less than five minutes from where we're standing right this second. But yes, I'll take the apartment. For now."

Her mother shot her dad a knowing smile. "I thought you might."

Her dad shook his head as he reached over to pat her shoulder. "You know your mother thinks you work too hard and need to find a man, but I'm just fine if you want to stay single. Or maybe it's another woman you're looking for? Which is also fine with us, I should add."

Emma's face flamed. *Lord, save her from meddling parents.*

She was thirty-four years old, and they still acted like she was fifteen at times.

"I'm not looking for a man *or* a woman." She forced a bright smile. "I'm going to have enough to do learning to run the clinic. I don't need anything distracting me. Or anyone."

"Well." Her mother busied herself spooning more stew into Emma's bowl, though Emma had barely put a dent in it. "If that's the way you want it, sweetheart. I'm sure there are plenty of other men around if someone snaps up that handsome Mr. Connolly."

"Five more of them at the range, Ellen."

Emma didn't miss the smirk on her dad's face, or the wink he sent her way. At least *one* parent had her back.

"Thanks, Dad. I'll keep that in mind."

Chapter Four

"Okay, give it your best shot," Blaze said. "Come at me."

The man facing him squared his shoulders. He was as big as a tank, impressively muscled like he spent a lot of time at the gym. Confident. Too confident if the way his buddies all smirked at Blaze was any indication. They thought he was going down in the next three seconds.

Amateurs.

The man shifted the baseball bat from one hand to the other. He glanced at his friends and grinned.

"Today," Blaze said. "I've got things to do."

Dudes like him had too much confidence in their ability. Just because the guy lifted didn't mean he knew how to block a punch or deflect an attack. But since he was the biggest man in their office, they'd chosen him to go first. His workmates stood to the side of the mats, waiting for the show, egging Big Guy on.

Blaze could have taken him out already, like when the guy took his eyes off Blaze to smirk with his buddies, but he hadn't. He'd wanted to give the guy false confidence.

This session was part of One Shot Tactical's corporate training program. It was not only a team bonding exercise, but also had real world applications as they showed people how to disarm an attacker.

Finally, the dude swung the bat. Blaze stepped into the guy's space, not out of it, and took the bat away before it connected. But Big Guy wasn't done yet. He aimed a kick at Blaze's knee.

"Aw, man, bad move," Blaze said as he grabbed Big Guy's heel and jerked him off his feet. Then he stepped into Big Guy's space and wedged the bat beneath his chin.

"Holy shit," someone murmured.

"Whoa."

"That was cool, man!"

Blaze stepped back and offered Big Guy a hand. He took it, and Blaze helped him up.

"I didn't see it coming." He shook his head. "That was badass."

"Thanks for being part of the demonstration," Blaze said. "And for being cool about it."

"Gotta admit, my pride is a bit dinged, but I'm not so stupid as to let that get in the way of learning how you did it."

"Good man." Blaze gave him a nod of respect. "That's exactly the right attitude to have. You guys ready to start some training?"

There was a chorus of "Hell yeah! Let's do this."

After the group was gone, Blaze rolled his shoulders to loosen them and went to the office where Chance, Seth, Ethan, Kane, and Ghost—no matter how Blaze tried, he couldn't think of the man as anything but Ghost—were gathered. Blaze grabbed a water and leaned against a table, crossing his feet at the ankles.

Chance grinned. "Man, saw you take down the big guy. His buddies were sure he was about to knock your head off."

Blaze snorted. "In his dreams. How'd it go at the range?"

They had an indoor and outdoor range, but outdoor didn't get much traffic yet. Too chilly for now.

"Guy trying to impress his girlfriend with a damned Desert Eagle," Chance said. "He one-handed it and about knocked himself unconscious. Before y'all say anything, I told him not to. He did it when I went to help Mrs. Snead clear a jam in her Walther."

"That must have been the guy that peeled out of here," Ghost murmured.

Chance nodded. "That's the one. He was pissed when I kicked him out. The girl was apologetic."

They discussed a bit more of what had happened at the facility that day and agreed on the need to hire a receptionist to staff the front desk and take care of booking classes. Right now, they took turns doing it. Not the best use of anyone's time the busier they got.

"I'll start looking," Ghost said. He waited a beat before continuing. "Let's adjourn to the SCIF. Need to talk."

They had a state-of-the-art Sensitive Compartmented Information Facility, built specifically for this mission, made out of a shipping container and brought to the site intact.

Nobody was allowed inside except the Ghost Ops team. They'd built walls and a roof around it, so it looked like part of the building. It was accessed through a door that led into a small hallway. At the end was the secure door for the SCIF.

Nobody would know it was there from the outside.

Anyone who discovered it from the inside, like a receptionist, would think it was storage since they wouldn't be able to get inside.

There were other containers on-site, not enclosed, where they stored ammunition and weapons as well as supplies for the range.

They followed Ghost into the SCIF and shut the door. Everyone took a seat at the conference table as Ghost fixed them with a look.

"Had a call from Washington today. We have orders."

A thrill of *hell yes* went collectively through the group. It'd been a long month and a half while they'd gotten things set up and running. The mission timeline was months, and Blaze had felt that ticking clock in the back of his head.

He was itching for action. They all were.

They hadn't been briefed on the scope of the top-secret project, but there was nothing unusual in that. They'd gone on plenty of missions during their careers, to protect or capture objectives, without knowing precisely what it was for.

"What's the target, boss?" Ethan asked.

"Royal Shipping. They have a warehouse over near the airport. They send and receive secure shipments for the government, among others. We need to go in and set up surveillance equipment. Watch the place, get a map of their movements and security. Watch what comes and goes, see if it processes through proper channels."

"That's it?" Blaze asked. Sending the six of them to set up surveillance was like using a cannon to go deer hunting. It was overkill.

Ghost took the toothpick he'd been chewing from his

mouth and tossed it in the trash. "For now. Remember, this mission is months, boys. Not weeks."

Nobody said anything for a long moment.

Blaze spoke first. "You've never steered us wrong. Best team leader I ever had. I trust your instincts. You agreed to this, and you handpicked the five of us to join you. That means something."

"Damn straight," Chance said.

Ghost nodded. "Appreciate it."

"Teaching ladies how to shoot isn't so bad," Kane said. "I'm liking this civilian gig, 'specially when I already got a date out of it."

"You sure that's a good idea?" Blaze asked with a laugh.

Kane shot him a puzzled look. "Why wouldn't it be?"

"Man, never date a woman you're teaching to shoot," Ethan said. "Rule number one of several."

"I don't see why not. Not all of us get to be Chuck Norris at the gas station like Shadow. Some of us gotta pick up chicks the normal way."

"I didn't pick up any chicks at the gas station. I tried, but she wasn't impressed."

Understatement. Emma Sutton had very clearly not enjoyed his company. She was polite, after being rude and apologizing, but that was the extent of it.

"I can't believe I gotta say this," Ethan said, "but the reason is that if you piss her off, she's liable to shoot your ass."

Everyone laughed. Kane did not.

"Ain't no little mama shooting my ass. I make the ladies happy, not mad."

"Until you give them the *sorry this isn't working, baby* speech," Ghost said. "Think Ethan's got a point."

It was almost comical to watch the way the truth of what they were saying sank in.

Kane looked like he'd swallowed a lemon. "Well, fuck. Didn't think that far ahead. I'm not used to teaching civilians how to shoot. 'Specially hot ones."

"Guess not." Ghost leaned back in his chair and tossed the pen he'd been playing with on the table. "Need an action plan, fellas. Get to work studying the outfit, finding their weak points. I'm expecting a schematic of the building to arrive any minute from Washington. Need Kane and Chance to visit the place with the idea we might use them for shipping legal weapons to buyers in other states."

"Copy that, boss," Chance said. "I'll set it up."

Ghost nodded. "We've got seventy-two hours to get the surveillance in place."

Ethan whistled. "That fast, huh? Okie-doke, we'll make it happen."

Blaze grinned. "There's the challenge. I was wondering why we were being sent to do kindergarten stuff."

Ghost laughed. "Nothing kindergarten about it, but I see your point." He got to his feet. "Who wants to go pick up some barbecue from the gas station? I'm starved."

Chapter Five

THE SCHEMATIC FOR ROYAL SHIPPING ARRIVED, AND KANE and Chance made their visit as prospective customers. Two nights later, the team suited up in black tactical gear, drove the ten miles to the facility, then infiltrated and placed surveillance equipment while avoiding the security guards who patrolled at night.

Blaze, Chance, Kane, and Ghost went inside while Seth and Ethan remained on overwatch duty.

The operation was textbook.

Four cameras and listening devices later, the six men melted into the night like ghosts, leaving no trace they'd ever been there.

Now the watch began.

Chapter Six

Blaze felt every one of his thirty-eight years tonight. He slotted his truck into a spot behind the Sutton building and rolled his aching shoulder before setting boots to pavement. His plan tonight was to drink a beer, prop his feet up, and binge watch the *Mandalorian*. Or maybe *Picard*.

Hell, he might even soak in the tub.

He was in peak form, but getting hit repeatedly during a long day of classes had a way of taking it out of a guy. Blaze entered the building and hit the stairs. The polished wood was smooth beneath his boots as he trudged up. The Sutton building smelled old. Not bad old, but the kind of old that came with history. It was bigger than it appeared, longer rather than wider, and older than anyplace he'd ever lived before.

Doc Sutton's offices took up the first floor. There was a front entry with a staircase on one side that went up to the second and third floors. There was a corresponding entry and staircases in the rear of the building. There were two apartments per floor, or there would be when the third floor was renovated. The Suttons could have probably made four smaller apartments on each floor, but they hadn't, which was how Blaze ended up with nearly two-thousand square feet.

Bigger than he needed, but he liked the location, and the rent was reasonable. The other guys had chosen to live in the two farmhouses on the property, but Blaze liked his own space. Needed his own space when the nights got bad.

He pushed the thought away in case it called up a nightmare. He hadn't had any in over two weeks now, and he didn't want one.

The building still had original features like plaster moldings and wood floors that looked hand-scraped but were naturally aged from years of people traipsing across them. It was on a corner, which meant he had windows on two sides. He could see the road leading into the historic district and the rear parking lot with all the quirky buildings that perched around it.

A bail bondsman, a law office, a store that sold incense and hosted séances from time to time. Colleen Wright was a kooky old lady, but harmless enough. She'd stopped him in the Dawg one day and told him not to upset Melvin. When he'd inquired as to who Melvin was, she'd informed him that Melvin was the ghost who lived in the Sutton building.

So far as Blaze knew, Melvin was happy. Blaze had never heard a chain rattling or a spooky voice groaning in the night. He didn't expect he would, either.

When he reached the top of the stairs, a small shape nearly plowed him over. Emma Sutton squeaked as she skidded to a halt. He steadied her with his hands on her shoulders, not quite missing the way she stiffened. He let her go, and she stepped back to put distance between them.

He hadn't seen her since the robbery a few days ago. But his palms tingled with that brief contact, his hands itching to touch her again. It annoyed the shit out of him, especially since she looked like she'd rather be anywhere but near him.

Emma's hair was piled on her head in a messy bun. She wore yoga pants and tennis shoes, but she didn't look like she was going for a run. She wasn't wearing earbuds either. Her phone was in her hand, which meant she'd probably been distracted by something on it.

She blinked at him through her glasses. "I'm sorry. I was reading and didn't see you. It's totally my fault."

He didn't mention that she apparently didn't hear him either, which was kinda impossible since the staircase creaked in spots. Whatever was on her phone must have been damned interesting.

"It happens. Would've been worse if you missed the step and tumbled down the stairs, though. Might want to be more careful."

She grimaced. "You're right. It won't happen again, I promise. I'm sorry for any noise, by the way." She hitched her finger toward the front apartment. "I'm moving in. Guess we'll be neighbors."

Her smile was forced. He didn't know if it was because of him or because she was awkward around others.

"I just got home. Didn't hear a thing."

"Oh. Well. Then I'm sorry for any noise you might hear later. Though I still need to shop for furniture, so I guess there won't be much noise until then."

She clamped her mouth shut and frowned. He wondered what that was about.

"I'm gone most days anyway. If you need help moving anything, just ask."

"Thank you. I think I'm good, but I appreciate it."

"You doing okay after the other day?"

"I'm fine. I dealt with trauma on a regular basis in the ER. You get used to it. I'm thinking of the robbery as something similar."

"Not a bad way to go."

She frowned. "I'm sorry for what I said to you. About bullet wounds. It was uncalled for."

"I'm already over it, Doc."

She nodded and gave a jerk of her chin before her gaze dropped to the floor. He sensed she wanted to say something else, so he waited.

"I hear you teach self-defense at your facility."

"We do. Beginning through advanced."

Her blue eyes lifted to his. There were storm clouds in those eyes. "I think I might need some training."

Chapter Seven

BLAZE CONNOLLY'S GAZE SHARPENED. "WHAT'S WRONG? Has someone threatened you?"

The way he said the words, all rough and soft at the same time, stroked her senses. But it was the way he cut straight to the chase that unnerved her.

"I d-don't know." She cursed herself for the hitch in her voice that made her sound like a squeaky wheel in need of grease. And for admitting something she hadn't intended.

She hadn't expected him to be so perceptive, though. To see into the fear she tried to keep hidden.

Truthfully, she didn't know that Simon was a threat anymore. She hadn't heard from him in the last few weeks before she'd left Chicago. It was as if he'd finally gotten the message and decided to leave her alone. She hadn't breathed any easier though. She'd known she wouldn't until she'd left the city behind.

She'd only been back in Alabama a handful of days but the feeling she was being watched hadn't dissipated. It was probably nothing, and yet that subtle prickle on the back of her neck wouldn't let her rest.

The only other time she'd felt it was when Simon was lurking around outside the hospital or her apartment.

"You want to tell me what's going on?" His tone was gentle.

Emma hesitated. She hadn't told anyone. But since the moment he'd disarmed the robber and put him on the ground, she'd been thinking about how confident he'd been. He hadn't hesitated. He'd done the job, and they'd all survived.

Clarence was back to smoking meat again, a bit bruised but suffering no ill effects from the mild concussion he'd gotten from falling to the floor. Britney's young life hadn't been cut short by an asshole looking for money, and Emma was standing there now, scared to say more but able to do so. They all had Blaze to thank for that.

"I lived in Chicago for four years. I kept meaning to take a self-defense class, but I never seemed to have the time. I thought I should rectify that now."

He gazed at her expectantly. "That's a good plan. But you said you didn't know if someone had threatened you or not."

Her throat tightened. "It's nothing. Really. I had a bad relationship that ended before I moved home. I haven't heard from him, but I sometimes wonder if he's out there. Watching me. It's crazy to think he followed me back here."

Her face flamed at how ridiculous she sounded. All she had was a vague fear, not evidence. It was nothing more than PTSD from what she'd experienced still reverberating through her life. It was normal, and she had to get used to it. One day, if she was lucky, it would fade. End of story.

She expected him to give her a pitying look. To tell her she was obviously wrong if she had nothing but a feeling to go on. And he'd be right.

"How does it feel when you think he's there?"

The way he asked the question made her limbs go soft inside, like sinking into a tub of warm water. It was a comforting feeling, one she hadn't had in a long time. "You believe me?"

"Yes."

Said without hesitation. She had to resist the tears welling up inside.

"Now tell me the feeling. How does it differ from usual?"

The bands around her chest loosened. "Like a prickle at the back of my neck, a coldness in my heart. My granny called it feeling like someone was walking across your grave. It's unsettling. But I don't know that I'm right. I've made a lot of changes in a short time, and I might just be feeling the effects of them."

He pushed a hand through his hair. His nostrils flared, and her heart skipped a beat. He was tall, muscled, and rugged in a way that had heat flaring in parts of her that needed to sit down and shut up.

She didn't need to be attracted to this man. She'd already proven that her judgment was suspect when it came to men.

Simon had been nice. Handsome, impeccable manners, treated her like a lady. He'd opened car doors and sent flowers.

He'd been playing a role. He was none of those things when her guard went down. When she felt like maybe she'd met a guy who could be The One with a little more time.

He was not The One. Not even close. He was a nightmare.

"I'm probably overreacting," she blurted as panic squeezed around the edges of her vision. *Breathe, breathe.* "I'd still like to take a class, though. I assume I can sign up online, or do I need to stop by in person?"

"Either is good. Now breathe," he ordered, echoing her thoughts.

She did as he said, nodding when the panic started to recede. It was still there, still ready to roar to life, but she could hold it together for a little while longer. "I'm okay. Just tired."

His frown hadn't eased. "If your gut tells you something's wrong, listen to it."

"Is that what you did in the military? Listened to your gut?"

"I probably wouldn't be alive today if I hadn't."

She thought a flash of anger crossed his features, but it was gone too quick to know.

"I, um, I should leave you alone. I'm sure you have plans that don't involve standing here talking to me. Thank you for the information, though. I'll sign up for class soon." She fumbled her phone in her hand as she started to walk past him.

"Doc."

His voice was filled with command, and she stopped, turned, and faced him again. She pasted on the bright, utterly fake smile she always had ready. Her heart tapped a drumbeat in her chest as she tried to appear casual. "Yes?"

"Listen to your gut. Don't ignore it or rationalize it if you feel like someone's watching you. Don't live scared to step out your door, but be aware of that feeling. If it happens again, note what you're doing and what you see.

Then I want you to tell me about it, okay? Knock on my door. Call me. I don't care. But don't go through this alone."

She swallowed the giant lump in her throat. "Okay. Thanks."

He took his phone from his back pocket. "Give me your number and I'll text you so you can capture mine."

The look on her face must have given him pause because his expression softened. "I asked if you were hungry the other day because I wanted to know you better. You said no. I accept that. I'm not asking for your number to blow up your phone with a bunch of bullshit. I want you to have mine so you'll have someone to talk to when that feeling hits again. I won't ask you out. Promise."

"Of course."

She gave him her number, and her phone lit up a second later. But her brain got stuck on the part where he said he wouldn't ask her out again. Why did it bother her that he'd given up the idea so easily, especially when she didn't want to go out with anyone?

She went through the motions of adding his name and saving him to her contact list, though it didn't stop her from obsessing about what he'd said. He was gorgeous, and she'd turned him down. Of course he wasn't interested in her. He'd had a momentary lapse brought on by the shared experience of the robbery, but he was over it now.

"I've got you now," she said. "Thanks."

The way his sky-blue eyes studied her made her stomach tighten. In a good way. She thought of those eyes roving her body as he peeled her clothing off. Heat pooled in her belly. What was wrong with her, mentally undressing him and thinking about what sex with him would be like?

She offered her bright smile again to cover her discomfort. "I'm meeting a friend over at the Dawg. I better get going. Have a good night."

"You too, Doc."

"You can call me Emma. I think of Doc as my dad if I'm honest. It was fine in Chicago, but it's a little odd here. I mean I am a doctor, but I'm not Doc. I hope that makes sense."

She clamped her mouth shut to end the babbling.

His grin sent another flutter through her that landed solidly in her core and made her ache.

"Have a good night, Emma. Call me if you need me."

Her ears were hot. She thanked him again, needlessly, and fled.

Chapter Eight

"I'm so happy you're home," Rory said for what seemed like the thousandth time that night. "I've missed you, Emma Grace."

Emma sat at the bar while her friend worked behind it, mixing drinks, pouring beers, and sorting out any snafus with the kitchen. Rory kept up a steady stream of chatter, which was good for Emma because it didn't require her to spill her guts about anything.

Not that Rory wouldn't get around to digging deeper about why Emma gave up her job in Chicago to come home, but so far she'd seemed to accept the answer Emma gave everyone, which was she'd missed home. Since her dad had recently decided to retire, taking over the Sutton's Creek Family Practice was a natural choice to make.

"I missed you, too." She took a sip of the white wine Rory had poured for her and smiled. It wasn't quite as forced with Rory as it had been with Blaze Connolly, but it wasn't entirely natural either.

Emma hadn't been inside a bar in months, and it made her nervous. Not that she'd ever spent a lot of time in bars with her job, but there had been times when she went out with some of the doctors and nurses on her shift. She'd stopped when Simon didn't like it.

Her gaze darted around the Dawg when Rory had to go take care of a table.

It was an old habit. Looking for Simon. For his disapproval.

He hadn't ordered her not to go out with her friends, but he'd made his displeasure known. Coolly, calmly, without anger or overt manipulation. Little had she realized just how much he was pulling her strings.

She'd always thought she was too smart to be an abused woman, but it wasn't like abusers wore signs and waved their control flags proudly before you got involved. They built a wall around you brick by brick until you couldn't see over it anymore. Then they bricked over the top until you were trapped.

Emma took another swallow of wine and let it burn its way down her throat. Simon was history. She didn't have that tickle on her neck tonight. He wasn't there, and she was going to learn to defend herself. Not because of him, but because it was a good idea.

"Sorry about that," Rory said as she popped back over to where Emma sat.

"Not a problem. You had beer to pour for the guys at the pool table."

A loud beep sounded. "Son of a bitch," Rory said, pulling her shirt up to peek at the glucose monitor on her abdomen.

"What can I do?" Emma asked, instantly alert.

Rory reached for the insulin pump clipped to her belt and tapped it. "Stop your hovering, Doctor. I'm just a little low on glucose. Don't worry, I pay attention to all the alarms and do what I'm told if the pump doesn't do it for me."

Emma pulled in a breath. Rory had been a type 1 diabetic since they were teenagers. She'd gone through hell as a kid with a life-altering diagnosis, but these days she wore a glucose monitor and an insulin pump and seemed to be in tune with her body.

Rory was the kind of person who never let anything stop her for long. She exercised, ate well, and paid attention to her levels.

Still, Emma's training kicked in when the alarm sounded. She wasn't Rory's doctor, but that wasn't going to stop her from trying to take care of her friend in the moment. The beeping stopped, and Rory sighed.

"It's still a pain in the ass, but at least I don't have to inject myself all the time anymore. And it's sooo fun explaining what these things are on my skin whenever I get hot and heavy with a guy. Not that *that's* happened in forever. It's been so long I think there are cobwebs in my hoo hah."

Emma snorted. They were alone in their corner of the bar, but that wouldn't have stopped Rory from saying it anyway. "Cobwebs, huh? I can give you a cream for that."

"Nah, just need some vitamin D. Have to find the right guy, though."

"Are you looking for hot sex or a relationship?"

"Hot sex, of course. But you'd be surprised how territorial some guys get. They start coming around and glaring at every dude who talks to me while I work. I don't have to tell you how much that pisses me off."

Emma suppressed a shiver. She knew *exactly* how territorial a man could get. "Ain't nobody got time for that," she teased.

"Nope. I just want a good shag from a hot guy every now and then. Is that too much to ask?"

"A shag, huh? What are we now, British?" Emma couldn't help but grin. Rory was a hoot without intending it sometimes. Or maybe she did intend it, but she was damned good at making it seem natural.

"I'm classing shit up around here. Is it working?"

"Oh yeah, definitely."

"Oooh, don't look now," Rory said, her brown eyes lighting up. "We've got a Hottie Alert."

"What kind of hottie?"

"Three sexy military men. *Former* military men. They work at One Shot Tactical, that new range over on the old Jackson farm." Rory's tongue was going to hang out any second as she stared. "Damn, I wouldn't mind climbing that like a tree."

"No fair, I can't turn around and look."

"You'll get a chance. I'll let you know when they're sitting down. You already know one of them. Blaze."

Emma's heart decided to start thumping like a drum. "He's definitely easy on the eyes."

"Girl, have you looked at his butt in those jeans? So fine." Her eyes sparkled. "Seth and Chance are the other two with him tonight. They're also gorgeous—but Chance is a prick. Not a fan."

"What did he do?"

Because Rory liked everybody, so he must have done something to piss her off.

She shot fresh club soda into her glass and took a sip. "He thinks he's God's gift. Flirts with every girl that passes his table, flashes that cocky grin at everyone. He had the gall to tell me Ole Miss is better than Alabama even though Alabama played in the championship game and his team did *not*. He's also bossy, telling me how to pour drinks like I don't know what I'm doing. He's just an arrogant jerk."

Emma suppressed a snort. Rory went to the University of Alabama where she got her business degree, and she took her Crimson Tide football very seriously. She wasn't just a fan by virtue of living in the state. She'd spent four years in Tuscaloosa. Bear Bryant sat at the right hand of God in her not-so-unbiased opinion. Nick Saban would surely join him when the time came.

Emma was a fan because she'd grown up with Alabama football on TV every Saturday in the fall, and her parents had met at a game when they were students. But she didn't get pissed off about it the way Rory did.

"Could be worse," Emma said dryly, tracing the rim of her glass. "He could be an Auburn fan."

Rory put up a hand, palm out. "No, no, I can deal with that. Usually. Okay, you can look. Over near the pool tables."

Emma twisted the bar stool. Blaze sat at a table with two other men who had that same sexy intensity he had. But neither of them made her palms sweat the way Blaze did. His head swiveled her direction. She spun around before he saw her.

Which was dumb because she'd told him where she was going when she'd talked to him in the hall earlier. If their gazes happened to meet across the room, so what?

"See what I mean?" Rory said. "They look like the kind of men who could rip a grizzly bear apart with their bare hands if it threatened you. Yum."

"I don't think that's possible."

"You know what I mean. Tough, masculine. Sexy as heck."

Definitely those things. She had a mental picture of Blaze disarming and taking down the gunman at the Gas-n-Go, and her belly tightened.

"I'm going to sign up for a self-defense class. You should take it with me," she said.

Rory blinked. "You are? I thought you were a pacifist, madam doctor. When I told you I bought a gun for home defense, you lectured me on gun violence and how most shootings happen by accident with legal weapons."

Warmth bloomed beneath her skin. "I *am* a pacifist for the most part. And I still think guns are dangerous. But knowing how to defend yourself is important. Besides, I'm pretty sure you don't have to have a gun for basic self-defense. It's knowing how to fend off an attacker, how to protect yourself." She shrugged. "I just think it's important."

Rory nodded. "Agreed. I was planning to shoot an attacker, but I see what you're saying. I'm still surprised *you* want to take a class though."

"Did you forget I walked into the middle of a robbery a few days ago and almost got my head blown off?"

She said it teasingly, but it still made a shiver roll down her spine.

Rory patted her arm. "Of course I didn't. I'm so sorry that happened, babe. But glad you had Blaze there to take care of the situation."

"Me too. I still don't know how he did it, but Blaze turned the tables on that guy so fast it was unreal. I want to know how he did it, so that's why I'm taking the class."

"I completely understand and agree. But you do realize that self-defense for women is usually about gouging out eyes and stuff, right? You already know how to do that."

"I know the weak points of the human body. But I

don't know what to do if someone grabs me from behind or drops a bag over my head. Or, heaven forbid, points another gun at me."

Being on the wrong end of the robber's gun hadn't been fun, but it wasn't the first time she'd had a weapon pointed at her. Yet another reason she really wanted to know how Blaze had done it.

Rory's brother emerged from the kitchen where he'd been cooking up comfort food such as meatloaf and mashed potatoes.

The Salty Dawg was more than a bar. It was a restaurant with bar food and hearty dinners, too. Fridays they had prime rib, but that wasn't until tomorrow. Today was meatloaf.

"Emma Grace!"

"Theo!"

Emma jumped off the bar stool and ran to greet him, throwing herself into his open arms. There'd been a time when she'd had a major crush on Theo, but that had been over for years.

He lifted her up and spun her around, and Emma laughed as she clung to him. It'd been a long time since she'd seen Theo. She'd gone to see Rory at home the day after she'd arrived, but this was her first trip to the Dawg. He set her down and raked his gaze over her.

"You're looking good, honey." He looped an arm around her and hugged her to his side as they went back to Rory and the bar. "We missed you, didn't we, Ror?"

"We sure did." Rory was pulling beers from the taps for Amber, the waitress who stood at the end of the bar, waiting for the order she'd collected from Blaze and his friends. Amber was pretty, with red hair and big boobs, and Emma felt a pang of jealousy when she slid her gaze over to the table with the three men.

Blaze looked right at her, and Emma glanced away. Or maybe she'd imagined it. He could have been looking at Amber. She let her gaze slide over to him again. He didn't look away. This time he nodded. She nodded back then shifted her gaze to Theo, who was saying something she hadn't paid attention to.

"I'm sorry, what?"

Theo grinned down at her. "You and Ror, both distracted by our One Shot Tactical guys. They come in here, and she trips over her tongue."

Rory stuck her tongue out as she finished the last beer and set it on Amber's tray. Amber winked and said, "Honey, we all do," before she sashayed away from the bar to deliver the drinks.

"Maybe Amber does, but I do *not*," Rory said. "Do you trip over your tongue every time some gorgeous woman with big boobs walks in the door?"

"Yup."

Rory rolled her eyes. "You do not. Stop making things up."

"In my defense," Emma said, "I was in a scary situation when Blaze Connolly saved the day. I was just giving him a nod. I can hardly ignore him."

"Thank God y'all weren't hurt." Theo gave her shoulders a squeeze. "The sheriff was in yesterday. He said the guy was a meth head from Decatur. Thought he'd cross the river and make a quick score."

"Seems like Sutton's Creek changed more than I thought when I was away."

"It's changed some, but we're essentially the same. Huntsville and Madison are growing this direction though.

Bound to bring more crime as more people move this way."

"They keep putting up subdivisions and apartment buildings in what used to be farmers' fields," Rory said. "I wouldn't be surprised if we get swallowed up in the next five years or so." Her gaze slid over to Theo. "We get approached about selling the farmland and this building all the time. I keep saying no, but I can't deny the money is hard to turn down."

"We aren't selling." Theo looked angry for a second. "This building's been in our family for three generations. Same with Emma Grace's. None of us are selling. Unless the Tennessee overflows its banks and starts flooding us out on the regular, we're staying."

"I know we aren't selling. You can't deny there are days you don't think about it, though."

Theo gave Rory a look that put a lump into Emma's throat. "Honey, if selling everything would get you a cure, I'd do it in a heartbeat. That'd be the *only* reason I'd do it."

Rory smiled at her brother. "You're a big sweetie pie, you know that?"

"Don't tell anybody or I'll deny it." He kissed Emma on top of her head. "Gotta get back to the kitchen. You want some meatloaf? I'll send out a plate."

"No, I'm fine. Rory already offered."

"She microwaved a dinner," Rory said with a grimace.

"Ugh, no. Emma Grace Sutton, you know better than that. You're a doctor for heaven's sake. Didn't they teach you anything about salt and preservatives in medical school?"

Emma laughed as she pushed him away. "I don't eat it every day, Theo. Sometimes the convenience is worth a little risk."

"Not on my watch, hon. Now that you're moving in practically next door, you've got no excuse. You can come over here for dinner or let us send somebody with takeout."

Emma couldn't stop the goofy smile that appeared. "Y'all are the best. I'm glad you're my friends."

She'd missed the comfort of being around old friends who'd known her back when she'd still been sitting in a highchair to eat. You couldn't replace that kind of history.

"Always will be, babe," Rory said. "We're both here for you no matter what. You can tell *me* anything, but I'd probably think twice about what you tell Theo."

Theo snorted before heading for the kitchen with a wave. Emma climbed back onto her stool while Rory went to fill a drink order. She was truly happy for the first time in days. Relaxed. It'd been so long since she'd been at ease in her own skin.

Maybe coming home wasn't such a bad thing after all.

She picked up her drink and took a sip. The back of her neck prickled with warning. A chill shot through her and she spun on her seat to glance wildly around the room.

The Dawg wasn't crowded tonight, and she could see most of it. Simon wasn't there.

Emma closed her eyes as she turned back to her drink. Was she paranoid, thinking something was wrong when it wasn't?

The moment she felt good about something, the fear roared to life. He *wasn't* there, but her mind wasn't going to let her stop fearing him.

As if she knew, deep down, that he wasn't finished with her yet.

Chapter Nine

Blaze didn't do jealousy. It wasn't his thing. If a woman wanted to date another guy, then he'd wave bye and move on to the next one.

But something about watching Theo Harper wrap Emma Sutton in his arms and hug her tight while she smiled made his gut tighten. Didn't know why.

Then Theo put her down and kept his arm casual around her shoulders. She hadn't shrunk away, hadn't looked uncomfortable.

She'd enjoyed every second until Theo returned to his kitchen. There was that kiss on her head, too. Brotherly more than anything, but that didn't mean there wasn't more going on beneath the surface.

Blaze shot a look her way. He'd intended to stay in tonight, but when Chance called and asked if he wanted to go to the Dawg, he'd said yes.

The reason why sat at the bar and chatted with her friend. He told himself he had no business being interested in Emma Sutton, but he reasoned that it wasn't interest so much as concern for her safety. She was scared of something, and he wanted to make sure she didn't get scared tonight.

He stole glances at her when he could, but mostly he drank beer and ate wings with his buds and talked about memories from other times, other assignments. Nothing too specific, of course. That time they were in a Costa Rican jungle and a giant spider landed on Seth's shoulder. Freaked him the fuck out. Dude still didn't like spiders, which meant he was fun to prank at Halloween.

They didn't prank him year-round because it wasn't fair, but Halloween was fair game. Seth screamed like a girl then took his revenge in other ways, like putting shaving cream in shoes or rigging buckets of glitter to drop on unsuspecting heads.

The glitter had been the worst by far.

Blaze took a drink of his beer and glanced at Emma yet again. She was alone at the bar, Rory presumably having gone to pour drinks or take care of a customer. That wasn't what bugged him, though.

It was the way she hunched over as if trying to make herself smaller. He scraped his chair back and stood.

"Something wrong?" Chance asked.

"I'll be back."

He headed over to the bar. Emma still had her head down, muttering something to herself, when he sidled up. She broke off and looked up at him. His heart squeezed at the look on her face.

Fear, loathing, confusion.

"You feel it again?"

She nodded.

"But you didn't see him, am I right?"

"Right." She sucked in a breath and took a sip of her wine. Her glass shook. "I must be losing my marbles. It's

PTSD. I think he's there, but he's not. And believe me, I'm very glad he's not."

Blaze really wanted to know what this guy had done to make her so scared. He wasn't going to ask, though. Not yet. She didn't trust him enough. She would, but it would take time.

"You aren't losing your marbles. It could be the stress, but that doesn't mean you don't need to listen to that feeling."

She gazed at him again, her blue eyes wide and wounded behind her glasses. He had a strong urge to wrap his arms around her and hold her close. Except that was Theo Harper's job, apparently.

Blaze bit down on the impulse and kept his hands to himself. "You listen to it because if you get into the habit of ignoring or dismissing it, because you don't see the danger you're looking for, then one day that danger really will be there—and you won't be prepared. You'll walk right into it because you told yourself you were losing your marbles. So don't do that, you hear me?"

She nodded. "You're really nice, you know that?"

She surprised him enough that he laughed. "Nice? No, not really. I'm the guy the bad guys don't want to see coming. Definitely not nice then."

Her smile was shaky. "I saw that in action."

He didn't tell her it got worse than what she'd witnessed. Disarming that punk hadn't taken much effort or thought. It was something he did on instinct. Kinda like breathing.

"I still think you're nice, though," she said, her voice whisper soft.

"Hey there, Blaze. Can I get you something?"

Blaze looked up to find Rory Harper on the other side

of the bar. She was pretty, with long blond hair and banging curves. She wore red lipstick and had long dark lashes and perfect eyebrows. Her nails were short and neat and matched her lipstick.

She was the kind of woman he usually liked. He'd never felt that flare of interest in her though. Maybe it was because of her brother. Theo was overprotective. Rory could take care of herself with handsy customers, and did, but Theo sometimes inserted himself in the situation and threatened to knock off heads.

Blaze would have done the same thing if she was his sister. Not that he had a sister, but if he did, he'd do whatever he had to do to make sure guys knew if they upset her, they upset him.

"Nah, just came to talk to Emma."

Rory's gaze slid to her friend. Whatever she saw must have been good because she didn't glare or tell him she was back now and he could return to his table.

"Heard you broke that guy's arm when you took his gun away."

"I never said that," Emma blurted.

"Didn't say you did, babe. I heard some people talking in here a couple of days ago."

"And you believed them?" Blaze asked.

Rory grinned. "Not necessarily. I just wanted to see what you'd say."

"I didn't break his arm. Might have broke his ass when he fell on the concrete though. Nothing less than he deserved after he scared Britney and Emma and shot at Clarence."

"You won't get any disagreement from me." Rory nodded at the other end of the bar. "I have to fill some orders. Be back in a few. You need anything, Emma Grace?"

Emma still had half a glass of wine. She shook her head. "I'm good. Probably going to head home as soon as I finish this."

Rory looked disappointed for a second. "Okay. I'm glad you came out tonight. I'll text you later about that class."

Blaze thought she winked but she turned away so fast he wasn't sure. "You been friends a long time?" he asked Emma when Rory was gone.

She turned her indigo gaze on him. "Since we were three years old and met in daycare at church. Thirty-one years, though it doesn't seem like it's been that long."

He didn't have a single friend he'd stayed in touch with. He also wasn't from a small town. He'd spent most of his childhood in Enid, Oklahoma, and he'd been planning his escape from the minute he'd realized his mother wasn't ever getting clean. She'd never married his father, and she'd bounced them between a succession of boyfriends, a.k.a. dealers, while she got drunk and high and generally sucked at raising a kid.

"Emma Grace," he said, dragging his mind from the darkness of his childhood. "It's a pretty name."

He thought she was blushing. "Everyone who knew me growing up calls me that. They run it together like one big name."

"Do you mind it?"

"Sometimes." Her expression was serious. A little troubled, maybe. "It's not their faults. It's mine. It makes me feel like I never left, like I never accomplished anything. I don't feel like Doctor Sutton. I feel like little Emma Grace, the doctor's kid. The nerd who loved science and biology and didn't much care for school dances or boys. Not that I wasn't interested in boys, just that I didn't spend a lot of time thinking about how to get them."

There was a lot he wanted to unpack in that little speech, but he decided now wasn't the time. "And I guess you aren't asking your oldest friend to call you Emma."

She shook her head. "Nope. It's my problem, not hers."

Blaze shrugged. "Seems to me like she'd want to know if something bothered you. I would if I was your friend."

She took another sip of wine. "You shouldn't be so logical, Mr. Connolly. It's annoying."

He laughed. "Sorry." He nodded at her wine glass. "You said you were going home when you finished that. I'll walk over there with you."

"You don't have to do that. You're out with your friends."

"Okay, but tell me this. Considering that feeling you got just a few minutes ago while you sat here alone, do you really want to walk home in the dark by yourself?"

"It's not far."

"No, it's not. But do you want to go alone?"

He saw the emotions cross her face before her expression fell. "No, I really don't."

"See? Wasn't hard at all."

Chapter Ten

Emma felt like she was going to burst from all the emotions swirling inside. She was grateful for Blaze's stoic, hulking, seriously badass presence as they walked the one hundred feet between the Dawg and the Sutton Building. She was also embarrassed that she'd caved into his suggestion he accompany her. Ashamed at the relief that had clawed its way up her throat when he insisted.

It shouldn't be so damned difficult to walk down the street in laidback Sutton's Creek, a town she'd grown up in and never felt a moment's concern for her safety.

Well, not until she'd been in the Gas-n-Go a few days ago. But, technically, the station wasn't in the town limits, so she could still say she'd never been scared for her life in Sutton's Creek. She'd walked *to* the Dawg so walking home again shouldn't be so difficult. Of course it had still been daylight then, and that wasn't quite as scary.

If she hadn't had that moment at the bar when she'd felt a chill, she wouldn't have accepted Blaze's offer. Maybe she shouldn't have anyway. Simon hadn't been there. If he had been, she'd have seen him. The Dawg hadn't been that crowded, and she'd had a clear line of sight around the entire space.

"Is that one of your ancestors?" Blaze tipped his head toward the statue across the street. The town square was lined with shops, offices, and places to eat. At the center was a small park with a fountain where a man stood tall in bronze, gazing out at the town with benevolent pride.

"Yes, that's Jacob Sutton. He founded the town in 1830 after moving from Mooresville, which is about eight miles northwest. I guess he had a falling out with someone over there and decided to make a town more suited to his liking. It grew and flourished for a few decades before the Civil War, then spent a lot of years just getting by. And now it's waiting to be swallowed up as Huntsville expands."

"Seems to be thriving, though. The Dawg is always packed, and there are stores and restaurants on the square that get a lot of traffic. It's got that small-town charm that people look for."

"Is that what brought you and your friends here?"

She wouldn't have thought small-town charm was high on his list, but then again he lived in her family's building, and it was full of old features. Just because he was a badass didn't mean he couldn't like original crown molding and aged wood floors.

They reached the front door of the building and stopped on the sidewalk. They could have gone out the back of the Dawg, but Blaze had said there were too many cars in the parking lot and led her to the front door instead. She hadn't argued.

He gazed down at her. Her heart did that skip thing it usually did whenever he was near. She wished everything were different. That she could step into him, put a palm on his cheek, and kiss him. Not that she'd ever been the kind of girl who made the first move. She thought about it and froze. Every time.

She wished she was more courageous, like Rory.

Rory wasn't afraid of anything. Never had been. Not even diabetes. That had made her angry.

"We were looking for a place to start our own business. Checked out a site in Mississippi and another in Tennessee, but we felt like we'd do better here. Property was the right price and, like you said, Huntsville's growing."

She glanced at the door. "If you want to go back to your friends, I think I can go the rest of the way by myself."

He tugged the door open. "Not how this service works, Emma. I take you to your door and wait for you to go inside. Only then do I leave."

She couldn't help but smile. "Like I said before, you're a nice guy."

His answering grin made her stomach tighten. "I'm honest and loyal. If that makes me nice, then I can deal with it."

They started toward the wooden staircase that led up to the second floor. The stairs were old, made of polished American oak that had darkened with years of wax. There were subtle grooves worn in the treads from generations of people climbing them.

The stairs were wide enough to climb side by side. There was a freight elevator in the rear of the building, but it was old and the last person who could work on it had passed away last year. It was hard to get parts, hard to find anyone who knew how to repair an antique.

Fortunately, since the stairs were so wide, it wouldn't be difficult to get furniture up to her apartment. All she had now was a card table and chairs and a folding mattress her parents had given her.

She hadn't told them she'd left everything behind in Chicago. They assumed she was expecting a shipment, but she wasn't. She'd sold it all. What she couldn't sell, she'd given away.

She didn't want anything that reminded her of her life there.

Emma's heart thrummed a little faster when they reached the top. She hadn't been to the gym regularly in months, and she was feeling it. She needed to start running again. Maybe she would when she was settled in. There was a treadmill in the office downstairs, or she could buy one of her own.

Blaze eyed her, but she didn't stop to catch her breath. Maybe she should have, but how embarrassing was that? She was thirty-four, and one set of stairs threatened to do her in.

She walked down the hall toward her door. Blaze was behind her. Since they'd come in from the front entrance, her apartment was first. She reached into her jacket for her keys, then plowed to a stop in front of the tall wood door, her heart lodging in her throat.

Was the door open?

Blaze pushed her back against the wall, his expression serious. Her stomach dropped. She turned to look at her door again. She hadn't been wrong. A slice of pale light filtered through the slim crack where the door stood ajar.

"Stay here," Blaze murmured.

She nodded, though part of her wanted to wrap her fists in his shirt and beg him not to leave her alone. But it made sense for him to go inside and see if anyone was there.

If Simon was there.

Blaze drew a weapon from behind his back, shoved the door open, and disappeared in a cloud of silence. Emma flattened herself against the wall. She couldn't hear anything past the rush of blood in her ears. She strained for any sounds that would tell her what was happening, turning her head right and left, peering down the hall in both directions. If someone was there—if *he* was there— what would she do?

A few moments later, Blaze appeared in the entry. "It's clear. Nobody inside."

The gun was gone. He had his phone instead, and he was busy tapping away on it.

Emma let out a slow breath. Her heartbeat didn't calm, though. "Maybe I didn't tug it closed well enough. It's an old building."

She'd pulled the door closed, held it tight, and locked it. She remembered that. Then she'd tested the knob. Nothing had happened. But maybe the wood swelled, or contracted, and the lock slipped. Anything was possible in an old building. She knew that from the house she'd grown up in.

"Do you really think that's true?" he asked, his sky-blue eyes searching hers as he slipped his phone in his pocket.

She shook her head. Her natural impulse tilted toward keeping her cards close to her chest, but for some reason she felt like she could admit the truth to Blaze.

"Here's how I see it, Emma. If you remember closing and locking the door, there's a slim chance you're wrong and it popped open on its own. But considering what you've told me about that prickly feeling you got earlier, we're not going to assume that's the case."

"Do you think someone was inside?"

"Maybe." He stepped out and pulled the door closed, took her keys from her hand, and locked it again. He did the same thing she'd done, tugging and pushing, and the door held. She thought he'd unlock it again, but he didn't. He handed her the keys, put a gentle hand on her elbow, and guided her down the hallway toward his apartment.

She thought she should object when he unlocked the door and ushered her inside. She didn't know him, not really, and he was a big man capable of violence.

She'd seen the violence, though it had been in service to her, Britney, and Clarence.

You can trust him.

It came from deep within, but how could she believe it when she didn't trust herself?

She thought of her father saying he felt like Blaze was a good man. John Sutton was one of the best judges of character she'd ever known. Growing up, she remembered times when he treated people who couldn't pay him. He took baked goods, crafts, labor, and many other things she hadn't understood.

He'd never been wrong about any of those people, even when he treated them first. They always showed up with payment.

Emma let out her breath and stood quietly as Blaze unlocked his door. He pushed it open and motioned her inside.

She crossed the threshold, not certain what to expect. The apartment wasn't as bare as hers, but it was pretty bare. There was a couch and chair, an end table, and a round table with four chairs in the adjoining dining area. Of course there was a big TV on a console.

"Have a seat. Can I get you a water or a beer? Afraid I don't have any wine."

Emma shook her head. "I'm good. Thank you."

She wrapped her arms around herself as she walked over to the couch and sat on the edge. Perched, really. She bounced her knees up and down and worked to hold back any tears. She told herself they were angry, frustrated tears —and they were—but they were also brought on by fear.

He didn't sit. Instead, he lifted his phone and put it to his ear. "Yeah? Okay, thanks." He dropped it on the table and raked a hand through his hair.

She couldn't help but notice the way the muscles in his arm flexed and rolled.

"I had my friends check out the surrounding area. They didn't see anyone suspicious."

"He wouldn't look suspicious," Emma said. Simon had always been proud of his ability to blend and look inconspicuous. He'd bragged about it more than once. To scare her, she'd realized later.

He'd succeeded.

Blaze dragged a chair away from the dining table and turned it around, straddled it with the back to his front. Now why was that sexy?

"Can you tell me about him? Give me a picture? Knowing his name and description could help us find him."

Emma blinked rapidly, then pulled her gaze away from his. "Why do you believe me? What if I'm a drama queen and all this"—she waved her hand around—"is to get your attention."

"Is it?"

She whipped her gaze back to him. He'd lifted one eyebrow in question. Heat flooded her. "No, it's not."

"Okay then. You gonna tell me what I need to know, or do you plan to keep worrying about this guy?"

Chapter Eleven

BLAZE HAD A KEEN UNDERSTANDING OF FEAR. HE'D LIVED it, experienced it, ate it for breakfast, and kept going anyway. Was he damaged because of it?

Probably. Wasn't going to stop him, though. Worst thing you could do was stop and let the fear engulf you.

Today's fears were different from the ones he'd had as a child. He knew how to deal with today. He was still figuring out the kid shit. Probably always would be, truth be told. None of it had been his fault, and yet he still sometimes caught himself thinking that if he'd been a better kid, his mother would have loved him enough to kick the drug habit.

He knew that was bullshit, but his inner eight-year-old didn't.

Emma Sutton was tougher than she looked, but she was in danger of being engulfed in her fear. He needed to know what was after her, what scared her, so he could keep her safe.

Because he damned well *was* going to keep her safe. It

was what he did. What he'd always done. It was risky to get involved, but this was protection, not a relationship.

After he'd cleared her apartment, he'd called Chance and asked him and Seth to reconnoiter the area. They hadn't found anything, but they were headed for Emma's apartment now so they could take a better look than he'd had time for. Look for anything out of place. Not that she had anything worth stealing yet, but that didn't stop someone from planting a camera or a mic if they wanted to spy on her.

He didn't reject any possibilities. He waited patiently as Emma swallowed and clasped her hands together around her knees. Her feet were still tapping the floor. He could feel his anger building. Not because she tapped the floor or hesitated to talk, but because some asshole had done this to her. Scared her half out of her mind.

Her eyes behind the glasses were big and shiny, and he knew she was fighting tears.

"His name is Simon Marsh. He's thirty-five, five-eleven or six-foot, with brown eyes and blond hair. Short hair. He has a tech consulting business. He builds websites for people, optimizes online branding and advertising, keeps their sites secure, that kind of thing. He works from home, which means all he needs is an internet connection to do his job. He doesn't have a boss or employees in the traditional sense. He has a virtual assistant, and he contracts out some of the work he needs done, but there's no job to go to, no one keeping up with where he is on any given day."

"So he could follow you to Alabama and nobody would miss him."

"Right."

He had so many questions. He started with a simple one. "How did you meet?"

She pulled in a breath. "At the gym. He was building their website, and he started to work out there. We said hello in passing, he started to talk to me, then he eventually asked me out." She closed her eyes. When she opened them again, they were harder than he'd expected. "It was a huge mistake to get involved with him, but he's the kind of man who says and does all the right things until the day he doesn't. He was controlling and verbally abusive, and it took me far too long to realize it."

Blaze thought if Simon Marsh walked through his door right now, he'd flatten the asshole. "Did he ever hit you?"

Her eyes flashed fire. But then her chin quivered, and she dropped her gaze to her lap. It killed him. He didn't even fucking know her, and it killed him.

"It's not your fault," he rasped. He could see his mother taking that shit from the men she dated, and it twisted him up inside as if it was yesterday. "It's *never* your fault, no matter what he told you."

She nodded. Didn't look at him. He wanted her to, but he wouldn't force it. She would trust him before they were through. He'd make sure of it.

"When I went to work the morning after, I knew I wouldn't go back. He was in *my* apartment, because he'd started staying there much of the time, but I wasn't going back for anything. I stayed at the hospital, slept there until a couple of the other doctors cornered me and made me tell them what was going on. I don't know what happened, not really, but they went to my apartment and had a talk with Simon. The next thing I knew, he was gone."

"But that wasn't the end of it."

Her knuckles were white. "Not entirely. He called, sent texts, swore he wasn't like that, that I needed to give him another chance. I ignored them all. He finally stopped, but by then the wheels were in motion for the move back to Sutton's Creek. My dad had decided to retire, and I jumped at the chance to get away from there. I wanted to feel safe again."

"You didn't see him before you left?"

She hesitated a moment too long.

"Emma. It's okay."

She sucked in a breath. "I saw him. From a distance. At the gym. At the grocery store. Across from my apartment building. At the hospital a couple of times. He didn't speak to me. He stared. Hard. That's when I started to feel the tingling sensation that I was being watched."

He was really fucking pissed at the way some men treated women. "Anything else?"

She shook her head. "No. Staring at me wasn't enough to call the police, so I didn't. And, um, I didn't report the assault. I should have, but I was embarrassed. I just wanted to forget the whole thing."

He hated that she'd been too scared to call the cops, but he also knew why she hadn't. He'd lived around too much of that shit as a kid. He knew the psychological toll it took on women and children. The excuses people made, thinking it was their fault, that they'd caused it, that the police already had enough to do and what was one more assault to them.

"He knew you were leaving?"

"I don't know, but he'd have figured it out if he was watching. I broke my lease, sold the furniture, donated what I didn't need, and packed my car. I could have taken more time. My dad wants to retire to travel with my mother. She had a heart attack last year, but she's fine now, and he's not quitting immediately. I took his decision as a sign when it happened after everything with Simon." She dropped her head to her hands and shook it again, slowly. "I'm talking too much. I do that when I'm nervous. And maybe I'm blowing this out of proportion. Why would he follow me here? He's an asshole, but there are plenty of other women for him to intimidate. Maybe I didn't engage the lock. Maybe the prickly feelings are just paranoia."

He understood why she questioned herself. Maybe she was right, but he wasn't going to dismiss her feelings so casually.

"Would he have known where you were going when you left town?"

"Probably. He knows where I'm from. Even if I took another job, he'd probably expect me to come here. He wanted to know all about where I grew up when we started dating. I was happy to tell him everything back then."

There was a knock on the door, and she flinched.

"It's my friends," he said. "I'm going to give them your key and let them have a look around."

"Okay." She offered her key ring.

He handed off the keys and returned to sit near her again. "Do you have a picture of him?"

It'd help if he had more than a description to go on. If he saw the guy lurking outside the building, or hanging around in the Dawg, staring at her, he could intervene.

Emma shook her head. "He was adamant about pictures. He didn't want to be in them. He never let me take any selfies of us on dates, or even just a picture of him to have back when I thought he was a nice guy."

Blaze frowned. It wasn't quite normal behavior, but it wasn't illegal either. He was careful about photos. All his guys were. They'd spent years relying on the basic anonymity that came from not having photos plastered all over the internet for others to find. Maybe tech bros like Simon were cautious about their online footprint because they worked online and saw how it could be abused.

Blaze had what he needed for now, so they talked about other things. Unimportant things like the weather and how good the banana bread over at the Kiss My Grits cafe was.

"Warm from the oven with a smear of butter," he said, and she nodded enthusiastically.

"Wendy bakes the best banana bread I've ever tasted. I got a piece this morning and savored it with my coffee."

Seth and Chance returned a few minutes later. Emma hadn't relaxed much, but at least she'd stopped tapping her toes and hugging her knees.

"Find anything?" Blaze asked his teammates when the introductions were done. He could have had the conversation away from her, but he sensed that was the wrong thing to do. Emma was scared, but she wasn't a child and wouldn't appreciate being treated like one. The woman was a doctor, which took crazy amounts of schooling and time. He was certain she could handle whatever they'd learned.

"Nothing inside. But the lock was picked recently. There are fresh scratches around the keyhole that didn't come from a key," Seth said.

Blaze looked at Emma. She shivered. Then she sat up a bit straighter and thrust her chin out. He didn't know if she was telling herself to be brave or feeling vindicated that it wasn't just her imagination.

"These locks aren't the best," Chance said. "Could use something a bit more secure."

Blaze thought so too. "I'll pick something up tomorrow. For both apartments."

Not that he worried about his ability to stop an intruder, but a better lock was warranted.

"I can help you install them," Seth said. "What about cameras?"

"Those too. At least in the hall. I'll have to clear it with Doc Sutton."

Emma seemed to shake herself from her reverie. "I don't want my parents to know why," she blurted. "I never told them about Simon. After things went wrong, I c-couldn't."

Her knuckles were white, the corners of her mouth tight. It wasn't his business why she hadn't told her parents. Maybe they weren't the kind of people you shared information with. He thought they were nice, but he wasn't their kid.

"I'm not going to tell them. I think after what happened at the Gas-n-Go, they'll be amenable to security measures."

"I hope so. But lots of people still don't lock their doors in Sutton's Creek." She swung a hand out, pointing vaguely west. "You could drive into the historic district right now and walk into just about any house without encountering a locked door. It's been that way for years."

Blaze exchanged a look with his teammates. "That may be," he said gently. "But the area's growing and more tourists visit every day. Adding security to public buildings is reasonable."

She nodded. "Just don't tell them what happened. Please."

"If I tell them, I'll say it was my door, okay?"

"Okay."

She sucked in a breath and climbed to her feet. She didn't even come to his shoulder. He wanted to wrap an arm around her the way Theo had, feel her slight body solid against his. Infuse her with confidence that he was going to keep her safe.

"I've imposed enough on you tonight. I should go."

"Can you sit for a moment? Let me walk the guys out?"

He thought she was about to tell him no, but she sank to the couch and started tapping her feet again. Blaze went into the hall with his guys and told them about Simon Marsh.

"I'll see what I can dig up," Seth said. He was their IT guy, and he was good at research.

"Thanks. Appreciate the help tonight."

They clasped hands all around, and then the two men disappeared down the hall. Blaze went back inside, closing the door behind him. Emma was where he'd left her. She looked up when he walked in. Her eyes were a little glassy, and he thought she must have been fighting tears. It made his gut tighten a little more.

"You can't stay in your apartment tonight. Whoever picked that lock could come back. It's not safe."

Her mouth opened. Closed again. She seemed to think about it for a moment. "I can't go back to my parents' house. I'd have to explain. I don't want to explain it to Rory, either. Or Theo. They don't know about Simon, and I don't want them to know. I have no choice. I'll put a chair under the door and call you if anything happens."

Blaze blew out a breath and raked a hand through his hair. He got her reasons, but her logic wasn't sound. Just like insisting earlier that she could walk home alone. She was stubborn as hell sometimes. Or maybe it was pride. He didn't know, but he couldn't let her risk it.

There was only one thing he could say.

"Then stay here tonight. With me."

Chapter Twelve

Emma was feeling more than a little wigged out
about the break-in, but she was trying not to let it show.
She was *trying* to be logical. She didn't want to stay in her
apartment, but knowing Blaze was here and she could call
him, she thought maybe she could manage it. She'd lock
the door, wedge the chair beneath the lock, and try to
sleep.

She wouldn't sleep, though. She would lie awake all
night, coming out of her skin at every creak and groan of
the building. She was used to old buildings, and she knew
how much settling they could do at night.

Still, it wasn't going to be easy when every creak meant
she'd picture Simon creeping closer and closer, his palm
wrapped around the butt of the pistol he'd threatened her
with the day he'd hit her. She hadn't told Blaze that part.
She didn't think she could. He would want to know why
she hadn't called the police for that alone.

She had no excuse other than she'd believed Simon
when he'd told her if she did, he'd make sure she regretted
it.

He'd said even if they arrested him, he'd be out on bond because he had no record and was a good citizen. That's when he'd find her and make her wish she'd kept her mouth shut.

"I can't impose," she said, her throat tight.

Can't impose? She heard the words leave her lips and felt the panic tighten her gut. What else could she do *but* impose?

"Honey, I don't know if you've noticed, but this apartment could house a whole family. There are three bedrooms, and two of them have beds. You can shut yourself in and lock the door if you like. You can have the bath in the hall, and I'll stick to the one in my room. We don't have to see each other until morning."

She didn't miss that he'd called her honey. She should say something about that, but she didn't actually want to. There were far more important things to worry about. Plus, she kinda liked the way he said it and the involuntary thrill that slid down her spine.

She could get a room at the Wheeler Inn, which was the closest motel to Sutton's Creek, but her parents would find out because Celia Lincoln would call and tell them. She'd been managing the Wheeler Inn since Emma was in diapers, and she wouldn't miss a chance to gossip about Emma's presence. Her parents would ask questions, and then what?

"I need to get my toiletries and clothes."

"Sure. You also need to check your belongings and see if anything is missing. If so, you might want to fill out a police report. You could do that anyway for the break-in."

He said it gently, as if he expected her to say no. Her heart skipped. How unreasonable must she seem to him?

"I'll see if anything's missing. If not, I don't want to call the police."

If she did, the whole town would know within hours. She wasn't ready to face that kind of scrutiny unless she had to. A picked lock with nothing missing wasn't enough. She didn't know if it was really Simon anyway. Was she supposed to tell Chief Vance that she had a *feeling*? How would that sound?

"Okay. Then I'll go over with you and stay in the hall outside while you get your things. When you've got every-thing, we'll come back here. It's that or tell your friends, because staying in a compromised location is not an option."

She stood, determined to get this over with. He was right. Only an idiot would argue with him.

"Then I'm choosing get my things for a thousand, Alex."

He arched an eyebrow. "A *Jeopardy* joke, Doctor Sutton?"

She couldn't deny the warmth that flowed through her whenever he smiled. "My granny loved it. I used to watch it with her whenever I stayed over at her house."

"Nothing wrong with *Jeopardy*."

He led the way to her apartment, then unlocked the door and swung it open. He didn't enter, though.

She hesitated. "Please come inside. I don't want you to have to stand in the hall."

The man was offering her shelter. It wasn't right to make him stand outside her door like a sentry.

He grinned at her again. "It's my job to watch for trouble. I'll stand in the door while you collect your stuff."

Emma felt weird going into the apartment, but she

pushed her feelings aside and went to get her suitcase and toiletry bag.

She hated Simon. Even if it wasn't him who'd broken in, she hated that she felt unsafe in the building her family had built. This was *home* to her as much as her family home, and for the first time in her life she was scared to be alone in it.

It took only a few moments to get what she needed and return to Blaze's side as a chill she couldn't shake seeped into her bones.

"Anything missing?"

"No. I only brought my clothes up today. Everything else is still in my car."

"I can help you with that tomorrow if you like."

"Thanks, that'd be great."

She'd feel better getting her stuff out of the car. Maybe she'd go furniture shopping this weekend. Rory was off on Sunday. Emma would ask her if she wanted to go.

Blaze locked the door behind them, checked that it was latched, and they went back to his place. Emma could breathe when she crossed the threshold. Didn't matter that she barely knew Blaze Connolly and she was spending the night in his apartment. It was safer than being alone.

His apartment was a mirror image of hers. Tall ceilings, plaster moldings, three bedrooms, a main bath and a full hall bath, a kitchen and dining room, a living room, and windows that ran along two sides of the building since they were on a corner. The wall between their apartments was where the bedrooms and bathrooms were, which meant they could be in bed at the same time and only inches apart if he'd put his bed in the logical place against the wall.

Then there was the shower. They could be naked at the

same time, only a wall between them as they soaped up and rinsed off and got ready for the day. Emma dragged her mind as far from the thought of Blaze naked in a shower as she could get.

It wasn't very far. She'd had a couple of lovers over the years besides Simon, but none had been as fit as Blaze appeared to be. That wall of muscle intrigued her more than it should.

"Make yourself at home," he said as he dropped his keys into a bowl on the kitchen island. "I've got sandwich fixings if you're hungry. There's beer and water in the fridge. Might be some crackers in the pantry."

Emma stood in the door to the kitchen with her suitcase and felt her heart start to return to its normal rhythm.

"I ate before I went to the Dawg, but thank you." She nibbled her lip. "And thank you for taking me seriously earlier tonight when I told you about the feeling I get when I think he's there. I realize this could have nothing to do with him, but if you hadn't come to talk to me at the bar, I'd have probably walked home alone. I'm glad I didn't."

He tipped his chin. "You're welcome. Something you should know is that I will always take you seriously."

Warmth slid into her bones. It was a welcome change from the cold that'd taken up residence there.

"I appreciate that, but the cynic in me feels compelled to point out that some people lie for attention."

"They do, and I'm pretty good at spotting it. You aren't looking for attention, Emma. You don't have to worry I'm gonna think that. I can tell the difference."

Her pulse throbbed a little faster. "Part of me wants to protest that I'm not that predictable. But that would be silly because I'd basically be suggesting you couldn't trust me to tell the truth."

His smile made the butterflies swirl in her belly. "Protest all you want. You aren't going to change my mind."

"I'm not going to try, really." She shrugged. "I just like to point out potential logical inconsistencies when I run across them. Consider it an adorable flaw."

Dear God, was she flirting with him?

He laughed. "Noted. You wanna stash your stuff in the bedroom and continue this discussion over a beer?"

She told herself she shouldn't. That she should thank him again, go into the bedroom, and stay there for the night. But she was keyed up, and a beer wouldn't hurt if she wanted to sleep at any point this evening. She'd had wine at the Dawg, but that was wearing off.

"Sure. Sounds good."

Chapter Thirteen

"All I've got is Monkeynaut," Blaze said when she returned to the kitchen. "Can or glass?"

Two blue cans sat on the island. There was a monkey in a space helmet on the can.

"Granny always said a lady drinks from a glass," Emma told him. "But a can is fine. Granny isn't here to chastise me."

Blaze slid the can into a Roll Tide koozie and handed it to her. Rory would approve.

"I didn't open it because I thought you might want to do that yourself."

Emma pulled the tab up and pushed down. "I wasn't thinking about that, but thank you."

He took a sip of his beer. "Never let a man you don't know give you an open container."

She smiled. "I'm well aware of what some men put into drinks. I've treated a few cases in the ER." She sipped the beer, her tastebuds unsure whether to wince or shout hallelujah. "Wow. Very hoppy."

"It's strong, right? I bought it because I wanted to try a

local brew and there was a space monkey on the can. Been my favorite since."

Emma studied the monkey. She wasn't sure if he looked happy or terrified to be going into space. "I was seventeen when craft beer became legal in Alabama. Before that it was just the national distributors like Budweiser who could sell beer here. Straight to Ale was one of the first breweries to open. I can honestly say this is the first of theirs I've had."

"Not a beer girl?" he teased.

She took another swig. The beer was cold and barely scalded her throat going down. It was strong, but good when you knew what to expect. She needed it to take the edge off, which she was positive it was going to do in the next couple of minutes.

"Corona with lime is more my speed."

He made a face. "Slightly better than beer-flavored water."

She laughed. "That's usually how I like my beer. Corona is a party. This is a sit-down meal with dessert." She swigged more of the surprisingly delicious liquid. "I could get used to this, though."

"Better go easy on that, Em."

Her insides melted just a little. *Em.* Nobody called her that. It was Emma Grace in Sutton's Creek. Emma or Doctor Sutton everywhere else.

When they were kids, Rory had called her Idgy from time to time, but she hadn't done that in years. Theo had never called her anything but Emma Grace. Same for everybody else. When you said it fast enough, it all kind of ran together and became its own nickname anyway.

EmmaGrace. Emagrayss. Kinda like if you cut the

word *immigration* off without the *-ion*. And without the *shh* sound.

Hmm, maybe not such a good comparison after all.

"I will." She sighed as the beer warmed her blood. "I suspect sleep will elude me tonight. I was hoping this would help."

It was more than she meant to say, but the infusion of fresh alcohol was already loosening her tongue. She turned away and walked through the big cased opening and into the living room. The walls were bare but there were curtains on the windows. Her mom had put those up because she had them in her apartment too. Tall, thick ivory curtains—neutral, bless her—that were meant to keep in heat in winter and repel it in summer.

Emma trailed her fingers along the back of the couch, then rounded it and sat at the far end. She leaned her head back on the cushion and closed her eyes. The stress of the past few weeks was still there, still sitting at the back of her head like a noxious cloud of burning rubber. She wanted it to go away, but she wasn't sure if it ever would.

"What happens next?" she asked.

She felt the couch sink as Blaze sat down. When she opened her eyes, he was at the opposite end. He picked up the TV remote and turned it on. Bluesy rock, instrumental, flooded the room. He notched it down a bit and tossed the remote on the couch beside him.

He'd propped his feet up and he was leaning back on the couch, one arm stretched along the back of it. He took another drink and leveled his gaze at her.

Emma's belly tightened. Warmth bloomed there, and lower. If she put her hand out, she could touch his fingers. She told herself not to do that, no matter how much her brain thought it was a good idea.

"If you want a different channel, let me know." He sucked in a breath, blew it out. "What happens next is that I change the locks and see about installing security cameras in the hallway and on the exterior of the building. Seth will do some digging online, see what he can find out about Simon Marsh. Assuming the guy isn't the paranoid type who uses a burner, he'll tag his location. We'll know if he's in the area sometime tomorrow."

Emma's pulse throbbed. "And if he is?"

"Not much we can do except watch and make sure he doesn't get close to you. You ever have any reason to believe he's capable of escalating further?"

Emma needed more beer. She took a gulp, then lowered the can and looked at him. "Isn't everybody?"

"When the circumstances are right, sure. But escalating a situation because you choose to and escalating because you feel threatened are two different things. I'm asking if he's the former."

"I think he is. He was normal until he wasn't."

Though honestly, the signs had been there. She just hadn't recognized them. He'd been overly interested in her schedule, shown up at the hospital unannounced, and asked pointed questions about any of the male doctors who spoke to her—or that she spoke to. He was possessive in public when men talked to her or acknowledged her in any way.

Any of those things were warning signs. All of them together were a red flag.

But the second she'd felt a tendril of unease, he'd smile and tell her she looked pretty. Or he'd whisk her to dinner, or send her flowers, or perform some other grand gesture that had all her gay and female coworkers sighing if they were around to witness it.

"You're so lucky." "He's so attentive." What a gentleman." "I wish my husband still sent me flowers." "Snap that one up, Doctor, because they don't make them like that anymore."

"You're thinking about something," Blaze interrupted.

She lifted the beer. It was three-quarters empty by now. "I was just wondering if I should ask for another or if I should call it quits for the night."

Because the truth was too embarrassing. She couldn't admit that she'd been so thoroughly deceived by Simon's good-guy act that she'd made excuses when he'd started losing his temper over her wardrobe, which hadn't been anything low cut or revealing, acting jealous, and texting or calling her a hundred times a day. He'd gotten angry if she didn't respond right away, but he'd always couched it as being concerned for her safety. Loving her so much that he immediately started to think she'd been hurt somehow.

Lies. Every bit of it.

"How about I get you some water? You drink that when you finish the beer. If you want another one after the water, I'll get you one."

"Sounds fair." It hit her when she agreed that maybe she'd done that too fast. Maybe she should protest. Simon used to tell her what to do, what to eat, how much to eat, what to drink. She hadn't fought back, and she should have. But Blaze wasn't giving her an order. Or was he?

"Hey," she said as he stood.

"Yeah?"

"What if I don't wanna drink water? What if I want another beer anyway?"

"Do you?"

She looked down at the can. "Maybe. It should be my choice if I want water or if I want more beer."

"You're right. If you want that beer, I'll get it for you."

"Then why did you suggest water?"

He shoved a hand through his hair and looked over her head like he was thinking. When his gaze landed on her again, her heart tripped over itself.

"I was a military guy, Emma. I've done my share of drinking and been with my buddies when they were drinking. I know that downing alcohol too fast can lead to regretful choices. Drinking water in between slows you down and gives your head a chance to clear."

He wasn't wrong. Her doctor brain knew it. She sighed and rolled her head back to gaze at the ceiling. "Fine. I'll have water."

"Coming right up."

Emma rolled her head to the side so that her cheek was on the back of the couch. She didn't need to watch Blaze walk away. Didn't need to focus on his ass in those jeans, the way the faded fabric hugged the curves of his impressive bottom. She definitely didn't need to imagine it naked.

Too bad she did all those things anyway.

Blaze came back with a bottle of water and set it on the end table beside her. She'd managed to look away before he returned so he couldn't know she'd been staring at his butt and fantasizing about him with no clothes.

Yum.

"You look a little flushed."

"I'm fine." Emma picked up the water and took a drink.

She'd finished the beer when his back was turned. She really did want another, but the room was pleasantly fuzzy, and her blood buzzed.

"What will you do to him if you catch him?"

"Depends on what my guys find out. If he's in the local

area, we'll have a talk with him and strongly suggest he go back to Chicago."

"Is that code for beating him up? I can't approve of that. I'm a doctor."

Was she slurring her words? She blinked to pull Blaze back into focus. Seriously, it'd been *one* beer. Was she really that much of a lightweight?

One beer and two *glasses of wine.*

Ohhh yeah, the wine. Plus, dinner had been a while ago, so it was no longer soaking up alcohol.

"Not beating him up, Em. Threatening him? Abso-fucking-lutely."

She liked the sound of that. "Threatening him with what?"

"Bodily harm, of course."

She couldn't help but grin. "I like you, Blaze Connolly."

He blinked and then his eyes narrowed. "I like you, too, Emma."

She took another drink of water and set the bottle on the end table. And then, because she couldn't remember why she shouldn't do it, she crawled across the couch and settled in the crook of his arm. Emma closed her eyes and sighed. "You smell good."

She thought he twisted a finger in a lock of her hair that had come free from her bun, but maybe she was imagining it. The room was spinning just a little bit, and she was tired. So much stress. So little sleep. Emma yawned.

"You do, too," he said, his breath ruffling her hair.

Was he sniffing her?

Didn't matter. Emma turned into his side, stretched her arm across his abdomen—whoa, so firm—and dragged her eyes open to gaze up at him. His were hooded as he studied her.

A portion of her brain was beating tambourines like it was Saturday night in a tent revival meeting, but the rest of her was saying one word. *Safe.*

"Sleepy," she said. "Thanks."

He slid down on the couch, taking her with him so that she lay against his chest, one leg thrown over his. That secure feeling intensified.

"Sleep, Emma. I'll protect you."

"I know," she murmured. "'S'what you do."

Chapter Fourteen

Blaze took note of the black SUV in the parking
lot when he arrived at One Shot the next morning. They
weren't open for another two hours, but someone was
clearly raring to go. He slammed the door of his truck and
strolled into the store portion of the range where their
offices were located.

Ghost leaned against a counter filled with Glocks, legs
crossed at the ankles, arms folded over his chest, pewter
eyes giving nothing away as he stared—somewhat narrow-
eyed in Blaze's opinion—at the man and woman across
from him. His sidearm was visible at his waist. His polo
shirt featured the One Shot Tactical logo over his heart—
gold on a navy background—same as Blaze's did. The
shirts had arrived day before yesterday, and they were all
wearing them now.

The couple turned as Blaze walked in. He clocked the
suits and the government look they sported—like being
constipated and pissed off at the same time—and revised
his opinion about potential clients. Even the SUV looked

government issued, but the tags weren't government. He'd have noticed if they were.

He was distracted this morning, but not so distracted he'd have missed a detail like that.

Having a pretty doctor fall asleep on his chest hadn't been on his bingo card for last night, but it had happened. He'd spent an hour lying partially under her, waiting for her to wake up, but she hadn't. He'd planned to carry her to the guest room, but instead he'd fallen asleep with a tiny woman sprawled across him and a dick that was more than a little bit aroused.

It was a nice change of pace from waking up sweating and shouting through a nightmare. Sex helped, but he never spent the night in a woman's bed—or let her spend the night in his. Too fucking embarrassing to have to explain himself if the dreams started.

He hadn't had any last night. He'd slept soundly, waking a few hours later when Emma stirred. She'd mumbled about having to pee then disappeared and didn't return. He heard the bedroom door close and the lock twist. This morning, she'd rushed out the door with nothing more than a quick thanks. She'd had her suitcase and toiletry bag in hand, and he knew she wasn't planning to return.

Or, hell, to acknowledge that *anything* had happened. He got that Emma Sutton had reason to avoid anything involving intimacy, but it bugged him anyway. She'd felt safe enough to relax with him. Were they going to pretend it hadn't happened?

Then again, did it matter? He couldn't get involved with her. The most he could do was hook up, but he didn't think Emma was the hookup type after what'd happened to her. She would need to trust a man, get to know him, feel like they had something worth exploring.

He wasn't that guy and couldn't be because his first priority was the job.

No matter how much he wanted it to be otherwise.

The federal agents—because what else could they be—watched him. Ghost did too, but his expression telegraphed annoyance at their unexpected guests rather than wondering what the hell was going through Blaze's mind.

Probably a good thing.

Blaze shrugged out of his jacket and slung it over the counter. "Morning."

It was as cheery as he could manage after last night.

"Blaze, these are Special Agents Diana Corbin and Clay Ackerman with the FBI," Ghost said on a drawl. "They've come to speak to us about Royal Shipping."

Blaze tilted his head like an inquisitive puppy. "Royal Shipping? Aren't they the private courier we were looking into for transferring licensed firearms to dealers in other states?"

"That's the one," Ghost said.

"Is there a problem with their service? Should we find another courier?"

Agent Corbin was a tall, leggy blonde with green eyes that gave nothing away. Her partner was her height, but rounder. He sported a wedding ring and a bit of a belly behind his suit jacket. Agent Corbin was the one who gave Blaze an icy stare before sliding it to Ghost.

"No problem," she said smoothly. "We're speaking to everyone who visited their facility on Tuesday."

"Why Tuesday?" Ghost asked. Tuesday was the day Kane and Chance had gone inside, and early Wednesday was when the team had infiltrated and planted their equipment.

Agent Corbin's cheeks reddened slightly, as if she'd given away information she hadn't intended. "Not important, Mr. Bishop. Our records indicate that two of your employees—"

"Partners," Ghost interrupted.

Agent Corbin blinked. "Pardon me?"

"We're partners. It was our dream to start our own business together back when we served in the military. And here we are, living the dream in Alabama."

His grin was wide. Blaze was the only one who knew that it was dripping a *fuck you* so big it could blot out the sun.

"Fine," the pretty agent said, sounding perturbed to be interrupted with what she no doubt considered unimportant details. "Two of your *partners* visited the facility Tuesday. We'd like to speak with them."

Ghost shrugged. "Sure. I don't know what they can tell you, though. We can't mail handguns through the postal service. When we make a sale to someone in another state, we need a private courier who can transport the weapons to a dealer in that state. Kane and Chance were doing research."

"I'm aware of it, Mr. Bishop. It's a federal law."

"Of course. And please, call me Alex." He smiled at her, but Agent Corbin didn't crack one in return.

"If we could speak to those employ—partners, Mr. Bishop?"

Ghost took his phone from his pocket and tapped the screen. "Chance, can you and Kane come to the office? Got a couple of federal agents here who'd like to talk to you."

He put the phone on the counter. He still hadn't uncrossed his ankles. He looked slightly less than harmless rather than what he really was. Neither agent had any idea the man they faced could kill them without breaking a sweat or knocking a hair out of place, or they'd be standing a few feet away and have their hands on their guns. Not that it would help in the slightest if Ghost wanted to kill them.

Blaze went over to the coffee pot, grabbed a mug from the cabinet, and poured himself a shot of caffeine. He hadn't made coffee at home because he'd been dealing with a skittish woman. When she ran out of there like her hair was on fire, he'd wanted to get out too and stop thinking about how she'd felt pressed up against him half the night. He'd gone to Kiss My Grits, but that hadn't worked out either since they were closed for a maintenance issue.

He took a sip of coffee and turned as Chance and Kane came in from outside. Ghost did the introductions, and Agent Corbin, who was clearly running the show, asked if there was someplace they could talk. Chance, Kane, and the two agents headed for one of the small meeting rooms.

Ghost arched an eyebrow as he shot Blaze a look. Blaze sidled over with his coffee and sipped. "Odd."

"Fuck yes," Ghost muttered. "We didn't leave a trail."

No, they hadn't. Getting in and out of places, achieving their objectives, was as natural to them as breathing. They'd spent years training, years doing. While it wasn't ideal to find two FBI agents in One Shot a couple of days after they'd broken into Royal Shipping, they'd handle it.

"Leak somewhere?"

"Possible. Our orders come from the president, but that doesn't mean she doesn't have a problem. There are a lot of people who don't like Marla Willis. I imagine there are quite a few in critical government agencies still smarting over her victory."

"Always happens when a new president takes over."

"It does, but we've got a lot of man babies out there who can't stand the idea a woman is finally in charge. I wouldn't be surprised if her problem is a lot closer to home than she realizes. The FBI director hasn't always been on her side, and neither have several high-ranking congressmen or a couple of the joint chiefs."

"She should have replaced the director."

"Probably. But she didn't. Wouldn't be surprised if he has an informant in the West Wing."

"Isn't that what Ian Black is for?"

Ian Black, billionaire CEO of Black Defense International, former CIA agent, once disavowed but probably not really, was the sort of man people in power hired to take care of problems quietly and quickly.

"I'm sure he's got his minions in the halls of government."

He very likely did. Blaze had wondered at first why Black's people weren't the ones moving to Alabama, but it turned out that President Willis wanted HOT operators, not spies. Ian Black and company had other jobs to do.

Blaze took his coffee to his desk and sat down to go over invoices. Ghost went back to arranging Glocks and wiping down the glass cabinets. Seth and Ethan arrived a few minutes later.

"Whose black Yukon?" Ethan asked.

"Feds," Blaze said. Ethan's eyebrows climbed his forehead. "They're in with Kane and Chance, talking about their visit to Royal Shipping."

This time his brows arrowed down into a frown. Seth's did too.

"Apparently they're talking to everyone who visited the facility on Tuesday," Blaze said, sipping his coffee. "They haven't said why."

The four of them exchanged a look. Nobody said anything. Ethan and Seth got coffee and went to do their tasks for the morning before the range opened. When the feds emerged a short while later, they stopped by the counter where Ghost was checking inventory on rifle scopes.

"Get what you need, agents?" he asked with a sunny smile.

Blaze would have laughed if he could have.

"For now," Diana Corbin said. She took a card from her pocket and slid it across the counter. "If you think of anything that might help us with our inquiries, give one of us a call. We'll be in touch."

Ghost picked up the card and dropped it in a drawer behind the counter. "Thanks. A pleasure to meet you both. If you'd like to join the range, we offer a discount for military and government employees."

Agent Corbin didn't crack a smile. "Thank you, but we're good," she said before turning on her heel and marching to the door.

"Have a nice day," Ghost called as the two agents walked out. Clay Ackerman acknowledged Ghost with a nod and said, "Thanks, you too."

Diana Corbin didn't stop her march into the parking lot.

"Don't think she liked you, boss," Chance drawled. He

was standing in the doorway that led into the hall, arms folded across his chest, grinning.

Kane was there, too. He was also grinning. "I wouldn't say she was all that friendly to us, but she was a lot nicer than she was to you. Maybe it's not me that needs to worry about pissing off the hot babes."

Ghost snorted. "Oh, you still need to worry, brother. What can I say, though? Agent Corbin likes a man she can boss around. Guess she could tell I'm not that type. What'd they want to know?"

"Nothing important. What time we visited, who we talked to, what we talked about. Did we get a tour of the facility? Did we see anything out of place? Bullshit questions."

"Equipment's still operational," Ghost mused. "So they didn't find the cameras or mics. Huh, wonder what they really want?"

"You gonna call Washington?" Blaze asked.

"Yeah, think so," Ghost replied.

Blaze followed him into the office. "Uh, boss, need to tell you something."

Ghost looked up with one dark eyebrow arched. "About what?"

Now why did he feel like he'd been called to the principal's office?

He gave Ghost the rundown about Emma Sutton and her problem. Ghost's gaze hardened while he talked. "She okay?"

"Seems to be. She's scared, though. That's why I suggested the cameras. And I asked Seth to check into it, see what he could find on Simon Marsh."

Ghost nodded. "All right. Do what you have to do to

make her safe. But careful how deep you get into this. We've got enough problems already."

"Just trying to help the lady out."

"I trust you to handle this, Blaze. What we're doing here is too important to risk."

"Got it, boss. You can count on me."

Ghost was studying him. "What happened in Afghanistan… That wasn't your fault. I hope you know that."

Blaze's insides tightened painfully. His throat squeezed shut. "It was my mission, my responsibility."

Ghost pitched his voice low. "Shit goes sideways, Shadow. It was a clusterfuck of bad intel and bad decision-making. Not yours and not HOT's. The CIA fucked that one up, and your team paid the price. Mendez tore 'em a new asshole over it, but that doesn't bring back the men we lost. None of that is on you."

"Yes, sir. Thank you, sir."

Ghost sighed. "You're still gonna think you could have done something different. I know that. But maybe stop blaming yourself so much. You're here because I trust you. Because I *know* you're the right man for this job. So help Emma Sutton out. Take her to bed and screw her silly if you want. Just don't let it go any deeper than that."

"Heard and understood, sir."

Chapter Fifteen

"I NEED TO SEE DOC SUTTON, NOT YOU."

Emma didn't let her smile falter as she faced the steel-haired woman sitting in the waiting room. If this was the worst she had to deal with these days, she could handle it. It was annoying, but there were far worse things.

Like falling asleep on a man you barely know?

Heat flared in her cheeks. Dammit, she didn't have time for this.

"I'm a doctor, Mrs. Croft. I'm helping my dad with patients."

Margaret Croft gave her the once over with skepticism.

"That's not possible, Emma Grace Sutton. I've known you since you were knee high to a grasshopper. You might've gone off to that fancy medical school and passed all the exams, but your daddy is my doctor, and he's who I want to see."

Emma prayed for strength. "Mrs. Croft, my father is retiring in a few months, which he's announced to all his patients, and I've come home to take over the practice. I assure you I'm qualified to examine you and prescribe medicine, should it be necessary."

Mrs. Croft looked like she'd sucked a lemon. "I didn't think he was serious. He knows how much we need him in this town." Her face screwed tighter. "Oh no, this won't do. It won't do at all. I'll have to go to Huntsville if he leaves, and I really don't want to do that."

Emma didn't have it in her to fight. It'd been like this since she'd started work a few days ago. People who'd been seeing her dad their entire lives didn't trust a young woman who, according to them, lacked life experience.

Never mind that she was thirty-four years old and had been an ER doctor in a trauma center. None of that mattered to the good citizens of Sutton's Creek because they'd known her when she was still playing with dolls and waving shepherd's crooks.

Yet another reason she'd never wanted to take over the practice. She'd known this would happen.

"You can go to Huntsville when he's gone if you like. As for today's issue, my dad's schedule is booked at the moment. You can reschedule and ask for him specifically, but it'll be at least two weeks. Maybe three. Or you can come back to the exam room, and I'll have a look."

Mrs. Croft stood with a great huff. She shouldered her massive handbag—it looked like she could store a boat in there—and stared down her nose at Emma.

"Fine, Emma Grace, I'll let you examine me. But I'm going to be watching you, I promise."

Did she think Emma was going to dive into that handbag and make off with her vault of priceless jewels or something?

"That's fine, Mrs. Croft. Whatever makes you comfortable."

Emma stood back and allowed the woman to sail past her into the hallway where the exam rooms were. After a few questions and a brief examination, Mrs. Croft left clutching a prescription for an antibiotic ointment for her skin rash and looking like she'd smelled dog poop. She didn't bother to say thank you, either.

Emma closed her eyes and rubbed them. She needed patience, and she didn't have a hell of a lot of it today. Her life had turned upside down and it wasn't finished yet if yesterday was anything to go by.

Her phone dinged in her pocket. Probably Rory asking if she was coming by the Dawg for dinner. Which she totally was because the idea of facing Blaze Connolly after last night made her stomach twist and her skin flame.

She pulled her phone out, her heart flipping at the message.

Blaze: I called your dad about the cameras. He agreed. They're going up this afternoon. Locks being changed, too. I convinced him we needed something better.

Relief flowed through her. Not to mention more heat. Seriously?

Emma: Thank you.

Blaze: You're welcome.

Emma stared at her screen. Three dots appeared and disappeared. Just when she was ready to put the phone away, his message came across.

Blaze: In case you were wondering, I didn't mind last night. I liked it.

Her face really was on fire. Which was ridiculous. She was a doctor. She understood vasodilator effects, so why couldn't she get better control of hers? Not that she could control blushing, because nobody could, but *why* was she letting her emotions get that far in the first place?

She should have a lock on her reaction to Blaze Connolly. She wasn't a teenager anymore. He was a gorgeous man, but she was a grown woman. As if that mattered a bit to her fluttering pulse.

Emma: Let us never speak of this again. I'm embarrassed enough already.

Blaze: If that's what you want. When are you coming for self-defense lessons?

Emma swallowed. *I'm not sure. It's very busy here.*

Blaze: Think you need to prioritize this, babe.

Emma stared at the casual *babe* tossed at the end of the sentence. She really should tell him not to call her babe. She'd gone to medical school, fought the misogyny there, and eventually graduated in the top five percent of her class. She'd worked hard to dispel erroneous beliefs about her skills in Chicago, almost always from older male colleagues, and she'd never stopped fighting for her place at the table.

She'd earned it. And then she'd thrown it all away because she'd had the misfortune to get involved with a charming psychopath. So telling Blaze Connolly *not* to call her babe really should be at the top of her list of ground rules for dealing with him.

But a part of her liked the way it felt coming from him. She *shouldn't*—really, really shouldn't—but it was somehow wrapped up in that safe feeling she got around him. It made her feel protected, which was crazy because it was just a word.

A door closed in the rear of the practice. Her dad strolled in, looking fresh from his early morning golf game, smiling wide when he saw her. Emma's heart filled with love and gratitude. She hadn't appreciated her dad's choice to take care of the citizens of Sutton's Creek nearly enough when she was growing up.

"There's my girl. How's it going, honey?"

Emma shrugged. "You know. Mrs. Croft wasn't pleased. Neither were the other three patients I saw today, but none of them called me by my given name and insisted I somehow didn't learn anything in medical school. That honor goes to Mrs. C."

Her dad frowned. "Sorry, honey."

"She'll come around, or she'll drive all the way to Huntsville every time her arm itches. How was your game?"

"Had a good time with the guys. Thanks for covering for me today."

Emma stood on tiptoe to kiss his cheek. "I'm glad I could help. Why are you here anyway? Thought you were having lunch with Mama."

"I am. Just stopped to see how you were doing."

"I think I've got a handle on it, Dad." Like most Southern girls, she usually called her father Daddy. Didn't matter how old she got, he was her daddy. When she was annoyed, it was Dad.

He raised both hands. "Okay, message received." He hesitated a moment. "Blaze Connolly called."

Her belly fluttered. "Oh yeah?"

"Mm-hm. Said he wanted to put up some security cameras and change the locks on both your apartments. Any reason why?"

Emma blinked. "I think he's just security conscious. That's his business, right? And you have to admit cameras on the building aren't a bad idea. Sturdier locks as well. After what happened at the Gas-n-Go, I'm all for it."

He nodded. "That's basically what he said. I told him

to give me a bill, but he refused. Said it was on him because he'd suggested it."

"I'm sure those guys get their equipment at cost, Daddy."

"Sure, but it's not free."

"I'll talk to him."

The second she said it, she wished she could call it back. Her dad looked at her with a raised eyebrow and a half grin. He was so going to tell her mother, who was going to call her up and grill her for details about how she'd gotten on such a friendly footing with Blaze.

"It's nothing," she said. "He's my neighbor. I spoke to him yesterday in the hall, and he mentioned the security cameras and locks to me. I said he should call you. That's it."

Because the rest was her business alone.

"All right, honey."

Her phone buzzed again.

Blaze: You avoiding me?

"Have to answer this," she said, holding up her phone. She didn't wait for a reply as she retreated to the office space she'd carved out in the stock room for the time being. She'd take over her dad's office when he retired, so no need to make another office even though he'd told her she should.

She sat at her desk and frowned as she stared at the screen. Then she typed, *No, not avoiding you. I have a job, you know. I was busy.*

Blaze: Which is why you need to make time for self-defense class. Got one starting Monday night at six. I'll save a spot for you.

Emma frowned hard. Then she sighed and tossed her phone on the desk. She couldn't avoid Blaze forever. Last night had been supremely embarrassing but she could legit blame it on the alcohol.

The trick was not to do it again. No matter how tempting his broad chest and solid muscles were.

Her phone buzzed. She snatched it up to see what he wanted now.

It wasn't Blaze, though. The sender was unknown. The message was simple.

I'm watching.

Chapter Sixteen

"You're telling me the fucker's still in Chicago," Blaze growled.

Seth was at his laptop, studying the screen. "Technically, yes. His phone is, anyway. He's either hired someone to intimidate her, or he bought a burner and left his phone at home."

"That's what I'm thinking."

Blaze was fucking furious. Acid scalded its way through his gut. He and Seth had gone to install the cameras and change the door locks that afternoon. He'd stopped by the doctor's office to tell Emma what they were doing. She'd shown him the message and he'd launched into protector mode, hustling her out of there and into his apartment while they worked.

"I'm only letting you do this because I've seen the last patient for the day," she'd said, eyes flashing fire at him as she closed up the office and followed him upstairs.

They were back at One Shot Tactical now, and Emma was currently on a tour of the facility with Kane. Charming Kane. Blaze had glared at his teammate, telegraphing that he'd better keep his damned charm under wraps. Dude could charm the panties off a nun if he tried, and Blaze wasn't having it.

If anybody was getting into Emma's panties, it was him.

Maybe.

"You know, I thought the doc was kinda standoffish when I first met her." Chance said when he walked into the office. "But she's not, is she? Plus she's kinda hot in that nerdy librarian way."

"Off limits," Blaze said, his teeth grinding.

Chance grinned. "Saw Kane showing her the ropes. You sure you wanted to do that, man?"

"He's already got a date with that cute chick that's been taking the ladies' beginning firearms class. What was her name? Lindsey? Laura? Lainey?" Seth said without looking up.

"Beats me. Never stopped him before, though."

"Emma Sutton's too smart for Kane Fox," Ghost said without looking up from his desk.

Blaze said, "I think you mean she's smarter than a fox."

Ghost pointed a finger gun at him. "Bingo. She's not his type if *Lainey* is any indication."

"Riiight, Lainey," Chance said. "Bleach blonde, big knockers, ass to die for."

"That's her," Seth replied. "Kane got there first or I'd have asked her out."

"What's taking so long with the rest of that report?" Blaze said.

"Uh, you realize we aren't back at HQ and the shit doesn't show up instantly, right?"

"I know. Sorry." Blaze clenched and unclenched a fist, thinking. "Emma's been feeling like someone's watching her, her apartment gets broken into, and now she gets a message from an unknown number. Unless she's got enemies in Sutton's Creek, it seems like Simon Marsh is the most likely suspect."

"Here it is," Seth chirped. "He doesn't have a record. No arrests. On paper, dude is ordinary. No mortgage, but he has an address, so he must be renting."

"He hit her," Blaze ground out. "And he intimidated her enough not to report it. He's probably done the same to other women."

"Gonna agree with you there," Chance said, his voice hard. Blaze knew his friend had grown up rough, like he had, but he didn't know the extent of it. Chance didn't talk much about his childhood, but they all knew it'd been difficult. His easygoing manner overlaid some serious trauma if Blaze was any judge.

Which he was since his own mother had been such a nightmare. So far as he knew, she was still alive. They didn't talk, though. He hadn't heard from her in about five years. She'd occasionally called asking for money when she was desperate enough. Never for any other reason. Not birthdays or holidays or anything else. Just money. The last time, he'd told her he'd pay for a treatment facility, but he wasn't sending money. Predictably, she'd ghosted him. It wasn't a loss. He'd always known he didn't mean jack to her.

"Any photos?" Blaze asked.

"No."

"Not even on his driver's license?"

"Still trying to access the file for that. Nothing's coming up so far."

The door opened, and Kane emerged with Emma. She was smiling, and Blaze's gut tightened. She hadn't smiled at him since last night when they'd been drinking beer together. Of course, she'd pretty much avoided looking at him since she'd fallen asleep sprawled across his chest.

"Did you find anything?" she asked, directing her gaze at him. *Finally*.

The tension he'd been feeling seemed to ebb a bit. "His phone is still in Chicago."

She frowned. "I guess I could be wrong. Maybe we scared whoever broke into my place before they could hit yours. They heard us coming and got out before they could really go through my stuff, such as it is. It could be a whole lotta nothing."

He could see the hope on her face. He hated to crush it, but he had to be real with her.

"It's also possible he left his phone at home and bought a burner rather than using a service like Google Voice to mask his number."

Marsh would have been easier to find if he'd done that, but either the dude was aware he could be tracked, or he was still in Chicago and they were wrong. He could send a shitty text from Chicago just as easily as he could from Sutton's Creek.

She closed her eyes for a second before gazing at him again. He watched the mask settle over her face, the determination to be strong. If his mother had mustered even an ounce of Emma's strength, maybe she wouldn't have searched for whatever it was she was looking for in bottles and needles.

"Okay. So now what?"

"We monitor the video feed for any sign of him or anyone else. And you have to promise not to go anywhere alone for a while."

He didn't tell her that they'd also see if Marsh's car had

gone through any toll booths between Alabama and Chicago, or that they'd pull footage from the parking garage at his building to see if he'd been leaving and returning regularly, or if he'd left and hadn't yet gone back.

Emma skated her gaze across the men gathered. "I don't see how I can do that. I have to work, and I might be in the clinic alone sometimes if my dad or the nurse isn't there. And what if I need to run upstairs to get something from my apartment? Or if I want to visit my parents at home? I can't upend my life again. I won't."

She'd wrapped her arms around her middle. Her eyes had widened the more she spoke. Blaze could see the fine edge of a panic attack about to happen. She'd been on the verge of one last night when she'd first told him she thought she was being followed. He'd told her to breathe, and she had. She'd managed to hold it off, at least so long as he was there. If she'd had one later, he didn't know about it.

"Breathe, Emma."

Chance produced a chair, and she sank onto it. She bowed her head and sucked in a breath. Blaze went and knelt beside her. "You got this, babe. Just breathe."

She nodded and reached a hand out. He took it, squeezing gently while she processed her way through the attack. Nobody said anything. Someone put a bottle of water in his free hand. Chance placed a blanket on the counter nearby in case she got chilled. It happened with panic attacks sometimes, and Blaze was grateful that his friend thought of it.

"You aren't alone, Emma. You've got me. You've got this room full of badass motherfuckers willing to stand between you and any asshole who tries to hurt you. I promise you that."

Her gaze lifted to his. Her skin was pale and her hand clammy, but she squeezed back. "I fucking hate this," she hissed through her teeth.

"I know, honey. It sucks. Been there a few times myself."

Her eyebrows climbed her forehead.

He nodded. "Yep, it can happen to anyone. Even big guys like me. Anxiety doesn't care who it gets, babe. It's getting to you right now, but it's gonna be okay."

She closed her eyes and leaned her head back. She was already breathing easier. He felt the tremors start in her limbs as a chill settled over her.

"I hate that I can't control my body. That I know what's happening but still can't stop it."

Chance handed him the blanket, and he settled it around her. The guys exchanged looks and then melted away so he could handle the situation alone. He appreciated that. He knew she would too. Emma was an accomplished woman who didn't like to appear weak. He'd figured that out pretty quick.

"I know. It doesn't work that way, though. I'd explain the science, but I think you probably understand it better than I do."

She attempted a laugh. It sounded rusty. "I hope so. There's an inciting incident to make the heart race—Simon's presence in my hometown, for example—and then the amygdala sends a distress signal to the hypothalamus. The hypothalamus fires up the adrenal glands, which in turn release adrenaline and cortisol. Pretty much a flight or fight response that floods your senses, diverts blood from non-essential regions, and fucks up your day for a while."

"A wise colonel I knew said once that a panic attack is

just fear of fear. So long as you know that, you can deal with it instead of letting it conquer you."

It was Ghost who'd said it. Dude was right, too. Not that panic attacks were easy, but it helped.

"Can't necessarily stop the symptoms, though."

"True."

She'd wrapped the blanket around her neck and sat shivering from time to time. Not as badly as she had before. "This is another one of those things that, when it's over, we need never speak of again."

A smile tugged at the corners of his mouth. "You mean we need to file it away with that other thing we can never speak of?"

"That's right."

"Sure, why not?"

She cracked an eye to look at him. "Like I said, you're a nice guy, Blaze Connolly."

"I am to you." He got up and grabbed a chair to tug over near hers. She'd let his hand go and clutched the blanket. The panic attack was ebbing, though she'd probably feel the shivery effects for quite a while. "We need to talk about protection, Emma."

She rolled her chin forward and opened her eyes. There was a question in them. "Protection?"

"For you. You need to be escorted to and from work, which is easy enough for me to do since I live next door. You shouldn't be alone in the office. Make sure your dad or the nurse is there. If they can't be, then call me. One of us will stay with you."

Her mouth fell open. "You guys have a business to run. You can't drop everything to sit with me for the hour or two I might be alone in the office. There'll be patients coming and going, so I won't be alone anyway. If I see

Simon anywhere—sitting across the street, walking in the park, whatever—I'll call you and 911 both."

"Not good enough, Emma. Any man who abused you the way he did, who controlled you and tried to intimidate you, who then follows you across state lines to a new town after you ended your relationship, doesn't have good intentions. If he's out there, it's not so he can apologize."

She shivered again. He didn't think it had anything to do with the panic attack this time.

"What is it, babe?" he prodded softly.

"There's something I didn't tell you before."

"So tell me now."

She dragged in a breath. "He has a gun. That last day, when he hit me, he held it to my head and told me what would happen if I ever left him."

Blaze swore. Emma shook her head, her eyes squeezing shut. "I know, I know. And telling you this doesn't make you less likely to tell me not to be alone. But when does it stop, Blaze? When do I get to live my life and stop worrying that some deranged control freak is going to pop up when I least expect it and do, well, I don't know what? I think he gets off on fear. I'm not sure he'd go so far as to kill. It wouldn't make any sense. He doesn't want to end up in prison."

Blaze gritted his teeth. "Not everyone is logical or sane. Some people are broken, and they do things that don't make sense. He threatened you, hurt you, controlled you. But you left him, and when he tried to get you back with apologies and promises he wasn't that guy, you didn't fall into his arms. Instead, you left your job and moved several states away. A guy like that is probably *pissed as hell* that you dared walk out on him. Maybe he wants to scare you, make you as uncomfortable in your new home as you were in your old one. But maybe it's more than that. He might want revenge, and none of us can say what form that's going to take in his head or what he's going to consider satisfying. Best you treat this like a dangerous, life-threatening situation until we get evidence otherwise."

She blinked up at him. Her face had gone pale, her mouth parting slightly. She swallowed and then nodded. "You're right."

He shoved his fingers in his hair and blew out. "I know you don't like this. I know it's not what you want. But anybody who'd use a pistol to threaten you isn't stable, Emma."

She was still pale, but her spine straightened, and her head tilted up.

Good girl.

"Tell me what I need to do."

Chapter Seventeen

EMMA WATCHED BLAZE CONNOLLY'S FACE. HIS SKY-BLUE eyes sparked as if he was choosing his words before he spoke.

She let her gaze drop a fraction, taking in the navy polo shirt with the gold One Shot Tactical logo that fit him like a caress. He wore a sidearm in a holster at his waist, and she knew he had a knife in his boot. She thought she should be repelled, but she wasn't.

He ticked it off on his fingers. "One, do what I already told you and never be alone, not even in the office. Patients don't count, Emma. Two, let me teach you how to defend yourself. Three, buy a gun and learn how to use it."

She felt the color rising to her cheeks until she blurted, "I don't know that I can do that. I've tried to piece people together while they bled out from gunshot wounds. It's horrific what happens to the human body—"

"I know what a bullet does to a body. I've shot people. I've been shot. It's not what anyone wants to do, but you don't go up against a man with a gun armed with nothing but your principles."

Emma's body tightened. He'd been shot? Her gaze skimmed over him as if she could see the bullet wound, but of course she couldn't. When her eyes met his again, he was watching her curiously. She cleared her throat and clasped her hands over the blanket in her lap.

"I'm sorry you were shot," she said, her voice sounding raspy and hoarse.

"Me too. But I'm still here." He leaned forward and tipped her chin up with a finger. His skin was smooth, not rough, and she wanted to lean into his hand and feel more of his skin on hers.

"Learning to fire a weapon, owning one, doesn't mean you'll ever shoot anyone. It just means you'll have an option if you find yourself in danger and I'm not there to protect you."

"I know how to use a shotgun. I'm a Southern girl."

"That's good, babe. Real good. I'll teach you how to shoot a pistol, okay? You can try as many as it takes until we find one that's a good fit. Because if something happens and that asshole points a weapon at you again? I want you to know how to fight back."

"I want to do what you did. At the Gas-n-Go."

"I'll teach you. But Emma, the smartest thing you can ever, *ever* do when faced with a gunman is get the hell out if you can. Don't confront them; don't try to disarm or shoot them. Just get out or hide if you can't escape. If they've got you held hostage, different story, but even then you need to really know what you're doing, or you could get killed. You got me?"

She nodded.

"Good girl," he said before skimming a finger along her jaw and down her neck.

Her heart rocketed into gear, her skin was suddenly too

hot, and the hair on her arms prickled as need stirred in her core. She watched his mouth, the sensual curl of his lips, and had a strong urge to press her mouth to his.

Her gaze skittered sideways as embarrassment and longing flooded her in equal measure. What in the absolute hell was wrong with her? He was trying to help her, and she was busy thinking about kissing him.

Not helpful, Emma Grace.

"You feeling okay? You're looking flushed."

"Fine," she croaked. "Maybe I should get some water."

He'd said he'd liked her lying next to him last night, but he hadn't actually kissed her. Maybe he was just being nice and wasn't as attracted to her as she was to him.

"Here." He picked up a bottle from the counter and handed it to her.

The plastic was cold when she wrapped her hand around it. She twisted off the cap and took a long drink, hoping the icy liquid would cool the flame burning low in her belly.

"What else?" she asked, clearing her throat and fixing her gaze on him again. She would *not* turn red. Not, not, not....

"We changed the locks on the apartment doors, put the cameras up in the hall and on the front and back of the building. But I'd prefer you weren't alone. I think you should stay with me for a couple of days if you're not comfortable telling your parents or Rory about this."

Heat scored its way across her skin. "I'm not, but I'm not sure staying with you is a good idea."

Except she *would* feel safe. She had last night. Apart from attacking him on the couch and sprawling across his chest to fall asleep, it'd been a good night. She hadn't lain awake worrying or jumping at every creak of the building.

"It's not forever, Emma. Just until we get a lock on this guy. You know the apartment is big enough. You get your own room, I get mine, and we don't have to spend every moment together. I'll get one of the guys to stay at your place, that way someone will be there if Marsh tries to break in again."

"I'm not sure I'm comfortable with any of you putting yourselves in danger."

His eyebrows lifted, and then he laughed. "Babe, I'm telling you, that's like worrying that a house cat's equal to a lion. Simon Marsh is no threat to any of us, no matter how big his gun or how clever he thinks he is."

She believed him. A small flame of relief flickered to life as she clutched the cold bottle in her hands.

"I feel like every bit of this is a lot to ask. We met a few days ago, and now you and your friends are going out of your way to help me when you have a business of your own to run. You're letting a stranger crash your space with no idea whether I'm a pain in the ass to live with or not. What if I leave dirty dishes everywhere and forget to throw away my trash? What if I leave rings in the bathtub and use all the toilet paper?"

He grinned. "It's a few days tops, Emma. If you're a slob, I'll politely ask you to put your stuff away or clean up your own messes. This isn't hard."

"I still feel like it is, but you make everything sound so reasonable."

"It *is* reasonable. How likely is your father to come upstairs looking for you?"

"Not at all unless invited. He's always been very particular about giving me my space. My mother isn't quite as good about it, but she knows not to show up unannounced. I won't have to explain why I'm not staying in my apartment." She chewed the inside of her lip. "I may have to tell Rory, though. Maybe not if she's busy enough at the Dawg and I go see her more often. Unless you tell me I can't go. Which won't make me happy, but I'll do it."

"You can go to the Dawg, but you can't walk over there alone."

"How long do you think it'll take to find him?"

"I don't really know. I'd like to say it'll be fast, but a lot of that depends on how reckless he is going forward. Still don't think it'll take more than a week though."

Her stomach tightened. "Maybe I should text him back. Make him think I'm not scared of him. He'd hate that."

"No." His voice was like ice. "Don't engage."

"I could help, Blaze. He'll slip up and make a mistake if he thinks I'm not freaked out enough."

He reached for her hand and enclosed it in his big, warm one. "I don't want you doing that. If he's watching you, he's staying somewhere close and he's gonna slip up. We'll find him."

Emma sighed. "Okay. I trust you."

It was both a relief and a shock to realize that she really did. Blaze Connolly was a hero. He'd put himself between her and a bullet once before. He'd do it again.

She just hoped he didn't have to.

Chapter Eighteen

It was Friday night, work was done, and they were planning to head to the Salty Dawg after a quick stop back home to check the cameras and locks. Blaze glanced over at Emma. She gazed out the window of his truck, her long hair hanging over her shoulder as she played with her ponytail, twisting it around and around her finger.

Blaze wanted to play with that hair. He wanted to take it down and spread it out, then he wanted to see it fanned across his pillow as he lowered himself into her willing body.

Shit.

He shoved the thought away at the first tickle of arousal in his balls. He didn't need to be getting hard over a thought that wasn't gonna happen. He wanted it to, but the fact she was under his protection now, staying in his apartment, meant he wasn't making any moves.

It wasn't professional, and it damned sure wasn't right considering what Emma had been through with Simon Marsh. She was still dealing with the fallout of that relationship. Last thing she needed was to get involved with him when all he could do right now was a few hot nights together.

Even when the mission was done in a few months, he didn't do long-term. Maybe it was his childhood that had fucked him over, or maybe he just wasn't cut out for it. He'd never met a woman he wanted to try with anyway.

He knew he wasn't parent material. He hadn't had a good example of that. The idea of having to be there for a kid, to give them a stable life free of fear that he might not come home one day, was too much.

And to be fair, there'd always been a chance he wouldn't come home again. Not because he was a drug addict who'd do anything for his next fix, but because his job was dangerous.

Still was.

At least before, he could tell a woman that what he did in the military was risky. Now he wasn't allowed to so much as hint at his status as an operator. *A mercenary*. Too much at stake.

Emma's phone dinged with a text. He could see the hesitation before she picked it up. He hated that for her. Hated that someone tried so hard to dim her sparkle.

She didn't stiffen or say anything. Instead, the corners of her mouth turned up as she started to type an answer. He felt something remarkably like envy that someone else had made her smile.

"Everything okay?" he asked because he was too fucking nosy where she was concerned. Could be Theo Harper texting her. He hadn't asked if there'd been anything between them. Wasn't his business. Yet he still wanted to know.

She looked over at him, still smiling. "It's Rory. She's funny sometimes."

Funny? He hadn't thought of Aurora Harper as funny. She was serious in the tavern, flirty when she served him and the guys—except for Chance, who she actively disliked—and completely no nonsense when dealing with any problems.

"You said before that you didn't tell her about Simon. Did you mean that he was abusive or that you didn't mention him at all?"

She huffed out a breath. "At all. It happened fast, and I didn't want to say anything to anyone until I was certain the relationship was going somewhere. Besides, Rory had a bad breakup a few years ago, and I didn't want to start talking about a guy and then it didn't work out."

Her head dropped as she studied her phone. "Honestly, we didn't talk a whole lot the past four years anyway. The job took it out of me, and time would go by without me realizing how long it'd been. I really don't deserve how sweet she is to me now that I'm back. I left town and abandoned everyone here. It's no wonder some people are having trouble accepting me as their doctor. I've been home three or four times a year in the past decade, and I never stayed more than a week. I told myself I was making a career, and that one day I'd have more time, but I wouldn't have. I'd have just stayed on the hamster wheel."

"You wanted out."

He understood the desire to escape. That was all he'd ever wanted. It was why he'd signed up for the military the day he turned eighteen.

"Yes."

Her voice was little more than a whisper, but he could hear the pain in it. He wanted to ask her why she'd wanted out, but he knew better. It was her story, same as his story was his. You had to be careful who you shared your truth with. Who you gave a piece of yourself to. He knew that, too.

"But you came back."

Her nostrils flared as she lifted her head and looked out the window. The Alabama countryside was brown at this time of year, the trees bare, though some evergreens were visible, yet it was still beautiful. Mother Nature was resting, but soon the ground and trees would burst with color. Cotton, soy, and corn would fill the fields. He imagined growing up here. He wasn't stupid enough to think he'd have never left if he had.

Everyone had their demons.

"My dad's retiring, and there won't be a doctor in Sutton's Creek when he does." She shook her head. "It's not what I ever wanted to do, and maybe I made the decision under duress, but it's not a bad decision. If it doesn't work out, I can go somewhere else. Maybe work in Huntsville or Decatur or Madison. Hell, maybe I'll join Doctors Without Borders and work there for a while. Maybe I should have done that in the first place. Simon would have never found me if I had."

He didn't like the way hearing her talk about leaving made the weight in his chest expand. It shouldn't affect him at all. "I'm sure your parents are happy to have you home. Clearly your friend is. And her brother. The patients will come around."

She laughed softly. "You're very confident. The older ones who knew me when I was a child don't think I know what I'm doing. One called me Emma Grace the whole time and said she didn't care if I'd passed my exams and that my daddy was still her doctor."

"Ouch."

"I told her she could go to Huntsville if she wanted, or she could let me see what the problem was and save her a trip. She let me examine her and took the prescription I wrote, but she stuck her nose so high in the air she'd have drowned if it rained." She spread her hands. "It was a little bit funny and a little bit exasperating. I know it'll take time to win them all over. And I know there'll be some who I'll never convince. I plan to take it a day at a time. If there comes a time when I can't stand it, I'll think about finding another doctor to take over so I can move on. Hopefully my dad will be well retired by then and enjoying himself too much to feel obligated to come back."

He eased the truck into the town limits, careful to drive the posted speed. The Sutton's Creek PD was small but mighty, and they loved giving tickets to unsuspecting drivers. He knew from experience.

"I like it here," he said as he drove along tree-covered streets toward the center of town. "People are friendly, food's good, and life is quieter than where I was before this."

"Where did you move from?"

He'd known that was coming. "Maryland. We planned to start our own business for a while. The time was finally right and all of us were ready, so we did."

"I think that's nice," she said. "Kinda crazy, too. Moving somewhere you've never been before. What if you hated it?"

"Nah, we weren't going to hate it. We're used to going where we're told and adapting to the circumstances. Being here isn't much different from that."

"And where are you from originally?"

Unease flared. He didn't like talking about his childhood. "I was born in Oklahoma. Left when I was eighteen to join the military."

"Do you go back often?"

"No. No family left, so I don't go back."

His grandparents had been dead for years, and he didn't have anything to do with the rest of the family. They'd cut his mother off long ago, and that had included him. He didn't blame his aunts for not wanting his mother around their families, but it'd have been nice if one of them had taken him away and raised him with her kids. Life might have been more stable, less frightening.

"I'm sorry to hear that."

"Don't be. I have my friends, and life is good."

"But no Mrs. Connolly?" She pressed a hand to her forehead. "Good Lord, don't answer that. Way too intrusive. I'm sorry."

"It's okay. I've never been married. My job in the military took me away a lot. I never met a woman willing to put up with that."

"My parents would love it if I got married. Mama wants grandbabies to spoil."

"And what do you want?"

She shrugged. "I'm not against kids, but I also don't see marriage and family fitting into my life just yet. Maybe. Someday, but not too far in the future since time's not on my side. Who knows?"

She seemed uncomfortable enough that he didn't pursue it. Besides, that was a heavy conversation to be having with a woman he only lusted after.

"Yeah, who knows? You think you got life figured out, and then something happens completely opposite of what you expect."

"Don't I know it," she muttered.

"Damn, I shouldn't have said it like that. Sorry."

"Don't be. It's the truth."

They reached the town square, and he took a left on First Street to drive around behind the buildings. The parking lot was filling up because it was prime rib at the Dawg tonight. Later, there was a live band on the stage that took up one corner of the tavern, across from the bar. A country band from Nashville, probably. Lots of small bands toured down into Alabama while they worked to pay their bills and get studio time. He'd never considered himself a country music fan, but he had to admit that was changing the longer he spent here.

"Wait for me to come around and get you," he said as he backed into a space.

"You don't have to do that. I don't expect you to open doors for me."

"It's not some kind of manly duty, Emma. It's protective. I make sure it's safe before I let you out of the vehicle. I escort you upstairs and make sure that's safe. Everywhere you go, I make sure it's safe."

Her jaw had fallen open just a little. She snapped it shut, but he could feel the irritation rolling off her in waves. He got it.

"I see."

"This is serious, at least until we know it isn't, okay? I'm not trying to control you or make all your decisions for you. In this situation, you're the movie star and I'm your bodyguard. I have to make sure the paparazzi isn't waiting to ambush you, understand?"

"When you put it that way... This isn't going to be easy for me, okay? I let Simon cut me off from my friends and colleagues at the hospital, and I got to where I was afraid to make a decision in case he didn't like it. You telling me I have to wait to get out of a car, that I can't go anywhere alone—well, it's logical and I get it, but it still makes me feel like it's happening again. And I'm not accusing *you* of that, just saying that it's Simon getting his way again. It makes me furious."

"Okay, how's this? I get to control your movements because I have to, but you get to pick all the TV shows we watch and all the food we eat. With the exception of broccoli. Have to draw a hard line there."

One corner of her mouth lifted. "Broccoli, huh? That's your line in the sand?"

"Well, yeah. There's nothing worse than that."

"I dunno. What if I like tripe or pickled herring? What if my idea of a hearty breakfast is pickled herring *and* tripe on toast or something?"

He put a hand to his stomach. "I feel like I'm turning green here, babe. Am I green? Are you sure you like those things? Can we add them to the list, or is it too late?"

She laughed. He loved the sound of her laugh, especially when she seemed genuinely amused like she did now. Sure, it was at his expense, but he liked it anyway.

"Nope, too late. Sorry. I'm going to need to hit the grocery store tomorrow so I can pick up supplies. You're gonna love my herring-tripe toast!"

"Put barf bags on the list. Think I'm gonna need one."

She cackled. Legit cackled. He loved it. He put his hand on the door to open it, but she stopped him by circling his other wrist with her fingers. Or trying, anyway. Her hands were small, and his wrist wasn't.

He lifted his gaze to hers, something tightening in his chest at the emotion in the depths of those baby blues.

"Thanks, Blaze. I appreciate that you're trying to make me comfortable, and I'm sorry if I freaked out a bit.

I know you're helping me. I'm grateful, and I owe you one."

"Nah, you don't owe me." His voice felt stretched out in a way. Strained with the effort not to let any emotion in. "I'd do it for anyone."

Her smile softened. "I know you would. That's why I like you."

Chapter Nineteen

"WHAT'S UP WITH YOU AND MR. TALL, DARK, SEXY, & Broody?" Rory asked, notching her chin toward the table where Emma had been sitting with Blaze, Chance, Seth, and Ethan. Kane and Alex were the only two not there.

After stuffing herself full of prime rib, a baked potato, and green beans, Emma had moved to the bar so she could chat with Rory while her bestie poured drinks. She was feeling more relaxed than she had in a long time. Simon was out there, somewhere, lurking like the noxious cloud he was, but Blaze was there too, watching out for her. Protecting her.

It was a comforting thing.

Emma toyed with her wine glass. She knew Rory was talking about Blaze in particular. No need to pretend otherwise.

"Nothing. He's my new neighbor. He invited me to join them for dinner, so I said yes. Gotta eat. Might as well eat with four sexy hotties, right?"

"Mmm, or let them eat you."

"Aurora Harper," Emma blurted. "You've gotten downright kinky."

Rory grinned as she topped off Emma's drink. Emma thought she should have put her hand over the glass, but Rory was too quick.

"Not really. I just read a lot of romance novels. I'm on a reverse harem kick at the moment."

"A what?"

"Reverse harem. You know, where the girl gets all the guys instead of one man having a harem of women. It's fun."

"Fun." Emma shook her head. "I think all four of those men at once would be terrifying rather than sexy. Have you seen the size of them? No thanks. I'll keep my sexy times one on one."

Rory laughed. "To be honest, as fun as the books are, I'm a one-on-one gal, too. I'd just like to *get* some this decade."

"There are four testosterone-laden prime specimens sitting over there. Pick one."

"You mean three, because Blaze is yours. But it's really two because Chance is an obnoxious prick." She leaned over to study the four men. "The other two are gorgeous, but they aren't doing it for me."

"Blaze isn't mine," Emma said. "He's just a neighbor."

"Mm-hm. I see the way he looks at you. And you're blushing, Emma Grace. That's not nothing."

Emma shook her head. "You are a truly annoying friend. Do you know that? Yes, he's beautiful. Yes, he makes me think dirty thoughts. But I've got too much going on right now. I need to get established and make sure my dad knows he can retire and start having fun with my mother because the practice isn't going to implode."

"I saw your mom at the Piggly Wiggly a few days ago. She looked great."

"Yep, she's fine. Her heart is good and strong, and Daddy keeps after her about her medicines."

"That's good news. Everybody was shocked when she collapsed at the Mardi Gras parade last year. Your mother always looks the picture of health."

Emma's chest tightened. She hadn't been home then. She'd taken time off and raced to Vanderbilt, where Mama had been transferred for emergency bypass surgery. Everything went perfectly, and Mama was home within a week. Her recovery had been stellar and all her tests good since.

"She does, and fortunately it's true now."

"Where do you think they'll go first after he retires?"

"Probably France. They went to Paris for their honeymoon, but they've never been back. This time they plan to go to all the places in France they couldn't afford the first time. Chamonix, the Loire Valley, Mont Saint-Michel, Aix-en-Provence. Other places I've forgotten."

"That's really cool. I'd like to go somewhere, but I think I'll probably be behind this bar until I die." Rory dropped a lime into a glass and filled it with club soda, flipped the cap off a beer, mixed a cocktail, and put it all on a tray before taking a sip from her glass of ice water.

"You love this old place," Emma said.

"I do." She wiped the polished wood bar with a towel and leaned against it. "There's no other job I'd want, but it'd be nice to get a vacation once in a while. Maybe when Theo and I get it back on firmer ground, there'll be time."

"That's one good thing about all the development around here. There are more tourists than ever. Has to help."

Rory nodded. "It does." She gave her head a little shake. "Don't mind me. Theo tells me I worry too much, and he's right. We're doing great, the place is crowded, and we've got a band coming on in half an hour. You gonna dance?"

Emma shot a glance over her shoulder at the dance floor. Her heart dropped as she spied a familiar profile. The crowd shifted as she strained to see the man in the corner, talking to a woman. Her heart pounded and her ears hummed. The crowd moved again, people leaning together to talk and then parting, others stopping to say hi and moving on—and Simon wasn't there.

"Emma Grace? What's wrong?"

Emma spun to Rory. "N-nothing. Sorry. I thought I saw—" She swallowed. "It was nothing. You know how you think you recognize someone, but it's just a trick of the light?"

"Uh, sure." Her gaze speared over Emma's shoulder. "Don't look now, but here comes your hot neighbor and he looks ready to break some heads."

Shit. Emma took a gulp of wine. Her hands trembled, and she swore silently. She really was freaking out over nothing. Blaze was going to think she was crazy. Then he'd get tired of dealing with her.

"Emma."

Blaze's voice washed over her, warming all the icy hollows inside her that had been exposed when she'd thought she saw Simon. His hand went to her back, a solid, comforting touch against her spine. She swiveled her head to look up at him and forced herself to smile, though her heart felt like a trapped thing beating the bars of a cage.

"It's fine. I thought I saw him, but I was wrong."

Rory had retreated to pop the caps off some beers, but

she was watching. A frown sat heavy on her face. Emma didn't know what to say to make it go away, so she tried to look casual instead.

"Where?"

She pitched her voice low but kept the smile so Rory wouldn't worry. "I turned to look at the dance floor. I thought I saw him in the corner, sitting at that table near the window and talking to someone. But it's not him. There are two women at the table and no sign of a man."

"I'll check it out. Don't move."

Emma stayed put until Blaze returned a few minutes later. She already knew before he shook his head that he hadn't found anything suspicious. After all the talk about Simon lately, she'd been primed to mistake another man's profile for his. Especially in a crowded bar.

"You ready to get out of here?" Blaze asked, sliding an arm around her.

Her breath hitched in. "Are you telling me or asking me?"

"I'm asking, but I'll resort to telling if you say no. And not because I can't protect you here, but because I can feel you trembling."

His touch on her spine was light, but it seared her skin anyway. She wanted to lean into that touch. She didn't, though.

"If we leave now, Rory will be suspicious."

Blaze bent his head to hers, his lips against her ear. "No, she really won't, babe. She can see the sparks between us, and she'll think you want to be alone with me."

The sizzle that went from her ear to her core left her throbbing and hungry in a way she hadn't felt in a long time. It scared her to feel this way, and it filled her with joy that she still could.

Before she could think too hard about it, Emma turned and palmed his cheek before curling her hand around his neck. She tugged his head down and pressed a kiss to his lips. She'd only intended a chaste kiss, but Blaze's mouth opened and she couldn't help but follow suit. His tongue stroked hers, and that aching in her core intensified. She was wet instantly, her limbs trembling for a different reason now.

Blaze swept her mouth possessively, turning her on the bar stool and fitting her between his spread legs. She had a brief moment of worry that he'd feel the heat between her legs. That he'd know how wet she was. But he didn't nudge in that close, thank God.

She'd lost control of the kiss the instant she initiated it, but she was quickly becoming too lost in it to care. She'd never felt this kind of fire simply from a kiss.

Desire was biological. It shouldn't be vastly different from one man to the next.

But somehow it was.

Blaze put his palms on her cheeks and then kissed her forehead. Her lips tingled, her cheeks were straight up fire, and she needed to take her jacket off.

"Whoa," Rory said. "I was about to turn the soda hose on you two."

Emma could hardly look at her friend. "Sorry. I was overcome."

Blaze looped an arm around her shoulders and faced Rory. "Think we're heading out." He laid a credit card on the bar. "Can you close out my bill? Put Emma's on mine. I'll make her buy next time," he added before Emma could object.

Rory took the card in two fingers and grinned. "Sure thing, stud. But you be careful with my friend here, or I'll ban you for life. Just so you know."

Blaze put a hand over his heart. "Now that's a threat that gets me right here. What would I do without regular meals from the Dawg?"

"Take care of Emma Grace, don't be a dick to her, and you'll never have to find out."

"Copy that, ma'am." He bent to kiss Emma's head again and whispered in her ear. "Gotta go tell my guys we're leaving. Don't move."

Emma could only nod as he walked away. Rory returned with the credit card and receipt. She was smirking.

"Looks like somebody's about to get some Vitamin D. I'm not in the least bit jealous."

Emma was going to remain permanently on fire. It was too early for hot flashes, but she thought this must be what they felt like. "I don't know about that. We're in the getting-to-know-you phase."

"Honey, you can talk as much as you like *after* he gives it to you good." Her gaze lifted to peer across the room, and Emma knew she was looking at where Blaze stood with his friends. "That is one fine ass, Emma Grace. I'm really trying not to be jealous here."

Emma laughed. "Ror, I say this with love—there are three other hot men over there. Go grab an ass and see what happens. Maybe even grab Chance's. Hate sex is a thing, you know. Might be pretty hot."

Rory snorted. "Not even if you offered me a million dollars. He already thinks he's God's gift. If I fucked him? He'd brag to everybody who'd listen. I'd have to endure all the old biddies around here lecturing me about guarding my treasure and not giving away the milk for free."

"Could be worth it. How will you know?"

Rory just shook her head. "You're goading me and it's not going to work. Chance Hughes isn't worth the aggravation, no matter how pretty."

Blaze returned and looped an arm around her. "Ready?"

Emma wanted to lean into the heat of him and stay for the rest of the night. "I'm ready."

"Night, you two," Rory said as Emma hopped off the stool and Blaze wrapped her hand in his. "Don't do anything I wouldn't do."

Chapter Twenty

"I'm so, so sorry," Emma blurted when they were outside and walking back to the Sutton building. "I didn't mean to do that! I got carried away with making Rory think I had a good reason to leave so early."

Blaze was still holding her hand. She hadn't pulled away when they'd gone outside. He told himself he really needed to put some distance between them. But he didn't let go.

The second she'd put her hand on his cheek at the bar, he'd felt a lightning bolt of electricity race straight down to his balls. When she'd pressed her mouth to his, his brain shut down and his dick took over.

Slipping his tongue into her mouth had been a mistake, but he'd been on autopilot by then. Kissing her set off a chain reaction that had him harder than stone within seconds. Thank God for the flannel shirt he'd tugged on over his T-shirt earlier. Putting his hand in his pocket and shifting the shirt a bit to the front had managed to hide the bulge in his jeans when he'd gone over to tell the guys he was taking Emma home. That and the dimmed lights in the Dawg. He'd gotten it under control, but for how long was anybody's guess.

Holding her hand now did things to his insides. Made them jump and roll in ways he hadn't felt before. Something about Emma Sutton made him want to lay claim to every inch of her sweet body. He didn't understand it, but it didn't change the fact.

"It's okay. I think I had a hand in letting it get out of control," he told her.

Understatement of the night. He'd been the one who'd pushed it over the line. But the second her mouth touched his, he'd lost all sense of control. Not usually an issue for him, but damn.

"I just wanted to be able to leave with you and not have Rory question me about it. I messed that up because now she's going to ask all kinds of questions, starting with were you good in bed and ending with am I going to do it again."

She sounded miserable. He squeezed her hand. "Tell her it was amazing and yes, you are."

"I shouldn't have kissed you without permission. I'm really sorry I did that."

They reached the front door of the building, and he tugged her inside and turned her until she was against the wall between the door and the window. Then he stepped into her space, nudging her legs open with one of his. He didn't miss the gasp she gave or the way the heat of her burned into his thigh as he leaned closer in.

"Stop apologizing, Emma. I don't mind you kissing me. I'd let you do a lot more than that, though I really shouldn't while I'm protecting you. But I have a feeling you're going to make that really fucking difficult for me."

"I'm sorry—"

He kissed her to shut up her apology. This time he was ready for her, and he had more control. Barely. Instead of thrusting his tongue in her mouth, he nipped her lips and sucked on the bottom one before releasing her. His hands wanted to roam, but they stayed on her hips, pushing her to the wall and holding her there the way he wanted to hold her as he thrust inside her.

Her arms went around his neck rather than pushing him away. Her back arched, bringing her body flush to his. His control hung by a thread. It would be so good. So fucking good.

He'd worship her body, make her scream and sob and beg in the best of ways. He wouldn't let her up until she'd come a dozen times.

Blaze dragged in a breath and stepped back, putting a little distance between them without letting her go. Her blue eyes searched his. She wanted him, and it confused her. He ached to erase her doubt, her fear, and replace it with joy and pleasure.

Still didn't make it a good idea, though. Getting involved with someone you were protecting clouded your judgment, made you susceptible to errors. Errors could get you killed. Worse, they could get the person you were supposed to be protecting killed.

He'd die before he hurt her.

"Babe," he said hoarsely. "Don't apologize for being as desirable and sexy as you are. It's my problem that I want you, not yours. Don't make it yours. I'll deal with it."

He could see the pulse thrumming in her neck and he lifted a hand to stroke it. She didn't pull away. Her eyes drifted closed and she sighed. "I feel safe with you," she whispered.

He allowed himself a touch of his lips to hers before pulling away again. "I know. I'm glad."

Her gaze lifted to his. "Thank you. For everything."

"You're welcome." He stood back and tugged her away from the wall. "Let's get upstairs and watch something on TV together."

She didn't pull her hand from his as he walked backward to the stairs, taking her with him. "What if I don't watch a lot of TV?"

"Then we'll listen to music."

"What kind of music?"

He stopped and picked her up, set her in front of him so she could go up the stairs with him immediately behind her. She'd squeaked when he did it, but she didn't squirm. She really did trust him, and that was remarkable when he thought about what she'd been through with Simon Marsh.

A man like that didn't deserve to call himself a man.

Blaze got that women were equals and wouldn't ever treat one like she wasn't, but he also took his role as protector seriously. A man was supposed to protect and cherish his woman, not hurt her.

"Whatever you want, Sunshine. You pick."

She turned and smiled at him when they reached the top of the stairs. "Sunshine?"

God, what was wrong with him? He shouldn't have said it, but now he had to explain. He opted for the simple truth.

"After the robbery, when I asked if you were hungry, you were staring at the horizon. Watching the sunset. The light made you look like you were standing in a shower of gold. I guess I think of sunshine when I see you."

Her smile was bigger than before. Not that fake smile

she sometimes gave him. She gave it to others, too. She probably thought nobody could tell. He could. Especially when he saw what she looked like right now.

"That's... incredibly sweet."

"Great," he grumbled. "First I'm nice, now I'm sweet. What will the guys say?"

She giggled. "Probably ask you to leave the range, give up teaching self-defense classes, and suggest you get a cat while looking for a customer service job of some sort."

They reached his door, and he slid the key in the lock. "I like cats," he said as he pushed the door open, clocked that the interior looked the way it should, and let her inside before locking the door behind them. He dropped his keys in his pocket and turned to find her watching him with a sweet smile on her face.

"Dogs or cats?" she asked.

"Cats. Except I like dogs, too. But cats are easier. No morning walks, no rushing home to let them out."

Emma shook her head as she laughed. "Not what I expected, big guy. Not at all. I thought you'd be the sort of man who had a Labrador retriever and went hunting every weekend with his trusty canine companion."

"Nah." He didn't tell her the only kind of hunting he did was for bad people. He hadn't felt like hunting animals, too. Animals at least were decent. Couldn't say that about a lot of humans. "What about you? Cats or dogs?"

"I had both growing up. If I had to have one now, I'd probably lean toward cats for the reasons you stated. My job can be unpredictable sometimes. A cat can handle it if you work a double." She frowned. "Though I guess I should say it *used* to be unpredictable. Not so much here."

"Is that a bad thing or a good thing?"

Her expression clouded for a second. "It's a good thing. Definitely good."

"You sure?"

"I'm sure. I'm still getting used to the change, that's all. Working in the ER was like riding a rollercoaster that never quit. Coming here is a bit of a full stop. It's not bad, though. Just different."

He felt like there were things she hadn't said. "Sometimes different is good."

"I know. I'm working on appreciating the good parts of being home. I'm not as tired as I used to be. I get to see my parents and my friends every day. And I can have Clarence's pulled pork anytime I want. Those are definitely good things."

He grinned. "That pulled pork is worth moving across the country for. Definitely one of the good parts."

She smiled. "Now that we've established Clarence makes the best pulled pork, I have to ask another question. Ocean or mountains?"

"Oooh, tough one. I'd have to say mountains, though. Nothing like waking up early and sitting outside watching the sun come up over the woods and peaks. Though I love a good beach, too. How about you?"

"Beach all the way. My family went to the beach every year. Mama and Daddy bought a house on Dauphin Island, and we always went every summer when I was growing up. Rory went most of the time too."

"Not Theo?" he asked.

"No. He was invited, but he never did." She nibbled her lip. "Rory and Theo's parents died when we were in elementary school. Their grandparents took them in. They were the ones who owned the Dawg. I think Theo was afraid to leave them in case they got in an accident, too."

Damn. He'd been prepared to dislike Theo if he and Emma had ever been a thing, but hard to feel that way about a kid who'd lost his parents and been afraid to leave his grandparents in case they died too.

"They're still alive?"

Emma shook her head. "Mr. Harper died about five years ago and Mrs. Harper went to join him a little over a year ago. That's when Rory and Theo inherited the Dawg, though they'd been running it for a while before that."

"Must have been hard for them both."

"It was. Their grandparents were their parents, really." She dragged in a breath. "You ready to watch a show of my choosing?"

"I am."

He could see the mischief sparkling in her eyes. "How do you feel about costume dramas?"

He didn't get a chance to answer before someone banged on the door. Emma jumped. Blaze went to answer it as Chance called out, "It's me."

He dragged the door open to find his teammate frowning. Chance had volunteered to stay in Emma's apartment for the time being. He held a piece of paper in one hand. He turned it so Blaze could see what was written in all caps.

YOU'VE BEEN A VERY BAD GIRL

"Found it when I opened the door. Somebody shoved it under there."

Blaze's blood ran cold. Fucking hell, the asshole had been inside without them knowing. They typically got motion alerts, but those had been off because of the contractors working late on the third floor. Marsh was either lucky or he'd known the best time.

Because he'd been watching.

"We need to check the video feed."

"I called Seth. He's having a look now."

"It's him," Emma said, coming over to stand behind Blaze. She'd wrapped her arms around herself. The light that had been in her eyes a few moments ago was gone now. In its place was fear. "I don't have to see him on a video to know. I thought I saw him in the Dawg tonight, but it was crowded and I decided I was wrong. But I don't think I was."

Blaze put an arm around her and tugged her close. She shivered against him, but she didn't push him away. "We need to get this motherfucker," he growled. "Soon."

He knew, even as he said it, that simply confronting Simon Marsh wouldn't be enough. Neither would a restraining order because abusive assholes like him didn't obey them. The man was a menace and he needed to be locked up.

"Agreed," Chance said.

"He saw us, Blaze." She turned to him, clutching his shirt in her fists. "He saw *you*. He probably saw me kiss you. He'll come after you to punish me."

Blaze would have laughed if she wasn't so serious. Instead, he put his hands on her cheeks and cradled her like she was the most precious thing on earth. He couldn't explain the need and he didn't even care that Chance was watching.

"Good. Let him come. If he focuses his anger on me instead of you, even better. Because I won't play games, Sunshine. If he tries to get a piece of me, all the better. I'll be waiting for him."

Chapter Twenty-One

Emma kept looking at her watch. It was nearly two in the afternoon, and she had another patient to see. Her dad was in the office today. Brenda, his nurse, was there too. Three of them in the office at once and it was broad daylight.

But she couldn't get over the thought of Simon shoving that note under her door. Seth had called to tell them there was a person who'd entered the building and went to the second floor, who bent over and pushed a piece of paper beneath her door, but he'd worn a hoodie and sunglasses.

He knew about the cameras, and he'd been taunting them.

Emma had looked at the still shots and knew it was him. She didn't have to see his face.

He hadn't come back over the weekend. They knew for certain because the only notifications were for her, Blaze, and Chance entering and exiting the building. Blaze had installed the app on her phone so she could get the notifications too.

Blaze had taken her to One Shot Tactical on Saturday

and started her self-defense training. He said they weren't waiting for an official class to start, and she'd been fine with that. She wasn't ready for pistols yet, but he'd taught her how to get out of a hold, what to do if someone tried to choke her—from the front and from behind—and how to take down a full-grown man with a few well-placed blows.

She knew the pain points in a human body. She knew how to find the ulnar nerve and how to drop a man to his knees with it, but she'd never had to. Nobody had to explain to her the result of ramming her palm straight up into a man's nose, or what her thumbs could do jammed into eyes. It was brutal and gruesome, and she rebelled as a doctor whose mission was to help people, not hurt them.

But Blaze kept putting her through the paces, kept hammering the idea into her that when it was her life or someone else's, she had to choose hers.

Of course she did. She knew it. When Simon had held the gun to her head that day, she'd frozen. She never wanted to freeze again. She wanted instinct to take over. That's why she drilled again and again. That's why there were bruises forming on her arms and legs and why her butt was sore from falling onto the mat so many times.

If Simon came for her, she wanted to be ready. She *would* be ready.

After Emma finished with her last patient, she was making notes in the file when her dad knocked on the wall beside the open door.

"Hey, Daddy. Everything okay?"

"Everything's fine, honey. Your mother wants me to ask you to come to dinner tonight. I told her it's very last minute, but she said to ask anyway."

Emma couldn't help but smile. "She knows how to text, right? I know she does because I've seen her do it."

"She thinks you can ignore a text easier than you can ignore me."

Emma gave a snort of mock outrage. "I would never ignore a text from her. I might not be able to answer right away, but I'd get there eventually."

"Same difference to her. What do you say?"

"I can't tonight. I have plans."

He arched an eyebrow. "Do you now?"

She swallowed. *Uh-oh.* "I do. With a man, so you tell Mama that. She'll forget all about dinner."

"Or she'll tell you to bring him," he said with a wink.

"No, no. It's too soon. Meeting the parents is serious stuff. I can't ask a man I just met to have dinner with my parents."

"Understood, pumpkin. I'll smooth it over with your mama. Keep her off the scent for a while longer." He hesitated, and she knew something else was coming. "Though somebody told her they thought you were kissing a man in the Dawg Friday night."

Emma's heart dropped. "Really? Who was it?"

"Who told her? Or who you were kissing?"

"Uh, both?"

"Not sure where she got the info if I'm honest. But the man was allegedly Blaze Connolly."

Busted.

"Isn't that interesting?" she said, her face heating.

Her daddy smirked. "It is. Especially to your mama."

"Oh brother," Emma muttered.

Her dad laughed. When he didn't say anything else, or move to leave, she met his gaze again. It was clear from his expression that he had something else on his mind.

"I've been meaning to ask, honey… Is everything all right?"

Her stomach turned over for a different reason. "Everything's fine. Why? Did I do something wrong?"

He held up both hands. "No, honey, nothing like that. You're a fine doctor. I have no problem with your treatment plans or anything you've done here. Brenda brags about you so much I'm beginning to feel like the third wheel." He chuckled as he said that part. "You're quieter and more serious than I'm used to, that's all. I know life can give us sorrows as we grow older. I also know that being an ER doctor in a trauma center had to have given you experiences you can't quite forget. The fact you're here at all, that you wanted to make this move, has me worried that something is going on and you aren't telling me."

Emma's throat tightened. She didn't want to worry him, and she definitely didn't want to worry her mother. Blaze and the One Shot guys had Simon handled. If she thought he was a danger to anyone but her, she'd tell her dad everything. Instead, she chose her words carefully.

"I loved working in the ER, but I was also tired of never having time to live my own life."

Very true, which she'd only realized lately. It was nice not to work doubles, to get enough sleep, to have a regular social life. To not lose patients because their bodies were too damaged by their injuries.

She went on. "When you said you were thinking of retiring, it seemed like a chance to make a change. It's a big change, though. I guess maybe I'm still struggling a bit with that."

He nodded. "I understand. But I always thought working in a trauma center was your dream."

His hair was grayer these days, and the lines on his face

were more pronounced. He still had that youthful sparkle in his brown eyes, though. John Sutton was the kind of man who walked into a party and had everyone gathering around him because he drew them like flies and always had.

That was the thing she didn't have, the thing that was going to make taking over the practice more challenging. If it was only a matter of skill, she'd nail that.

It was more, though. It was that empathy and kindness that radiated from him. The gentle manner that had people willing to talk about their troubles and what pained them. She could learn a lot from her father.

"I thought so too. But four years sometimes felt like forty. And I can still make a difference here, like you have."

He sighed then. "You've always wanted to save people, pumpkin. I just wanted to say that if you're doing this for me, to make it easier for me to retire, then maybe it's not the right thing to do."

The lump in her throat grew. They never spoke about what was behind her drive to help people, but did they need to? From the moment her mama had found her baby brother not breathing in his crib, Emma had wanted desperately to fix him. She'd thought, with the wisdom of a nine-year old, that maybe if she became a good enough doctor, she could fix other people, protect other families from the soul shattering grief that'd gripped her family for so long.

Emma stood and hugged her daddy tight, pressing her cheek to his chest. Hearing his steady heartbeat was the kind of comfort she needed right now. His arms went around her and tightened.

"I'm fine, Daddy. What we want changes as we learn

new things about ourselves and others. I've realized that emergency medicine is only one way to serve."

And that was the God's honest truth.

He hugged her a little bit harder. "Okay, Emma Grace. But maybe you could find a part-time position at one of the bigger hospitals nearby, keep your skills up while working with me. You might even want to specialize. I'd understand if you did."

"You're supposed to be retiring."

"Maybe I could go part-time, too."

She leaned back to give him a look. He chuckled.

"You look just like your mother when you do that. I meant part-time with time off for travel. When we're home, I could help out."

"We'll talk about it. But you'd better talk about it with Mama first."

"I will." He kissed her forehead. "You about done for the day?"

"Yep. Just finishing up these notes, then I'm going upstairs to get ready for my, uh, date."

It felt funny to call Blaze a date, but she certainly couldn't say she was temporarily living with him.

"Do I get to know the name of this lucky guy? Assuming it's not Blaze, of course."

Her heart thumped. "Never you mind. I need to see how it goes first."

"Fine, fine. But if this mystery man gives you any trouble, he'll have to answer to me."

"Don't worry, I'm signed up for one of those self-defense classes at One Shot Tactical. If he gives me any trouble, I'll drop him to the ground and make him wish he'd never met me."

Her dad arched an eyebrow. "One Shot Tactical, huh? What brought that on?"

Emma's face flamed. She'd said too much.

"Mama mentioned they taught classes. I thought it was a good idea."

Her dad studied her a little too closely. "Who's the instructor?"

Dammit.

Emma shrugged. "It was Blaze the first time. Could be any of the guys though. I think they take turns teaching the class."

"That right? You should have called your mother. She's been talking about going since they opened."

"Honestly, I didn't think she was serious. Plus it just kind of happened."

"Before or after you kissed Blaze in the Dawg?"

"Oh my God," Emma groaned. "You're as bad as Mama."

Her dad laughed. "For the record, your mother is dead serious about a lot of things. You most of all."

He winked before he turned and walked away.

Emma dropped into her chair, put her head on the desk, and groaned one more time for good measure.

———

EMMA: *Don't show your face in the office. Wait for me on the stairs.*

Blaze: What happened?

Emma: My mom had my dad ask me to dinner. I said I couldn't because I had a date. I didn't know what else to say! He said to bring the date over. I said no way, it's too soon to meet the parents. So he can't see you waiting for me. Plus someone told them I kissed you in the Dawg on Friday. Small towns!

Blaze: You're ashamed of me.

Emma: This is serious! Don't tease me. You don't know my mother. She'll be planning a wedding and wanting to know how many kids we're going to have. It's bad enough she knows about the kiss.

Blaze: Is ten too many?

*Emma: *facepalm* You're not helping.*

Blaze: Just winding you up, Sunshine. I won't show my face. I'll text you from the stairs so you can skulk out like a teenager hiding from her parents.

Emma: I'm not hiding and I don't skulk.

Blaze: Sure thing, kiddo. See you soon.

Chapter Twenty-Two

When Blaze stepped out of his truck onto the pavement, Colleen Wright was waiting for him. Her gray hair was streaked with red, pulled back into a thick bun at her nape. She wore a flowing purple caftan with a diaphanous purple layer that floated behind her when she walked. A cigarette hung from her mouth and a large necklace in the shape of an eye perched on her ample bosom. The pupil nestled in a sea of white, painted blue with a black iris.

Creepy.

"What have you done to Melvin?" she demanded as she strode toward him.

"Ma'am, I have done nothing to Melvin. I haven't heard a peep out of him."

She stopped in front of him and popped her hands on her hips. "How would you know? He's not going to talk to you."

Blaze didn't have an answer for that. "Did he say something to you?"

"He didn't have to. Something's not right in the Sutton building, which means *he's* not right. His spirit is troubled."

Blaze would have shivered if he believed in that kind of shit, which he did not. "Did you see something? Someone sneaking in or out?"

Colleen looked affronted. "Indeed not, young man." She tapped her fist to her chest. "I feel it in here. Melvin is unsettled, and so am I. That's a bad thing. You need to be careful."

Blaze wanted to walk away from her woo-woo silliness, but he had to know. "Why is it bad?"

The woman huffed. "It's bad because it is! Don't upset him further!"

On that note, she spun on her heel and stalked back toward her shop. Blaze shook his head as he turned and headed for the back of the building. He took his phone out to text Emma that he was there. She texted back that she'd be out in a minute.

He waited on the back stairs until she emerged from the office. She hurried toward him, glancing over her shoulder as she went. She still wore her white lab coat over a pair of gray slacks and a maroon turtleneck sweater. Her hair was in a high ponytail and her glasses perched on her cute nose, making her look nerdy and hot at the same time.

"Quick, get upstairs," she shout-whispered.

He went up and waited for her just out of sight of the back door, amused at her insistence. She hurried up the stairs, her face red. He couldn't help but grin as she approached. He wanted to swing her around in his arms and kiss her. He refrained, but barely.

"What's up, Doc?"

She stopped and glared. He thought it was cute.

"You have no idea the trouble you're in if Ellen Sutton

gets wind of this. My mama is the sort of woman who could maneuver you into jumping out of an airplane because it's a pretty day and the sky is blue. Trust me on this."

Blaze laughed softly. "Babe, I've jumped out of planes. I'll be fine."

"You aren't taking me seriously, Blaze. Southern mamas with wedding fever are especially diabolical. Swear to God."

"Why does yours have wedding fever?"

She waved her hands around as if it were obvious. "Because I'm in my midthirties and single. Because I just left a busy job in a big city and moved home. Because she wants me to be happy. Because my eggs are aging as we speak. I don't know all her reasons, but I'm telling you, if she even thinks we're dating, she'll start her campaign for a wedding. And since I told my daddy I had a date, and *somebody* with a big mouth told her I kissed you, that ship is about to launch."

She put her hands on her temples and shook her head. "It just popped out. I should have thought of something else. But I couldn't say I couldn't go to dinner because you're sticking to me like glue. Then she'd have wanted to know why."

"And you don't want to tell them about Simon."

"Not if I don't have to. My mother had a heart attack last year. And though everyone says her heart is fine and she's fit as a fiddle, I'd prefer *not* to add the stress of knowing about Simon if it's not necessary."

"Got it."

"You aren't mad about the date thing?"

He snorted. "No. Considering Colleen Wright just accosted me about upsetting Melvin, I'd say things are already weird around here. If your mother decides I'm the guy you need to marry, I'll deal."

He walked into his apartment with Emma grumbling behind him. "You say that now, but you won't be so nonchalant about it when it happens. This is a disaster."

Blaze laughed as he put his hands on her shoulders and turned her to face him. "I can handle it, Emma. Promise I've been through worse. Besides, I think you need to give your mother some credit. She's not going to want you to marry a guy she thinks you just started going out with."

"You don't know that. She already thinks you're hot, and she knows you're single. If she thinks I'm dating you, she's going to start grilling you. Then what? I can't ask you to lie and say we really are dating if we're not."

"Promise I can handle it, and I won't lie. We're adults, Emma. If we date or not, we don't have to tell anyone the details. I don't, anyway."

She nodded, her brows drawing together. "What does Colleen think is wrong with Melvin?"

"You believe in Melvin the ghost?"

"Not really, but she does. Sutton's Creek is a hotbed of paranormal activity according to her. Oh, and alien sightings. There's a particular field over toward the river where the UFOs hover about once a month or so. She takes pictures of white lights, blurry of course. Did I mention she uses a flip phone for this alien investigation?"

Blaze snorted. "Of course she does. I have no idea what's wrong with Melvin other than she says he's unsettled and that's a bad thing."

Emma frowned. "Maybe she saw Simon sneaking in."

"I asked. She said she hasn't seen anyone, just that Melvin communicated his displeasure to her."

"It'd be nice if Melvin would tell her where Simon's

staying. Though I don't know what good it would do. The Sutton's Creek PD won't arrest him for a vague text or a note shoved under a door."

"No, they won't. But knowing where he is would be a good thing."

The only intel they'd been able to uncover on Simon Marsh was that his car had left his building's parking garage the day Emma left town and then returned a day later. It hadn't moved since. Which meant he'd probably rented a car, though a search of his credit cards hadn't returned any rentals.

In fact, his credit and bank cards hadn't been used in weeks. His bank account had a couple thousand in it, which wouldn't even cover the rent for his apartment. If he had other accounts, Seth hadn't found them yet.

Emma's shoulders slumped. "What can you do really? There's no proof he picked the lock to my apartment, no witnesses that saw him coming or going. He could waltz down Main Street and, so long as he doesn't do anything illegal, I'll just have to live with him being around. He could move to Sutton's Creek, set up his business here. He could go to the Dawg every night and stare at me from across the room. I can't stop him. Neither can you."

What she said was true, but Blaze wasn't going to let that happen. He had five other guys with him, and they all knew how to conduct covert ops. If they needed to run an abusive asshole out of town, they could do it.

"Let me worry about that."

She studied him, her head cocked to the side. "I feel like I should ask for details. But I also feel like I don't want to know."

"You don't. Get changed and I'll take you to dinner

somewhere that isn't Sutton's Creek. Then we can swing by One Shot and try some pistols."

Her face paled. "Pistols? I don't know, Blaze."

"We're just going to try them. You don't have to carry one. Nothing but a little target practice. If you don't have fun, we'll stop."

She chewed her lip. "I get to choose the food, right?"

"That's the deal."

"Okay then. But it's my turn to buy."

"If that's what you want."

She smiled. The warmth of it slid into the dark corners of his mind, chased all the shadows away. He could get addicted to that smile if he wasn't careful.

And he had to be careful. Emma Sutton wasn't for him. Even if he'd been free to start a relationship, she deserved better. He had too many secrets, too much darkness.

She was still smiling as she walked backward toward the hallway and the room she was staying in. He marveled that she could go from hopeless to happy in the space of a few heartbeats. It was a sign of her resilience, something he admired about her.

"Let me change into something more casual, and I'll be right out. I'm starved!"

"Me too."

Except he wasn't talking about food.

Chapter Twenty-Three

THEY WENT TO NEARBY MADISON AND ATE ITALIAN FOOD, then stopped at the range on the way back. Ghost was still in the office. He came out to say hello with a curious glance flicked at Blaze, probably for the late hour, then went back inside to continue what he was doing.

Blaze wondered if it had anything to do with Royal Shipping and the cargo container that had arrived today. It'd bypassed inspection and been put under guard. Seth had downloaded all the footage, and Ghost had retreated to the SCIF to report it to Washington.

When he'd returned, he'd said the president's team was discussing it.

Who knew what they'd decide? Or if it even had anything to do with the top-secret project they were here to protect. Could be a drug shipment for all anyone knew.

The most frustrating thing about this mission so far was the waiting. Ghost had said it was unlike anything they'd done before, and that was certainly true. Blaze was glad to be here, but he'd be lying if he said he wasn't itching for more.

The team met in the SCIF daily to discuss the state of the surveillance and to hear any new orders from Washington. Ghost had reported the FBI's visits and was told it'd be handled.

Maybe it had.

Special Agents Corbin and Ackerman hadn't been by in days, so maybe someone had reassigned them or given them another case to focus on. Why they'd homed in on the One Shot connection to Royal Shipping in the first place was a bit concerning, but it could also be that Diana Corbin lacked a personality and rubbed everyone the wrong way. She could just be harassing everybody who'd visited the shipper the same Tuesday Chance and Kane had.

But why? Did she know something they didn't? It would be nice if Ghost could just ask her, but that wasn't happening.

Blaze went over to the gun safe and chose a Sig Sauer P238 and a P938. He also chose a Glock 19, his preferred weapon, and a Ruger SR1911 9mil Luger. Four weapons, four different experiences. He gathered ammo and returned to the counter where he'd left Emma.

Her eyes were big as she surveyed the weapons on the tray. "I don't know, Blaze."

He tipped her chin up with a finger and fixed her blue eyes with his. "Babe, you can do this. We're going to shoot at targets, and I'll be with you the entire time. You don't have to shoot if you don't want to. But come into the range with me and let me show you how to handle a weapon. Then I'll shoot, and you can watch. If you want to try, I'll guide you."

She swallowed and nodded. "Okay."

He grabbed a pair of hearing protectors that slipped

over the ears and had her try them on. After he made sure they fit well, he grabbed a pair for himself and picked up a small stack of silhouette targets that he handed to her. Then he led her through the two doors that opened into the range. First door put them in a small chamber with a sink and a sticky mat for use on the way out again. Second door put them in the range. There were six bays on the side he chose, and they were all empty because the range closed at eight.

The bays were clean because they'd swept up the shell casings earlier, but the smell of spent ammo never went away. It was a comforting smell to him, but Emma seemed a little wild-eyed.

Blaze set the tray of guns on the back table along with the boxes of bullets. He chose the Sig P238 first because the kick was less and the gun was small enough to not be quite as intimidating. He turned and chose a bay, placing the gun onto the carpeted shelf where he would load it. Then he took the targets from Emma, laid all but one on the back table, and pressed the button to activate the pulley that would bring the clip for the target closer. Once he had it secured, he sent the target backward, selecting the ten-yard distance for demonstration. He'd move it to three yards if he got her to shoot.

"I'll show you how to load it," he said, motioning her forward. She hesitated a moment before stepping up beside him. The feel of her there, small and warm, seemed right. He knew she was reluctant to use a gun, but the urge to protect her was strong.

He needed her to learn this. Not that he intended to let her out of his sight when she wasn't at work, but if the team got a go order in the middle of the night, he needed to know she could handle a weapon.

Blaze pushed a couple of .380 bullets into the magazine and then handed it to her so she could finish. She drew in a breath and loaded the rest of the bullets. He'd chosen full metal jacket for shooting, but if he got her to carry, he'd give her hollow points. They did more damage, which he figured she was well aware of, plus there was no danger of them going through a body and hitting someone else.

Brutal, but necessary. When it came to personal protection, he didn't give a flying fuck about the damage hollow points would do. So long as they stopped the attacker, that's all he cared about.

Emma handed him the magazine. The P238 was easy to load by hand, but the rest would be harder. Especially the Glock with its extended magazine.

He made sure the gun was cleared then pushed the magazine into the grip.

"You push it in until it clicks." He ejected the magazine, cleared the chamber—though it was already clear—and handed her the weapon. "You try."

Emma nibbled her lip. He'd noticed she did that when she was unsure of something.

"There won't be a bullet in the chamber yet," he said gently. "And the safety is on. You aren't going to accidentally shoot anything."

She huffed a breath. "You must think I'm ridiculous. I swear I've loaded and unloaded a shotgun before, but that's different. And it was a very long time ago."

"You aren't ridiculous. Guns should be treated with respect. They're meant to kill. I don't care what anyone says otherwise, that's the ultimate purpose. A gun is a deadly weapon and should be treated with care. It's not meant for waving around like a toy, or pointing randomly at people or animals, or using it to make yourself feel important. You pick this up with purpose. You get trained on gun safety and you know what you're doing. And you never, *ever* point it at anything you aren't willing to shoot."

Her brows drew together in concentration as she shoved the magazine into the gun and felt it click.

"Good girl," he said. "Now eject it."

She pressed the button to release the mag, and it dropped into her hand. She looked up at him with a grin.

He took the gun from her. "Let me show you how to clear the chamber."

He tugged the slide a couple of times to show her there was no bullet in the chamber, then pointed the weapon at the target and pulled the trigger. It clicked. He gave her back the gun, took the magazine and set it on the shelf, then had her clear the chamber on her own. It took her a couple of tries, but she did it.

"Now point and shoot. One hand is fine for this. There's no bullet and it's not going to bang."

She did as he said then grinned again. He liked seeing her smile. Emma wasn't comfortable with guns, and he got that, but everything she did that he told her to do, every smile she gave him in this range, made his heart beat a little harder.

"You ready for some noise?" he asked. "I'll shoot and you can watch."

"Yes, I think so."

"All right. Hearing protection on, then I need you to stand back here, to my right, so you can see. I'll walk you through the steps."

They both put the protectors over their ears. They could still hear, but it was muted. Blaze explained everything as he inserted the magazine into the gun, demonstrated the process of getting a bullet into the chamber, flicking off the safety, the proper way to hold the gun—though he was capable of single-handed firing, he used two because that was how she was going to hold it—and how to line up the sights. Then he fired a single bullet into the X in the center and another into the target's head.

"Oh my God," Emma said when he placed the gun on the shelf, barrel facing the range, safety on, and turned to her. "That's impressive. And a little bit frightening, really. That kid at the Gas-n-Go has no idea how lucky he was."

"I wouldn't have shot him unless I'd had no other option. It's never the first choice, by the way."

She nodded. "I'm glad to hear it because you are dead-on accurate with that thing."

"Lots of practice. You don't just pick up a gun and hit what you aim at. You want to try it?"

He hoped she would say yes. She nibbled her lip again, uncertainty stamped on her face. Just when he thought she was about to tell him no, she nodded.

"Yes. I do."

He pressed the button to bring the target in and changed to a fresh one in case she wanted to keep it. Some people did after their first time. When he sent it back, he set it at three yards.

"Okay, stand over here."

He showed her where to put her feet and how to face the target. "Now pick up the gun, keeping the barrel pointed downrange. The safety's on, so it's not going to fire."

She did as he said. He adjusted her hands, explained the best way to hold the pistol, then helped her use the green dots on the tritium sights to line up the shot.

"Use your thumb to push the safety down. Either side

because it's made that way. Then keep your focus on the sights and what you see through them. When you're ready, squeeze the trigger softly. Don't yank, just squeeze. The gun's going to jump a little in your hand, but it's nothing to worry about. I'm right here with you."

Emma drew in a breath and moved the gun a little. He could see her concentrating on the target. And then she squeezed the trigger and the bullet exploded from the barrel. Emma squeaked but didn't let go of the gun. She kept her firing stance and glanced up at him. The bullet had missed the target entirely, but he wasn't telling her that. She'd dropped the barrel when she'd squeezed which was why she'd missed.

"Can I do it again?"

"Yes. Don't shut your eyes when you pull the trigger. Don't anticipate. Just do it softly, like it's an extension of your body, and pull that trigger back toward you. Don't move anything else."

She adjusted herself and tried again. This time the bullet hit the target, but not the silhouette. An improvement, sure, but shooting accurately took work.

"I think I probably suck at this."

He stood behind her so close the back of her fitted to the front of him, slid his hands along her arms, and sighted down the barrel. He put his lips behind her ear where she'd be able to feel his words and didn't miss the shiver that stole through her.

"You don't suck, Emma. Did you do any surgery the first day of med school?"

She shook her head, the perfume of her shampoo invading his senses. His dick was getting hard. Another few seconds and she'd know it.

"It took time," he growled. "This takes time. We'll do it together so you can feel what I'm talking about."

Blaze cupped her hands in his, slid his finger against hers, and pulled the trigger. The bullet hit dead center of the target. He moved his hands back to her wrists and adjusted his stance so his erection wouldn't become obvious.

"One round left. Make it count."

She took her time, adjusted the gun a hair. He didn't adjust it back though he could see she wasn't going to hit center. Finally, she pulled the trigger.

"I hit it!"

Blaze took the gun and laid it on the shelf, then turned her in his arms so he could look at her smiling face. For a woman who'd been uncertain of her ability and scared to pick up a gun, she sure looked happy.

"I'm proud of you, Sunshine."

"I know I missed the important bits, but there's a hole inside the silhouette. I think that might stop somebody for a few seconds, don't you?"

He kissed her nose. "I do. Think you can fire a few more rounds? We'll move to a different gun after you do another round with this one, see how you like it."

"I can do that."

"Eject the magazine and clear the chamber before we load it again."

She did as he said, then smiled up at him as he handed her the box of ammo. "Thanks, Blaze. I still have mixed emotions about this, but you're right that it doesn't hurt to know how to use a gun. Sometimes it's necessary, though I hope I never have to."

After she fired six rounds into the target with varying accuracy, he walked her through the next pistol and the next. By the time they were done, another hour had passed and Emma was getting better at putting rounds into the silhouette. He wouldn't call her competent, but at least she was open to the idea of learning.

They exited the range and he put the guns away while she checked out the merchandise in the cases. He heard her phone ring and then her answering with a cheery, "Hey, Rory." Her tone changed in the next instant. "What? Are you sure?"

Blaze returned to her side, instantly alert. She was ashen as she stared up at him. The fear on her face made him want to tear Sutton's Creek apart until he found Simon Marsh and sent him back to the hole he'd crawled out of.

"Okay, thanks. I'm going now."

"What is it?" he asked.

Her eyes glittered with tears. "Somebody broke into my parents' house. Theo heard it on the scanner. I need to get over there."

Chapter Twenty-Four

There was a police cruiser with lights on in front of her parents' house. Emma jumped out of Blaze's truck and ran toward the side door where she could see them standing with two officers. Another police cruiser sat in the driveway, but the lights weren't on.

"Emma Grace," her mother cried out. "What are you doing here?"

Emma skidded to a stop in front of her mother, who'd been standing beside her father as he talked with the police. "What happened? Rory said it was on the police scanner. Did you really expect I wouldn't race over here?"

"It's nothing, honey. Oh, my."

She didn't miss her mother's face when she spotted Blaze strolling toward them in the darkness. Ellen Sutton was clearly pleased as punch at the sight of the tall, gorgeous man who'd obviously been the mystery man Emma had spent the evening with.

Or not much of a mystery considering what she'd heard from her anonymous source.

She should have asked him to wait in his truck.

Then again, why? Blaze was her rock lately. And he'd said he could handle her mother's expectations. She guessed they were going to find out.

"Mama. Focus."

Her mother dragged her gaze back to Emma. "Your father and I went to see a play in Huntsville when the Garbers gave us last minute tickets. When we returned, we noticed the back door was open. Someone broke a pane and unlocked the door."

Emma's heart throbbed. She could feel the tension rolling from Blaze as he stopped beside her.

"What about Coco?" Emma blurted.

"Coco is fine, honey. She's still at Antonio's. He was running behind before we left and said he'd bring her by when we got back tonight. I called to tell him what happened, and he's keeping her until we can stop and get her. Hello, Mr. Connolly."

"Hi, ma'am."

Emma shivered. "That's good. Dog groomer," she explained to Blaze. "Barkingdales."

He nodded. "Is there anything missing, Mrs. Sutton? Anything that looks out of place?"

"I don't know. We called the police as soon as we saw the glass. I haven't been inside yet."

"You need to go to a hotel tonight," Emma said. "Don't stay here."

Panic was starting to close in. She forced herself to breathe through it.

"Nonsense, sweetie. It's probably just neighborhood kids playing pranks."

"I'm guessing you don't have a home security system?" Blaze asked.

"No. We've lived here for thirty-five years when John's

parents moved to a smaller home nearby and gifted the family home to us. It's never had a security system."

Emma's belly was churning with fear and fury. "Might be time to get one, Mama. Sutton's Creek isn't as isolated as it once was."

Her dad finished his conversation with the police and turned around. He looked a little surprised to see Emma and Blaze, but he recovered quickly, offering his hand to Blaze to shake and looping an arm around Emma to hug her.

"What happened, Daddy?"

"I assume your mother told you the door was open and a pane of glass was broken. The police have checked the house and found nobody inside. We can go in now and see if anything's missing. They're going to dust for prints on the door, and Vernon says they'll patrol the neighborhood hourly tonight and for the next few days."

"Emma Grace says it's time we get a security system, John."

Her dad shook his head. "We don't need that. Don't need folks cutting into the walls and mounting cameras everywhere."

"Daddy, you're planning to travel. You'll be gone for two or three weeks or more at a time. I think a few cameras are the least you should do. Unless you plan to hire a house sitter every time?"

"It's possible to put a system in with minimal impact, sir," Blaze said. "Everything's high tech these days. Cameras can be mounted without being obvious, and you can have door and window sensors that'll set off an alert to the police if breached. Everything would be controlled on a panel in your bedroom and an app on your phone when you aren't home."

John Sutton was frowning. "And if we're the ones who set it off by forgetting to turn something off or on? We don't need the police showing up every time that happens."

"You'll know if you've done something to trigger the alarm. The monitoring company will call to make sure the alert is real before they send first responders. It's very intuitive, sir."

"I'll consider it. Who would do this work for us?"

"I can give you recommendations for a couple of trusted firms in the area. They'll come out and estimate what you'll need and how much it'll cost. I can look over their suggestions if you want my opinion."

Her dad nodded. "Okay then, I'll do that. Give Emma Grace the names, please, and I'll set something up."

"Yes, sir."

Her mother slipped her hand into her dad's. "Emma Grace, would you like to bring Mr. Connolly in for a beverage?"

"We can't stay that long, Mama. But I'd like to check out my room, see if anything is missing."

Her mother blinked. "Of course, if you'd like to look. I'm a bit more concerned about the silver, myself."

Her parents went inside, and Emma and Blaze followed. They sheared off and went up the wide central staircase that led to her room on the second floor. Her heart beat with anger and dread. If Simon had broken into her parents' house, what did that mean? Was he letting her know he could get to them? Or was it a message that she couldn't hide from him?

Emma pushed open her bedroom door. The room still looked the same as it had when she'd left for college. Her mother had a way with home decor, and Emma's room had been the perfect combination of stylish and homey for a teenage girl. Her bed was a four-poster with white and pink linens, and her walls were cream.

There were framed photos of her and her family on the dresser, her and Rory dressed for homecoming, her and Granny when she'd still been alive. Her, Gramps, and Granny from years before that. There were pictures from the beach, pictures from horseback riding lessons and dance recitals.

Blaze stood just inside the door, gazing at her room with a blank look on his face. Embarrassment flooded her. She knew what he saw. The big house. The antiques and oil paintings. The large, fluffy bed and big room that had been hers alone. She even had a small sitting room.

"It's a lot for one kid, I know."

He seemed to shake himself, his gaze meeting hers. "It's nice."

She ducked her head shyly. "Thank you."

"Is anything missing?"

"I don't think so."

She wandered around the room, looking at everything, trailing her hand over the picture frames and then over the outlines of furniture. It wasn't until she got closer to the bed that she saw it.

"What is it?" Blaze growled, stalking to her side. She loved that he could tell, without a word, when something was wrong. "Goddammit," he growled as he saw it too.

In the center of her bed, hidden by the fluffy comforter folded at the end and only visible when she'd walked over, was a Barbie doll lying in a large red pool of what looked like paint. It had brown hair, wore a white lab coat, and there was a noose around its neck. It lay on its side, its hands bound behind its back. There was a piece of what looked like duct tape over the doll's mouth.

Blaze was still growling. "We need to get the police up here."

She trembled, tears stinging her eyes. "I don't want to scare my parents."

Even as she said it, she knew it was wrong.

Blaze wrapped strong arms around her and tugged her against him. His chin was on top of her head, his solid body comforting against hers. She melted into him as his heat seeped into the ice surrounding her.

"Babe, I understand. But you don't have a choice. If the police start looking for Simon, that's a good thing. Give them a rundown of what happened in Chicago, tell them you suspect this person is harassing you. Give them a description. It's safer for you and your parents. They're staying here, not going to a hotel. They should know what's going on. The danger isn't only to you anymore."

Her heart pounded. "You're right. Of course you're right."

He pushed her back just enough for their eyes to meet. His were serious. "You're strong, Sunshine. He hit you, held a gun to your head, and you left. You didn't go back. There was a line in the sand, and you held to it. Not everyone can do that. You did. Now tell the police about the man harassing you. Tell them he's obsessed with you, because he is, and let them do their job. I won't stop protecting you, and my guys won't stop either. But having more people looking for him puts pressure on him, and that's a good thing. It also lets others in your life keep themselves safe."

Emma inhaled the comforting scent of him. Spent gunpowder, pine, and leather. It was outdoorsy and so much nicer than the antiseptic and vague citrusy scents she associated with hospitals.

She felt like the lid to an old musty trunk had been flung open inside her heart. She'd been ashamed for not being smarter, for letting Simon into her life, but she couldn't keep it a secret any longer. It wasn't right or safe to do so.

And it was a relief not to have to anymore.

"I'll tell them everything I know about him."

Blaze hugged her to him. "Good girl," he whispered against her hair.

The shiver that cascaded through her then had nothing to do with Simon.

Chapter Twenty-Five

Somehow, Emma got through the next hour of telling the police and her parents about what she'd found in her room and who she thought was responsible.

There were questions in her parents' eyes. Fury in her father's. Worry in her mother's.

It was a relief they knew because now they knew to be vigilant. Her dad had looked at Blaze and said he wanted that security system ASAP. Part of her hated that it'd come to that. Another part said it was about time because Sutton's Creek wasn't so isolated anymore.

Emma closed her eyes as Blaze drove them the short distance to downtown. Her skin crawled with the knowledge of what Simon had done. He'd broken into her childhood home, poured red paint on her bed, and left a bound and gagged doll in the middle of it.

To terrify her. To let her know he could get to her.

She shuddered. Blaze's big, warm hand closed on her fisted one. His touch instantly soothed her.

"You did the right thing, Emma. Your parents needed to know for their own safety, and now the police are looking for him. Both those things are good because this was an escalation."

"I know. It's just so sickening that anyone would do such a thing. If he wanted to make me feel unsafe in my childhood home, he's succeeded. I don't know that I'll ever be able to sleep in that bed again."

"Don't let him ruin a place you were happy. Don't let him put a black mark on your childhood."

"I'm trying not to. I'm trying to think of all the good times I had growing up in that house. The sleepovers with Rory. Christmases when my mother decorated my room and put up a tree in my sitting room window. I got to pick the ornaments for it, and we added a new one every year. My room was my sanctuary when I was a kid, and he defiled it and made it feel unsafe. And now my parents are going to a hotel for the night because my mother doesn't feel safe either."

"I know, honey. But it sounds like you had a wonderful childhood there. The kind a lot of kids don't get."

There was something in his voice.

"I did," she said softly. "But I also had problems. It wasn't perfect, Blaze."

He shot her a look of surprise. "Of course not. Nobody's life is perfect. We all have problems to work through."

She hesitated, but she suddenly wanted to know. "What about you? Did you have a happy childhood?"

His knuckles whitened on the wheel. "Not really. My mother never married my father. She had a string of boyfriends. Moved us from place to place. I didn't often have my own room. I shared with other kids until Mom and her flavor of the month broke up and we moved on."

Her heart ached for the little boy he'd been. Never

having a home that was his. "I must sound like a spoiled princess to you."

"Why would you say that?"

"Because I'm going on and on about a single act of defilement that doesn't change my childhood or the mostly happy home I grew up in. It's self-indulgent and whiny."

He pulled into the parking lot behind the Sutton building, shoved the truck into park, and turned to look at her. "Babe, you're allowed to be upset about what happened. You're allowed to freak out and have trouble processing that it happened in what's always been a safe space for you. You aren't spoiled for what you're feeling. No, I didn't have what you had as a kid. I had a somewhat volatile childhood, but it made me who I am today. I like who I am and what I do. I've made a difference to people's lives in my career, and that counts for a lot. You don't have to apologize because you grew up the way you did. We don't all get the same start in life, but it's what we choose to do with the chances we get that count."

She had an overwhelming urge to kiss him. But if she did that, if she crossed the space and pressed her mouth to his, she didn't know when or where it would end. Not to mention the fact that Simon could be out there, watching them.

The thought made her stomach twist.

"Thank you for saying the right thing when I need to hear it."

He took her hand in his, threaded their fingers together, and lifted their joined hands to kiss the back of hers. "You're welcome."

The warmth of his breath on her skin made little shivers chase up and down her spine. She was instantly wet, her body aching for his. She'd have thought it impossible to want to get naked with a man this soon after the last one, but the fact was that she did.

Desperately.

Didn't make it a good idea, but she still wanted it.

His expression was hot on hers one second and cooling the next. Her heart thumped at the way he seemed to shut off the heat in his gaze. The need. He smiled a friendly smile and let her go. Disappointment stung.

"You know the drill. Sit tight and I'll be around to open the door for you."

She nodded because she didn't trust herself to speak. They trudged toward the building and up the stairs, stopping in front of his door. She was thinking about what to say, how to ask him why he kept shutting down, when the door to her place opened and Chance Hughes stepped out. He looked more serious than she'd ever seen him.

"Hey, man. Got a call from that client I told you about."

"Oh yeah? How'd it go?" Blaze asked. There was tension in the set of his shoulders, the stiffness of his back.

"Good, good. Gonna need to head back to the range in a bit. He's only in town for tonight."

"When do we need to go?"

"Fifteen minutes."

"I'll be ready."

Chance went back inside, and Blaze opened his door and went in first. She was used to letting him check the place out before he let her inside, so she stood patiently until he motioned her forward. She shut the door behind her and locked it out of habit, though Blaze would check it again if this were a normal night.

But it wasn't normal. He was leaving her to go to the

range with Chance, which meant he was going back out and she would be alone.

Emma wrapped her arms around herself and shivered.

"I don't know how long this will take," Blaze said as he strode back into the living room with a black gym bag in one hand. He set it down and came over to where she stood. "Hey, you okay?"

Emma nodded as he put his hands on her arms and rubbed them lightly up and down. "I don't want to stay here alone. Can I go with you? I won't get in the way."

It was hard to ask, but she couldn't get the idea of Simon in her childhood home out of her mind. Being by herself meant she'd keep thinking about it, imagining him in her bedroom, remembering the day he'd put the pistol to her head and cocked it.

Threatened to kill her.

Was that his end game now? Had she misjudged his willingness to commit a crime? Just because normal people had a healthy fear of getting caught and going to prison didn't mean that he did.

Sympathy flared in Blaze's eyes, followed by sorrow. "I can't take you, Emma. I don't know how long we'll be gone, and you have work tomorrow. You're safe here. You have the app for the cameras on your phone, and you'll know if anyone breaches either entrance. I'll call when we return so you'll know it's me, but if an alert goes off and you haven't heard from me, call 911."

Her fear bubbled higher, but she wouldn't beg him. He'd already done more for her than she could have asked for. "Okay."

He kissed her forehead then swore softly and took her mouth with his. The kiss was hot and sweet and held the promise of more. Her insides turned to jelly, her knees wobbling as she clung to him.

The kiss ended too soon. He set her gently away from him and searched her gaze with his.

"I'll be back as soon as I can. Don't unlock that door until I return."

"I won't."

He kissed her again, quickly, and then he was gone.

Chapter Twenty-Six

Blaze climbed into the passenger seat of Chance's SUV. "Thanks for picking me up."

He'd asked for a ride so his truck would be in the parking lot, even going so far as to meet Chance at the corner. He didn't want Marsh to see him leave if he was watching.

"No problem. Emma okay?"

"Yeah. Shaken up, but okay." He scraped a hand over his head. "I'll tell everyone what happened when we get there."

"Copy."

Blaze didn't like leaving Emma alone, especially tonight, but he had no choice.

Ghost Ops wasn't optional. When the call came, they went. And he'd known something was coming, just not when. He guessed Washington was done discussing the shipment.

He'd wanted more action. Just not tonight.

Blaze comforted himself that the police were doing extra patrols. He had to believe that was enough to keep

Simon Marsh in the shadows for the time being. The police station was literally two blocks away. If Emma called, they'd be there faster than a greased pig.

The man was certainly growing bolder, showing up at the Dawg to watch her, shoving notes under the door despite the cameras in place, and now breaking into her parents' house and leaving a grisly message in her bedroom. He was toying with her.

And with them since he didn't seem concerned about being caught.

Rage flared in Blaze's gut. He wanted to find Simon Marsh and double-tap the bastard into oblivion.

Not that he'd actually shoot without a stronger reason, but the fantasy comforted him.

He should be with her tonight, not flying down a country road toward One Shot Tactical and his team. But the mission came first, and it would keep coming first until the project was successfully launched and the president gave the order to stand down.

Which meant his life wasn't his. It belonged to his country and his president. All he had to give to anyone else —to a woman he was starting to care about—was scraps of himself. Not fair to her. Not fair at all.

He clenched a fist as he thought about her asking him to take her along.

And his refusal. It had killed him to say no.

Holy gods, that kiss. She'd have given him everything tonight if he'd stayed.

Wasn't a good idea, but he couldn't help thinking about it.

They pulled into the parking lot, grabbed their bags, and swaggered into the range. Of course it wasn't a client waiting for them. It was Ghost and the rest of the team.

"How are Emma and her parents?" Ghost asked. Everyone knew her parents' house had been broken into, though they didn't know the extent of it. Blaze gave them the lowdown.

"Jesus," Ghost said. "Sick fucker. Is Emma safe tonight?"

"She should be. She knows not to leave or let anyone in, and the police have beefed up their presence. The outer doors are locked, so if she gets an alert they've been opened, she'll call 911."

"Good." Ghost leveled them with a look. "Sorry to call everyone in this late, but we're gonna need to get a closer look at what's sitting in that cargo container. Top priority."

"Now?" Ethan asked.

"Correct."

"Took them long enough to decide," Kane grumbled.

They all felt it, but they wouldn't have gone in before this time of night anyway. And they were already prepared. They'd been planning this mission since the moment they'd been tasked with setting up surveillance.

Seth brought up the camera feed on the monitor against one wall. "We already know they have 24/7 security, but they've stepped it up the past couple of days with four guards rotating patrols and watching the cameras in the guardhouse."

"Great," Chance said. "More guards."

"They're predictable, though," Ghost said. "It takes fifteen minutes to do a circuit and they go every half hour. Theoretically, we've got a fifteen-minute window to get inside and break into the cargo container before they start another round."

All the team had to do was change into their assault suits and tactical gear, which they did right there in the

SCIF, shedding clothing and donning equipment. It took scant minutes before they were ready to go.

"Do we have any clue what we're looking for?" Blaze asked as he slipped his earpiece into place.

"Not until we get a look inside that container," Ghost replied. "I know this seems like child's play compared to things we've done before, but we can't underestimate the risks. Getting caught is not an option, you feel me?"

"Hooah," five men said in unison.

"Let's roll, gentleman."

Chapter Twenty-Seven

ROYAL SHIPPING'S WAREHOUSE SAT ON THE EAST SIDE OF the airport. There were other businesses and warehouses perched along the access road for several miles. Traffic was lighter than during the day, but there was still enough of it at night that a couple of trucks belonging to the Ghost Ops team didn't stick out.

They parked in a dark lot about half a mile distant from the warehouse. Seth stayed behind to monitor the camera feed on his laptop and the rest of them hurried for the target. They were able to skirt along the sides of buildings, staying in shadow, until they approached Royal Shipping's warehouse. The company logo featured a three-pointed yellow crown on a black background.

The fence surrounding the complex of warehouses and office buildings was easily scalable. Chain link, no razor wire, nothing but three strands of barbed wire at the top. Not a problem for men like them.

They dropped behind the fence and made their way to a side door they'd used the last time they inserted. It was locked, but that was hardly a problem. Kane had it picked in record time, and they were in, making their way around the perimeter toward the container they needed. Their watches were synced, and they knew when the guards would patrol.

Ethan and Chance peeled off to guard the perimeter as Ghost, Blaze, and Kane headed for the target.

Seth spoke into their earpieces, guiding them around shipments toward the one they needed. A small, rectangular air freight container sat on a pallet near the front of the warehouse, a bit too close to the guard area for comfort, but there was nothing they could do about that.

The container was a little over five feet tall, which meant they had to crouch, and almost eleven feet in length. Made of steel, it had two doors on either end. They chose the door farthest from the guards and Kane set to work on the lock.

A sound came from the direction of the guard shack, and they froze, staring at each other with hard eyes. It didn't stop them from working, but they were aware things could go to shit in a heartbeat. Bugging out before they discovered what was in the container wasn't an option. Temporarily incapacitating guards was an alternative, but not one they wanted to use unless there was no other choice.

"Phantom," Ghost whispered into the mic. "Status."

"Smoke break," Seth said into their ears. "Two of them. Next round in ten minutes."

"Copy," Ghost said. "Demon, little faster with that lock. Wraith, prepare for a distraction."

"Getting there, sir," Kane said.

"Copy," Chance said.

It was as natural as breathing to fall back into their

mission patterns. Call signs and respect for leadership was part of who they were when they did this kind of work.

A thrill that he hadn't known was missing tore through Blaze. But there was regret too. Regret that he had to hide this side of his life from Emma, that it meant he couldn't be with her, couldn't explore the tangle of feelings she'd made take up residence in his chest.

"In," Kane said as the lock clicked. Blaze took a small can of spray lubricant and aimed it at the hinges. Kane lifted the handle, turned carefully. There was no sound. He pulled the doors open.

If they were expecting weapons or explosives, they were sorely disappointed. The boxes weren't big enough. Ghost sliced the tape on one and opened it.

"Computer parts," he said, pulling out a thin package wrapped in plastic and bubble wrap. "Made in Taiwan."

He tucked the package into his vest as Blaze peered inside the container.

"All the boxes look identical from here."

Ghost frowned. "They do. And we don't have time to dig through and find out. Six minutes before the guards start their round. I've got a sample. Let's tag the shipment and get out."

Blaze pulled a white tracker tag from his pocket and peeled off the adhesive cover. Then he pushed the tag against the container's top. The container was white, and the tag would blend in unless someone looked carefully.

Ghost took pictures of the interior and the container's serial number while Blaze did a circuit to find the manifest. It was on the opposite side. He tugged it from the plastic and quickly took a picture of the front and back before replacing it.

"They're on the move. Five minutes early." It was Ethan's voice sounding urgently in their ears.

Shit.

"Copy," Ghost said. "Moving out. Wraith, Dragon, let's go," he added for Chance and Ethan.

"Copy, sir," Chance replied.

A noise boomed like a wrench falling onto concrete. It reverberated through the warehouse, echoing from the rafters. The guards shouted. Kane locked the container and the three of them took off at a run.

They were out the door, flying toward the fence, hearts pounding, breath razoring in and out, when a gunshot shattered the night.

Chapter Twenty-Eight

"And your parents are really okay?" Rory asked. "Nothing stolen?"

Emma rubbed her forehead as she sat on Blaze's couch and talked to Rory on the phone. She could hear the music thumping from the bar, but Rory was in the office, so it was quieter.

It was almost midnight and Blaze had been gone for nearly two hours. What kind of client expected the range to open especially for them at almost ten o'clock at night?

She hadn't asked because it was their business and they could run it how they liked. Seemed a little odd though.

Especially since he wouldn't let her go with him.

"Nothing stolen." She hesitated, thinking how best to tell Rory what had happened. In the end, she simply started at the beginning and told her friend everything from meeting Simon and dating him to the breakup and the Barbie tonight.

"Oh my God, sweetie. I'm so sorry you went through that. Are you okay?"

She heard the unspoken questions, the sympathy, in her

friend's voice. It helped break down another wall inside her. She'd been hiding her trauma from everyone, and it hadn't helped a bit. Sometimes you needed the sympathy of others to let you know you weren't alone.

Emma pulled in a breath. "Yes. Mostly. I don't know why he's here, if he really wants me dead or he's just harassing me because he's angry. But I need you and Theo to be careful. He knows you're my friends, and he might try to use you to get to me. Or target you in some way because it'll upset me."

"Don't you worry, babe, we've got your back and we'll be careful. Do you have a picture of him? I'll put it on the wall in the Dawg and make everyone aware."

"No pictures." She described him like she had for Blaze. "I know a lot of men fit that description. He can be very charming, too, so watch for any guy who's a little too suave. I doubt he'll show up in the Dawg now that the police are looking for him, but be on the lookout just in case."

"Got it. Sick fucker. Are you safe alone? Do you need me to come stay with you?"

Emma's heart throbbed. "I'm, uh, staying in Blaze's apartment. In the guest room," she emphasized at Rory's intake of breath.

"Oooooh, and you were with him tonight when I called you."

"How did you know that?"

"I didn't until just now." Rory cackled.

Emma's skin heated. "There's nothing going on. He was teaching me to shoot."

"Shoot what?" Rory asked with more than a hint of wickedness.

Emma laughed. "A gun, Rory. I told you nothing

happened between us the other night. Yes, we kissed and he walked me home. That was it."

"I know, and I believe you because why would you lie, but dang, girl, you need to jump that man and let him take you to the moon. Especially if you're staying *in* his apartment!"

"I'm getting to know him first. And then *maybe* I'll sleep with him."

In reality, she'd have slept with him tonight after that kiss. Maybe she still would.

"What about you? Did you squeeze Chance's ass yet?"

"Girl, no. I told you there's no way." Rory hesitated a second. "But I did meet someone tonight. A guy from Huntsville. He came into the bar, and we talked. A really cute guy, too. Kinda shy and awkward, though. He didn't ask, but I gave him my number. So we'll see. Before you ask, he doesn't match the description of Simon and he wasn't exactly charming. Awkward, like I said. But cute."

She definitely would have asked. "Aw, that's good, honey. Is he a Vitamin D prospect?"

"I think so. Need to talk to him some more, see if the good impression holds."

"There's no rush, Rory. There are other ways to take care of that itch, you know."

"I know, and believe me I have. But Gus isn't nearly as satisfying as a real man."

Emma nearly choked. "Gus?"

"Gus the Glamorous. He lives in my bedside drawer and takes care of Mama's needs."

"Oh Lord, you absolutely kill me sometimes," Emma said with a laugh. "I missed you and I'm so sorry I let too much time go by without calling you more often."

"Hey, you had an important job to do. You were *busy* saving lives. I get it. You don't have to apologize."

Warmth radiated all the way to her bones. "Thank you, but I should have made time."

"You'll make time now."

"I will."

"Good. Because I'm immature and I need somebody to be immature with me."

"But not too immature."

"Of course not," Rory said with a sniff. "All right, though I'd rather talk to you, let me get off here and finish the books for tonight so I can go home. Maybe I'll see if Gus is feeling particularly amorous."

"TMI, Ror."

Rory snorted a laugh, and Emma laughed with her. When the call ended, Emma got up to wander into the kitchen. She didn't need a snack, but she wanted one. She found a piece of cheese and ate that while considering whether or not to go to bed. She was tired, but she wouldn't sleep if Blaze wasn't there.

Instead, she went to the couch again and turned on the TV. Not too loud because she wanted to hear if anyone was in the hall. The outer doors to the building, both front and back, were locked now, but that didn't stop her from worrying about Simon breaking in anyway.

She needed to hear him if he did. Just in case the camera app didn't warn her.

She knew Blaze kept a pistol in a drawer in the kitchen. It was loaded and ready. She hated that it made her feel better knowing it was there.

Grabbing it and using it was a whole other thing, but she'd worry about that if it happened.

By the time her phone rang, she'd dozed off on the

couch. She jumped, fumbling for it, finally getting it to her ear with a rusty, "Hello?"

"It's me, Sunshine. We're coming inside the building."

Relief left her feeling weak as she pushed to her feet and ran over to the door. Her phone dinged with a notification as she twisted the lock and yanked the door open. She could hear Blaze and Chance on the stairs.

"Told you not to open the door, Emma," Blaze said tiredly when he spotted her. He didn't sound angry though.

"I know, but you called and said you were here, so I saved you a step."

"What if Simon was holding a gun to my head and made me say it?"

Emma crossed her arms and glared. "He could also hold a gun to your head and make you unlock the door, so why would he force you to call me first?"

"Smart-ass."

He looked tired. Chance did too. Emma frowned as she studied them. Were they drunk?

Maybe Chance was because he looked a little glassy-eyed. Blaze looked clear-eyed but tired. She ran her gaze over them both, then jerked it back to the dark spot forming on the sleeve of Chance's sweatshirt.

"You're bleeding."

Chance glanced at his sleeve. "Crap, it must have opened up again. It's nothing. Just a scratch."

"Judging by the rapidly expanding blood stain, it's not a scratch. Let me see."

Chance waved a hand. "No need. It's fine."

"It's not. Get inside. Now."

"Emma," Blaze said, glancing at his friend. "I'll bind it for him again and leave him at your place. It'll be fine."

Emma pulled herself upright, stiffened her spine, and

glared at the two of them like she'd had to glare at men during most of her career to get them to take her seriously. "I'm a doctor. I've had my hands in more guts than either of you have ever seen in your lives, guaranteed, and I've never lost my cookies. So either you let me take a look at that *scratch* or I'm calling an ambulance."

Both men blinked. "For a bleeding scratch? You'd call an ambulance?"

She thrust her chin out and nodded. She was blustering, but they'd scared her.

"Hell yeah, I would. I only have your word that's what it is but at the rate I'm seeing blood, somebody needs to make sure you haven't shot yourself."

Chance's face paled. A stone formed in her gut.

"Holy shit, you *were* shot, weren't you? Downstairs, now."

Blaze closed his hand around her arm as she started to turn. "Babe, no. The bullet wound is only a graze. But there was some barbed wire and he, uh, fell against it. Sliced his arm open."

Her mind boggled. Shot *and* sliced? "I'm still going to look. At *both* wounds. Downstairs."

"Not downstairs. That's official. Inside the apartment, okay?"

She wanted to argue, but she could tell it was a battle she wouldn't win. "Fine."

She walked inside and the men followed. Blaze closed the door and Chance went over to sit at the kitchen island where the lights were brightest. He peeled off his shirt to reveal his arm. A bandage was wrapped around his upper arm, soaked through.

"You idiots," she hissed, unwrapping the bandage so

she could get a look at the wound. "He needs stitches. Where's the gunshot?"

Blaze was frowning. "We cleaned it and applied a clotting agent before binding. It didn't look that bad at the time. The shot grazed his right thigh."

"Okay, pants down."

Chance looked a little wild-eyed. "Uh, it's fine. Really."

"Pants. Now."

"Better do it," Blaze grumbled.

Chance stood, unbuckled his belt, and dropped his jeans to reveal his thigh. She resolutely didn't look at his tighty-whities as she lifted the bandage and peered at the graze. It was ragged but not deep. Grazes were never stitched, and it looked as if they'd cleaned it. Still, she'd clean it again just to make sure it was done right.

"I need supplies. Can you go down to the practice and get them for me?" She threw the words at Blaze.

"Yes."

Emma told him what she needed and where her keys were, and he ran out the door. He was back in a few minutes, dumping supplies on the island.

"The clotting agent did the job it was supposed to, but you've opened it up again. What the hell were you two doing, anyway?"

"We work at a shooting range, Doc," Chance said. "Shit happens."

She gave him a hard look. "Really? Barbed wire happens in the middle of the night when you've gone to the range to open it for a special client? And you get shot too? Seriously, any client who calls you out that late is clearly not right in the head. Maybe you should think about that the next time. And don't play with barbed wire *or* guns."

"Yes, ma'am."

She shot Blaze a look. He was frowning but didn't offer any explanation as she got to work. She treated the cut first, injecting lidocaine to numb the area and then irrigating the wound before she started stitching. When it was done, she applied a fresh bandage then got to work on cleaning and patching the graze. She told Chance how to care for both as she stripped off her gloves.

"I'll remove the stitches in a week or so."

"I can take them out," Blaze said. "You don't have to."

She stared at him. Then she shrugged, though she was angry deep down. "Suit yourself. You're done, Chance. Try not to tangle with barbed wire again."

"It's always the goal, Doc."

She went over to wash her hands again. "You do know I'm supposed to report a gunshot wound, right? I'm going to assume neither of you want me to do that."

Blaze shook his head. "It's an accidental wound, Emma. You aren't required to report that. And we're in my apartment, not your office."

"Which is why you wanted it done here. And you're right, I don't have to report an accidental wound. But I don't personally know that's what it is, do I? All I have is your word for it."

"It was an *accident.* Chance went downrange to retrieve the target because the pulley wasn't working right. Unfortunately, the idiot in the next bay didn't get the memo. We've learned our lesson about this client. He's not welcome back again."

"And the barbed wire?"

"An unfortunate accident when he lost his balance and fell against the fence as we were leaving. He might have, uh, had a shot of whiskey or two to ease the pain in his thigh."

She studied them both for a long moment. There was tension in their features. She didn't know why, and it bothered her.

She hadn't smelled whiskey. Chance had taken a strong painkiller, not alcohol.

Did they really think she was so stupid she didn't know the difference?

Or that she believed the crap they were laying down?

Whatever they'd been doing, it had resulted in one of them getting winged by a bullet and tangling with barbed wire. But what could it have been?

Robbing a bank? A gas station?

No. That was ridiculous.

And it was literally none of her business what kind of shit they'd gotten involved in.

Hell, it was probably better if she didn't know. Even if the fact they didn't trust her enough to tell her punched deep.

She'd been feeling things for Blaze, wanting him, so maybe this was her reality check. Don't get involved with men you don't know, no matter how heroic they seem.

Emma rubbed her eyes. "You know what? I'm tired. I'm going to bed. I'm glad you're both okay, and sorry you got shot, Chance. Maybe get that pulley fixed and don't ever walk onto the range when you have clients on the premises, huh?"

"Yes, ma'am," Chance said, sounding more chastened than she'd ever heard before.

She looked at Blaze again. His eyes spoke volumes, but she wasn't willing to stand there and figure it all out.

"Thank you," he said.

"You're welcome."

She went into her room and locked the door.

Chapter Twenty-Nine

Blaze stood in a hellish landscape, his heart pounding so hard he could barely hear the gunfire raging around him.

His team was falling apart. The gunfire was coming from all around, tracer rounds exploding against a background that was oddly blurry. Blaze was screaming into the comm, begging for air support.

Except he couldn't remember the words. All that came out was, "Help! Help!"

It was his fault his men were dying. Because he couldn't get the right words out. That's all he could think of. His team was falling apart around him, men bleeding out on the desert floor, and he'd forgotten his words. What kind of fucking operator was he anyway?

On the other end of the comm, the voice maddeningly kept asking what he needed. Who he was. Where he was.

Nothing felt right about it. Nothing at all. He'd been doing this job for years, knew how to call for air support, and he couldn't fucking find the words.

He sank to his knees, screaming in frustration. A bullet whistled through the night, coming straight for him. Any second it would hit. Any second and his misery would be over. It would all be over. He bowed his head, waiting…

But it didn't hit. Instead, someone pounded on a wooden door that he hadn't realized was there. To his left. Pounding, calling his name—

Blaze woke up. It was Emma pounding on the door, Emma calling his name.

"I'm okay," he said, his voice hoarse. From screaming, no doubt.

Embarrassment crawled over him. And despair.

It'd been almost a month since he'd had a nightmare, but he'd known in his gut they weren't gone. Just slumbering, waiting for a trigger. Like always.

He pushed upright, his body wet with sweat, the covers pooled at his feet. He shoved a hand through his hair and gulped in air.

Fuck.

"Blaze, open up."

"It's fine. Go back to sleep. Just a dream."

"Does it happen often?"

His heart hammered and his head pounded. Did it happen often? He didn't think so, but what was often anyway? For him, anytime it happened was too often.

"It happens when it happens. Go back to bed, Emma."

She didn't say anything for a long minute. "Okay, fine. But if you want to talk about it, I'm here."

Talk about it? Hell, he didn't want to talk about it at all. He just wanted it to stop. He should have known tonight would trigger the dreams. He'd gone on plenty of missions that hadn't ended badly. Hundreds of them. So why did he obsess over the one that had? It was years ago, and it still haunted him.

Ghost said it wasn't his fault. But he still felt responsible. Always would.

He'd been due to dream. It'd been weeks since the last

one. Then Chance took a hit while they were escaping tonight, one small hit that created a bigger problem when he was clumsy going over the fence, and Blaze had to go and spiral down a rabbit hole in his dreams.

Chance was fine. In a bit of pain, but fine.

He shoved a hand through his damp hair. The dreams were why he lived here instead of on the farm. If his team knew he still woke up drenched in sweat, hoarse, his body trembling, they'd probably think twice about trusting him to have their backs on any mission, let alone one so important it had involved them separating from the military and moving across country.

Chance's misstep tonight had been his own, but what if it had been Blaze who'd caused his teammate to get injured?

"I'm good," he called out, swallowing. "Thanks."

"Okay… What if *I* want to talk?"

Blaze dropped his head to his hands and squeezed his eyes shut. It had been a tough night for Emma, too. He couldn't forget that or that he'd promised to keep her safe.

She'd been upset with him earlier. He'd thought about that kiss on the drive home, wondered if she'd be waiting for him. About kissing her again, where it might lead.

If he was up front with her that it was just sex, maybe she'd want it anyway. She'd just gotten out of a bad relationship. Wasn't likely she wanted another one.

Blaze sighed. He wasn't getting back to sleep right now, so he might as well get up. If Emma wanted to talk to him, maybe she'd gotten over it.

"I'll be out in a few minutes."

"Thank you."

He got up and went into the bathroom, turned on the shower, and stood beneath the spray to wash away the sweat. Then he toweled off, brushed his teeth, and slid on sweats. He grabbed a fresh T-shirt but didn't put it on right away. He was still too hot, so he slung it over his shoulder and stalked out of his room.

Emma was on the couch, legs curled beneath her, a cup of something hot in her hands. He didn't smell coffee, so it must be tea. Her gaze slid over him. He didn't miss the intake of her breath, and he started to think maybe he should have dragged the shirt on anyway.

He knew what she saw. A few scars, the pucker of a bullet hole in his side where he'd been hit during the mission he still hadn't gotten over.

Shit happened on the teams. Nobody got out without a few scars here and there. Not all of them were physical, though.

He tossed the shirt over the back of a chair and stalked into the kitchen to grab a beer. One cold beer would do him good. Maybe help him get back to sleep.

He was conscious of the desire for it, but he never let it get the best of him. He was Mary Connolly's son, and he knew the addiction gene was locked away inside him.

If he let it, it might rule him the way it ruled her.

He would never allow that to happen. One beer, maybe two, and he was always done.

"I'm sorry if I woke you," he said as he returned to flop onto the chair opposite her, beer in hand.

"It's okay. I wasn't sleeping all that well anyway."

"But you *were* asleep."

She shrugged. "Yes, but like I said, it wasn't good sleep. I kept dreaming that Simon was standing over me. The instant I fell asleep, he was there, hovering, waiting. So I'd wake up again and he wasn't there at all. But I can't seem to stop it from happening."

"I'm sorry, Emma. It'll get better, but what he did tonight—last night—is too fresh for you. You'll probably sleep like a baby tonight."

She nodded. "Will you?"

"Yes." The word was clipped. A warning not to push.

He took a pull of the beer. It slid down his throat, rippled heat through his stomach despite the cold.

"I'm sorry I had to leave you alone earlier. I should probably explain that it happens like that sometimes."

"I admit I don't understand why you can't make people wait until normal business hours, but it's not up to me how you run things."

"Some clients are old contacts from the military. We go when they can be there. Things like what happened tonight—that was an accident. It's not typical."

He sure as hell hoped not anyway. They were better than that, but shit went sideways sometimes.

What'd happened was that Chance knocked a crowbar off a container. He hadn't seen it lying there because it was above his head, but when he headed back toward the exit, he hit it with his helmet.

Because the damned thing had been on the edge of the container, it fell before he knew what was happening. He'd still been trying to figure out what had beaned him when the clatter broke the sound barrier.

One of the guards made a lucky shot when he winged Chance.

Fortunately, they'd run like hell, scaled the fence, and despite Chance getting tangled up, got out without having to disable a guard.

"I hope not," she said softly. "I have to admit it scares me to think you could get shot doing your job."

"I'm not going to get shot," he said roughly.

Hell, he couldn't promise that, but he was going to anyway.

Her gaze dropped to the puckered scar beneath his ribs. "Looks like you weren't so lucky before."

"It was a long time ago."

She sipped her tea. Her small hands curled around the mug, and he thought of the way she'd sewn up Chance earlier. Delicate stitches. Even.

In combat, you patched up your teammates with clotting agents and bandages. You applied tourniquets and pressure, and you figured out how to keep someone alive until you could get them back to the base.

They were all capable of it, because they had to be, but it wasn't their main skillset.

Without Emma here tonight, he'd have applied more clotting agent, bound the wound tighter, and checked it in the morning.

Chance had antibiotics and pain relievers, and he knew the drill. Blaze had told him to stay in the farmhouse with the others, but he'd wanted to come back to town, stay in Emma's apartment. Be ready to help if Emma needed it.

"Were you in combat?" she asked.

"I was." There was no point in lying when the answers were written on his body.

Her eyes were big as she stared at him. He thought he might drown in those eyes given a chance. What he wanted, more than anything, was to drag her beneath him and lose himself inside her body.

"Is that why you have nightmares?"

He took another swallow of beer, closed his eyes, and leaned his head back on the chair. He didn't talk about this shit. He'd had to talk about it after the mission because they'd all had psych evals and counseling—those who were left—but he didn't talk about it now.

Maybe that was the problem.

"I chose to join a combat unit. I was good at my job, and what I did mattered."

"You were screaming for help."

His eyes snapped open, and his heart rate picked up. Of course she'd heard him. She'd been pounding on the door for fuck's sake.

"Not every…" He searched for the word he wanted. Not mission. "Deployment. Not every deployment went as planned. But I'm still alive, and sometimes I dream about the ones that went wrong."

She dropped her gaze to the rim of her cup as she traced it with a finger. "I'm sorry, Blaze. I know it's not my business. I'm here because you're helping me, which means I should probably be grateful and keep my mouth shut, but my job is to help people, too. Differently, sure, but it's hard for me to see someone in pain and be unable to fix it."

"I don't need fixed, Emma."

His voice came out colder than he intended, but he wasn't prepared to open a vein for this woman, no matter how much she wound him up inside. Not only that, but he couldn't.

The more he said, the more questions she would have.

And he couldn't tell the truth. He hated lying to her, but he had no choice.

He got to his feet, emotion roiling his gut. "I know you mean well, but I don't want a prescription, I don't want a counselor, and I don't want to talk it out like bestie girlfriends at a sleepover, okay?"

"Okay."

She looked chastened, and he hated seeing that look on

her face. Knowing he'd put it there. But it had to stop. She had to know there was a line she couldn't cross. He wasn't going to risk the mission or, more importantly to him, her safety by getting her involved.

"We done? You say everything you wanted?"

"Yes."

Her voice was hardly more than a whisper. He wanted to sit beside her and drag her into his lap, hold her close. Apologize for being a dick.

He couldn't, though. He couldn't let her mean that much.

He gave her a sharp nod and walked away.

Chapter Thirty

She'd messed up. Emma dragged in a breath and took a sip of her now cold tea. Why had she pushed him? He was angry with her, and she couldn't blame him. They weren't besties, or lovers, or even in a relationship. She had no right.

And yet her heart throbbed at the idea he wasn't willing to share his pain with her. She'd told him things about her life she hadn't told anyone else. That he wouldn't do the same hurt.

It shouldn't, but it did.

"He's not your boyfriend," she muttered. "You don't want a boyfriend anyway."

Emma got up and took her cup to the kitchen, washed it out in the sink, and set it on the drying rack. The sky was starting to lighten outside. The wind howled because it was the beginning of March. A profound sense of loneliness invaded her heart.

If she were still in Chicago, it'd be a lot colder out. There'd probably be snow, too. And if she couldn't sleep, like now, she'd grab her bag and go to the gym.

She couldn't do that because she wasn't leaving the building alone, but she could go down and use the treadmill in the office. The front and rear doors of the building were locked. It was safe.

She chewed her lip, thinking. Blaze wouldn't like it, but she really needed the physical exertion to clear her head, to ground her. Her life was upside down, again, and she felt like she was going to come out of her skin if she didn't do *something*.

Emma hurried to her room, rummaged through her suitcase, put on her workout gear, and grabbed her phone. Blaze had given her his spare key for the time she was staying with him. She locked the door behind her and slipped it into the hidden pocket on her leggings.

The building was quiet, and the hall was dark. For a moment she wondered if she should go back inside Blaze's apartment and stay there. Her heart hammered in her chest as she listened for movement, but there was nobody waiting for her.

Simon wasn't superhuman. He needed sleep like everyone else, and she knew his patterns. Unless he'd changed them, he stayed up until midnight or one, then slept until about eight. He wasn't waiting in the dark on the chance she'd emerge alone.

Emma went down the stairs and opened the office with her key, then locked that door behind her and entered the small room at the back of the building where the treadmill was located. Her dad had a television above it so he could watch videos while he walked.

She grabbed the remote, punched the *On* button, and signed into her YouTube account, paging through options until she found a video on baking she hadn't yet watched. With the droning of the woman's voice explaining how to knead bread, Emma turned up the speed of the treadmill until she was walking at a good clip.

It'd been too long since she'd gone to the gym regularly, and she knew she had to start back easy, no matter how much she wanted to crank that sucker up and run until she collapsed.

Frustration snapped at her as her feet slapped the belt. Nothing was the way it was supposed to be.

Simon was in her hometown, disrupting her life, threatening her parents with that break-in, invading her childhood bedroom, and threatening her with a bound and gagged doll—and Blaze wasn't quite the easygoing nice guy she'd thought.

There was something going on with him and Chance. Probably with the entire group of them. Who went shooting at ten o'clock at night, got shot, sliced, and then insisted very strongly on not going into a doctor's office for treatment because she might report the gunshot?

Somebody with secrets, that's who.

Emma shivered. Was she really that terrible a judge of character?

She'd thought Blaze and Chance were the good guys. Still did down deep.

But what if she was wrong? Just because they were helping her didn't make them good. A man didn't have to be abusive toward a woman to be a bad guy.

Emma punched the speed higher. She was tired of not having it figured out, tired of people being different than she thought they were.

It was supposed to be easy. The only problem she'd been supposed to have was settling into Sutton's Creek again, dealing with patients who'd known her when she was in diapers or when she'd gone to high school with them. She'd expected that part to be difficult, to have to work to make people trust her.

There'd been a family physician in Sutton's Creek for two generations. That doctor had always been male, and now she was there, a small woman who'd left home years ago and hadn't been around to put people at ease before she took over.

Emma hiked up the speed until she had to break into a run. Her heart throbbed as sweat ran down her face and between her breasts. The woman on-screen talked about punching the bread down.

Emma wanted to punch something.

Simon's face. His arrogant, lying, stupid face. Her life had fallen apart because of him.

Emma growled and punched the speed higher. She was sucking wind, her limbs ached, and she felt like she would fly off the treadmill any second. She wasn't ready for this much speed, wasn't in shape for it.

There was a sudden pounding on the door. She lost her balance and stumbled. The emergency brake clip popped off the treadmill as she fell. The machine died. The sudden stop propelled her forward until she sprawled across the controls, her arms wrapped awkwardly around the bars at the sides.

The pounding continued.

"Emma! I know you're in there. Open the fucking door."

It was Blaze's voice. Not Simon's.

Thank God.

"Just a damn minute," she yelled between breaths.

She managed to lever herself upright again. Her right arm hurt where she'd pressed all her weight on it. The pull on her tendon was sharp.

Great. Fucking great.

Emma stumbled to the back door on rubbery legs and unlocked it. Blaze loomed in the entry. He was blazing mad. She might have giggled at the pun if he didn't look so utterly dark and serious.

"What the hell were you thinking?" he growled.

She hobbled back to the room and picked up a towel to rub over her face. The woman on television was kneading the loaf now.

"I was thinking I needed exercise."

Her shirt clung to her, wet with sweat, and her heartbeat was still erratic.

He'd stalked into the room behind her. His gaze slid over the treadmill, the television, then back to her. "You aren't supposed to leave the apartment without an escort."

Frustration pounded in her brain, her temples. "Look, it's five in the morning, the front and back doors are locked, and you get alerts on your phone if they're opened. I didn't go out, I simply came downstairs—and locked myself in, I might add. I did everything safely."

"I don't care if you locked it, you aren't supposed to step out the door without letting me know. What would you have done if that'd been Simon at the door just now?"

She spread her arms, then winced at the pain sizzling through her elbow and down her arm. "It wasn't, okay? It was *you*—"

"What's wrong with your arm?"

She rubbed her tendon, feeling angry and confused all at once. "I slipped when you started pounding on the door like a maniac. The clip came undone, and the treadmill stopped."

He had the grace to look contrite. Sort of.

"I'm sorry."

She huffed. "I'm not an idiot, Blaze. I judged the situation safe and acted accordingly."

"Jesus," he growled, shoving a hand through his hair. She refused to dwell on how his muscles flexed with the movement.

He was a jerk. A hot, sexy jerk who didn't trust her to make her own decisions or to talk to about what bothered him.

He knew so many things about her, personal things, and all she knew about him was that he'd had a crappy childhood and he'd been in the military and experienced combat at some point. She only knew that because his body told a story he couldn't deny.

The rest of it? Blank.

"What you don't seem to understand," he said, still growling, "is that when I tell you not to leave the apartment without me, that's exactly what I fucking mean. I can't protect you if I'm not there. If I don't know you're going out. You hurt your arm—what if it was something worse?"

"It's not worse, and I wasn't going out."

He closed his eyes a second before glaring at her. "Out the door, Emma. The one that encloses my apartment. I think you know that's what I meant."

She reached for the glasses she'd taken off and pushed them on her face. Her skin was starting to cool, the sweat chilling her body. "I need a shower."

"We aren't done discussing this."

She whirled on him. "Oh yes, we are. *I'm* done. My arm hurts, I'm sweaty, and I want a shower before I have to go to work."

"Fine."

He shot a glance at the television, his gaze still dark.

She could see the visible effort he made to rein in his temper. As if he could tell that continuing to insist they talk about this wasn't going to work out the way he thought it would.

She was practically nuclear she was so angry. She snatched up the remote and stabbed the *Off* button.

"You into baking?"

It was an attempt at civil conversation. And she was having none of it.

"None of your business. You don't get to keep *your* secrets—of which there seem to be many—and ask me to spill mine. I'm done telling you things. As you pointed out, we aren't besties, and this isn't a relationship. You decided to help me with a problem, which I appreciate very much, but I've told you all you need to know about that situation. Nothing else is relevant."

His eyes sparked. Might have been anger. Might have been chagrin. She decided she didn't care.

"You're right," he told her. "But you still need to follow my guidance about your personal safety. That means no leaving the apartment without me."

Her temper flared. It wasn't just that he was telling her what to do. It was how easily he agreed with her. He didn't fight back or say he was wrong. He just agreed.

Like the time they'd spent together was nothing but a job for him even though he'd held her tenderly when she'd needed it, kissed her like a man starved, and called her Sunshine.

His empathy, his understanding, his vow to keep her safe—it all meant nothing. He was utterly disconnected from her as a person, and it *hurt*. She could be anyone and he'd do the same.

Rory. He'd hold Rory, call her babe or Sunshine, and keep her safe. It wasn't personal *at all.*

Emma lifted her chin, angry at herself more than him. For believing she was special when really he was just a man who hadn't pushed her away when she'd escalated things.

Kissing him. Lying across him half the night. Hugging him when she wanted comfort.

Seeing meaning where there was none. It was *humiliating.*

"I want my apartment back. The police have Simon's description. They're patrolling more often, the locks are sturdy, and we've got security cameras with alerts. You've taught me how to defend myself and I know better than to go anywhere alone. But not being able to walk downstairs in a locked building without your permission is too much control, and I won't do that again."

"Emma." Her name was a growl.

"No, Blaze. *No.* I won't be treated like that ever again. Not by you or anyone."

He shoved a hand through his hair. It was spiky and sexy, and she hated that she noticed. Hated that it sent a current of desire throbbing to life inside her.

"All right." He blew out a breath. "I'm not trying to control you, Emma. Keeping you safe is a job, and I know how to do that job. I think you need to stay close to me until Simon is in custody, but if you want to go back to your place, I can't stop you. I advise against it strongly, though. I think it's the wrong move after last night."

She trembled inside. She hadn't forgotten the doll. How could she? It was on her mind all the time, even when she tried to think of other things.

Part of her wanted to cave in and stay with Blaze. It was the easy choice.

But another part rebelled. She'd been in this place before, a place where a man slowly squeezed the fight from her, bent her to his will. Trapped her.

Blaze wasn't Simon, but she *needed* her own space back. "It's what I want. You'll be next door, and I won't change how I do things. I'll still wait for an escort. I'll let you know my movements. I won't be alone except in my own home."

He looked pissed, but then he schooled his features into a carefully blank expression. "If that's how you wanna do things."

"It is." She glanced at her watch. "I need to get ready for work. I assume we can go upstairs?"

"We can. I go first, same as usual, got it?"

"Yes."

He strode to the door, then hesitated with his hand on the knob. "I get that you're pissed at me, and I don't blame you for it. I like you, Emma. But anything deeper—I can't. It's better for us both this way."

Heat flooded her. Embarrassment or anger, she wasn't sure.

"What makes you think I want more from you? I've had enough of men for a while, thanks. No offense."

His lips flattened, but he nodded. "Not offended. Glad we got that straight."

"Me too."

"I'll talk to Chance when he wakes up. You can stay in your apartment tonight."

"Awesome." She smiled her fake smile and nodded at the door. "Can we go now?"

He yanked open the door and strode into the hallway. She stopped to lock it then followed him up the stairs. It wasn't until she was in the shower with hot water beating down on her that she let the first tear fall.

Chapter Thirty-One

CHANCE SLUNG HIS DUFFEL BAG OVER HIS SHOULDER AS HE locked the door of Emma's apartment and dropped the key into Blaze's hand. Chance moved a little stiffly, but he didn't complain.

Not that Blaze expected him to.

"This about last night? My injuries?" Chance asked as they walked down the back stairs.

"No."

His teammate eyed him. "Then why are you so pissed off?"

Blaze ground his teeth together. "It's my fault. I lost my shit with her earlier."

Lost his shit and pushed her farther away than ever. He'd told her he liked her but they couldn't have anything deeper. Even though it'd killed him to do it. Wounded him somewhere deep inside that he hadn't known existed.

He'd hurt her when he'd said the words. He'd seen it in her face before she'd told him she'd had enough of men and pasted on her fake smile.

"I'm not so sure. She was mad when she did my stitches."

Blaze shook his head. "Nope, it was all me."

He'd already explained that Emma had gone down to the office to use the treadmill. He'd also said that Emma wanted her space back. He hadn't elaborated.

"Damn, dude. What did you say?"

"I told her it was a stupid thing to do and not to do it again."

It was way more than that, and he knew it. It was everything about last night. Chance's wound, Blaze's nightmare. His unwillingness to talk about any of it.

She was mad because she'd shared deeply personal things with him and he wouldn't do the same.

When he'd wanted to pull her close and hold her tight, he'd pushed her away. When he wanted to sink into her body and not come up for air, he pretended an indifference he didn't feel.

For the first time in forever, he'd met a woman he liked enough to want to spend time getting to know. And he fucking couldn't because the mission took precedence.

What he needed was to head over to Huntsville one of these nights, meet a woman in a club, and take her to a hotel so he'd stop thinking about what Emma would look like when he hooked her legs over his shoulders and licked her until she screamed.

Except the thought of going to a hotel with a random stranger didn't do it for him. Not since he'd met Emma. She was the one he wanted, which meant he was fucked. And not in the way he wanted to be.

"Gonna give the key to Emma," he said when they hit the bottom floor. "Meet you outside."

"I'm going over to Kiss My Grits for coffee and a biscuit. Want anything?"

"Yeah. Coffee, three creams, and a sausage biscuit." He reached into his pocket for money, but Chance shook his head.

"I got this. You go talk to the doc."

"Thanks, brother."

Blaze pulled his truck keys from his pocket and tossed them at Chance, who caught them one-handed. It was understood that Blaze was driving this morning since Chance needed to take it easy on the arm.

Chance went outside and Blaze took out his phone and texted Emma. He could have knocked on the door, but her dad might have answered. Or Brenda.

He wanted to see Emma. Needed to see her. He didn't know what the fuck he'd say, but he was doing it anyway.

Got your key. Standing in the hall outside.

It took a moment before he saw the three dots.

Emma: I'll be out in a second.

It was more like three minutes, but finally, the door opened and she stood in the entry, dark hair pulled back in her signature ponytail, blue-rimmed glasses perched on her nose, expression mildly annoyed. She wore a white lab coat over a cream V-neck sweater and a pair of black pants tucked into black ankle boots.

Blaze held out the key. "It's up to you what you choose to do, Emma, but I advise sticking to the plan we had before. Don't go anywhere alone, and always wait for an escort until Marsh is found."

She nodded as he dropped the key in her palm. There were two spots of color in her cheeks as she drew her hand back. "I'm not stupid, Blaze. I know Simon is still out there. The only thing that's changed is I'm going home to my apartment when you go to yours."

"Call me if you need me for anything."

"I will."

He looked past her toward the interior of the medical practice. "Thanks. For last night. Fixing Chance."

Her jaw tightened. "Of course. I won't tell my dad, in case you're wondering. Brenda keeps track of the supplies, but I'll apologize when she notices and make up an excuse. If it happens again, I won't cover for you. Just thought you should know."

"Much appreciated. How's your arm?"

"Strained, but it'll get better. No shooting or self-defense classes for a couple of weeks, I think."

"We'll start again when you're better."

She nodded with her lips pressed tightly together.

There was nothing more he could say, though he wanted to stay until she smiled at him. Which wasn't happening anytime soon, he guessed.

"See you tonight then."

"Yep."

"Can't leave until you lock the door, Sunshine."

She frowned as she stepped backward then shut the door harder than was probably necessary. He waited for the twist of the lock, then turned and walked out the door without looking back.

The air was cool and crisp, but the sun shone bright. He took a deep breath and felt like he'd be happy if not for the woman in the building behind him.

If he could wake up in this place and kiss her good morning—kiss all those babies her mother wanted her to have good morning—that would be perfect.

The thought stunned him, made him hesitate.

He'd never wanted kids, not after the way he'd been jerked around from place to place, living in uncertainty. Wondering if he'd have enough to eat, a bed for the night.

But with Emma Sutton?

He shook his head and took the steps down to the parking lot. It was sparse with cars at this time of the morning, but that was because it was early and not everybody was open yet.

The Dawg opened for lunch and stayed open until midnight most nights, aside from Sunday and Monday. They didn't do breakfast, but Kiss My Grits did.

Chance wasn't at the truck, so Blaze went over to the cafe where he picked up coffee and breakfast most mornings. Chance had discovered the pleasures of Wendy Cochran's coffee and breakfast sandwiches while staying next door for a few days. No wonder he'd looked so dejected when Blaze told him he had to clear out.

Blaze went in the back door and halted at the sound of raised voices.

"You're so wrong, Chance Hughes," a feminine voice grated. "Ole Miss is *not* better than Alabama. Eighteen national championships. You have *three*."

"Yeah, but Nick Saban retired, darlin'. Y'all are sunk without him. He made the team."

"You have *no* idea what you're talking about. And don't you even breathe Coach's name in my presence, you hear me?"

"Hotty Toddy, baby."

"Roll Tide. Now go away and stop bothering me."

Chance snorted. "Bothering you? I'm just ordering breakfast. You're the one who walked in here with a chip on your shoulder."

"Argh! You're so irritating!"

Blaze strode into the cafe. Chance and Aurora Harper were facing off by the counter. Rory's hair was pulled back in a glossy ponytail, and she wore workout gear. A gray zip-up sweat jacket that read *Roll Tide* and had an elephant with a big A on it was paired with black yoga pants and pink tennis shoes. She had lipstick on though, which didn't say *workout*.

"Yeah, and you're annoying," Chance said. "All I said was *nice jacket*, and you attacked."

"It was the *way* you said it," Rory grated. "I know sarcasm when I hear it."

Chance raised both hands. "Babe, I didn't mean a thing by it. I was serious. Looks good on you."

Blaze had to admit it did. Rory had a great rack. Not that Blaze cared because he didn't.

But she filled out the sweatshirt in all the right places. No doubt that's what Chance had noticed because, who wouldn't?

"Hey, Rory. Do I need to step between you two or what?" Blaze asked with a grin.

Rory turned flashing eyes on him. They softened as she smiled at him. "Hey, Blaze. Not at all. I would not deign to lay a finger on your slimy friend."

"Hey," Chance said. "I am *not* slimy. I showered and everything. Want to check?"

Blaze groaned. Chance's mistake was arching his eyebrows and wiggling them up and down at least twice.

"Jerk."

Rory promptly forgot her vow not to touch him when she hauled off and punched him in the arm.

His bad arm. Chance sucked in a breath as his face paled.

"Jesus," he hissed as he clasped a hand over his wound.

Rory looked confused. "Are you faking that I hurt you? Because I didn't hit you hard and you know it."

"Yeah, I'm faking. Little thing like you?"

Except Chance's face was still pale, and Blaze knew he was feeling that blow.

"Stop antagonizing her," Blaze growled. "Chance tangled with some barbed wire out at the range. He's got stitches in his arm, and you just landed a punch dead center."

Rory slapped her hands over her mouth. "Oh my God, I'm so sorry. I didn't know. Are you okay?"

"Fine," Chance said between clenched teeth. "Just need a minute."

"Need to see if it's bleeding again," Blaze said. "Maybe we should go see Emma."

"Just give me a fucking moment and I'll look."

"I'm so, so sorry, Chance. I didn't mean to hurt you." Rory's face was pale now, too. "I shouldn't have hit you. No matter what you said to me, I shouldn't have let my temper get the best of me."

"I'm not going to die, Rory. You don't have to be nice to me."

"I know that, you idiot. And I'm not being nice. I'm apologizing for crossing a line, which is something you wouldn't know how to do if the line bit you on the ass."

Blaze took out his phone and dialed Emma as he stepped away from Chance and Rory. He was reasonably sure they wouldn't come to blows now that Rory knew Chance was hurt, but he kept an eye on them anyway.

Emma answered promptly. "Yes?"

She sounded cool. He hated it, but that was the way it needed to be.

"Hey, I'm over at Kiss My Grits, and Rory just

punched Chance on the arm. That arm. Don't know if it's bleeding yet but he's in pain."

"Rory punched… Oh for heaven's sake. What is wrong with her?"

"I don't know," Blaze said truthfully, though right now she looked miserable as she stood next to Chance and frowned up at him.

"Bring him over. Brenda is here but my dad isn't. I'll have a look."

"Thanks. Be there in a few. Want anything from the cafe?"

"No thanks. I've got a protein bar, and Brenda made coffee."

Before he could say another word, she hung up on him. Blaze sighed as he tucked his phone away. He deserved that, probably, but it bugged him anyway.

"We're going over to the doc's office," Blaze said to Chance.

"Christ, you're as bad as a mother hen, you know that?"

"Better to have it looked at now than get halfway to the range and have to turn around."

"It's five miles away."

"Yeah, and it's my gas we're using, so I'm opting for getting it checked now."

Their order was called. Chance grabbed the bag with one hand while Blaze got the coffees. Rory still looked miserable as she waited for her order.

"I'm really sorry, Chance. Come over to the Dawg later and I'll give you dinner on the house."

Blaze elbowed Chance in the side when it took too long for him to respond. "Dude, accept graciously before you put your foot in your mouth."

"Thanks, Rory. You don't have to do that. It's not your fault."

"It is my fault, and I know I don't have to. I want to."

"Not sure I'll get over there tonight. Maybe."

Rory looked chastened. Maybe Chance was enjoying it.

"Okay, well, the offer stands. I'm so sorry."

Chance grunted.

The door opened and a man walked in. He was stocky with reddish-brown hair, a scruff of a beard, and he wore a ball cap that said Roll Tide.

Of course he did.

He saw Rory and smiled. She smiled back.

"I have to go. See you guys later."

She went over to join the man. He gave her a peck on the cheek, and they took a table in the corner. He sat with his back to them, but Rory was visible. She looked animated, happy.

Chance watched her with a frown. And, whether he realized it or not, *longing*.

"Take the dinner," Blaze said. "She feels guilty enough to be nice for a while, so maybe you can talk to her without pissing her off for a change."

"I don't try to piss her off. Just happens."

"Yeah, you open your mouth and bullshit comes out. Stop teasing the woman about her football team for starters."

"It's a friendly rivalry. Ole Miss and Alabama have always been that way."

"Yeah, but you didn't go to college, and you don't actually give a shit about a school."

Chance gave him a look as they headed out the back door to the parking lot. "You don't have to *go* to a school to love the team. I was raised in Mississippi. Ole Miss is in my blood, even if I never spent a moment on campus."

Blaze rolled his eyes. "Yeah, fine. But if you want to end the war and maybe have a shot at getting her between the sheets, and I think you definitely want that, you'll zip it about the Hotty Toddy stuff. What the hell does that even mean anyway?"

"It's part of the school cheer. Like saying Roll Tide for Alabama, God forgive me for letting those words pass my lips. And what makes you think I wanna get with Rory? She's pretty, but there's lots of pretty women around here."

"So go find one of them and get laid. Stop antagonizing Rory Harper for the hell of it."

They strode across the parking lot, Chance grumbling the whole way. "I just said the jacket was nice. She's the one who got prickly."

"Like I said, lay off that Old Miss shit and she won't be so annoyed."

"Ole Miss. Not old."

"Whatever." Blaze reached the back door of the building and pulled it open. Chance went inside and Blaze followed. Emma was waiting for them at the door to the practice.

"Pissing off Rory again?"

"I wasn't trying. Must be PMS or something."

Blaze cleared his throat as Emma's eyebrows climbed her forehead.

"What?" Chance said. "That's not a thing? I thought that was a thing."

"Get in here and shut up," Emma said, holding the door open.

She didn't seem angry though. Instead, Blaze thought she was trying not to laugh. He missed that laugh now that she seemed determined not to be friendly with him. They'd laughed a lot at dinner last night.

Hell, was it just last night? Seemed like a lifetime ago, but they'd gone to dinner and then she'd learned about the break-in when they were at the range. After dealing with that, Ghost Ops had gotten the call to move on Royal Shipping.

Yeah, a lifetime ago and everything was different.

Chance shoved the bag of food at Blaze. He caught it in the crook of his arm as Chance reached for one of the coffees. Blaze didn't know if it was the right one or not, but Chance didn't seem to care as he slugged it back.

"My arm hurts like a sonofabitch, but I know she didn't mean it."

Emma directed him to an exam room and followed him inside. Blaze trailed after them, half expecting her to tell him to get lost. She didn't, though. He leaned against the door jamb as Emma took Chance's coffee and set it on the counter. Then she directed him to remove his jacket and shirt.

He grumbled and winced, but he got it done. The stitches were intact, but blood leaked from the wound. Not a lot, but enough that it was clear Rory had probably caused it when she'd hit him.

Emma tutted and made sympathetic noises as she cleaned the wound. "You know, I've known Rory my whole life. She's passionate and headstrong, no doubt. She's quick to anger and slow to forgive. But all that passion and anger hides a vulnerable heart."

"If you say so, Doc. All I know is she hates me."

"I seriously doubt that. I think, if you got to know her, you'd find out she doesn't hate anyone. She's suspicious, sure. Wary. But maybe if you don't press her buttons so hard, you'll find out she's a good friend to have."

Chance looked slightly militant, but he didn't argue. Dude wanted more than friendship with Rory, that much was clear. Maybe Rory was the kind of woman who'd be up for a few nights in the sheets with no strings. Blaze didn't think Chance was going to find out, though. Not when he couldn't seem to help putting his foot in his mouth whenever he was near her.

And not when she'd seemed to be into the dude who'd met her at the cafe just now.

"Still," Emma said, "she shouldn't have hit you, no matter how mad you made her."

"She hit many people?" Blaze asked.

Emma didn't look at him. "Not to my knowledge. She seems especially annoyed by Chance if I'm being honest."

"I don't know why," Chance grumbled.

"I don't either."

"It's his face," Blaze joked. "He's got one of those faces you want to punch."

Chance snorted. "Thanks, bro. Appreciate it."

"Anytime, bud."

Emma shot him a look, their gazes tangling for the first time since he'd walked in. Blaze found himself wanting to reach for her, tuck her against his chest, and tell her everything was going to be okay.

She broke the eye contact first, bandaged Chance's arm, and peeled her gloves off. "All good. Try not to get into any more fights today, okay?"

"Yes, ma'am," Chance said, reaching for his shirt and tugging it on. "What do I owe you for patching me up?"

Emma blinked. "After everything y'all have done for me? Not a damn thing."

"Thanks," Chance said as he stood and picked up his coffee again. "But you don't have to do that."

"Not negotiable." Emma's chin lifted in what Blaze recognized as her stubborn look.

He shifted upright. "We appreciate your help. I'll let you know when I'm headed this way again. Rory invited Chance to the Dawg for a meal on the house, so I figure I'll eat there too. If you want to join us."

"Hey, I don't know that I'm taking her up on that tonight," Chance interjected.

"You definitely are. She felt terrible and she wants to make it up to you. You have to go."

Blaze didn't take his eyes off Emma. She'd folded her arms over her chest and looked at him coolly.

Something about that lab coat got him going anyway. He wanted to muss her up, make her look less like a medical professional and more like a woman who'd been thoroughly kissed.

Wasn't going to happen though. Not now. Not here.

"I'll go," Emma said. "But I'm sitting at the bar and talking to Rory while she works."

"Understood." He headed for the door behind Chance, then stopped and held her gaze. "See you later, Sunshine."

She stiffened but didn't shift her stance. "Yep, later."

Blaze turned away.

"Y'all be sure not to walk onto the range while you have shooters in the bays this time," she called. "There are some things I can't patch up, no matter how hard I try."

Chapter Thirty-Two

Emma got a text from Blaze around three that said he was headed back to town. She stared at the words on the screen for a long moment. She wanted to respond with words of her own, but she stopped herself. Instead, she did a thumbs up on his text and continued with her paperwork.

Her dad stopped in the door to her makeshift office, and Emma looked up.

"You okay, honey?"

"I pulled a tendon in my arm this morning but otherwise fine."

"I'm sorry to hear that, but it's not what I meant."

Emma's pulse throbbed. "Yes, Daddy. I'm fine."

Mortified that he knew what Simon had done to her and how he'd systematically undermined her confidence in herself, but fine, nevertheless.

"You know you can talk to me if you need to, right?"

"I do. I'm fine. Really." She sighed and put her pen down. "I didn't know what Simon was like when I started dating him. He wasn't that way at first. I feel like I should have seen it, though. The potential. But I didn't. And I'm really sorry he broke in and made Mama feel unsafe."

John Sutton came over and dropped to his knees beside her chair, dragged her into his arms, and held her. Emma put her arms around his neck and told herself *not* to cry.

"Baby girl, don't apologize for that. It's not your fault. Your mother and I are concerned about *you*. He could have burned the house down, and though we'd be devastated, it's nothing compared to how we feel about your safety and wellbeing. He *threatened* you. That Barbie wasn't a joke."

"I know. But I'm safe, Daddy. Blaze Connolly's making sure of it." She huffed a laugh. "He won't even let me leave this office until he arrives to escort me upstairs. He also doesn't let me go anywhere alone, just so you know. He makes sure I'm locked in my apartment safe and sound for the night, and he gets alerts on the cameras he installed. So do I, by the way."

Her dad squeezed her tight before leaning back to look at her with a watery smile. "I'm glad to hear it, pumpkin. I know your mama drives you a little crazy with her match-making, but you couldn't do better than Blaze. If you were interested, I mean."

Her heart thumped painfully. "It's a bit too soon for that, really. I think he's a good man, though."

Even if she wasn't certain what he'd been up to last night.

Her dad nodded. "He is indeed."

Her phone buzzed on her desk, and she glanced at it.

Blaze: Slight delay. Be there soon as I can.

"I can walk upstairs with you when you're ready," her dad said. "If he isn't here yet."

"It's okay. I've got to finish this paperwork, and I'm sure he'll get here soon."

She didn't tell her dad that Blaze had an entire routine he did with entering the apartment first and checking for intruders. Not that one could get past the cameras unobserved, but he wasn't the kind of man to take chances.

"All right then. I'm not leaving yet, just wanted to check with you. Do you think you could bring Blaze to dinner one of these nights now that your mama knows he was your date?"

Emma's insides quaked at the thought. "Let me ask him when he's available. But we aren't really dating, Daddy. He's a bodyguard. That's all. Despite the kiss," she added.

"I'll impress that fact upon her, but you know your mama. She's going to hope."

"She's always loved her romance novels," Emma said with a smile.

"Unashamedly."

Rory did too, but Emma had stopped reading them when she'd headed off to college. Maybe it was time again. She remembered sneaking her mother's books and sharing them with Rory, but now she wasn't so sure she'd been sneaking them at all. Mama always left them where she could pick them up and never asked where a book had gone.

Mama didn't just read romance. She read the classics, biographies, non-fiction, literature, and she'd encouraged Emma to read them too. It'd been a long time since Emma had sat down with a good book that transported her. Maybe she should ask Rory for one of those reverse harem things.

Emma finished her paperwork, closed her computer, and went to see how Brenda was getting on with her inventory. Emma had an excuse ready for the missing bandages, needle, and thread, but Brenda didn't ask.

"I think I may have used some things without keeping track," Emma said, unable to let Brenda think she'd miscounted.

Brenda was an older woman who'd worked for her father for at least fifteen years that Emma could remember. She gave Emma a kindly smile.

"You're the doctor. It's what you do. Don't you worry about keeping up with the little things. It's my job to make sure we have enough and order more when we need it. That's it, Emma."

Emma smiled. She'd gotten brave enough to ask Brenda to call her Emma, and the woman hadn't detoured to her full name since.

"Thank you. I appreciate that."

"It's my job, Doctor. You just worry about taking care of people and I'll take care of the rest."

Emma leaned against the door frame. "Do you think we could use a new receptionist, Brenda? Would that make things easier around here?"

Brenda stopped what she was doing and gave Emma a look. "Wouldn't hurt. When Beth left last year, your daddy planned to hire someone else, but then your mama had her heart attack and, honestly, I think he's had his hands full with life since. I've handled it, but we could use someone."

"What do you think about another doctor and nurse? Down the road, if things go well?"

Brenda smiled big. "Expanding the practice? I think that's a fine idea. We're a small town, but there's development going up everywhere near us, more people moving in all the time. I think folks will drive a few miles to Sutton's

Creek just as easy as they'll drive to Madison or Huntsville."

Emma hadn't known she was going to say such a thing until it popped out, but it felt right. Maybe leaning into her new life and seeing what she could make it was the best thing she could do. If it didn't work out, it wouldn't be from lack of trying.

Her phone buzzed with a text.

Blaze: I'm here. Got something to show you.

Emma donned her cool, controlled, not-into-you-at-all face and tapped a reply. *Be right out.*

She said goodbye to Brenda, then popped her head into her dad's office to say bye to him. He came around to give her another hug.

"I'm on my way out the door in just a minute, too. If you need anything from me or your mother, we're a phone call away."

"I know, Daddy."

He held her by the shoulders and gave her a serious look. "You don't have to hide the bad things from us, you know. I'm your father, and if I could get my hands on that man, it wouldn't be pretty."

She started to protest, but he shushed her.

"That said, I know it's best to leave it to the police. But if I had to commit violence to protect you, I wouldn't hesitate. Neither would your mother."

Emma couldn't help but smile. "Thank you. But I'm going to hope it doesn't come to that."

"Have a good night, sweetheart. Say hello to Blaze. I assume he's waiting for you?"

She could feel the blush creeping into her cheeks. "He is."

When she exited the office, Blaze was in the hall. He

sat on one of the steps going to the second floor and he held a bundle wrapped in a towel.

Emma had slipped into her mask of indifference before walking out the door, but she could feel it slipping as the bundle moved.

"What's that?"

Blaze stood to his full height and came over to her. He peeled back one edge of the towel as he dipped forward so she could see what he held.

A little black and white face peered up at her before the bundle mewed.

"Oh my goodness," she breathed. "Where did you get a kitten?"

"She was in the parking lot at the range, meowing her head off."

Her heart pinched. "Oh no, did you see any others?"

"Just this one." His face went hard for a moment. "Somebody probably dumped her off."

Emma could feel the shields she'd put into place crumbling away. She wanted to stay mad at him, stay detached, but the man made it impossible. He was sweet beneath that hard exterior, kind and caring.

"What are you going to do with her?"

"For now, take her upstairs and put her in the bathroom. Then I'm going to make a run to the pet store and pick up some supplies."

The kitten mewed again, and Blaze stroked a big finger over her tiny head. "It's okay, little baby. I've got you."

Emma's heart melted. "I can watch her while you shop. My apartment is still pretty much empty, and she can run around the living room."

The corners of his eyes crinkled. "That'd be great. Want to hold her?"

She nodded and he handed over the squirmy bundle. The kitty purred as Emma rubbed under her little chin. "Do you intend to keep her?"

"I don't know, but I won't take her to the shelter."

"There are some rescue foundations in the area that take animals and help them get adopted out. She wouldn't have to go to the shelter."

"That's an idea. Still need to get her some things, though. She's probably hungry."

Emma cuddled the little bundle, bouncing a bit like she was holding a baby. She didn't know why she did it except the kitten was tiny and maybe all babies liked to be bounced.

"I'm sure she is. I don't have anything in my fridge. You have ham, right? We could try to give her a little bit of that, see if she likes it."

"Even better, I think I have some shredded chicken. It's not spicy. I can run in and grab it."

"That'll work."

They went up the stairs and stopped at Blaze's apartment. She waited in the hallway while he went inside for chicken. He came back with two saucers as well.

"She'll need water and I think she's too little for a bowl."

Emma couldn't stop the warmth welling up inside. Or the sudden surge of moisture that stung her eyes. She sniffed back the tears and kept her attention focused on the tiny bundle. She'd been angry at Blaze for pushing her away, for yelling at her, but now all she wanted to do was hug him for being so attuned to what a small kitten might need.

He made her wait outside while he did what he called clearing her apartment, which basically meant making sure

Simon wasn't inside. When he returned and held the door for her, she walked in with her bundle. The emptiness of her apartment smacked her as she made her way to the kitchen.

She didn't have furniture yet, aside from the temporary chairs and table, but Blaze did. He had beds while she had a fold out mattress. The loneliness of her apartment over-whelmed her after spending a few nights in his.

He filled one of the saucers with water and set it on the floor. Emma put the kitty down and loosened the towel. The little thing tottered out on four shaky paws.

Blaze handed her a small container of chicken. "You feed her."

"She's so cute," Emma said, taking the container and opening it. She squatted and held out a little piece of chicken for the kitten, who sniffed and then gobbled it up before meowing plaintively. "Okay, okay. You can have more. But not too much. Don't want to get sick."

The kitten had black and white on her face and a couple of black patches on her back. The rest of her was white, or would be once she was clean.

"I wonder what happened to her tail." Emma touched the kitten's black tail. It was a stub, but it was bent at the end.

"I don't think it's an injury. There's no wound. Prob-ably a birth defect."

"Oh thank goodness. I'd hate to think this little baby had been hurt."

"She's too friendly for that. Came right to me when I bent down to look under the car."

Emma's stomach twisted. "She was under a car?"

"Yeah, but I heard her. I checked carefully for others.

The guys helped. There were no cats, no kittens. Just this little thing."

Emma fed the kitten another bit of chicken then placed her in front of the water. The kitten stuck her face in it, sneezed, then lapped it up as if she hadn't had water in a long time.

"I've never had a kitten before," she said, stroking the tiny back as the kitten drank.

"You could keep her," Blaze said. "You aren't working those crazy shifts anymore."

Emma felt tears welling in her eyes. "I could, couldn't I? My parents wouldn't care." She thought of Simon, of the doll in the puddle of red paint. "But I can't risk it. If Simon got in here again, he'd hurt her to spite me."

She shook her head, whether to shake away the tears or the idea that someone would hurt a kitten, she didn't know. "Until he's no longer a threat, I can't get close to anyone or anything. Especially not something so helpless."

Blaze hunkered down beside her and stroked the little kitty. She toddled over to him and rubbed against his shoe. "I'll keep her for you, Sunshine. Until this is over. Though I have to point out I have no intention of allowing him to get inside this apartment."

"I know." The kitten bounced over to Emma and she picked her up and cuddled her. She was rewarded with a loud purr. "But I can't risk it."

"Then I'm keeping her until you can. Problem solved."

She sniffed. Why was she so emotional about this? "You would do that for me?"

His smile made her heart ache. "I'd do a lot for you, Emma."

She dropped her gaze, suddenly feeling confused and frustrated. Just a few hours ago, he'd said that he liked her, but that was it. So why did he keep showing up for her? Rocking her emotions with the gift of a kitten? Telling her he'd do a lot for her?

That sentence was charged with meaning, though maybe it was just her. Maybe she was the one hearing things that weren't there.

"Thank you."

Because what else could she say?

Their eyes locked and held. She thought he was going to say something more, but he rocked back on his heels and stood.

"I'll head to the pet store. Be back as soon as I can. You know the drill."

She got to her feet, too. "Lock the door, don't open it for anyone."

"Right."

He walked out the door and turned to wait for her to close it. She lingered in the opening, one hand filled with a tiny kitten and the door in the other. Their eyes stayed locked together.

"I know you're a good man, no matter what you and Chance were up to last night. I appreciate your protection and your friendship more than you know, and I'm sorry if I was too pushy about things you'd rather keep personal."

Emotion crossed his face before he beat it back. But his voice was rough when he spoke.

"You make me want to share everything with you, Emma."

"Then why don't you?"

He closed his eyes a beat before they speared into her again. "Lock the door, Sunshine. Let me go get kitten food and supplies so we can make that baby happy."

Emma swallowed the knot in her throat and did what he told her.

239

Chapter Thirty-Three

The Salty Dawg wasn't too crowded, but Emma still found herself looking into all the corners as soon as they entered, searching for a familiar figure.

Beside her, Blaze tensed. "You feel something?"

She shook her head as she glanced up at him. "Nothing. I'm just paranoid, I guess."

"It's a good idea to look for danger whenever you enter a room. Note the exits, places to hide if there's trouble." He nodded toward the bar. "That's solid oak and it'll provide temporary cover if there's any gunfire."

She thought she should feel terrified at what he said, but she was oddly comforted. Blaze was always looking out for her, even when they were at odds.

Rory was behind the bar, filling orders. She looked subdued tonight. It didn't take long for Emma to guess why when her gaze landed on Chance sitting with Kane, Seth, Ethan, and Alex.

Rory was no doubt feeling the embarrassment of having lost control and hitting a man where he was already hurt. Blaze had given her a rundown of the circumstances that had led up to the incident when they'd been setting up the kitten's litter box and bed in his master bathroom.

It was typical Rory in Emma's opinion. No matter what she said about Chance being a jerk, if she wasn't attracted to him, he wouldn't get beneath her skin the way he did.

Blaze's friends saw them and waved. Emma found herself walking over with him, though she'd planned to eat at the bar.

"How's the kitten?" Alex asked. He was a strikingly handsome man with dark hair and piercing eyes. He had an aura of command about him that was hard to ignore.

"She's got food, water, a bed, and a litter box now," Blaze said. "When we left, she was eating."

"That's good," Alex replied. "Did you name her yet?"

Blaze shook his head. "Not keeping her. Just helping out." He glanced at Emma, and she felt the warmth of that gaze slide into her skin. "Emma's going to keep her, though."

She wanted to curl her hand into his, but she resisted the urge. It wasn't that long ago she'd been angry at him, or that he'd told her there could be nothing between them. She'd apologized for pushing him, but nothing had really changed between them. The fundamental problem was still there.

"I'm calling her Kitty at the moment, but it's not permanent. How's your arm, Chance?"

He jerked his attention to her from where he'd been watching the bar. Watching Rory, no doubt. "Uh, great. Thanks."

"Good. Let me know if you have bleeding, swelling, or redness."

"I will," he said sheepishly.

"You joining us for dinner, Doc?" Kane asked.

"Oh, I, uh…"

Six pairs of eyes in six handsome faces watched her expectantly. It hit her that she liked these men. Really liked them. They didn't have to lift a finger to help her out, but they had. Cameras, time to install them, teaching her to defend herself. The way they'd given her privacy during her panic attack but still managed to provide water and a blanket for her without comment or judgment. Blaze was always there to protect her, too, and that had to involve some kind of understanding with his partners.

"Yes, thank you, I'd love to join you."

She could visit with Rory afterward. Alex pulled out a chair beside him and she sat down. Blaze sat across from her. It was somehow worse than having him beside her. If he was beside her, she could be aware of him but not looking straight at him.

Now she had to meet those sky-blue eyes with their depths that hinted at secrets he would never share. Again and again, their eyes met, held, and her reservations dripped away like ice beneath a winter sun.

She found herself wanting to press her mouth to his, lose herself in the deliciousness of his kiss.

And more. She'd seen his naked chest last night. The broadness of it, the honed muscles, the warrior's scars that marred his perfect skin in places. She wanted to see all of him, wanted to slide her body against his and feel his possession when he took her.

He'd told her there couldn't be anything between them, but the things she saw in those eyes when they held hers said otherwise.

It was exciting and frustrating and confusing all at

once. She didn't *need* to be hung up on this man, and yet she feared she wasn't going to be given a choice.

"I want to thank you for helping out last night," Alex said as she cut into her chicken-fried steak and tried not to stare at Blaze too often. "And for your discretion."

"You're welcome. I admit I don't quite understand what happened, and I think y'all need to take a hard look at some of your business practices, but helping people is what I do. I'd never want any of you to think you couldn't come to me for care."

"Appreciate that, Doctor Sutton."

Because she was feeling brave and edgy and so many other things she wasn't quite sure how to name, she gave him a meaningful look. "I won't turn a blind eye to any illegal activities if I see them, but I also won't ask what's going on. That's not my priority."

His eyes glittered but he nodded. "Appreciate that, too."

Emma cocked her head. "You aren't going to protest about my illegal activities comment? Assure me that's not the case?"

"Nope. That's what guilty people do. We're just a group of friends who opened a business together. We're new at the business and we may make some mistakes, but mistakes aren't illegal."

"Mistakes can be deadly, though."

"They can. Hopefully we won't make those kind."

She smiled at him. "I hope not. I can fix a lot of things, but not that."

He laughed. "Guess not. We'll be mindful in future, I promise."

A change came over him in the next moment. His chin lifted, his eyes flashed, and his jaw tightened. He was looking at something behind her, but she shouldn't turn and look. But what if it was Simon?

That was the thought she needed to make her swivel around anyway. It was rude to stare at people, rude to make it seem like you were looking at them on purpose when you didn't know them, but the woman who'd walked into the Dawg was so striking Emma couldn't help but stare. Tall with hair the color of golden wheat and sunshine, she surveyed the room like a queen.

Emma had never seen her before, but that didn't mean anything since she'd only been back in Sutton's Creek for a short time. Whoever the woman was, she hadn't grown up here.

"Excuse me," Alex Bishop said before he was on his feet and moving toward the golden-haired woman in the jeans and navy silk shirt.

Emma turned to find Blaze also looking in that direction. His gaze dropped to her, and he gave her a half smile. "You doin' okay, babe?"

Her heart thumped at the endearment. "Yes. You?"

He patted his unfairly flat belly. "Full as a tick. Isn't that what y'all say in the South?"

Emma grinned. "We do. It's not a very appealing comparison though, is it?"

"Nope, but it fits the bill when you eat a hamburger the size of that one."

"Nobody made you."

"Just Theo Harper and his Big Dawg Burger."

"Theo loves to cook. Thankfully he's good at it." Emma glanced over her shoulder at Alex and the newcomer. They were at the bar and the woman was looking at the menu. Alex was standing beside her, saying something she nodded at.

"Who is that?" she asked when she turned back to Blaze. "I've never seen her before."

"She visited the range a few days ago. I don't remember her name."

"She's very pretty."

Blaze's eyes sparked. "So are you."

Emma felt a blush heat her cheeks. "I didn't say that for a compliment."

"I know, but it's true."

Chance was beside Blaze. He took a drink of his beer and nodded. "It's true, Doc. You're very pretty."

Blaze growled, "Mind your own business, Chance."

Emma laughed. "It's okay. I don't mind when handsome men tell me I'm pretty."

Chance elbowed Blaze. "She said I'm handsome."

"You *both* are."

"Yeah, but which one of us is better?" Chance asked with an eyebrow waggle.

She knew he was only doing it to rib Blaze. "Find your own girl," he growled.

Emma's body softened at the way he said those words. Like she was *his* and Chance was poaching. Did he want her to be his? Or was he pushing his friend away with no intention of acting on his own desire?

Emma pushed her chair back and stood as her body heated again. "You know what? I'm going to go talk to Rory now. Y'all duke it out and let me know who's more handsome when I get back, okay?"

Chance laughed. "It's me, Doc. No need for fighting."

Emma waved a hand over her head and kept going until she reached the bar. She took a seat at the end and waited for Rory to finish pouring an order. Rory looked beautiful tonight. Her hair was down, curled at the ends, and she'd taken time with her makeup. She wore jeans and cowboy boots with a long-sleeved red plaid shirt unbuttoned over a white tank top.

"Looking hot tonight, Ror," she said when her friend strolled over and plunked a glass of white wine in front of her. "Any reason?"

Rory didn't so much as glance at Chance. "Nope. Just put on some clothes."

Emma wasn't sure she believed that for a second. "Okay. Thought maybe you were looking for that Vitamin D tonight."

Rory snorted. "I wish. The guy from Huntsville is promising, but I'm not quite there yet. I had breakfast with him this morning, and I liked him. But he might be a little *too* nice, you know?"

"Not sure I do, but I trust you." Emma sipped her wine. She'd had water with dinner, so she didn't feel like she was in danger of imbibing too much. "Who's the stunning blonde?"

Rory looked in the direction she'd indicated. "I'm not sure. Haven't seen her before tonight. Looks like she's gotten the attention of one of our One Shot guys though."

"Yeah, he physically reacted when she walked in the door. I was sitting beside him, or I wouldn't have noticed, but it was like a stallion scenting a mare. I swear every cell in his body went on alert."

Rory sighed. "Must be nice. All I get are the assholes who've had a little too much to drink and think I'm an easy lay." She paused and her eyes flashed. "You know, I think I'm sick of men. I should just stick to Gus and save myself the hassle."

Emma reached over and squeezed her hand. "The right one will come along. You just haven't met him yet."

"I don't know that he will, Idgy. I've tried before and it doesn't work out."

Emma couldn't help but grin. "You haven't called me that since we were teenagers."

EG for Emma Grace had morphed into Idgy when they were kids. Emma hadn't heard it in years, not since they'd grown up and gone their separate ways.

"You haven't seemed like an Idgy for a long time."

"I do now?"

It was Rory's turn to squeeze her hand. "Yes. You belong here, girl. In Sutton's Creek. I know it's a big change for you, and maybe it's not going to be easy, but right now you seem happy. That's what I want for you."

Warmth flooded her. "Thank you, Ror. I'm mostly happy. I didn't know how much I needed a change."

She'd always thought that working harder and longer would get her where she wanted to go in life. She'd envisioned succeeding at a level that would awe everyone who'd ever known her. But what was the point in that if she was overworked and unable to enjoy the life she'd built?

Life wasn't perfect, far from it, but she was enjoying working with her dad and Brenda, even if the patients weren't quite as welcoming as she'd like. And then there was Blaze and her kitten, coming to the Dawg whenever she wanted, and seeing her friends and family almost every day.

The only thing keeping her from being happy was Simon. A chill shivered down her spine.

"I'm glad you came back."

"Me too." She twirled the stem of her glass. "What happened this morning with Chance?"

Rory's face turned red. "I don't know. He makes me so

mad that I do stupid stuff like sock him in the arm. I swear I didn't know he had stitches though."

"I know you didn't, babe. But maybe don't hit people, hmm?"

Rory dropped her chin and shook her head. "I know better, I swear I do. It was a stupid thing to do, and I've apologized and given him dinner on the house. I think I just need to avoid him in the future, though. He makes me see red and I don't know why."

"You want to know what I think?"

Rory looked wary. "Not sure I do, but you want to tell me so go ahead."

"I think he gets to you because you're attracted to him. So maybe bang him and get it out of your system."

"Not going to happen." Rory looked militant. "I am *not* attracted to him. I mean sure, he's sexy and he's got those damned muscles, but he's a player, Emma Grace. I don't get involved with players these days."

"I know, honey. Mark did a number on you, and I get why you're cautious, but are you going to let that asshole affect the rest of your life after all these years?"

"I don't want to, but somehow he does anyway. We were only weeks from the wedding when I caught him screwing Tammy. And now they're married and have two kids. Thank God they moved to Decatur and I never have to see them."

Decatur was across the Tennessee river, not more than fifteen miles away, but Mark's job was there. Tammy was busy getting involved in the Junior League and posting on social media about the big house they'd bought in the historic district and their perfect children. Emma wasn't friends with her, but Tammy's posts sometimes came across her feed because other people she knew shared them.

Made her mad every time, but she never said a word to Rory.

"They deserve each other, and I hope they're miserable. But how is a one-night stand to get a man out of your system getting involved with anyone?"

Rory glanced toward the table where Chance sat with his friends. "What if he's so amazing in bed that I want more? Then my emotions get involved and, boom! He marries some skanky woman who pretended to be my friend while screwing my man behind my back." She shook her head. "Not gonna do it."

Emma sighed. "Okay, fine. I get it. Just a thought."

Rory slipped away to pop the caps off a few beers for Amber before returning with a smirk. "Speaking of banging hot men, why haven't you gotten naked with Blaze yet?"

Emma blinked even as fresh heat bloomed inside. "Ouch. Guess I deserved that. And the answer is, it's complicated."

"Always is."

"I want to," she admitted, her heart pounding to hear the words coming from her mouth. "And I think he does, too. But he says he doesn't want to get involved, so nothing happens even when I think it might."

"Dang."

"Right. Dang."

Rory sighed and leaned against the bar with a defeated kind of sigh. "It's a fucked-up world, isn't it? Handsome, sexy as sin men moving to our town without any girlfriends or wives, yet neither of us can manage to get laid because either they have hang-ups or we do."

"I'll drink to that," Emma said, lifting her glass to clink with Rory's water before taking a big swig. The wine burned going down, but she didn't care. "He gave me a kitten."

Rory's eyebrows lifted. "A kitten?"

She nodded. "He found one at the range and brought it back with him. Then he went to get food and litter while I watched her. Of course I fell in love that fast, and now she's mine. I've never had a kitten before."

"Oh my God, the man gave you a kitten but won't give you some hot lovin'?"

Emma laughed. "I know, right? He does sweet stuff like that and even when I get mad at him, I want him."

Rory looked intrigued. "What does he do to make you mad?"

"Well, he bosses me around when he's teaching me to defend myself. And he bosses me around about stepping out of the apartment without him as my fire-breathing shadow."

"Dunno, babe, but with that weirdo stalker you've got, you might want to listen about that one."

Emma sighed. "I know."

She told Rory about going to use the treadmill when Blaze was still asleep and how mad he'd gotten. She left out the part about how Chance got his stitches or Blaze's nightmare because those weren't her stories to tell.

"He was a bit angry when he banged on the door," she finished. "But he admitted it was safe to go downstairs before the building was open to the public."

"So you got your apartment back and he gave you a kitten in return."

"Yep."

Rory smirked. "And now you want to jump him again."

"Is it that obvious?"

"Yeah, girl. Totally. But I'd be pissed off too if I were

you. He makes hot eyes at you, kisses the fire out of you, and then does nothing about it. Think he got in some kind of accident where the parts don't work and he just doesn't want to have to admit it?"

Emma laughed. "No. Pretty sure the parts work just fine. I've felt the evidence even if I haven't *felt* the evidence."

"Welp, I'm at a loss." Rory frowned. "We should make a pact that if we reach forty and we're unmarried and childless, we marry each other, maybe adopt a kid or two, and be a platonic lesbian couple for the rest of our lives."

"Oh God, Rory," Emma said after she managed to swallow her wine without snorting it through her nose. "Don't say things like that when I'm drinking."

Rory grinned. "Hey, it's an idea. Put it on the back burner and we'll talk about it again in six years. Also, don't look now, but Mr. Tall, Dark, Sexy, & Broody is on the way over here." She cocked her head. "Hmm, wonder if he's gay? Maybe that's why he doesn't want to be hands on."

Emma's insides were fluttering. She couldn't see Blaze approach, but she felt him. "He doesn't kiss like he's gay."

"Bisexual then, and you aren't his dream man."

Emma snorted. "I love you, Ror."

"Love you, too," Rory said with a wink. "Hey, Blaze. Need a refill? Or maybe you'd like Theo's number? He's not gay, but you could try."

Blaze stood at the end of the bar, his gaze darting between them in somewhat adorable confusion. Emma bit the inside of her lip to keep from laughing.

"Uh, no thanks. Not gay, not planning to try it."

"Whatever. Drink?"

"No. Came to ask Emma if she wanted to head back home and check on her kitten."

Emma swallowed her mirth and blinked up at him. "That would be great. She's probably lonely all by herself."

Rory gave her a meaningful look as she hopped off the barstool. "Remember what I said."

"Hard to forget, Ror," Emma said with a grin. "See you tomorrow."

"Should I ask what that was about?" Blaze said when they went out the front door into the cool evening.

It was windy, which was typical for March, and the wind bit into her cheeks.

"Rory and I are getting married in six years. If we're both still single, that is."

"Uh, okay."

"A platonic lesbian relationship where we're done with men but live together and maybe adopt a kid. It was Rory's idea."

He laughed. "I see. And she thinks I'd like to marry Theo or something?"

Emma followed him through the front door of the Sutton building. Her belly was warm from the wine, and her inhibitions were maybe slightly less strong than usual.

"No, she suggested you might be gay. You know, since you don't actually want to sleep with me even when we both know I'd say yes if you asked."

Chapter Thirty-Four

BLAZE COULDN'T STOP HIMSELF FROM GETTING HARD. JUST like that, he was ready to go. Ready to kiss his way down her body and bury his face between her legs before sliding deep inside her and taking them both to nirvana.

Took him a moment to realize he was staring at her. That he'd stopped moving toward the stairs and turned to face her. She tilted her head back and smiled up at him in a way that made his fingers itch to bracket that face in his hands and kiss the daylights out of her.

"I never said I didn't want to," he finally managed when he got his brain back into gear.

We both know I'd say yes if you asked.

Emma shrugged. "It doesn't matter what you say, Blaze. It's what you *do*. And you don't do anything."

She sailed past him and started up the stairs. He watched her cute ass sway from side to side, imagined gripping those cheeks in both hands while he lifted her pussy to his mouth and licked her until she saw stars.

Blaze closed his eyes for a second and got a mental hold on himself before following her up to the second floor.

She walked past her apartment and straight to his, turning to face him when she got to his door.

"I want to see my kitten. I want to take her home, but I don't want to confuse her when we have to move her back in the morning. If I can just play with her for a little while, I'll leave you alone."

"You can stay, Emma. Be near her and stay with me until we find Simon. You know it's what I want you to do anyway."

"I know. But I fought to get my place back. What does it say about me if I agree to return after only a few hours? I haven't even stayed a night in there yet."

"It doesn't say anything except you want to be near your kitten and you trust me to take care of you both."

She pinched the bridge of her nose. "Dammit, Blaze Connolly, why did you have to find a stray kitten?"

"Because she needed my help."

Emma's eyes glittered when she met his. "Just like I did when you first met me. Always charging in to help people in danger or innocent animals."

"It's the right thing to do."

She looked as if she were wrestling with herself. "Okay. I'll stay. But if I want to go downstairs to hit the treadmill before the building is open, then I'm going."

"Already agreed to that."

She nodded her head with a jerk. "Just want us to be clear."

"We're clear."

She pointed a finger at him. "I had *one* glass of wine, by the way. I'm not drunk. But my filters aren't as strong because my give-a-crap factor is weak. I'm done with being agreeable and polite about absolutely everything. If I don't like something, I'm going to say so."

"Wouldn't want it any other way."

"Okay. Good. Perfect."

She was fucking adorable, and he wanted to push her against the wall and kiss her until she melted.

"Want to get your stuff before we go inside?"

"That's a good idea."

They went to her apartment, he checked it out, and she retrieved all the things she'd taken back that morning. Then they returned to his place. Before she could put her stuff in the guest room, he stopped her.

"You can have my room. That way you can be with your kitten. She's so small I'd suggest keeping her in the bathroom overnight, especially since she probably won't let you sleep if she's out. But then you can see her when you want."

Her expression softened as he spoke. "Oh Blaze, I can't take your bed."

"It's fine. I don't mind."

He could see her wrestle with the idea, but he knew the kitten was going to win. "Okay," she said softly. "If you're sure."

"I'm sure."

He led her to his room and grabbed the book he'd been reading from the bedside table. The kitten started to mew when she heard them, and Emma went over to open the door and squatted down as the little thing barreled out.

"Oh my goodness, you are so cute," she cooed as she picked up the mewing bundle of fur. "And sassy too."

Blaze's heart squeezed at the sight of her cuddling the kitten. The tiny thing was dirty and had fleas because she hadn't been to the vet yet, but Emma didn't seem to mind.

"Sassy might be a name for her," he mused.

Emma smiled at him. The kitten was still mewing and

trying to climb onto Emma's shoulder. "Sassy. I like that. She is pretty sassy, isn't she?"

"Yep. For a tiny, dirty, helpless little speck of fur, she's got plenty of attitude."

Emma held the kitten up in front of her face. "Are you Sassy? Does that sound good to you?"

Sassy mewed again, softer this time, and Emma laughed. "Sassy it is. Did you eat, little Sassy?"

Blaze went into the bathroom to get his toothbrush, razor, and shampoo. "Looks like she ate a good amount."

"Oh, that's so wonderful. Sweet little baby Sassy. I'm so happy you're here." Emma's voice had gone up about a hundred octaves as she talked in a baby voice to the kitten.

That voice hit him square in the chest as he pictured her talking to a human baby. Their baby.

He'd never really wanted kids, not after the childhood he'd had, but the thought of having a baby with Emma didn't scare him the way it once would've. She was a doctor, a stable, smart woman who had a loving family and had grown up with support from those around her.

She wouldn't endanger her children, ever. She wouldn't choose her own selfish needs and wants over what their kids needed.

He could picture it. Picture her with a child on her hip as he bent to kiss her before he headed to the range.

The range.

Of course it couldn't happen. None of his fantasies could happen. He had to maintain his distance, no matter how difficult it was getting. He was in Alabama for a job, not for a new start on a new life.

"I'm gonna head to bed," he said. "If you don't need anything else."

Emma's head swiveled in his direction. "No, I'm good. Is this about something I said?"

It was only eight o'clock, so of course she'd wonder. "Nope. Worked hard today, so I'm kinda beat. Gonna settle in and read my book for an hour, then lights out."

She set Sassy down on the floor when the kitten wiggled, and she took off like a shot, zipping under the bed before zipping back again.

Emma was grinning when she looked up. "Understand. Thank you, Blaze. For bringing me a kitten I didn't know I wanted. For letting me stay in your room. For believing me when I told you about Simon. For protecting all of us at the Gas-n-Go. For everything."

It was everything he could do not to wrap his arms around her and hold her close.

"I'd do it for anyone," he said roughly.

The light in her eyes dimmed a fraction, and he knew he'd said the wrong thing.

"I know. But thanks anyway."

Chapter Thirty-Five

It was the shouting that woke her. Emma lay in the bed, staring at the ceiling, her heart pounding, and wondered if she'd been dreaming. But no, there it was again.

Blaze calling out in his sleep. Asking for help.

It broke her heart, that plea. And there was no way she could ignore him, even if his dream had been the beginning of the end the last time.

Emma threw the covers back and strode into the hall. When she got to Blaze's door—her door just last night— she knocked.

The hoarse shout of his voice stopped. She waited, straining to hear through the silence. Sassy mewed in the bathroom. She'd hated to put the kitten in there for the night, but Blaze had been right that she didn't want to settle down. Kittens were primed to jump on everything that moved, and legs were no exception when they shifted beneath the covers.

Emma had put her in there with her food, water, litter, and a kitty bed—and then there'd been silence.

Not anymore.

"Blaze? Are you awake?"

The door was yanked open and her big, growly, sexy protector stood there looking disheveled and a little bit lost. Not drained like last night, but tired and resigned.

He was shirtless again, and her blood hummed in her veins at the sight of all that muscle and skin.

"Sorry."

Her heart pinched. "There's nothing to be sorry for. You've had a trauma of some kind, and your brain calls it up when you sleep. I know you don't want to talk about it and I'm not asking, but if you'd like to talk about something completely random, I'm here. Or maybe you'd like to come and play with Sassy? I'm going to have to let her out for a little bit. She heard me get up, and now she's meowing."

He shoved a hand through his hair, apparently unconcerned—or probably unaware—with the way it spiked over his head. She thought he would refuse and close the door, but he sighed.

"I think I'd like company."

"Meet you in the living room? Or do you want to come into your bedroom for a while? We could sit on the bed and let Sassy bounce around between us."

His gaze sharpened for the briefest of moments. "Yeah, that. Kittens and puppies make everything better."

"Then you'd better come join us when you're ready."

Emma went back to her room, aware that he was following closely behind. She heard the snick of the door as he closed it, but she didn't turn around. Every cell in her body was aware of him, but she told herself to cool it. The man was having a nightmare, and he was there to talk and laugh at kitten antics, not be her own personal wet dream.

Her skin heated as she thought about what she'd done earlier. After she'd put Sassy in the bathroom and couldn't sleep, she'd let her hand drift down to the soft wetness between her thighs. She'd pictured Blaze's face as she'd teased herself, gasping at the electricity when she skimmed her clitoris.

She'd thought she would need to ask Rory where she got Gus the Glamorous since shoving her fingers into her channel hadn't been nearly satisfying enough when she'd orgasmed around them. She'd lay there panting, seeing stars, and still wanting more.

She'd truly thought she didn't miss sex until she'd started stroking herself.

The truth was she didn't miss it with *Simon*. She craved it with Blaze.

Craved it and wasn't going to get it, which was about as satisfying as lying beneath Simon while he got himself off and then turned over and went to sleep.

Her ears were hot as she went to open the bathroom door. Sassy came bounding out of the room and ran between Emma's legs. She laughed as she turned and watched Blaze scoop the kitten up in one big hand.

"Hello, little Sassy Pants. Have you been a good kitty for your mommy?"

Emma grinned even as her heart throbbed a little faster. "Not precisely. She wouldn't go to sleep with me, like you said. She attacked my feet and legs until I had to put her in the bathroom."

"Takes time," Blaze said, sinking onto the far side of the mattress and leaning against the headboard. He set Sassy down and she promptly attacked a ripple in the covers. "The fleas aren't helping either, but we'll get those taken care of ASAP."

"You've had kittens?"

His expression was guarded. "Once, when I was a kid. We stayed in one place for eight months that time. But I had to leave them all when Mom found a new supplier."

Emma's heart stuttered. "Supplier?"

He tilted his head back and closed his eyes. "I said my mom moved us a lot because she had a lot of boyfriends. What I didn't say was that those boyfriends were usually her suppliers. She's a drug addict. Or was. I don't know if she's still alive or not. Don't really care since she didn't care about me enough to put me first once in a while."

Emma's throat squeezed. She didn't know what to say. "I'm so sorry. That must have been terrifying for you."

Inadequate, but all she had.

"I was scared a lot when I was little, and then I just got used to it. It was my normal. But I hated leaving those cats. I'd never had a pet before, and then I had five of them until the day I didn't."

Emma wanted to cry. And she wanted to hug him tight. He'd been a little boy who'd had nothing permanent in his life and no adults he could count on. When he had something good, something he loved, it was taken away.

Maybe that was why he didn't want to get involved with her. Maybe he didn't do relationships because they were messy and painful and he'd had enough of that in his life.

"You didn't have to give Sassy to me. You could have kept her."

He rolled his head on the headboard until he was looking at her. "I wanted you to have her. I still get to play with her, so long as we're neighbors."

Emma went to join him on the bed, sinking carefully

onto the opposite side. Sassy pounced on the ripples in the covers as they wrinkled anew.

There were so many things she could say—wanted to say—but she decided to stick to the simple things.

"Will you be able to sleep again?"

"Should. Can't guarantee I won't dream, though." He shoved a hand over his head and yawned big. "Haven't had them in a while, now they're back. Never go away completely."

"I had bad dreams in medical school. They were brought on by anxiety about my classes and exams. I know it's not the same thing," she finished on a rush, chiding herself for bringing up her own experience. Nowhere *near* the same.

"You don't have to explain, Emma. Stress happens to all of us." He blew out a breath. "It was Afghanistan. The Hindu Kush. My unit was after a warlord who'd been hijacking supply convoys. We had information about where his stronghold was, and we went after him. But the intel was wrong, and we walked into an ambush."

Her heart pounded as if she were watching a military action movie. She pictured Blaze in full gear, helmet, vest, rifle slung across his chest, taking fire and shouting for help. It made the desperation she heard when he'd shouted in his sleep all the more poignant.

"I lost five men that day. Three of us walked away, though walked isn't quite the right word for it. In my dreams, I need air support, but I can't remember the words to call for it. In reality, I called for air support, but it was too late."

Emma reached across the bed and wound her hand in his, squeezing. He squeezed back.

"Thank you for telling me."

She wanted to tell him to go to counseling, to consider medication, but she sensed he didn't want to hear those things. And she wasn't going to cross the fragile line between them by barreling over it with well-meaning but unwelcome advice.

"Thank you for listening. Before you ask, I've been to counseling. It's required, and I was released to duty again after I completed the sessions."

"I wasn't going to ask."

"You wanted to."

She saw no point in lying. "I did."

"I know you want to help, Sunshine. I appreciate it. But I know I might always deal with the survivor's guilt and helplessness. If it gets unbearable, I'll see someone. This shit doesn't magically go away, though, and you know it."

"I know. Just so long as you're self-aware enough to get help if you need it. That's the important part."

"Trust me, I know. And I will. There's been a lot happening lately, and I was due for a rough night or two. Always happens."

"Chance getting shot didn't help, did it?"

She felt the tightening in his body. "No. It was nothing in the scheme of things, but it reminded me."

"Understandable. Wouldn't life be great if bad things just never happened? Impossible, though. We're all carrying some emotional tragedy around inside and trying to smile like everything is perfectly normal. Which it is a lot of the time, until something throws us off kilter."

He hadn't let go of her hand. She took comfort in the warmth and solidity of it. He was here, with her, and even if they weren't together, they were friends. She trusted him more than she'd ever trusted a man before. It was a good feeling, but sad too since she wanted so much more and he didn't.

"It would be great, but I don't think that's how life works. We need the pain to make us human, to remind us that every day we wake up and have choices is a damn good day."

"Wow, look at us, philosophizing in the middle of the night with a kitten between us."

He grinned. He looked tired, but his smile had the power to make her melt. He was a handsome man, beautiful and rugged, his body honed like finely chiseled marble. She couldn't help but be aware of him, of the heat rolling from him and the need blossoming in her core.

"Who knows, we might solve world hunger or find the solution to world peace right here tonight."

Emma laughed. "Maybe."

His expression changed, turned serious. "I'm glad you're here with me, Emma."

Her heart thumped a quick beat. "I am too."

His eyes were beginning to droop. Sassy pounced a couple more times and crawled onto his lap before turning around and around. He stroked her tiny head.

"I should go. Let you get back to sleep."

"I think you should stay. Let Sassy use you as a bed."

"Looks like she already is."

"Then you definitely can't go."

His summer-sky eyes were warm when they slid over her. "Can't think of anywhere else I'd rather be."

Chapter Thirty-Six

Blaze slept soundly. More soundly than he had in a long time. Until something tiny with claws and teeth pounced on his hand. He woke with a start to find Sassy in attack mode.

She was still adorable. He gently pried her away, pleased when she stopped biting immediately. Kittens didn't know how sharp those pinprick teeth and claws were, but they could be taught to be gentle.

Sometime during the night, Blaze had slid down until he was lying on top of the covers. Sassy must have been sleeping on him for much of that time. A short distance away, Emma lay on her side, facing him, her eyes closed, mouth slightly open.

She'd dragged a blanket over herself, and her knees were curled up in a semi-fetal position. Not quite that tight, but close.

Sassy bounded up and down between them and Blaze was afraid she'd wake Emma. He sat up as gently as possible, picked the kitten up to cuddle her, and took her to the bathroom. She dove into the food and started crunching, and Blaze studied his reflection in the mirror.

He ought to go back to the guest room, but he didn't want to. He felt *settled* lying in bed with Emma. Since he planned to stay near her, he took a swig of mouthwash from the bottle sitting on the counter and went back into the bedroom, closing the door softly on Sassy.

Emma had moved to her back, one arm flung out, a black brace around it beneath the elbow, her face creased from the pillow. She looked younger than her thirty-four years, and impossibly innocent. He knew she wasn't, not with a job like hers. She said she'd had her hands in more guts than he or Chance had ever seen, and he figured she was right.

Emma Grace Sutton was one tough, badass woman, even if she didn't realize it, and he wasn't going anywhere tonight.

The next time Blaze woke, light streamed between the gap in the curtains. His arms were filled with soft woman. He lay on his side with Emma spooned against him. The sweet curve of her ass fit perfectly in the cradle of his hips. His cock nestled into the indent between her cheeks.

He was, of course, harder than stone.

"Shit," he muttered.

Emma moved then, pressing her ass back against him in her sleep as she stretched. It took everything he had not to groan, especially when she turned and threw a leg over his. Her hands rested on his chest, and she sighed as she pressed her cheek into his shoulder.

If he'd thought having her ass against his dick was bad, having her facing him, her leg over his thigh, was worse. She wore pajamas, complete with pants and a button-down top, but he could feel the heat from her pussy. It wouldn't take much of anything to reach down and cup her there, rub her through the pajamas.

He wouldn't, because she wasn't awake and he didn't have permission, but God above, how he wanted to.

Blaze closed his eyes and bent his forehead to hers as he worked to keep from coming just because she was so close. He'd never done so from something so tame before, didn't think he would now, but the truth was he didn't know. She fucking excited him.

She sighed again and wriggled against him. His dick pressed forward, seeking more. It was delicious torture, her body rubbing against his.

And he couldn't let it keep happening. Not when she wasn't aware of it. Felt like a creeper thing to do.

"Emma," he whispered. "Babe. Sunshine."

Her eyelids drifted open, the blue depths fuzzy with sleep. He thought she might scramble away from him when she realized, but she only smiled. "Hi."

God, this woman. "Hi."

She blinked sleepily. "Is Sassy okay?"

"Everything's fine. Sassy's asleep, but probably not for much longer."

Emma stretched against him, and Blaze bit back the groan in his throat as she brushed his dick. His very hard, very ready dick.

"Oh," she breathed, her eyes widening.

"Yeah."

They studied each other for a long moment without speaking. He could feel the tremor in her body, the way she waited for him to be the first to break the silence.

"I'm gonna get up and start the coffee," he growled. "Give you a chance to breathe. You still want to say yes after that, I'm not saying no this time."

Because he couldn't anymore. He'd tried. For the mission, for her, for his own sanity.

It wasn't working. Short of packing up his truck and driving away from Sutton's Creek for good—not something he could actually do without being considered a traitor to his country—he wasn't getting her out of his head. He didn't even think that would do it, really.

"If you *do* say yes," he continued, "you need to realize I can't promise you a future. All I can give you is right now. No promises."

"Didn't ask for promises, big guy."

"I know, but I gotta say it anyway."

"Hooah."

He blinked. "Did you just say *hooah*?"

"I did, and I believe it was proper usage. Heard, understood, and acknowledged."

Blaze laughed. He was still hard, still horny, but she cracked him up. "You got it, Sunshine. Damn, you surprise me sometimes."

She gave him a cheeky smile. "I'm a nerd, Blaze. I know things."

He kissed her forehead and reluctantly slid away from her embrace. "You're the prettiest nerd I know," he told her. "Now, I'm going to fix that coffee and pray this erection subsides."

"I know a cure for that." She propped herself on an elbow, her dark hair cascading over one shoulder in a thick tangle. So fucking pretty.

"I do, too. But I don't make major decisions while horny or in need of coffee. Neither should you."

Emma grinned as she threw the covers back. "I don't think anyone's ever said that to me before."

"It's a Blaze Connolly original, learned the hard way, har-de-har."

Emma laughed. "Cute. You should paint that on a sign and sell it on Etsy. You'd make a fortune."

He loved the banter with her. He could picture mornings making love to her, then fixing coffee and breakfast, bringing it to her in bed, laughing and teasing each other before they ended up getting naked again. He'd go to work with a huge fucking smile on his face, and Emma would look dreamy and satisfied because he wouldn't ever fail to please her. It'd be his mission to keep her happy.

The thought of missions made his gut tighten. It'd only been two nights since they'd infiltrated Royal Shipping and Chance got shot. They didn't even have word on what the computer parts were for yet or what their next move would be.

Didn't have to be a betting man to know this mission was nowhere near over.

"Hey," Emma said softly, dragging his attention back to her. She was standing now, looking adorably rumpled in her pajamas, but her eyes were filled with concern. "You okay?"

"I'm great, Sunshine. There's a beautiful, sexy woman in my bed, a kitten in my bathroom, and coffee on the horizon. How could I be anything but?"

"You looked far away, that's all."

He closed the distance between them and took her in his arms. She came into them willingly, pressing her cheek to his chest and closing her eyes. She tangled him up inside, but he liked it because she made him feel more alive than he had in a long time.

"I'm right here, babe. Like I said last night, nowhere else I'd rather be."

Chapter Thirty-Seven

Emma showered and washed her hair, toweling it dry before she slipped into yoga pants and a sweatshirt, put on a pair of socks, and went to join Blaze in the kitchen. Sassy was loose and playing with a wine cork that Blaze had given her, batting it around the kitchen and pouncing like her life depended on catching breakfast for herself.

Blaze looked up, and her stomach squeezed. He'd showered, too, but he hadn't put on a shirt. His hair was damp, a pair of jeans hung low on his hips, and his skin rippled over muscle when he lifted an arm to reach for a coffee cup out of the cabinet.

Emma's heart hammered as she thought about how she'd awakened. Plastered to Blaze's hot body, his hard cock nestled between her legs. In that moment, if he'd slipped it inside her, she'd have died and gone to heaven.

She'd *wanted* him to do it. Wanted him to drag her pajama bottoms off, free himself, and fill her until she moaned.

She still wanted it, but now she was shyer about it. Now that they'd showered and put that distance between them that he'd insisted on, she'd lost the boldness she'd had in bed with him. He'd told her he wouldn't say no this time. She didn't want him to.

Except he'd also told her he wasn't offering her a future. He was giving her right now.

And maybe that was enough. She was still reeling over the changes in her life because of Simon, and Blaze had baggage of his own to deal with. His childhood with a drug addict mother who'd never given him a stable home life, and at least one mission in the military that'd resulted in everyone dying except for him and two other guys.

That would be *a lot* for anyone to deal with. No wonder he couldn't promise more than the present moment.

He handed her a cup of coffee, fixed the way she liked it with plenty of cream, and she took a sip, closing her eyes to savor it. Blaze made good coffee. He ground his own beans and brewed it strong, though not too strong.

"Sleep okay? Aside from me waking you up in the middle of the night."

"You and Sassy both, you mean," she said with a smile. "Honestly, I was already tossing and turning a bit before I heard you."

"Because of Marsh."

"Him. And you."

"Why me?" He had the audacity to look puzzled.

"I think you know why," she said, her heart thrumming a little harder now.

"I think I do," he said softly as understanding crossed his features. "But I need you to be sure any desire to get naked with me isn't brought on by gratitude for my help, or proximity, or even the gift of a kitten."

Emma wanted to pinch him. She settled for rolling her eyes instead. "For God's sake, Blaze, even if those *are* my reasons, they aren't bad ones. You're a decent man who's upended your life and routine to protect me, and now you're housing me *and* a stray kitten. And you bought her all that stuff, which you need to let me pay you for, by the way. But damn, there are worse reasons to be attracted to someone."

"There are. And no, you can't. Consider it a gift. For both of you."

Emma shook her head slowly. "See? It's stuff like that right there. *That's* why I like you. Sure, you're big and growly and you've got that protector thing going that makes all the women at the Dawg want to throw their panties at you, but you're also thoughtful and kind. None of that is why I want to get naked with you, though."

"It isn't?"

"No." She set the coffee down on the island and went to him. It was bolder than she normally behaved, but nothing felt wrong with him. He made her feel safe, both physically and emotionally.

Right here, right now, she was happy again.

Emma slid her palms over the warm skin of his chest. He was silk and velvet and heat. Beneath that, he was steel. She pressed a finger to the pulse in his neck, felt a soar of triumph that it beat faster than normal.

"Attraction and arousal are complicated phenomena. You have to have the right amount of sympathetic nervous system activity. Your heart races, you tingle and feel jumpy. That's the fight-or-flight reaction. But then you have the parasympathetic nervous system which regulates the physical signs of arousal, like genital swelling and releasing sexual fluids. Add in the dopamine hits that come from being around you, and it's a perfect storm of need and desire."

"That's your reason?" he asked, his voice hoarse. "It's biological?"

"Mmm," she said, dropping her mouth to kiss his chest. God, this was so unlike her, but it was also precisely what she wanted to do in the moment.

His breath hissed in, his hands closing gently around her upper arms. He didn't push her away, though.

"It's biological, yes," she said. "But it's mental, too. Because you're you, and everything about you makes me want you. Whether it's biological, evolutionary, chemical— I don't really care. It's a need in my belly, in my core, that I haven't felt before. Nothing about this makes sense to me. And I feel like if I fight it, if I don't express to you that I want whatever you can give, that I'll regret it on some level. I'm tired of living scared. I want to live with the kind of wild joy that comes from choosing to get on the roller-coaster."

His hands slid around her body to cup her ass. Emma had to bite back a groan at the feel of those big hands on her bottom.

"I'm a rollercoaster, now?" he asked with a laugh before he bent to nibble her earlobe.

"You might be," she breathed. "But I want to take the ride."

Chapter Thirty-Eight

SHE WAS NERVOUS, BUT EXCITED TOO. BLAZE HAD HIS hands full of her ass as he pressed her back against the counter. Emma's palms were still on his chest, but they slid up and around his back to grip his shoulders as he lowered his head and claimed her mouth.

If their previous kisses had been hot and sweet, this one was raw and full of the kind of heat that incinerated. Blaze claimed her lips, her tongue, sucking and devouring in a way that made her whimper with need.

Only Blaze was capable of the kind of kiss that filled her soul with sweetness and made her want to climb his magnificent body and ride him until she collapsed from exhaustion and pleasure.

When he lifted her onto the counter, she could only gasp at the power and speed at which he did so. His hands were free to roam then. He wrapped one hand around her throat, beneath her jaw, gently holding her there while he devoured her mouth. She thought maybe it should terrify her, but it didn't.

Blaze was safe. Blaze was her protector. Whatever he did, he did for her.

And that made her feel more powerful than she ever had before.

Emma leaned into his hand, giving him all her trust, and he made a sound in his throat that strummed her senses with the rawness of it.

"Emma," he whispered, breaking the kiss to trail his tongue down her throat where his hand had been. "Beautiful, sexy Emma."

His words thrilled her. Nobody had ever called her beautiful and sexy in the same sentence. She was nerdy and sexy sometimes in a naughty librarian kind of way, but never beautiful.

She felt beautiful now. With him.

"Please," she said, though she didn't know what she was saying it for.

Blaze stepped back and ripped her sweatshirt off in one smooth motion. She hadn't put on a bra yet. Her breasts were small, a B-cup, nothing like the great rack Rory had, and she felt the first prickling of unease when Blaze's eyes dropped to take them in.

What if he was a boob man?

She was going to be so disappointing without her pushup bra.

"Gorgeous," he said as if sensing her burgeoning unease. His electric gaze caught hers. Held. "You're gorgeous, Emma."

"I'm glad you think so." Her voice sounded small.

"Stating a fact, babe," he said. "Any man would think so because it's the truth."

He made her feel effervescent inside. Filled with happy bubbles that popped and fizzed like the finest champagne.

"Careful, or I'll have to tell you I love you. Because that's an amazing thing to say to a woman, in case you didn't know. And if I do say it, then things are gonna get awkward because the L-word has entered the building, and we haven't even had sex yet."

She was babbling, but he seemed to find it amusing because he snorted a laugh.

"How the hell do you make me laugh and want to eat you up at the same time?"

"I dunno. Comedy isn't normally in my wheelhouse."

"Damn, Sunshine. You're one of a kind, you know that?"

She wasn't sure if it was a good or a bad thing, but she settled on good when he dropped his mouth to a nipple and sucked it between his lips.

Emma's fingers curled into the muscles of his shoulders. "Oh my God," she breathed as her head fell back.

Blaze sucked just hard enough to make her squirm. To make a thread of need ache from her nipple to her pussy. She could feel the swelling of her labia, her clitoris, the subtle signals that indicated arousal. Or not so subtle considering how wet she already was.

Blaze blew on her nipple. It hardened into a tight point as he sucked the other one.

Emma put a hand behind her so she could thrust her breast into his face. Her other hand clutched the back of his head, holding him to her as he suckled and nibbled while she closed her eyes and let sensation cascade over her like a shower of sparks on the fourth of July.

"Need to taste more of you," he growled, reaching for the waistband of her yoga pants.

Emma yelped as he started to drag them down. He paused.

"Here? On the kitchen island?"

"Why not? There's plenty of time to make it to the bed… or the couch. Unless you prefer the bed?"

She shook her head. Prefer it? No. It was just that no man had ever stripped her naked on a granite island before. She lifted her hips and Blaze tugged her pants off and dropped them. Emma felt the tops of her ears go hot. She had an urge to cover herself with her hands, but she purposefully put both behind her on the island.

"Open your legs, Emma."

She was going to die of embarrassment. Thank God the curtains were closed, or downtown Sutton's Creek would be getting quite a show. Still, she managed to spread her legs very slowly until she was completely exposed to his gaze.

"Damn, Sunshine, you're so fucking perfect."

He curled his fingers and brushed his knuckle down her abdomen before sliding one finger into the hot seam of her pussy.

"Wet," he growled. "So fucking wet for me."

"You've kept me waiting," she whispered, heart hammering. "I've wanted you for a while now."

He slid that finger into her channel, and she moaned. "Have you?"

"Yes."

"Did you touch yourself while you thought about me, Emma?"

He added his thumb to the mix, skimming her clit until she was ready to beg him not to stop. "Yes," she blurted. "I did. I touched myself, made myself come, but I wanted your cock instead of my fingers."

He pulled his finger from her body and sucked it into

his mouth. "Mmm," he said. "You taste sweet, Emma. Like honey and cream."

She didn't think he was serious, because tasting like those things wasn't possible, but it was one of the most erotic things anyone had ever said to her.

"You said you wanted my cock. What about my tongue?"

A fresh wave of arousal flooded her system, dripped down the insides of her legs. She was so wet it should be embarrassing.

"Yes," she whispered. "I want your tongue."

"Where, baby?"

His jeans bulged where he strained against the faded fabric. She thought if she could pull her phone out and take a picture of the way he looked with his jeans low on his hips and that massive hard on, she could get off to that every night when this was over.

No. Don't think about the end yet.

She slid her hand over her mound, down to curl a finger around her clit, and then pushed two fingers inside herself before brushing her clit again. "I want your tongue here. Inside me, on my clit, making me come. And I want you to take your jeans off."

"Whatever you want, Sunshine."

He started to unzip his jeans but she grabbed his hand and tugged him closer so she could do it herself. Their eyes met and held while she slid his zipper down and pushed the jeans open. His cock lay against his belly, held in place by his boxer briefs.

She peeled those back too, then pushed them down his hips. Blaze took over, kicking them off until he stood naked before her.

Everything—and she did mean *everything*—was perfection. Yes, he had some scars, the round pucker of a bullet hole, the slash of a knife, faded hairline scars from older, more minor injuries.

But his skin was beautiful the way it moved over lean muscle. He had abs, and he had a visible inguinal ligament, or Adonis belt. That lean groove on either side of his abdomen that pointed the way down to a very hard, very erect penis.

So sexy.

She reached for his cock, but he stepped back. "Not yet," he told her. "I get to play first. Now lean back. Can you do that with your arm?"

"I can lean to one side."

"Then do that. Tell me if it gets uncomfortable."

Emma did what he told her to do. He took an ankle and lifted it until he could place her foot on the island. Opening her to him.

Excitement drummed in her veins, her sex, throbbing through her with the need to be touched. The need to find release.

He leaned over her and sucked her nipples again while he played with her pussy. And then he kissed his way down her abdomen before sliding his hot tongue into the groove of her sex.

"Oh my God," she moaned.

Blaze opened her with his thumbs. When he sucked her clit between his lips, she couldn't help but sob his name. She was so freaking close. He'd licked her pussy for fifteen seconds max, and she was going to blow.

Emma lay back on the island and closed her eyes. The granite was cool beneath her skin, but it didn't stop the fire sizzling through her.

Blaze fucked her with his fingers, sucked her clit rhythmically. One second Emma was trying to hold off her orgasm, trying to make the sensations last, and the next she was arching off the island, calling his name as her body splintered into toe-curling pieces.

He didn't stop the motion of his fingers, though he gentled the pressure on her clit as she moaned through her climax. When it was done and she was limp as a wet noodle, she stared up at the old tin ceiling of the Sutton building and gulped in air.

She hadn't done anything besides come loud and hard, but she felt like she'd run a marathon.

Had any of her ancestors shattered like they were made of spun sugar while a gorgeous man made them scream beneath this ceiling before? If they had, she didn't think it could have been nearly as good as what Blaze Connolly had done to her.

Wow.

He worked his way up her abdomen, stopping to worship her nipples, before continuing up her throat to her mouth, which he took as if he owned it.

She gave it to him, too. Because, hell, so far as she was concerned, he *did* own it.

Nobody had ever made her shatter so completely as he had just now.

And he wasn't done yet if the erection against her thigh was any indication.

Blaze kissed her hard and deep, cupping her face in his broad hands as he took what he wanted. When he was done, his mouth hovered above hers.

"I'd spend a lot more time eating your pussy if this thing between us was typical, but it's not, and I need to be inside here."

He cupped her mound in his hand and pressed the heel

of his palm against her. A thrill shot through her at how he touched her. How he just *knew* the right way to do it.

"I need that, too."

He straightened. "I gotta say, as hot as I think it'd be to fuck you on this island, I don't want that to be our first time together. Couch or bed?"

"Couch is closer."

"Damn straight."

She thought he'd help her down, but instead he scooped her up and carried her to the couch, laying her back more gently than she expected he would.

"Gotta get a condom. Be right back."

He kissed her quick and headed toward the bedroom. Emma watched his perfect ass as he walked away. She could hear Sassy pouncing on her cork in the kitchen and batting it around. The kitten was happy, and so was she.

Blaze was back in an instant, a strip of condoms in his hand. Emma laughed as she propped herself on an elbow.

"How many times do you plan to do it?"

"As many times as I can."

He tore one off the strip and ripped it open. His cock was still hard, and when he took it in hand to roll on the condom, Emma felt a knot form in her belly. It wasn't an unhappy knot, though.

It was need and desire and anticipation all rolled into one. This gorgeous, wet dream of a man was about to slide that beautiful cock inside her and fuck her until she couldn't walk straight.

She couldn't wait.

He didn't pounce on her, much as she wanted him to. Instead, he grinned as he sank to his knees and put his hands beneath her ass, lifting her to his mouth.

"One more, Sunshine," he murmured before he feasted on her again.

Emma shattered within seconds, her eyes squeezing shut as light exploded behind them. It had been so long since she'd felt this good. So damned long.

Blaze rolled up her body like a wave, settling between the legs she had to spread wide to accommodate him.

"I've been dreaming of this," he whispered as his dick slipped into her entrance.

"Me too."

His eyes held hers as he slid home. It wasn't sweet and it wasn't rough. It was something in between, and it stole her breath away.

"You good?" he asked.

"Very."

She could feel every inch of him. Every hard, thick inch.

So good, and he hadn't even started to move yet.

"Babe, need you to know you're in control here. You don't like something, you tell me. You want to be on top, tell me. Need me to stop, tell me."

Emma lifted herself until she could kiss him. "If it doesn't feel good, I'll tell you, okay? But right now, it feels fucking incredible."

"Mmm," he said, lifting himself enough to gaze down at where their bodies were joined. "Looks incredible, too."

"Take me to the stars, Blaze," she whispered.

He withdrew and drove deep, again and again, the power of his thrusts pinning her to the couch. Emma took everything he had to give, opening herself to him, rising and falling with him, her hands on his back and then, later, gripping his ass as she hurtled toward the most powerful orgasm she'd ever experienced.

It broke over her, cascading like a chain reaction through her nerve endings. She saw stars.

Literally couldn't speak beyond the animal sounds in her throat as her body imploded.

Blaze was still moving, still dragging his cock against the base of her clit as he pounded into her, drawing out her release.

And then he stiffened and she felt him pulsing deep inside her as he came, his voice a hoarse shout in her ears.

It was long moments before she could move. Before Blaze shifted his weight off her and let cool air slide between them.

Her skin was damp. Her muscles trembled. And for the first time in months, she felt whole again. In control.

Blaze disappeared, presumably to take care of the condom, but then he was back, sliding down beside her, dragging the blanket off the back of the couch and draping it over them as the air turned chill on their heated bodies.

Sassy was in the living room, chasing her cork. Emma sighed as she pressed her cheek to Blaze's chest. She could stay like this for hours.

"I need to get ready for work."

"Me too."

But neither of them moved.

"Thank you," Emma said a few moments later.

"You're welcome. What are you thanking me for?"

"Oh, I don't know. Three amazing orgasms before breakfast, maybe?"

"Then I need to thank you, too. My toes are still tingling."

Emma snorted. "So are mine. We won't even talk about my vagina."

He leisurely skimmed a finger up and down her back. "Pretty sure I want to hear it."

"There's tingling for sure. And a bit of, um, soreness. Not bad," she hurried to add. "But I won't move today without thinking about you."

He chuckled. "I know I should apologize, but I like that you'll be feeling me every time you move."

"Caveman," she teased.

He kissed the top of her head. "I like my woman to know I'll take care of her needs, whatever they may be."

His woman. She liked the sound of that, but she didn't point it out.

"Right now, I think I need to get dressed. Brenda will be opening the practice in half an hour."

He flipped the covers back and slid down her body until his shoulders were between her legs, pushing them open. "Just enough time to make you come again before breakfast."

"I don't know if I can—"

Whatever she started to say was lost when he swiped his tongue against her slick flesh.

She *could* come again. She did. More than once.

Chapter Thirty-Nine

It was a bright, sunny morning when Blaze deposited Emma at the door to her office, backing her against the wall and kissing her silly before he managed to break away and leave her with a dazed look on her face.

He was hard as he walked out into the parking lot, but by the time he reached his truck and climbed inside, he was getting himself under control. He started the vehicle then turned to look at the back of the Sutton building.

Damn, what had he gotten himself into?

Because there was no way this was a one-and-done kind of thing. He'd already fucked her twice just this morning, and he wasn't nearly satisfied yet.

The second time, he'd only intended to make *her* come before letting her up to get dressed. By the time she'd shattered, he'd been harder than steel again.

And even though she'd said she wasn't going to move today without feeling him, he'd rolled on a condom and pounded into her until they'd both shuddered and groaned.

"You okay?" he'd asked in the aftermath, feeling guilty for taking her when she was already tender.

"Yes. And don't you dare apologize for any of it," she'd whispered in his ear before nibbling his earlobe and sending a shiver of fresh excitement into his balls. "I'm happy."

He was happy, too.

When Blaze turned into the parking lot at One Shot Tactical, the sight of a familiar black Escalade made his gut tighten. Maybe it was nothing. Maybe Agents Corbin and Ackerman were back to join the range.

Or maybe Agent Corbin wanted to tangle with Ghost again. There'd been sparks between those two, whether they admitted it or not.

Ghost might, but Blaze was pretty sure Diana Corbin would *not*.

She was beautiful, but too cool. Not Blaze's kind of woman at all, though she might be Ghost's. Who knew?

He shifted into park, grabbed his range bag, and stepped onto the pavement. When he entered the building, Chance and Kane were in the break room, Ethan and Seth were on range duty, and Ghost was nowhere to be found. Neither were the FBI agents.

"What gives?" Blaze said as he set his bag down and grabbed a donut from the box on the counter. He didn't need a donut, but the eggs and toast he'd had for breakfast weren't doing it after the exertions of the morning.

"There was a break-in at Royal Shipping a couple of nights ago," Chance said as if none of them were aware. "Shots fired. The FBI's talking to everyone who visited the facility in the last, I dunno, two weeks?"

Blaze frowned. "How shocking. They say anything else?"

"Nope," Kane said, polishing off the donut he'd been eating. "It's Corbin only today. Alex is, uh, taking her on a tour."

"Guess we'll find out what she wants when they return," Blaze said, biting into his donut.

"How did Emma do alone last night?" Chance asked. "She call you for anything?"

Blaze swallowed and tried to look nonchalant. "She decided it was wise to stay with me after all, though it was mostly for the kitten. She doesn't wanna keep Sassy in her apartment in case Marsh tries to break in again."

Chance's face hardened. "Because she's afraid he'll hurt the kitten."

"She thinks he's capable of it."

"Motherfucker," Kane muttered. "I can't stand any asshole that hurts animals."

"Agreed. But that's not going to happen because we're gonna find the prick and make sure he never bothers Emma again, am I right?"

"Damn straight," Chance said.

Blaze wished it was that easy, but Simon Marsh had done a good job of evading detection so far. If he'd rented a car, they couldn't find a record. His cell phone and credit cards still hadn't been used. He knew how to keep from leaving a digital trail, and so far he didn't seem to have any online presence that Seth could find.

It was possible that once he'd planted that Barbie on Emma's bed and the police started looking for him, he'd decided to stay away from Sutton's Creek until the pressure eased.

Maybe they'd get lucky and he'd stay away, but Blaze wasn't relaxing his vigilance an inch until they found the fucker or the police did. No sane person left a bound and gagged doll in a pool of what was supposed to be blood and then left for good.

"How'd it go with Rory last night?" Blaze asked.

Chance's face went blank as he shrugged. "You were there. I got dinner, she was polite, the end."

"Yeah, but I left early." Blaze slid a glance at Kane, who was more than willing to spill the goods.

"Rory was polite, but our man here fucked all chances he might have had to get into her panties because he ignored her all night. No matter how nice she was, no matter that she spoke to him without a hint of her usual annoyance at his mere existence, he gave monosyllabic answers and pretended *she* didn't exist."

Chance looked mildly constipated as he snapped back. "Look, she was nice to me last night, but it isn't going to last. If I'd been nice to her, she'd have yanked the rug out from under me already. She was nice *because* I ignored her."

Blaze shook his head. "Dude, your call, but like I said before, if you'd just talk to her normally, she wouldn't be so prickly. You might get somewhere then."

"Who said I wanted to get anywhere?" Chance managed to look affronted.

"She's gorgeous, man," Kane said. "If you don't want to get all up in that, I sure do."

"Nobody needs to get up in that," Chance growled. "Rory Harper is off limits because I don't feel like listening to you assholes complain when either she or Theo kick you out of the Dawg and ban you for life because you pissed her off or broke her heart or whatever. Food's good, beer's good, and it's right here in town. Do you want to drive to Huntsville for a beer at a bar? Neither do I, so forget that woman exists."

Kane held up both hands. "Fine, fine. Just pointing out

she's hot and you're an idiot for not getting to know her better when she gave you the chance."

Chance rolled his eyes. "She wasn't trying to give me a chance. She was feeling guilty for punching me. Besides, she met a guy for breakfast yesterday right after she hit me, so I don't think she cares if I talk to her or not."

That bit of info effectively ended the conversation. The back door opened with a chime, and the three of them looked at each other. Voices carried down the hallway, though they couldn't hear what was said. A moment later, Ghost walked by with Diana Corbin.

Blaze went to the break room door to listen in on the conversation happening out in the hall.

"That's the facility, Agent Corbin. You've seen where we keep the ammo and weapons shipments, the training ground, the range, and these offices. I'm not sure what else I can offer. I'm also not sure how this helps your investigation, but like I said, we aim to cooperate."

"Mere curiosity, Mr. Bishop. Your company's was the most recent inquiry into Royal Shipping's services."

"I didn't think that was a crime. We need someone impeccable to handle weapon shipments."

"I never said it was. As I said before, we're following all avenues of investigation, no matter how unlikely. It's my job to be thorough."

"Of course," Ghost replied. "I understand. But we're new to the area, and this is beginning to feel a little like harassment. We're inquiring about services from several shipping companies. We just happened to pick Royal Shipping first because it's close, and their website is slick."

There was a moment's hesitation before Diana Corbin's voice, smooth and unflappable, spoke again. "As I said, we're following all avenues of investigation. I assure you no harassment is intended. Though I have to admit you've intrigued me with the use of that word."

"I don't see why. I'm trying to run a business here, ma'am, and I've cooperated as thoroughly as I can. I didn't tell you to get a warrant for my containers, did I? I showed you how we're using them. I'd have thought the FBI would applaud us for taking extra measures to secure our equipment."

"I can see you're upset, Mr. Bishop. I'll show myself out."

"Not upset, Agent Corbin. And I always walk a lady to the door."

"As you wish," Agent Corbin said. Sounded like her teeth were firmly clenched when she spoke that time. "Before I go, however… Did I mention we've viewed security footage from Royal Shipping's cameras? There were five men, all dressed in tactical gear. We were able to see where they went over the fence."

"I would expect nothing less," Ghost replied, sounding bored. "Isn't it fairly standard for warehouses like that to have cameras these days? Anybody can put in a system with equipment ordered online anymore. Doesn't mean it's the best system possible or has the highest resolution. Probably should have put one inside too, though. Might have gotten a better look at those guys. Did they steal anything?"

"It doesn't matter," she replied, ignoring the question about what was stolen. "We've had a forensic team do a thorough investigation for evidence. They found blood and fabric on the barbed wire where the men went over. It's being analyzed as we speak. I expect we'll have an ID within days."

Blaze turned to exchange a look with Chance and

Kane. Why was this woman so persistent? It was as if she knew something about them, which should be impossible. Their records were sealed. They were ordinary. Everything about their cover had been carefully thought out and executed. Their DNA wouldn't turn up in the system. The bloodwork would come back inconclusive.

That was going to piss her off.

"Wow," Ghost said, sounding shocked. "That's amazing y'all can work that fast. I'm truly impressed. But should you be telling me this? I'm a civilian these days, not a military man or even an FBI agent. Or are you here to recruit us? Former military guys do make pretty good agents, I understand. Is this a test?"

Kane smirked. Blaze suppressed a chuckle.

"Not here to recruit anyone, Mr. Bishop. Just thought you'd like to know we're not wasting any time finding out who broke into Royal Shipping two nights ago."

"Pleased to hear it, ma'am. Gives me confidence in law enforcement. Let me walk you to the door now. I'm sure you have a busy day ahead."

Soon as they heard the tinkle of the bell, Chance whistled low.

"Damn, she's like a dog with a bone. She's not giving up easily." He put his hand on his arm. "Gotta admit she worries me."

"It'll be fine. HOT and Ian Black were in charge of our information. They wouldn't let our DNA stay in the system."

Ghost stalked in, looking like someone had pissed in his cornflakes. He went over to the coffee pot and slung more coffee into his Stanley.

"That fucking woman," he muttered after he'd taken a sip.

"She seems mighty fixated on us," Blaze said.

Ghost nodded. "I can't figure out *why*. The surveillance equipment hasn't been disturbed, so they still don't know it's there. Even if they'd found it, there are no prints or identifying information. She was here the day after you two visited the facility. And she's showing up at the Dawg now. I talked to her last night, and she didn't say one fucking thing about any of this shit. Just said she'd like a tour of the facility because she was thinking about joining."

"You didn't believe her, did you?"

"Fuck no. She's fishing. That woman either has extraordinary instincts, she's psychic, or someone's leaking information at a higher level, which could explain a lot."

"I thought the FBI was being handled," Chance grumbled. "Not gonna be happy if she shows up here with handcuffs and hauls me off."

"That's not happening," Ghost said. "Your blood won't match. As for the FBI, I don't fucking know what's going on. But you can bet I'm about to find out."

He slugged some coffee from his Stanley and growled that he was heading into the SCIF to make a call.

"I'd hate to be on the other end of that phone," Kane said.

"Me too. But there's no way he's calling the White House and bitching out President Willis," Chance said. "At least I hope not. I'd rather not be jobless and homeless by nightfall."

"Nah," Blaze said. "He's definitely about to chew some ass, but it won't be hers. Somebody on her staff, probably. Bet Special Agent Corbin is packing her bags for a new posting by the end of the day."

A door banged and someone came running down the

hall. Seth slid into view, holding his phone up, screen visible. Not that they could see what was on it. "I just got an email about Simon Marsh."

Blaze's gut tightened. *Hallelujah.* "Please tell me he's been arrested."

"Not quite. He's dead—"

"Dead? How?"

"That's what I'm trying to tell you. He's dead. He's *been* dead for three years."

Chapter Forty

"I don't understand."

Emma stared at Blaze, at the intensity in his sky-blue eyes, and tried to make sense of what he'd said. When he'd called and said he needed to speak to her about something important as soon as she had a free moment, she'd told him to come at lunchtime. He'd shown up with pulled pork sandwiches from the Gas-n-Go and a serious look on his face. She'd known then that they weren't going to have a peaceful lunch.

"Simon, whoever he is, isn't really Simon. He stole Simon Marsh's identity. The real Simon Marsh died three years ago. His body was found a couple of months ago but only recently identified."

"Murdered?"

Blaze's hand on hers tightened. "Yes. The back of his skull was smashed in. His body was buried on private property in northern Kentucky. It was sold about a year ago and developers moved in to build houses. They found the remains while clearing the land."

Emma felt sick. She managed to swallow her nausea as she squeezed Blaze's hand. "Who is he?"

"We don't know yet. The police are actively looking for him now that he's been tied to a murder. The pressure on him is getting hotter, whether he knows it or not."

"He's the murderer."

"I think he probably is. The real Simon Marsh disappeared, and this guy took over his identity. Seems deliberate."

"He did it." Emma was trembling. She'd never been so certain of anything in her life. Simon—whatever his name was—had been so charming and perfect until he wasn't. He slipped in and out of personalities like other people slipped in and out of clothes.

"I'm sorry, Emma."

She shuddered. "I should have known. I should have never gotten involved with him."

Blaze put an arm around her and tugged her in close. They were sitting on the couch in his apartment. Sassy was bouncing around like all was right in the world; cars were moving along the street outside; patients were coming and going from the office; Theo was cooking in the kitchen at the Dawg; Rory was probably wiping down the bar; and everything was just so normal.

Except for her. How could everything be normal when Simon was a killer and she'd spent three months with him, never realizing the depths of his evil?

"How could you know?" His breath ruffled her hair where he'd rested his chin atop her head. "Do you blame women for being victims just because a man was charming before he raped or murdered them? Do you blame kids for being molested? Or abused?"

"Of course not." The whisper was forced out of her tight throat. He was right, but it still bothered her that she'd fallen for Simon's act without seeing through it. There'd been glimpses after they'd started dating, but she'd dismissed them all as him being stressed over work or having a bad day.

"Then don't blame yourself, Sunshine. He pursued you like a normal guy, you went out with him, liked him, and kept seeing him until he showed his true colors. You got out as soon as you could."

"How did he get away with being Simon Marsh for so long? Didn't anyone miss the real Simon?"

"The real Simon had no roots. He'd been a software engineer in his old life, but he'd left that behind. He worked in construction jobs, moving around where the jobs were. When he didn't turn up to work, people thought he'd moved on again. His boss called the police, but he never filed a missing person's report. Simon had a cousin, and while she was accustomed to him being gone and out of touch for long stretches of time, when she didn't hear from him after a year, she filed a report in Oregon where he was from. The body was IDed through the database."

"His poor cousin."

"Yeah. She'll have been told by now."

Emma thought the real Simon's cousin must want justice. Emma did too. She wanted fake Simon caught and put away forever. She wanted him gone and then she never wanted to think about him again. She rubbed her palms along her thighs, soothing herself with the movement.

"I still don't understand how he could have killed someone, stolen their identity, and made up an entire life in Chicago. He had an apartment. A BMW. He worked on websites. I saw them."

"The real Simon Marsh was a software engineer

before he worked construction. Fake Simon probably accessed his bank accounts and drained them, then set himself up in Chicago. His apartment lease was up a couple of months ago and there's no evidence he owned a car. Whoever lives in the apartment now is the one whose car is in the designated parking spot. As for the web work, did you ever actually see him coding or did he just show you the sites?"

She could feel her cheeks heating. "He showed me the sites. He even pointed out features and talked about why he'd designed it that way. Oh my God, the whole thing was a con. He wasn't working on the gym's website either. He just pretended he was. The car—he only drove it once. We took mine or taxis if we were going to dinner. He said parking was too difficult and he preferred to use the car for trips out of the city."

She felt stupid. So, so stupid. "I went to his apartment a couple of times, but it was sparsely furnished. He claimed to be a minimalist. By the time he hit me, he was staying with me most nights."

Her chest tightened as the edges of her vision started to blacken. He'd lied about *everything.* He wasn't Simon. He didn't have a car or an apartment. He didn't code websites.

And he'd *murdered* someone. The ugliest, most brutal thing imaginable. How had she not known?

"You need to breathe, Emma."

She focused on Blaze's voice in the sucking blackness. It didn't surprise her he could tell.

"I'm trying." She sucked in air and let it out rhythmically. The last thing she wanted or needed was a panic attack. Not now. She had to get back to work. Her dad was depending on her.

She needed to work so she didn't sit around in a darkened apartment and think about what Simon, who wasn't Simon, had done.

"You've got this, babe. There's no reason to panic. I'm here. I've got you. My friends have got you too. We're on your side."

She felt the cold prickle of panic start to recede as she worked to push it away. As she focused on Blaze.

It could come roaring back, but this was a victory. She hauled in a deep breath and squeezed Blaze's hand.

"I know. I just feel like such a blind idiot. Maybe I couldn't have known he was a murderer, but when he started controlling me, why didn't I get out? Why did I let it happen?"

Blaze lifted their joined hands to his lips and kissed the back of hers. "Because he didn't do it all at once, babe. He targeted you, took his time, and tried to break you. But you didn't break, Emma. He didn't succeed."

Tears pricked her eyes. She squeezed his hand. "I should get back to work. I have a patient in fifteen minutes."

She didn't want to return to the office, but she couldn't cancel on her patients. Not when she was still trying to win their trust and prove she was worthy of being their doctor.

"Okay, babe. I know you want to be busy."

She nodded. He stood and pulled her up. She went into his arms without hesitation. She loved being close to him, loved how safe he made her feel. Blaze wouldn't let anything happen to her.

"I need to put Sassy in the bathroom," she said.

"I know. I made a vet appointment for her by the way."

"Dr. Lamott?"

"Yes. Tomorrow afternoon at one. I'll come get her and take her over there."

"I'll try to go, too. You shouldn't have to pay for her vet check when you gave her to me."

He tipped her chin up. "Told you before, I take care of my girls. That's you and Sassy by the way."

Emma's insides were jumpy and twisty today, but not all of it was bad. The parts that had to do with Blaze were good. "I'm glad we're your girls. I like it."

"I like it too."

His head moved toward hers, she closed her eyes, and then he was kissing her, every bit of it perfection.

She could love him. So easily. Her heart thumped hard.

He'd said he couldn't give her anything more than this, and she'd said she didn't want more.

She'd lied. She wanted so much more. She wanted everything.

With him.

"Gotta stop," he muttered as he set her back a step. "Or we'll both be late getting back."

Her throat ached as she looked up at him and smiled.

"Hey," he said, his voice gentling as he took in her expression. His finger skimmed along her jaw, and she shivered at the soft touch. "You okay, Sunshine?"

She nodded. "I will be. It's been a lot to take in. I'm overwhelmed, quite honestly."

"I know, and I'm sorry. I'll protect you until he's caught, you have my word. I don't want you to worry about that, okay?"

"Okay."

He kissed her forehead and bent to scoop up Sassy, who'd started climbing his leg. When he kissed the top of Sassy's head, Emma thought she'd melt right there.

"Let me put this pocket tiger away and I'll walk you down. You wanna kiss her?"

"Of course."

Emma kissed the little black and white head, and Blaze carried Sassy into his room and put her in the bathroom. Once she was a few weeks older, she could stay out, but for now she needed to be confined for her own safety.

Blaze returned with a smile, her big strong warrior man who kissed kittens and made her body sing with a touch. He made her tingle, and he wasn't even touching her.

"Ready?"

"Yep."

He took her hand and led her downstairs, pressing her against the wall beside the door to the practice for a long minute as he framed her face in his hands and kissed her again, his tongue delving into her mouth and making her ache.

"I'll be back around four, and then I'm gonna take you upstairs, strip you naked, and make you scream my name at least three times before I take you to dinner. Sound good?"

Anticipation snaked down her spine and sizzled into her core. "I can't wait."

"Me neither."

Chapter Forty-One

"I HOPE IT'S A GOOD DREAM YOU'RE HAVING 'CAUSE YOU sure look like it."

Emma started, her eyes snapping to Brenda, who stood inside the door to her temporary office and smirked knowingly.

"Oh jeez, you scared me."

"Mm-hm. I spoke to you three times, Doctor."

Emma's skin was on fire. She'd been thinking about the last couple of nights with Blaze, how hot and dirty they'd been. With Simon still loose, Blaze had insisted on sticking to his protection plan, which meant walking her downstairs in the morning and waiting for her in the afternoon so he could escort her back up.

She didn't mind, considering they usually ended up naked the second they walked through the door. Sometimes they made it to the bedroom. Sometimes they only got as far as the couch.

The man was magical with his tongue and cock.

"Doctor?"

"Sorry, sorry. What can I do for you?"

Brenda smirked knowingly. "Nothing, hon. It's quitting time, and I was telling you I was going unless you needed something else."

Emma glanced at her watch. Sure enough, it was four p.m. on Friday afternoon and work was over. Her daddy had started taking Fridays off to golf or do things with her mother, and Emma and Brenda handled the clinic. They closed at three and spent an hour or so doing paperwork and other tasks before locking the doors and heading home.

"I don't think there's anything. I've got to finish these last couple of charts and then I'm done, too."

Brenda nodded. "I'll lock the door behind me then. You tell that man of yours hello for me. And if any of his friends are single, my sister would like me to say she's back on the market since she kicked the last one out two weeks ago."

Emma grinned. "I'll tell him. Though if she's interested, she needs to show up at the Dawg. They're there on the regular."

"I'll tell her. Night, Emma."

"Night. Thank you, Brenda."

Thirty minutes later, Blaze texted to say he'd arrived. Emma turned off the lights and went to meet him. He smelled like gunpowder and pine, same as always, when she stood on tiptoe to kiss him.

"How was work?" he asked as they started up the stairs. He looped an arm around her waist then let it fall to her ass, where he caressed one cheek as she climbed. Such a simple action, and it made her shiver with longing.

"It was pretty good. That patient I told you about before, the one who called me Emma Grace and insisted she wanted to see my daddy only? Well, she came back in today to tell me how well the cream worked on her rash. And she managed to call me doctor not once, but twice."

"That's great, babe."

Emma laughed. "Sorta. Because then she called me Emma Grace again and said something about the time I peeled my dress off in church and my mama had to chase me down and put it on again. I would have been horrified, but this apparently happened when I was two. How was your day?"

He chuckled. "Fine. Went to train a corporate group at their workplace today about how to respond to an active shooter situation."

"I hate to think about that. We had casualties in the ER from a workplace shooter once. It was horrifying."

His hand wrapped into her ponytail and slid through the strands. "I'm sorry, Sunshine. Hopefully, it won't happen here."

"Me too. I hate that guns are so easy to get." She thought of Simon putting a pistol to her head and shivered.

"I don't have a solution for that, but I do know how to help people be prepared if it happens to them, so that's what I'm gonna do."

She hadn't been able to practice shooting or most of her self-defense moves since she'd strained her arm, but she couldn't say he hadn't taught her things that would save her life if she needed them.

They reached his door and he let go of her hair to get his keys.

"I'm sorry I said that about guns. It's not your fault, and you don't make the laws."

He bent to give her a peck on the lips. "It's okay. I want to know what you're thinking. Always."

Her heart throbbed. She was pretty sure there were things he didn't want to know. Like the fact she was almost certain she was falling for him. This was supposed to be temporary, but her heart was having a hard time remembering it.

His brows drew down as he studied her. "What are you thinking about now?"

"Who said I was thinking of anything?"

He touched the tip of his finger to the spot between her eyes. "You get a crinkle right here. You also nibble your lip. It's distracting as hell by the way."

"Which part?"

"All of it, because I know there's something you don't want to say. But mostly the nibble because it makes me want to suck your lip and give you something to moan about. So what is it, Sunshine?"

"I'll tell you inside."

They went into the apartment, and he disappeared into the hall that led to the bedrooms. A moment later Sassy bounded out, and Emma scooped her up to kiss her.

"You're getting so big, little kitty."

Blaze strolled in, peeling off his jacket to reveal muscled arms in his One Shot Tactical polo shirt. God she loved that shirt and the way it stretched across his chest, molding to all the parts she hadn't yet gotten tired of exploring.

"All right, baby. Spill."

She wasn't going to tell him she'd been thinking about him and love, so she blurted the next thing on her list. "Mama wants me to bring you to dinner. Tomorrow night."

"Okay."

"That's it? Just okay? You'll go?"

He came over and looped his arms around her and Sassy. "Yes. Your mother wants me to come to dinner so she can grill me about my intentions, or maybe she wants to start planning that wedding you say she wants so badly. I can handle it."

Emma studied him. "I would have thought being around a woman who actively wants her daughter married and producing a grandchild would give you the hives. You said you didn't want either of those things. So are you sure about this?"

"It's not going to give me hives, Sunshine. What someone else wants from me doesn't obligate me to provide it, right?"

She nodded.

"Problem solved, then. Unless you'd rather I didn't go?"

"I might rather you didn't, but not because of you. I'm more worried about what they might say."

"Up to you, then."

She put her forehead against his chest and groaned. "She won't stop if I don't get you over there, so I think we have to. It's been a few days since the break-in, and she probably thinks she's shown a lot of restraint."

He chuckled softly. "See. Not so hard after all."

"You are really going above and beyond, Mr. Connolly. First you save my life during an armed robbery, then you save me again when I tell you about my stalker ex, protect me, let me move in, teach me self-defense, get me a kitten, and give me orgasms. On top of *allll* that, you're willing to endure dinner with my matchmaking mother. Either I give the best blow jobs ever or you're not all that bright. I'm not sure which."

He snorted. "Your blow jobs are amazing, and I'm not

stupid. I also didn't know how good you were gonna be at sucking my dick when I did most of those things, did I?"

Arousal flared in her core. Just hearing him say the word dick did things to her that could only be solved by getting naked with him.

"This is true."

He shifted against her, his growing arousal evident. "Damn, when you talk about blowjobs, I can't help getting excited. Think we've got time before we need to meet everybody at the Dawg?"

Emma set Sassy down on the floor so she could play and put her arms around Blaze's neck, arching into him and his erection. "Does it matter?"

Blaze's eyes sparked. "Not in the least."

Chapter Forty-Two

Emma was boneless. She lay on the bed, legs sprawled, an arm over her eyes, trying to catch her breath.

The bed shifted beside her as Blaze stood and went into the bathroom to get rid of the condom. She cracked an eye open to watch his very fine ass stride away from her.

Her body still tingled with the aftershocks of her orgasm as she closed her eyes and put her arm over her face. This thing between them was intense, hot, and addictive.

Sex with Blaze made her feel like she'd run a race, and also like she was more alive than she'd been in maybe ever. Which was ridiculous. She'd had plenty of amazing moments so far in her life.

Doubt gnawed at the edges of her happiness. Would they crash and burn? Fizzle out like a dying ember? Or would one of them crash while the other walked away?

That's what she feared most. Him walking away once Simon was in custody and she no longer needed protection.

A small furry creature landed on her pillow and Emma started with a squeak.

"How did you get up here?"

Sassy merely bounced around on the pillow and then flopped against Emma, putting her head against Emma's cheek.

"Aww," Emma whispered, reaching up to pet Sassy with a finger.

"She climbed up the blanket that's hanging on the floor," Blaze said as he swaggered toward her. Sassy took the opportunity to jump up and bounce happily toward the edge of the mattress as he approached, her tiny body practically vibrating with excitement.

Me too, girl. Me too.

She could look at that body all day. Anatomy textbooks had taught her what all those glorious muscles were called, how they attached to the bones and ligaments, how they moved, and yet none showed her the perfection of a honed male body the way watching Blaze walk across a room did.

"Keep looking at me like that and we're never making it to the Dawg tonight."

Emma sighed and stretched, laughing as she managed to push herself onto an elbow. "As much as I'd love to take you up on that, I'm starved. I haven't been over there in days, and Rory's been texting me that I'd better make it tonight. They've got a new band. Oh, and Rory has a date."

"A date, huh?"

"It's not Chance. She keeps insisting that he might be hot but he's a jerk, even if she feels guilty for hitting his arm. This guy is from Huntsville. An engineer of some sort she's started to see. We're crawling with engineers in northern Alabama in case you didn't know."

He scooped up the kitten and bent to kiss Emma. "Then I guess we'd better get dressed and get over there."

Emma let her gaze slide down his naked chest to his hips and the half-erect penis that jutted between his legs. She loved his dick. It was big and thick and hit her nerves in just the right way as he stroked in and out of her body.

It was, in fact, the best dick she'd had. Not that she'd had all that many, but the sampling she'd experienced was severely lacking when it came to the technique and stamina Blaze Connolly was capable of. Him and his amazing dick.

"What are you thinking?" he murmured.

Her eyes snapped up to his. There was amusement in those eyes.

"Uh, nothing much. Just thinking about Anatomy 101 and average dick size."

He snorted. Then he set the kitten on the floor and reached for his jeans where he'd shucked them beside the bed. "Nothing average about this dick, Sunshine."

"No, definitely not."

"Nothing average about you either."

She warmed inside. "That's sweet, but I know I'm not stacked in all the right places. Not like Rory."

He stopped when his jeans were on his hips, but the fly was still open. She'd watched in fascination as he'd dragged them on without underwear.

"You're stacked right for me, babe. I happen to be fascinated with your perfect tits and pretty ass. And your pussy?" He put a hand over his heart. "Being inside you is perfection. Eating you is perfection. It's my favorite place in the world right now."

Nervous laughter bubbled into her throat, but she didn't let it out. He was serious. *Serious.*

She sat up and hugged her arms around her knees.

"Thank you. Nobody has ever said anything like that to me before."

"Not my fault the men before me were dumbasses." He pointed a finger at her as if he knew what her next thought would be. "And it's not yours either."

"Seriously? I'm the one who chose them. I'm a little at fault."

"Okay, so you had marginally bad taste in men. And then you met me."

He finished that sentence with a cocky smile, and Emma couldn't help but laugh. "Then I met you, and you saved my life. But I didn't want to go out with you if you remember."

"I remember. But then you got smart, so I guess it turned out okay."

It had definitely turned out okay. She'd had the best sex of her life, and she was ravenous for more. She didn't remember ever feeling that way. She'd even wondered at one time if she had a low sex drive, but talking with other med students at the time had made her realize that she was simply tired. Stressed and tired like so many of them were.

And the pressure hadn't eased in the ER, either.

Blaze dragged on a T-shirt and then a button-down shirt that he left open and untucked. God, he made her heart throb when he looked like that. She climbed from the bed, reluctantly, and padded naked into the bathroom. Blaze's hand on her ass made her shiver with delight as he gave her a caress when she passed by.

She studied herself in the mirror. Her hair was a wild tangle on her head. She had beard burn on her neck, her lips were red and puffy from kissing, and her nipples were hard little points that still ached. She brushed her teeth, splashed some water on her face, twisted her hair into a knot—after taming it enough to do so—and then slipped into new panties and a bra.

She opted for a soft cashmere sweater in cranberry red, a pair of black jeans, and heeled booties. After she put Sassy in the bathroom with fresh food and water, she joined Blaze in the living room.

He looked her up and down with appreciation. "Damn. I'm about to stroll into the Dawg with the hottest babe around."

She blushed again. "I don't know why I let you make me blush, but I can't seem to help it."

He grinned as he took her hand and led her to the door. "You blush because you like it."

She stood on tiptoe to kiss his cheek. It was roughened with stubble, and it made her belly clench. He'd scraped those cheeks across her thighs earlier, and she'd loved every delicious moment of it.

Loved it because he knew exactly how much pressure and where. The combination of rough and soft had driven her over the edge much quicker than she'd wanted.

They went out the door, he locked it and checked that it held, then they walked to the Dawg. He put her between him and the buildings, and he kept both hands free in case he needed them. He was alert to everything, scanning the street, the park, the cars, until they reached the Dawg's ancient wood and glass doors and passed inside.

It was crowded tonight, but that was to be expected because it was Friday. Theo's prime rib special was on, and people packed the tables. Rory was behind the bar with Amber, who often helped fill drink orders when the place was hopping. There were at least five servers on duty carrying plates to and from the kitchen.

Emma loved to see the hustle. It meant Rory and Theo

were doing well. When their grandfather got sick, the manager at the time hadn't done the best job keeping the place running at a profit. Their grandmother had been too distracted by her husband's health to dig into the operations, and they'd bled money for years. Owning the building was probably the only thing that had saved them, which neither Rory nor Theo had realized until their grandmother passed and left it to them along with the farmhouse.

Blaze ushered Emma over to the usual table that his One Shot guys occupied with a hand against the small of her back. They were all there. Alex—tall, dark, and very mysterious, with a vibe that said don't ask questions because you won't like the answers. Flirty Kane, serious Seth, grumpy Chance—tonight anyway—and easygoing Ethan.

She liked them all. Trusted them all. She still wasn't sure about their late night at the range and Chance's injuries, but their explanation was reasonable. Until somebody gave her a reason to think otherwise, she wasn't going to question it.

The guys turned toward them as Chance called out for them to take a seat.

"Y'all order yet?" Blaze asked as he pulled a chair out for her.

She was beside Alex again and across from Blaze. It kind of annoyed her that Alex wouldn't move over, but he showed no inclination.

"Nope, it's been busy, and the waitress hasn't been by yet," Kane said. "What took you so long?"

His gaze bounced between her and Blaze, and Emma's skin grew hot.

Blaze was unflappable. "I gave Emma that kitten I found, remember? She had to be taken care of first."

"Oh yeah. How's she doing?" Kane asked, turning to her.

Emma couldn't help but smile. "She's a bouncy little thing and so sweet. She makes me laugh. We took her for shots and deworming a few days ago. She's about nine weeks old."

She could see Alex out of the corner of her eye as he turned to Blaze.

Blaze shrugged.

She didn't know what any of that was about, but it seemed like disapproval. Or maybe she was overthinking it.

Nikki came over to take their orders and then left again. The guys talked about work for a while, including her as much as possible. They told her about a woman who'd been learning to shoot and yelped every time she pulled the trigger and about a man in one of the self-defense classes who ripped his pants on a karate kick nobody had asked him to do, and they laughed about stories they had from their military days.

They were a family. And she realized, after a while, they seemed to be the only family any of them had. They didn't talk about parents or siblings or cousins. They didn't talk about ex-wives, children, or girlfriends either. It was the six of them, and nobody else.

Maybe that's what made Alex wary of her. She wasn't one of them. She was an outsider in their group. But how silly was that, because it was clear they weren't monks. Kane was busy making eyes at Nikki every time she walked by, and she kept cutting her gaze at him and smiling.

Looked like a hookup waiting to happen. Alex didn't seem phased by that at all.

Rory sashayed over with a tray of drinks. "Evening, gentleman. Emma Grace. Y'all come in for the prime rib?"

She started handing out beers and waters as everyone confirmed they had. She set Emma's wine glass down and gave her the big eyes for a second.

"Haven't seen you in days, Idgy. But you look relaxed. Bit of a glow, too," she added.

"I have a new kitten. She makes me happy."

"Mm-hm. Guess that kitten keeps you busy." Rory leaned in close and whispered in Emma's ear. "I think somebody's been petting your kitty, babe. And petting it just right, too."

Emma's skin was never going to recover from all the blushing. She laughed. "Damn you, Ror," she whispered back. "You're incorrigible."

"But right."

"You could get your kitty stroked too, you know. He's right there, pretending not to notice you."

"Sorry, didn't hear you." Rory straightened, eyes bright. "Y'all got everything you need?"

They affirmed they did.

"Your food will be out shortly. Enjoy!"

She spun on her heel and marched away. Chance followed her with his eyes all the way to the bar. Emma met Blaze's look across the table. She hadn't even taken a sip of wine, but she felt like she'd downed the whole glass as she stared at him.

She was drunk on him, craving more. Addicted.

She wanted that feeling for Rory, too. Maybe Chance wasn't the one, but she wanted it for her friend anyway.

Her phone buzzed with a text. She dragged her gaze from Blaze and picked it up.

Rory: OMG, he fucked you! Finally!

Emma: Guess he's not gay after all.

She added a laughing emoji.

Rory: I'm jelly. Like really, really jelly.

Emma: It's just sex, Ror.

She wanted it to be more, but it wasn't.

Rory: Suuuureee. Have you seen the way he looks at you? Because I have. Looking at him right now and I can assure you he's got it bad.

Emma glanced up. Blaze was watching her. He dropped his gaze to her phone and back up.

A question. She melted a little more as she turned her head and indicated Rory. He nodded and turned back to his conversation with Kane.

If he'd been like Simon, that silent inquiry would have made her feel differently. Sick inside. Instead, she knew he was concerned. Making sure it wasn't something bad, like Simon sending another anonymous text. Once he knew it was Rory, he went back to what he was doing. Not hovering. Not controlling.

Protecting.

Rory: Earth to Idgy. See what I mean? Dude is obsessed. So are you.

Emma: I like him. A lot.

Rory: Damn it, gotta fill an order. Come over here and tell me everything when you get a chance. I want allll the dirty details!

Emma: I'm not telling you details! Don't you have a date tonight?

Rory: No, sigh. He got called in. Some sort of rocket engine test at the Arsenal tonight.

Emma: Is he Vitamin D material yet?

Rory: I'm taking it slow this time. No rushing into things. Okay, really gotta go!

Emma tucked her phone into her purse. She looked over at Chance, who was staring into his beer like a country music character who'd gotten his heart broken and lost his dog all in the same day. Seth said something to him, and he looked up, pasted on a smile, and answered with a cocky tilt of his head like always.

Maybe she was wrong and he wasn't interested in Rory at all. Maybe his arm just hurt and he was moody about it. He might have been watching Rory walk away because he was still mad at her.

It could be any of those things, or none of them. And really, she couldn't fix her friend's dating problems no matter how much she might want to.

The food arrived and they tucked into it. Emma had considered ordering a salad, but she was glad she got prime rib. Theo had made twice-baked potatoes, plus there was a grilled shrimp add-on for those who'd wanted it. The vegetable was grilled broccoli with bacon. Maybe not all that healthy with the bacon, but out of this world delicious.

Theo came by to check that everything was to their satisfaction once the orders had slowed down enough he could escape. He put a hand on her shoulder. Her first instinct was to shrink away because Blaze was watching.

His expression didn't change, though. He didn't bow up, his nostrils didn't flare, and he didn't glare at her. Emma covered Theo's hand with hers and squeezed.

"Thanks, Theo. It was amazing."

Theo bent to kiss her on top of the head, a move as natural as breathing for him. She squirmed as six sets of eyes looked on.

"Glad you enjoyed it. Y'all let Nikki know if you need anything else."

Theo moved on to the next table, Alex got up and stalked toward the pool tables at the back where Emma thought she'd spied the sleek blonde from the other night, and Blaze moved over beside her. He dragged his chair around next to hers and slipped an arm around her. Emma leaned into him, her head on his shoulder.

"I could tell you were worried what I'd think," he murmured in her ear.

"I was."

"I'm not jealous of your friendship, Sunshine."

She almost wished he was, just so she'd know where she stood, but she told herself that was ridiculous. She'd been down that path with Simon, and she never wanted to go there again.

"Thank you."

"But I gotta tell you, if he'd kissed you the way I kiss you, I might have reacted differently."

"I had a crush on Theo when I was a teenager. Nothing ever came of it. If he kissed me now, I think I'd be grossed out. And so would he. We're like family, we've known each other so long."

"Understood."

His fingers moved up and down her arm. Softly. Surely.

"I don't think Alex likes me."

Blaze's fingers hesitated before they kept moving. Soothing her.

"He likes you just fine. It's me he's worried about."

"You?" She slipped away to look up at him. He shrugged.

"The six of us planned this business and gave up a lot to make it happen. I think maybe he's afraid I'll lose my focus."

"Will you?"

"Will you fuck up patient care because of me?"

"Of course not."

"Same. I'm committed to the job, and I'm not going to fuck it up."

He looked troubled for a second. She put a hand on his cheek, uncaring who was watching. She liked that she was allowed to do so.

"Hey, it's not brain surgery. Just don't walk downrange when you've got a live shooter in a bay, okay?"

"It's not my plan."

She smiled. "Then you won't get shot, will you? Everything else is a piece of cake compared to that."

"Yeah, true."

A moment later, he reached into his pocket for his phone. Seth was already on his feet. Kane popped up beside him, looking fierce.

"It's an alert for the Sutton building," Blaze told her as his chair scraped back.

Emma shot up too, reaching for her phone to see the alert.

"You have to stay here, Sunshine. Yo, Chance."

Chance turned from where he'd been talking to one of the women at the next table. "Yeah?"

"Stay with Emma. We need to check the doors on her building."

"I want to go with you," she said.

He shook his head. "No, Emma. Let me handle this."

She sucked in a breath, not sure whether to cry or scream. Her heart hammered.

What if Simon had come back? What if he had his gun and he was waiting for one of them to walk into the building?

"It's okay, honey. I know what I'm doing."

She swallowed. He did. She knew that. "Okay."

"Good girl." He kissed her swiftly, then turned and stalked from the building with Kane and Seth on his heels.

Chance took her elbow in a gentle hand. "Hey, Emma. Let's sit down. Let them secure the building and they'll be back in no time."

Emma's throat tightened. She feared for Blaze, which was somewhat ridiculous considering what she knew he could do, but Simon had murdered a man.

Not only murdered, but done so in a way that he'd gotten away with it for three years.

Panic danced on the edges of her vision, but she held it off by forcing herself to think logically. If Simon was planning to kill again, he wouldn't do it by breaking into the building and waiting for her or Blaze to show up.

A sudden chill danced across her skin, skated up the back of her neck.

She whirled, peering into dark corners, looking for the source of the bad feeling. Blaze said to trust that feeling, and she did.

But Simon wasn't there. *He wasn't.*

She was imagining things because she was happy and she didn't want it taken away from her. She squeezed her hands tight under the table and waited for the feeling to pass.

It never did.

Chapter Forty-Three

THE BACK DOOR HAD BEEN JIMMIED OPEN AND PULLED SHUT again. Blaze was really going to have to talk Emma's dad into updating the building's locks too.

He exchanged a look with his guys as the three of them drew weapons. A second later, they were ghosting into the building, clearing the darkened corners of the downstairs before they crept up to the second floor.

The light in the hall was on like he'd left it. Both apartment doors were secure. They stood for a moment, thinking, and then the floor creaked above their heads. Another silent look and they split, heading for the front and back stairs.

Blaze and Seth took the rear while Kane took the front. The light was on in the hallway on the third floor. There were two apartments, same as downstairs, but they were still being worked on before they could be rented out.

Both doors were closed. Blaze gave Kane a signal. On the count of three, they burst into the two apartments simultaneously while Seth took the hall watch just in case.

Blaze didn't get all the way through the rear apartment before he heard a scream coming from the other.

He quickly wrapped up his search and sprinted for the front apartment. Seth was already there. Kane stood, feet spread, gun held low in front of a small woman with red hair who was sitting against the wall, knees huddled to her chest, a blanket lying haphazardly on the floor nearby and a small battery-powered lantern giving off a dim glow.

"Who are you?" Kane demanded.

"Please don't shoot. Please." The woman's hands were palms out beside her head, her eyes wide as she stared up at Kane.

"He's not going to shoot," Blaze said.

The woman's gaze slewed to him as if realizing for the first time there were other men in the room. "I-I'll go. Please. Just let me go."

"Kane."

His voice was firm. Kane glanced at him and holstered his weapon. They all did.

"We're not going to hurt you," Blaze said. "But you *are* trespassing. Care to explain?"

The woman's eyes were still big. They darted between the three of them as if she didn't trust that one of them wouldn't shoot her anyway.

"I'm sorry. I, um, I needed a place to stay. I knew these apartments were empty. I thought I could shelter here. I wasn't going to steal anything. I'm looking for work. I-I had nowhere to go."

"What's your name?" Kane asked, softer this time.

"D-Daphne Bryant."

"Can't let you crash here, Daphne," Blaze said. "The heat's not on, and it's still a construction zone."

Her lip quivered before she sucked in a breath and made it stop. "Okay. I understand."

Her shoulders sagged as she reached for a backpack sitting nearby. She dragged it toward her, stuffing a book that had been lying beside her into it. Then she reeled in the blanket and started to fold it. Tears slid down her cheeks as she worked, and Blaze felt like he was watching himself as a kid. Back when his mother would tell him they had to get out of wherever they were staying and he needed to hurry.

He never had much stuff, and he'd worked hard to cram everything he could into his backpack and the worn athletic bag that had been held together with duct tape. Clothes, books, school supplies, any treasures he'd collected like a pretty rock or something shiny he'd found in an alley. Once, he'd found a GI Joe doll and kept it because GI Joe looked tough in his military uniform with his dark hair and beard.

He'd lost that when one of his mom's boyfriends called him a sissy and said only girls played with dolls. Explaining that he didn't play with it, he only kept it because he was going to be a soldier one day, had earned him a slap across the face.

"What's your story, Daphne?" he asked.

She swiped beneath her eyes and stashed the blanket into the backpack before reaching for the over-turned lantern. "I was cleaning rooms over at the Wheeler Inn, but they let me go three days ago when one of the older maids wanted her job back. I knew these apartments were empty. I didn't think anyone would notice if I was really quiet. It's just for a few days. Just until I find another job."

"Your landlord didn't give you a grace period?" Kane asked, his voice gravelly with anger.

Her chin dipped to her chest. "I've been staying in my car."

"Why didn't you stay there tonight?"

"Because somebody broke a window, and it's too cold when the sun goes down. I tried."

"Have you eaten?"

Her chin came up, but it quivered. "I had some potato chips and beef jerky. I'm fine."

"Jesus," Kane said, shoving a hand over his head.

Daphne flinched, shrinking into herself.

Kane lifted his hand, palm out. "I'm not mad at you, Daphne. I'm mad for you, okay? Get your stuff and we'll take you to the Dawg. You can have dinner, and we'll find somewhere for you to stay until you can get work, okay?"

She blinked as she straightened again. Her gaze darted between them. "You would do that?"

"Yes." Kane gave them a look, and Blaze felt that look down to his soul. "We rescue people. It's what we're good at."

"Thank you. I'll pay you back, I promise."

"It's okay," Kane replied. "It's just dinner and a pillow. Nothing fancy."

Apparently nobody had ever told Kane that prime rib was fancy to some folks. It sure was to him since he'd never had any beef but hamburger before he'd joined the military and had a little bit of money of his own.

"You see anyone else around here? A man, about six-feet, blond?" Blaze asked.

"Um, I watched the place today. I saw a lot of people. There's a doctor's office on the first floor."

"But nobody fitting that description tonight?"

"No. Just you and the woman who left together earlier. Nobody else."

That was a relief at least. "Okay, thanks."

Daphne shouldered her backpack and clutched the lantern to her chest. She looked wary of them, as if she was afraid they were lying about the hot meal and the place to stay. It made him wonder what kind of life she'd had, how badly she'd been treated. He didn't blame her for being suspicious. A woman couldn't be too careful, and they were three big guys who'd burst in with guns.

"We're not going to hurt you." Kane had sensed her unease too. "I'm Kane, by the way. This here is Blaze and that's Seth. We work together at the range. One Shot Tactical. Maybe you've heard of it?"

"I s-saw it on my way into town."

"That's us. Sorry if we came on strong, but our friend is being threatened by a guy who broke in here before. We thought you were him."

She seemed to relax a fraction. "That's why you asked if I'd seen anyone."

"Right," Blaze said. "He's another good reason we can't let you stay."

She clutched the lantern tighter but didn't say anything.

"You ready?" Kane asked gently.

Daphne nodded. Kane offered his arm. She hesitated but then looped her arm into his. Kane escorted her from the apartment like she was a queen instead of a vagrant.

"Think she's in some kind of trouble?" Blaze said as he and Seth followed behind.

"Yep. And Ghost is going to flip his lid when we insist on helping this one, too."

"He won't stop us. It's not in his DNA to turn away anyone in trouble. Even if he might wish it were."

Seth looked thoughtful. "Except maybe Special Agent

Corbin. She seems to get under his skin pretty bad. They were frowning at each other when we got the alert. I don't even think he noticed us leaving."

"If we're lucky, she's been reassigned and only showed up tonight to get one last dig in before she leaves town."

"Hope you're right."

Blaze hoped so too. Because Diana Corbin struck him as the type of person who wouldn't quit until she'd nailed them to the wall.

Chapter Forty-Four

EMMA DIDN'T RELAX UNTIL THE MEN RETURNED. WHEN Blaze walked back into the Dawg, looking the same as when he'd left, relief made her sag into her chair.

He was fine. Simon hadn't been there. She knew he hadn't by the way Blaze swaggered over to the table. If Simon had broken in, Blaze would look a whole lot angrier. And satisfied, maybe, because they would have caught him.

There was a woman with Kane. Slightly built, red hair twisted into a knot at the base of her neck. She carried a backpack slung over one shoulder and… was that a lantern?

Kane pulled out a chair for her. She took a seat, looking apprehensive.

"Hi," Emma said, holding her hand across the table. "I'm Emma Sutton."

"Daphne Bryant."

Kane plunked beside Daphne, looking for all the world like a bear with a tooth ache. A big, grumpy, protective bear. "Order anything you like," he said as he dragged a menu across the table and put it in front of her.

Blaze sat down and put his mouth close to Emma's ear.

"She lost her job at the motel and has nowhere to stay. She broke in and set up a place to sleep in the front apartment on the third floor."

"Oh," Emma breathed. "Poor girl."

"You think she's from around here?"

"She didn't grow up in town if that's what you mean. Could have moved here at any point in the last ten years and I wouldn't know her. Rory would, though. I can ask her."

"Thanks, Sunshine."

"Where will she stay tonight? She could have my place if there's nowhere else."

"Not a good idea while Simon's out there. We'll make sure she has shelter."

Nikki came over to take Daphne's order, and Emma excused herself to go talk to Rory.

"Nope, never saw her before." Rory peered across the room. "You said she was cleaning rooms at the motel?"

"Yep."

"Not everyone comes to the Dawg. I'd have remembered if she had with that hair." Rory arched an eyebrow. "Looks like Kane's decided to be her personal protector. Or he wants in her pants."

Emma shot a look at the table. Kane was still hovering like a mother hen. He'd stopped flirting with Nikki for the time being, which had her pouting as she threw him looks whenever she walked by with an order.

"He's flirty, that one," Emma said. "Took me on a tour of the range and had me giggling like I was twelve."

Rory looked amused. "How did Blaze take that?"

"I didn't tell him. But it was before we'd started, uh, doing anything. So I doubt he'd care."

"Oh, I bet he would." Rory jumped then pulled her phone from her pocket. The screen lit up and she smiled.

"The engineer?"

"Yes."

"You planning to tell me his name?"

Rory grinned as she thumbed a reply. "Casey Kyle. He's very sweet, always checking up on me. I wish you could have met him tonight."

"Me too. How's the test going?"

"Boring. He wishes he were here."

"Seems like you really like him."

"Like I said, I'm taking it slow. He's nice. Good-looking, but not rugged the way those One Shot guys are. He's more of an indoor cat, I think."

Emma laughed. "You're saying Blaze and his friends are outdoor cats?"

"Scrappy toms who mark their territory and fight tooth and nail. Casey has glasses. And his hands are soft. I don't think he's ever thrown a punch in his life."

"But does he make *you* spark inside?"

Rory shrugged. "I don't know. I haven't let him kiss me yet."

"But you're attracted to him, right?"

"Duh! He's very attractive. Not too tall, a little bit stocky, but fit. Brown hair with some red in it, a beard, tanned, perfect teeth. I want to kiss him, but I don't want to ruin anything. That's why we're going slow. He's fine with it by the way. He's been burned in love, too. His ex-girlfriend cheated on him with a guy she'd just met. Moved in with the guy and everything."

Emma didn't like the way that sounded. "He's not on the rebound, is he?"

Rory swiped the bar with a towel. "It happened over a

year ago. He's just dipping his toe in the dating pool again."

"Well, be careful. He might have baggage."

Rory's eyes flashed. "Of course he does, Idgy! But so do I. That's why we're perfect for each other. Neither of us want to get hurt again."

Emma didn't want her friend to see her doubt, so she smiled instead. "Okay, Ror, but don't give up passion and heat for safe and boring."

Rory frowned. "There's nothing wrong with safe."

"No, there's not." Emma put her hand over Rory's on the bar, stopping the motion of the towel. "But safe can also be exciting. It shouldn't be boring."

"Speaking of excitement..." Rory waggled her eyebrows. "How is Mr. Tall, Dark, Sexy, & Broody in the sack?"

The subject change was lightning fast, but Emma understood. She wasn't going to keep pushing.

"Not giving you details, Ror. I told you that."

"Fine, no details. But is he at least, you know, a *decent* lay? Knows his way around the lady bits? Not afraid to kiss the kitty?"

Emma cursed the pale skin that made every blush noticeable.

Rory cackled.

"You did that on purpose," Emma said.

"Yep. Now answer the questions. Vaguely is fine."

"Okay, yes," Emma said, pitching her voice low so the people nearby couldn't hear. "He knows his way around, not afraid of the kissing. And he's in no hurry for any of it. He's very thorough."

"Yep, I'm jealous. But who knows? Maybe Casey will prove himself quite adept when the time comes."

"Or you could saddle up Chance Hughes and go for a ride. Just dropping it out there."

Rory sighed. "Emma Grace, I love you, but you gotta let that idea go. I'm not letting a guy who pisses me off so thoroughly, who's such a jerk, get anywhere near my bits. It might be worth the annoyance in the short term if he's as hot in bed as he looks, but never in the long-term."

Her gaze drifted over to where Chance was standing with his arm against the wall, leaning toward a woman whose back was to it. She laughed as he said something, and he trailed a finger over her jaw and into her hair where he twisted a long blond lock.

"Ugh, see? Total player. I'm sure he says all the right things, but he doesn't really feel any of them."

Emma lifted both hands and shook her head. "You win. I won't mention it again. I can't wait to meet Casey. Whenever you're ready to share him, I mean."

Rory smiled and leaned over the bar to loop an arm around Emma's neck. "Thank you, babe. Love you."

"Love you, too."

"Now get back to your man and stop interrupting me while I'm working."

"You only say that because I won't share details."

Rory grinned and shooed her away. Emma made her way back to Blaze. He stood at her approach and folded her into the circle of his arms, pressing a kiss to her forehead.

She wanted it to be this way always. Wanted to walk into his embrace in public, kiss him, and know he was hers. But she'd have to take what she could get, which was this moment right now.

She had to be happy with that.

Emma looped her arms around his waist, uncaring

who saw them. She didn't feel that itch on her skin, and she wasn't worried about Simon. Even if he was there, Blaze would protect her. She believed it with her whole heart.

The warm-up band started to play a slow song, and Blaze led her to the dance floor. Then he pulled her in close, breast to hip to thigh, and swayed to the music without ever taking his eyes off hers.

She could feel the eyes of envious women following them. Wondering what Blaze must see in her. Wondering how long it would last. She wondered how long it would last, too. How she'd manage to come to the Dawg when it was over and see him with someone else.

"You're thinking awfully hard, Sunshine. Everything all right?"

She pasted on a smile. "Everything is perfect."

"Liar. I can tell when the smile isn't real, you know."

No, she didn't know. And she didn't know what she thought about it. Was she bad at hiding her feelings, or was Blaze very good at reading people?

"I was thinking there are a whole bunch of women in this place who wonder what the heck you're doing with me."

He arched an eyebrow. "Seriously?"

She nodded.

"If they wonder that, then they're either blind or just plain dumb. You're perfect, Emma. Remember that."

This time her smile wasn't fake. "Hardly perfect."

"Mmm, true. You hogged the covers last night. That's a serious flaw."

"I could go back to the guest room if it helps."

He frowned, clouds chasing across his eyes. "You may want to if I have another nightmare."

Her heart ached for him as she put a hand on his cheek. "If you have another nightmare, I'll be right there with you. You don't have to go through it alone, and I won't push you to talk about it."

He curled his hand into hers, pressed his lips to her palm, and bent to kiss her right there on the dance floor. "Thanks, Sunshine."

Chapter Forty-Five

"Are you sure you want to do this?" Emma asked.

"Yes," Blaze lied. "It's fine, babe. Let's go inside."

In truth, he was oddly nervous. The grandeur of the Sutton home, perched on a green lawn with mature trees and a wrought iron fence on a large corner lot in the historic district, made him feel out of place. Like he didn't belong in their world and never would.

He wasn't used to being nervous. Hadn't expected it to happen today, but the gravity of the situation hit him approximately three minutes ago when they'd pulled into the driveway and he'd gotten a look at the house's facade in the daylight.

Fancy people lived here. Not kids with drug-addicted mothers and no roots.

Emma climbed the back steps and turned, her hand on the screen door. She was not in the least bit calm either, which reminded him that his nerves weren't important. It was how she felt that mattered.

Her grip on the handle tightened. "She's going to subtly grill you about your life and relationships," she whispered to him. "It's nothing to do with your suitability to be her son-in-law and everything to do with finding out if you're even interested in the position. She's going to ask about kids, too. I'll do what I can to derail her."

Blaze chuckled. "You said all that before."

"I know. I'm just, I dunno, *terrified* she'll make you think twice about being with me. I mean I know this isn't a relationship and we aren't getting married or anything, but I like what's been happening with us, and I want to keep it for a while."

He wanted to keep it, too. He didn't know if she was saying those things about relationships and marriage because he'd told her he couldn't give her anything more than a few nights in bed or if she meant them.

He didn't like the way it made him feel to think she'd dismissed the idea of a future with him. He wasn't looking for a future, and yet...

"She's not going to rattle my cage that badly, Emma. I've seen a thing or two in the military. Your mama, no matter how diabolical, doesn't compare."

"I think you underestimate her. You remember the signal?"

She'd given him a signal so he could let her know when he wanted to leave. He wasn't using it, though. "I tug my ear three times."

"Exactly. Do that and I'll save us both. Somehow."

The door opened behind Emma, revealing her mother in a flowery print dress, low heels, and a red head band that held back her blond hair and made her look like a mother from a movie set in the 1950s.

"Emma Grace, are you going to stand on the stoop and talk all night or do you plan to bring Mr. Connolly inside for dinner?"

"Of course, Mama. We were just discussing something that happened at the Dawg last night."

She was a bad liar. It almost made him laugh. Especially when her mother shot him a wink that said she knew better. He refrained, though.

Emma stepped inside and Blaze followed. He'd seen the kitchen the other night, but now he had time to pay attention to it. It was massive, with white cabinets, marble counters, a large island in the center, and the biggest stove he'd ever seen outside a restaurant kitchen.

Better than that, however, it smelled divine. Pots bubbled on the stove and the smell of fried chicken hung in the air. His stomach took the opportunity to rumble.

"What happened at the Dawg?" her mother asked, the picture of innocence.

"Oh, um, there was a great band. And Blaze's friend, Kane, found a woman who'd lost her job and had been sleeping in her car. He bought her dinner and found her a place to stay for a few nights."

More like he'd paid for a room at a local B&B and started lobbying to hire her as their receptionist. Ghost wasn't against it, but first they had to make sure she knew how to use a computer and answer phones. Not that answering phones was difficult, but if she wasn't good on the phone, then what was the point?

Ellen Sutton radiated genuine concern. "Oh no, poor thing. Is she okay? She's not a local, is she?"

"No. She was working at the Wheeler Inn and lost her job. I guess someone wanted their job back, and Celia let her go because she had less seniority."

"That wasn't nice of her. But Celia Lincoln has never been particularly nice, I'm sorry to say. I'm glad Mr. Connolly's friend was there to help." She turned to him, her smile welcoming and warm. "Mr. Connolly, we're so happy you've joined us tonight."

"Please, ma'am, call me Blaze."

"And you must call me Ellen. John will be down in a few minutes. I hope you don't mind, but we're having fried chicken. It's not fancy, but I thought a homey meal would be better than a fancy one."

"It smells terrific, ma'am. Ellen."

"Why, thank you." Ellen beamed. "Emma Grace, I thought we'd sit at the eat-in instead of the formal dining room tonight. Can you and Blaze set the table for me?"

"Sure," Emma said, going over to one of the cabinets to pull out plates. She handed the stack to him and went to collect silverware from a drawer.

"I starched napkins this afternoon, so we'll use those," her mother said as Emma led the way to the round table tucked into one end of the kitchen.

Emma's eyes met his. She looked less worried than she had before, but he knew she was still apprehensive about what her mother would say tonight. He wanted to tell her she didn't have to worry about that, but he knew she wouldn't listen.

It was clear to him that her mother had her number. Ellen probably knew exactly what Emma expected. She'd either play into it or she wouldn't. He was almost looking forward to the performance if she did.

John Sutton entered the kitchen when they were setting the table. He greeted Blaze with a warm handshake and a smile, hugged Emma and kissed her on the head, then went over to give his wife a kiss on the cheek.

It was wholesome and happy, and Blaze was envious of how much the Suttons cared for each other. How they didn't even question that this was how a family behaved.

He'd known his life wasn't normal when he was a kid. He'd gotten used to it because it was all he'd known.

His mom cared more about her next fix than him. He'd never understood why she'd dragged him from place to place instead of leaving him behind, but it'd finally dawned on him years later that she'd done it so she wouldn't have to go alone.

He was her companion between fixes. The person she forgot about until she needed him again.

He'd survived her bullshit and the crapshoot that had been his childhood, but it'd made him an emotional loner. He didn't let people in. Too risky.

His team were the best friends he'd ever had. They were his family. They were all fucked up in their own ways. Nobody wanted too much from anyone else, but they'd be there for each other through hell and back if they had to be.

That'd always been enough.

But what would it be like to really let someone in? To be vulnerable because you loved them and needed them in your life?

Would it be like the picture the Suttons made, or was that an illusion?

A shiver tripped down his spine at the idea of being vulnerable. And yet he wanted what the Suttons had more than he'd ever wanted anything.

To belong. To know he had a wife and kids who loved him as much as he loved them. To keep them safe and give them everything without holding back a part of himself.

Jesus.

He watched Emma as she placed starched white napkins on top of the plates and straightened the silverware beside them. She glanced up at him and smiled, and he felt that smile all the way to his soul.

It terrified him and somehow filled the empty spaces inside him simultaneously.

"Blaze, could you carry this chicken to the table?" Ellen called out, and he felt like he was in a dream as he turned and went to collect the platter from her.

She smiled and thanked him. His heart raced, and little beads of sweat broke out on his forehead.

Seriously? After everything he'd done, all the dangerous situations he'd found himself in over the years as a special operator, it was the idea of domesticity and being in love that made him sweat?

"Here, can you grab the biscuits too?" she added before he walked away.

He picked up the basket and carried everything to the table. Soon all the food was there, the glasses were poured with water, wine and beer had been offered and poured, and they sat down to eat.

They made small talk for a while about the weather (windy), the temperature (warming but a frost was imminent so don't plant flowers yet), and how Blaze and his friends were liking Alabama (just fine, thanks).

Blaze was appropriately complimentary about the food, which was as good as any restaurant, and Ellen blushed a little while thanking him for it. Now he knew where Emma got those soft blushes.

John asked if he played golf. Blaze admitted that he really didn't, though he'd played a few times in the military. What he didn't tell Doc Sutton was that the games he'd played were meant to be done while drinking with his buddies so that everyone was drunk at the end.

Silly team bonding stuff that didn't make sense to

anyone else and certainly didn't result in learning any golf skills.

He was on his second helping of fried chicken when Ellen winked at him and asked, "So tell me, Blaze, what are your thoughts about children? Do you want a big family?"

Emma, who'd been sipping her water, sputtered. Blaze reached over and patted her back as if she were choking, which she wasn't, and met Ellen's gaze.

"Ideally, I think ten is a good number. Would you agree?"

"Oh, most assuredly. They can clean the kitchen, wash the car, mow the lawn, and fetch the remote. Quite useful."

"But if there were eleven," he mused. "You could field your own family football team."

"Very true. Girls and boys both, I assume?"

"Why not?"

Emma's gaze darted between them before she shot him a glare. "You two planned this, didn't you?"

He laughed. "Not at all, Sunshine. But your mama winked, and I was pretty sure she was putting you on."

Ellen took a prim sip of her wine while John chuckled.

"You give me no credit for good sense, Emma Grace. I know you were reluctant to bring Blaze over because you thought I'd start planning a wedding. And as much as I might like to do that for you someday, I'm not going to start envisioning wedding bells the instant you move back to town and start seeing someone. Gracious. Now that we have that out of the way, would anyone like dessert?"

Everyone did. They ate banana pudding that was sweet, creamy, and delicious and talked for another hour before Blaze and Emma said their goodbyes.

He'd had one beer, water, and a coffee, but he felt

drunk on his feelings as he drove them back to the Sutton building. He liked her parents. Liked Sutton's Creek. Liked the life he was leading here, even when it involved clandestine parts he wasn't allowed to talk about.

That thought made his gut twist. He liked Emma most of all, and he couldn't tell her the truth. He hated that more than anything. Hated lying about what he'd been doing the night Chance got hurt.

"It wasn't bad, was it?" She sounded relieved.

He glanced over at her. She was watching him with big blue eyes, and he wanted to stop the truck, drag her into his arms, and kiss her right there.

"It was great. Your parents are good people."

"I didn't realize my mother was such a joker."

She almost sounded sad.

"Is it a bad thing?"

"Her joking like that? No. But me not knowing?" She hesitated. "It reminds me how long I've avoided being home and how much I missed. I should have returned more often."

He hadn't asked her before now, but it was an opening, and he was going to take it. Helped keep his mind off his own churning thoughts.

"Care to tell me why you were avoiding it? You seem happy here, you have great friends, and your parents appear to be normal. I know that's not always enough by the way."

"It's all true." She studied her lap. "My parents are great, the extended family—who you've not met yet—is great. Though Great-Aunt Bernice is a little crazy. My friends are great, and life here has always been good. I was teased in school for being exceptionally nerdy and awkward, but it wasn't anything that scarred me for life. That's not what made me stay away, though."

He waited, sensing she was working up to it in her own time.

"I had a baby brother. He died in his crib when I was nine. SIDS."

His gut twisted at what that must have done to the happy family he'd witnessed tonight. "I'm sorry."

"Thank you. I remember my mother crying all the time, my dad with red eyes as he tried not to cry. I remember wanting to be with her, sit in her lap, have her attention, and she wasn't able to give it. I was nine and I didn't understand. Of course I understood my brother was gone, and I cried too. I wanted to fix him, which is where I think my desire to be a doctor came from. Or maybe it's in the blood and I always would have wanted to do it."

She shrugged. "Mama did the best she could, I know that. She was depressed for a long time. She got better with medication, and I got her back again. But then my panic attacks started when I was twelve. Who knows why? Fear of something happening again, fear of being alone. Fear of dying in my bed at night the way Jay did?"

"Baby," he said, his throat tight. He could imagine that little girl in her pink canopied bed, her heart racing with fear, chills shivering over her body. Not understanding why, thinking she was dying.

He reached for her hand and squeezed.

"I started to work really hard to get the best grades, make my parents proud. I was a serious kid made even more serious by tragedy, and it made me believe things that only a kid would think were reasonable. I thought if I was a perfect daughter, then nothing bad would happen to me or them. And I guess I also thought I had to make them miss my brother less by being good enough for both of us."

He thought he understood. "You wanted to escape because the pressure was too much."

She sucked in a breath and nodded. "Yep. Pressure I put on myself, which makes absolutely no sense. I felt like I could breathe when I wasn't living in Sutton's Creek."

"And now?"

"I'm still working on it. But I'm enjoying being back. I love seeing my family, love having Rory and Theo nearby. I love the historic district and the downtown, the coffee at Kiss My Grits, the library, the shops on the square, Piggly Wiggly, and Clarence's barbecue. I even love kooky Colleen and her mystical shop of crystals and Tarot readings."

He wanted to ask what else she loved. He didn't. Instead, he lifted her hand to his lips and kissed it.

"I'm glad you're here, Emma. I'm glad I met you, even if the circumstances weren't the best."

She smiled softly. "I'm glad, too. You are definitely one of the parts of Sutton's Creek I enjoy."

He'd take it. For now.

Chapter Forty-Six

THE SEX BETWEEN THEM THAT NIGHT WAS BLINDINGLY HOT. There were no other words for it.

Emma had teased him about conspiring with her mother as they'd walked into the building. She'd shrieked with laughter as he'd tossed her over his shoulder and carried her upstairs with a firm hand on her ass.

They'd lost their clothes in a trail to the bedroom and then he was inside her, driving her across the mattress while she moaned and begged him for more.

The sex was hard and soft that night, dirty and sweet, and Emma saw constellations behind her eyelids again and again.

He wore her out, wore himself out, until they found themselves in the big clawfoot tub in the bathroom, lit candles on the vanity where Sassy couldn't yet jump, soaking languidly while sipping Monkeynaut from the same can.

Sassy had been set free to run around the apartment. She flew in to check on them sometimes, then bounded off again to chase one of the toys Blaze had bought her.

"Happy?" Blaze asked when Emma leaned her head back on the rim and closed her eyes.

He sat opposite her, his legs stretched on either side of her body. She sighed as she lolled her head to look at him. "Yes."

"Me too."

After telling him about her baby brother, her panic attacks, and the reason she'd wanted to escape Sutton's Creek, she felt as if a burden she'd forgotten she was carrying had been lifted from her shoulders.

Someone else knew why she'd wanted to leave, why she'd stayed away.

And he didn't judge her for it. Didn't think she was ridiculous or dramatic or crazy.

He'd said none of those things. He'd kissed her hand and told her he was glad she was there, glad that he'd met her.

Her baby brother had died, her mother had been depressed, and she'd started having panic attacks. Then she'd bargained with herself in a way that only a kid could that being the best at everything meant she wouldn't die, too.

Being home from college, or during the holidays when she'd been working, sleeping in her childhood bed, had always blurred the edges of her regimented life in a way that made her apprehensive. She'd known by then she wouldn't die in her sleep like Jay, but it still brought all that childhood anxiety to the fore.

Moving into the Sutton building the first week she was home had been just what she'd needed.

Blaze had been what she'd needed.

"Would you really want a lot of kids if you got

married?" she asked, thinking about his banter with her mother.

His eyes glittered in the candlelight. "Not a lot. One or two. Or none if that's how it turned out. Not sure I know how to be a dad if I'm honest."

Her heart ached for him. "I don't know if that's entirely true. You have a strong protective instinct, and that's probably the first thing you need. After that, I think it's something you figure out."

"Maybe so."

She ran a toe along the inside of his leg. "Any man who saves kittens and lets them sleep on his chest all night isn't going to be a bad father. Pretty sure I'm right about that."

His grin made her toes curl and her belly tighten.

"Why are you asking?"

She studied the way the candlelight lit his face, the dark hair that had curled at the ends when the bathroom had still been steamy. He made her heart throb and her body tighten in anticipation before melting like hot wax beneath his touch.

"Just making conversation."

"Okay. How about you? You want kids, or is that your mother's dream?"

Her throat tightened. "I think it'd be great with the right person. But it's okay if it doesn't happen. I'll be fine with it, but not sure she will."

"You could adopt. There are kids who need families pretty badly."

She thought of him as a child being dragged away from the kittens he'd considered his by his mother. She'd never met the woman, didn't know anything about her other than she was a drug addict, but Emma didn't like her. At all.

"That's true."

His fingers circled her ankle before skimming upward, along her inner thigh, almost to her aching core, before sliding back down again. "There are things I wish I could tell you, Emma. But I can't. I need you to know that."

Her heart gave a painful thump in her chest. "I wish you could, too. Does it have anything to do with the other night?"

He didn't pretend not to know what she was talking about. "It does, and that's more than I should admit. It's not my choice, though."

Emma swallowed. "Is it illegal? What you're doing?"

"I would never do anything illegal without a damned good reason that had nothing to do with personal gain and everything to do with saving lives. Ever."

"That's not really an answer, Blaze."

"I know, babe. It's the only one I can give."

She nibbled the inside of her lip. "That's an answer a fanatic could give, you know."

"I do. It's up to you if that's good enough for you. If you want to end this, I'd understand."

The thought of ending what they had made her stomach churn. She didn't know what he was doing, the things he couldn't tell her, and yet she knew he was a good man. Believed it with every ounce of her being.

Safe.

Emma pushed up to her knees and went to him, straddling his hips. He was already hard and her insides liquefied just thinking about what they were going to do.

She bent to kiss him, her lips skimming his softly and then harder. He gripped her ass in his hands, fingers splaying over her cheeks, one tracing along the seam of her body and making her gasp.

"Need a condom," he growled.

There was a fluttering in her belly, and lower. "Simon always used a condom. But I've tested clean since I was last with him, and I have an IUD."

He gazed up at her, his eyes hooded. "I haven't been with anyone in a very long time, and always with a condom. But damn, I want to be inside you bare. You have no idea. You sure you're good with it?"

Emma lifted herself up, careful not to put too much pressure on her sore tendon, and reached for his cock, positioned it so she could slide onto him. Their eyes held while she lowered herself until she was full of him.

"More than fine," she whispered.

"Fucking hell," he grated, gripping her hips and keeping her still when she would have moved. "You feel like heaven, Emma."

If her heart beat any harder, she'd pass out. Except there was a large, well-endowed man between her legs and she wanted to feel every moment of what he did to her. She let her gaze slide down his chest, over those washboard abs, down to where his cock disappeared inside her.

Glorious. It was glorious.

"You can move now, babe. Or I will."

His voice was raspy and raw, and she loved the way it scraped over her nerve endings. She lifted herself with her thighs, sank down to the root of him, over and over again as the sensations inside her grew so big she didn't know if she could contain them much longer.

"Fuck, you're gorgeous."

He splayed a hand over her back, brought a nipple to his mouth, and sucked while she rode him faster. Water splashed around them, splashed over the edge of the tub. It was hot and sexy and incredible. She'd never had such wild, passionate sex, never known how desperately she could want another person.

"Oh God, I'm close," she gasped. "So close."

"Come for me, Sunshine."

Blaze sucked her other nipple, put his hand between them and plucked at her clit until her voice was lost, stuck in her throat as she threw her head back and came in wave after wave of shattering pleasure.

Then she collapsed against his shoulder, her body too heavy to hold up.

But he held her. Held her hard and tight as he thrust upward, deep and sure, slamming into her until he stiffened.

"Fuck, Emma," he groaned, bowing his body up into hers until he was spent.

They deflated like a balloon as he took them down into the cast iron tub, leaning back to cradle her. He was still inside her, still hard, as she settled against his chest and closed her eyes.

Utterly spent. Utterly happy.

Utterly in love.

Chapter Forty-Seven

"Do you have the faintest idea what the fuck you're doing?"

Ghost glared at him, arms crossed over his chest, pewter eyes flashing fire.

There was an answering fire in Blaze's gut. "No, but I know you don't throw this kind of thing away. Emma is special."

He'd eaten with her family yesterday, listened to her spill her secrets, and lost himself in sex with her. The best sex of his life.

Because it was with her.

Emma Grace Sutton was an addiction. Not the kind he'd always feared, being the son of an addict, but the best kind.

Still scary, since she could leave him swinging in the wind tomorrow when she realized he wasn't worthy of her. But the high he got from being with her, being inside her, was gonna be worth the pain.

Or maybe she'd fall for him, he'd marry her, have that kid, and live happily ever after.

Why the fuck not?

Ghost closed his eyes for a split second before glaring again. "No family ties. No serious relationships. Sound familiar? Makes it easier to operate. If we have to disappear, or sacrifice our lives, there'll be no Medals of Honor, no warrior's burial. And there'll be no explanation. You want that for her?"

Blaze swallowed. He didn't have to answer because Ghost raked a hand through his hair and plowed on.

"Jesus, you're getting serious with this woman. You had dinner with her family. You live in their building. You gave her a kitten. Not to mention plastering yourself to her on the dance floor in the Dawg Friday night and those lovesick expressions you two wore when I wouldn't move chairs. Can't you just stick to fucking her?"

Blaze's gut tightened with anger. "Prefer you don't use words like that when talking about my woman. *Sir.*"

Ghost tipped his head back and widened his arms to the sky as if beseeching the Almighty. "His woman. Holy shit, you hear that? By all means, have sex with her. Nobody cares about that. What I care about is you getting *involved.* Setting up house with a woman and having to explain things to her *and her family*, having her *observe* things. *That's* what you aren't supposed to fucking do!"

Blaze knew the others could hear them. The range was empty except for the six of them. It was Sunday and they typically had shorter hours and a skeleton staff, but Ghost had called all of them in for a meeting.

Then he'd motioned Blaze into the SCIF and told the rest of the guys to wait a minute.

That's when Blaze knew he was about to get his ass reamed. He didn't care.

"Respectfully, sir, I don't see what the difference is

between seeing a woman regularly for sex or actually caring for one. Nobody told us we had to be monks. I'd have remembered that."

"Maybe they should have. Be a helluva lot easier if we could all keep our dicks in our pants."

"Could be useful having a doctor around, sir."

Ghost fixed him with a squinty stare. "First, knock it off with the 'sir' shit. Second, are you actually suggesting we bring the doc in and tell her we're in Alabama on a top secret mission to keep this country safe but she can't tell anybody or we'll all get in trouble?"

It did sound a little out there when he put it like that.

"Not quite. But hear me out. Emma sewed up Chance. She wasn't happy about it, but she didn't tell anyone. If she knew a little more—who we are, that we're on a mission, that it's important—then we might have someone who can perform more than field medicine looking after us if something goes wrong. She was an ER doctor."

"We can't *afford* for anything to go wrong. We're a skeleton crew doing Ghost Ops as it is." He blew out a breath, his nostrils flaring.

He called for the other guys to join them. They filed in, shooting sympathetic looks at Blaze.

Ghost stood with hands on hips, looking like he could chew nails. "Diana Corbin's breathing down my neck over these break-ins. She's pissed as hell her blood tests were inconclusive, by the way. Told you it'd be fine," he said to Chance as an aside before eyeing them all again. "Here's how it's gonna go, fellas. I don't care who you sleep with. I can't stop you and I don't feel like trying. If you sleep with the same woman every night and dance with her at the Dawg, that's your business. But we aren't calling it a relationship, you feel me? There's too much at stake and we can't risk compromising the mission."

"What if I want to marry her?" Blaze asked as everything inside him rose in rebellion.

The room went silent.

Ghost blinked. "Do you?"

"I dunno. Maybe."

"She means that much to you?"

He could deny it, or he could go ahead and admit the truth. To himself and to these men he respected.

"I don't know what love feels like, but I think this is probably it. I wanna wake up with her every morning, see the smile on her face when I bring her coffee and kiss her. I wanna listen to her laugh at Sassy's antics and watch her blush when I whisper something naughty in her ear. And I damn sure want to find that asshole who's terrorizing her and rip his head off. Then I'm gonna make damn sure nobody ever hurts her again."

"I'm no expert, but sounds like love to me," Ghost said.

"I don't want to get you in trouble, but I've never… This has never happened to me before."

Ghost leaned his head back on the chair he'd sank into. "Hell, I'm already in trouble. You think they chose me for this assignment because of my winning personality? No, they chose me to run this because they know I'm the right bastard for the job. I admit this is a curveball I didn't see coming, but I shoulda known at least one of you assholes would find Southern women irresistible."

Blaze looked at his teammates. They were all wearing grins.

"I still have a shot," Chance said. "She called me handsome."

"Fuck off," Blaze growled back.

Chance laughed. "Dude, you're a lucky fucker. I know she prefers you. Just like to see you riled when you think about her going out with me."

"Any of the rest of you harboring deep feelings for a woman you haven't told me about?" Ghost asked with a fresh glare.

"Not me," Seth said, hands in the air.

"Nope," Ethan chimed in.

Kane snorted and gestured to his body, running his hands up and down in the air. "Not about to shut down this magic ride for one woman. I like the thrill of the new too much."

"Chance?" Ghost asked.

"Me?" Chance pointed comically at himself. "Of course not, boss. I'm allergic to commitment."

"Good. One of you in love is enough to deal with. I'm happy for you, Shadow. Really. But I can't have you distracted. Date the doc. Shack up with her and give her a litter of kittens if you want. But let's keep weddings and engagements until after we've completed this mission successfully, okay? There's nothing more important."

Blaze's throat burned. It wasn't the freedom he'd wanted, but it was more than he'd expected. "Yes, sir."

Ghost leaned back in his chair. "Let's get down to business. I sent the package we lifted to Washington so they could analyze it. On the surface it's a shipment of microprocessors.

He hesitated. "What I'm about to say, I'm not authorized to reveal. I'm doing it anyway because I think keeping my team in the dark is bullshit. What you've been asked to do—to give up—means you deserve to know. Especially now that Blaze here has fallen for the doc."

A chill slid down Blaze's spine. He glanced at his

friends, knowing they felt the same. That their team leader, a man who'd been a top Army officer and second in command of the Hostile Operations Team, was willing to go against his orders on something this important said volumes.

About his trust in them, about his belief in the mission, and about his willingness to do whatever it took to get the job done.

Blaze already had mad respect for the man. If he could offer to have Ghost's baby, he'd do it. He was pretty sure everyone in the room felt the same.

Ghost threw down the pen he'd been tapping and looked them in the eye. "We're here because of a top secret national defense system known as Athena. Satellites with the capability to create what is essentially a protective shield over the continental US. It prevents other nations from launching missile attacks, nuclear or chemical. It's even designed to prevent an EMP weapon from taking out our grid and sending this country back to the 1800s, which is a threat that grows bigger every day. Everything about how this project works is centered in Huntsville. The researchers, the software engineers, even the rockets that will deploy the satellites. Athena has been one-hundred percent effective in small-scale tests. When it's operational, nobody can launch ICBMs at us. Not Russia, not North Korea, not a future rogue state. Nobody."

Kane whistled. "That's some space-age techno shit right there."

Ghost nodded. "It's revolutionary. Considering the instability in the world right now, this system is critical to our national defense. Ideally, we'd deploy the system and the president would inform other heads of state that we have it. But someone leaked the existence of the project, and now it's in jeopardy. Enemy agents are actively working to sabotage it while also trying to steal the technology for themselves.

"It's a shitstorm and we're in the middle of it. If an enemy gets the tech and deploys the system first, they can launch a nuclear strike anywhere in the world while remaining impervious to retaliation. This technology in enemy hands would change the global balance of power in an instant and put our people at risk of annihilation."

"Good God," Chance breathed. Blaze was pretty certain they all felt the same.

"Right. *That's* why we're here. The president needs a way to act quickly, without informing Congress or waiting for a consensus from squabbling partisan leadership, and we're it."

"Why us though?" Seth asked. "Why not the CIA, FBI, or Homeland Security? They're bigger and have more resources. And this is a pretty huge fucking deal. The potential impact is enormous."

"Because we're ghosts. Because we're fast, good, and expendable if the shit hits the fan. Easy to deny us, call us rogues, if this mission goes tits up. We're outside of the normal bounds of operations. We can be made to disappear or made examples of. Something to remember when going home to your pretty doctor every night."

That hit home in a way Blaze hadn't expected. Was it right to involve her in his life when the stakes were so high?

"We're not going to let that happen," Ghost added. "Because we're good and we're gonna get the job done the way we're meant to. As for the microprocessors, they were intended for the command and control network. And of course they're programmed with a backdoor that would allow someone to steal information and potentially take control. There's a real shipment expected in the next few days. Washington speculates this rogue shipment was meant to be switched with the legit processors before being sent onward to Griffin Research Labs. That's where the command and control software is designed and tested."

"Where are the processors we tagged?" Seth asked.

"Still at Royal Shipping. The legit processors will come through them as well, which means someone there has to be involved. If not with the actual sabotage of the project, then they're being paid to make the switch without caring why."

"What do we do now?"

"We'll make sure the switch doesn't happen. We've got to go back in and destroy the microprocessors we tagged."

"Timeline?"

"Washington wants it done yesterday. Which means we gotta plan and execute this thing as soon as possible."

"Anything else we need to know, boss?" Seth asked.

"Yeah. Make sure the op is foolproof. If Diana Corbin has her way, the FBI's going to be squatting outside Royal Shipping from now until the cows come home. We've got to get in and out fast. And nobody's getting fucking shot this time, you hear me?"

Chapter Forty-Eight

It was late morning when Emma woke alone. She pushed herself upright on her good arm and frowned. Then she vaguely remembered Blaze kissing her on the forehead earlier and telling her he had to go to the range.

She stretched as she reached for her phone, wincing at the pull in her tendon as she did so, and looked at the time. Shock rolled through her at the display. Nearly ten.

She *never* slept that late.

But staying up late with Blaze, talking, making love, sleeping, waking to talk some more and make love again, had taken it out of her.

That and the way she'd stressed so hard over dinner with her parents. But it had turned out fine.

One of her favorite parts was Blaze and her mother playing off each other without any prior agreement to do so.

She hadn't loved it at the time, but she did now. It meant that Blaze was comfortable with her parents, and they seemed to like him too.

Her heart ached as she thought about all they'd said

and done last night. She didn't know where they were going, but he'd given her the chance to end it. More importantly, he'd said he didn't want to when she'd asked him.

Maybe it was crazy to throw herself headlong into this thing with him when there were still things he hadn't told her, *couldn't* tell her, but she didn't really have a choice.

She loved him.

And that meant she was sticking by his side until she had a damn good reason why she shouldn't.

Yeah, it was scary. Yeah, she was worried. But going about her business without him, seeing him around town, and not being able to touch him or kiss him was too shattering to contemplate.

So she was in it, and she hoped like hell it didn't explode in her face.

Emma let Sassy out and padded into the kitchen, where she found a note from Blaze that said all she had to do was turn on the pot for fresh coffee. Emma grinned to herself as she hit the button. She was sure it was a goofy grin as she hugged herself and went over to open the curtains.

The sun shone brightly. It was still slightly chilly outside in mid-March, and the wind swayed tree branches, but the promise of short-sleeve weather was evident in the daffodils sprouting all over the downtown area. Easter was still a month away, but the daffodils, tulips, and hyacinths would be in full flower by then.

Emma had missed spring in the south the past few years. Chicago was still windy and cold and would be for quite some time. Hell, it'd been cold in May every year she'd been there. She'd grumbled her way through it, eager for June when it finally got warm enough to feel like she wasn't going to freeze her Southern ass off.

After she'd poured a cup of coffee and picked up Sassy, who purred as she snuggled in close, Emma set about fixing toast one-handed. Sassy swiped at it as Emma lifted the buttered slices to her mouth, and she laughed and called Sassy a tyrant before setting her down again so she could race across the living room and bat one of her balls around.

Her phone lit up with an incoming call from Theo. Emma swiped to take it.

"Hey, what's up?"

"I was wondering if Rory is with you."

Emma's blood chilled. "Not with me. She isn't answering her phone?"

"No. We were supposed to meet at the Dawg at nine-thirty to go over the receipts for the week, but she didn't show up. She usually calls if she's running late, but I haven't heard from her. I thought maybe she'd stopped to see you and lost track of time because y'all were gabbing."

The thread of panic that uncoiled inside her was icy cold. If Rory weren't diabetic, Emma wouldn't go from zero to a hundred on the worry scale so quickly.

"I haven't talked to her since last night. You need to get to her house and make sure she hasn't had a problem with her insulin."

"That's my next move. I'm already headed for the car."

She could hear his booted feet traveling down the stairs of the building where the Dawg was located.

"I'll meet you there. I need to grab some supplies just in case, but I'll jump in the car and be right behind you."

She wasn't supposed to leave the apartment without Blaze, but she wasn't going to sit inside while her dearest friend in the world might have a potential medical emergency.

Sure, she could call 911, but they were farther away than she was. She could be there in five minutes. It'd take an ambulance ten.

Insulin pumps were extremely reliable, and Rory was a pro, but it was always possible to fail to get the cannula into the skin properly. She could think it was fine when it wasn't, and that's where the danger came in. If she didn't get her doses on time, she could go into diabetic ketoacidosis and be confused or lethargic and too tired to insert the pump properly.

Emma didn't think Rory was that careless with her insulin and glucose monitoring, but stuff happened, and Emma would rather act than find out later her friend could have used her help.

Emma dressed quickly and headed for the door. She called Blaze on her way downstairs to the practice.

It went to voice mail.

She frowned and tried again as she unlocked the door and went inside for a medical kit and insulin supplies.

Voice mail.

Emma's heart hammered as she went outside alone. She hadn't been without an escort in a while now, and it was odd. But the parking lot was bright, and Colleen waved from her table on her rear patio where she was chain-smoking cigarettes after smudging the area. Emma's car was parked in a slot where Colleen would see her as she got inside.

If Simon was waiting, Colleen would know it.

Emma waved back, unlocked her car, and tossed in the bag, looking at the back seat where her belongings used to be piled high but no longer were thanks to Blaze, and got inside to start the vehicle.

She tried Blaze again as she fired up the car and drove out of the lot.

Voice mail.

"Blaze," she said when the beeping stopped. "Theo hasn't heard from Rory and we're afraid she's had an incident. She's diabetic, which you may not know, and this could be an emergency. Theo is headed to her house. I'm right behind him in case she needs help. An ambulance would take too long, and I'm not staying in the apartment and wringing my hands when she could be in trouble. I'm sorry. I hope you understand. I'll call you when I know more, and I won't go anywhere alone, I promise. Theo will be with me at her house, and if we have to go to the hospital, I won't leave until it's safe. I—"

Emma swallowed as she cut off the words. She'd started to say *I love you*, but maybe now wasn't the time. Blaze would be upset when he got her message, even if he understood why she'd disobeyed instructions, and that wasn't the time to hit him with those words.

So she calmly told him she'd see him later and hung up the phone.

When she turned into the long, tree-lined driveway that led to the house where Theo and Emma had grown up, her heart was beating fast and hard. Theo hadn't called her to say he'd found Rory yet. She didn't know if that was good or bad.

Bad if he'd found her and she wasn't responsive.

Good if he'd found her and was giving her hell for not answering her phone or keeping their appointment.

Emma hoped it was option two, though she couldn't

imagine what would keep Rory from calling her brother or answering the phone.

Theo's car was under the big oak tree in front of the house. Rory's car wasn't there, but it could be in the detached garage her grandfather had built behind the house about twenty years ago.

Emma grabbed her bag and supplies, slipped her phone in her pocket, and hurried up the steps to the front door. She didn't bother knocking. She simply turned the knob and stepped into the living room.

Into a nightmare.

Chapter Forty-Nine

The scene inside Rory's house wasn't what Emma had expected when she'd walked through the door. She'd been thinking of Rory asleep, too lethargic to change her insulin pump, and planning how to treat her friend and get her to the hospital for monitoring.

But Rory's pump wasn't the problem.

The man standing in the cased entry to her dining room *was*.

"Hello, honey," Simon said. "Did you miss me?"

Emma's insides turned liquid. It was everything she could do not to puke up her guts then and there.

Rory sat on her couch, hands bound in front of her body, a piece of duct tape over her mouth. There were tear streaks on her cheeks, but her eyes flashed angrily as she glared up at Simon. It was quickly replaced by fear, which tore at Emma's heart.

Theo was handcuffed to a chair and his mouth was also duct taped. The hatred shining in his eyes would have made Emma recoil if it had been directed at her.

Simon didn't care. Of course he didn't.

"Let them go. Your problem is with me, not them."

Simon swaggered toward her. His hair was reddish brown, and his eyes were green. Contacts, of course. He was also wearing clothing that made him look stocky.

Her insides were ice. Stocky, the way Rory had described her engineer from Huntsville.

He had his gun in his right hand, hanging loosely at his side. Emma considered her options.

She could swing the bag at his head. Step into his space if he got close enough and try to disarm him before he knew what she was doing.

But he stopped just out of range and lifted the gun until it was pointing at her chest.

"You're fucking right my problem is with you. I *chose* you, Emma. I had a plan, and you fucked it all up."

Emma's heart hammered. "How did I fuck it up? You're the one who hit me."

His expression was vicious. "You weren't supposed to leave. I said I was sorry. Isn't that what you bitches like? A contrite, apologetic man who kisses your ass and tells you how sorry he is and that he'll never do it again?"

"You weren't sincere."

Simon snorted an ugly sound. "I told you what would happen if you left me. I'm here to make good on that promise, baby."

Emma shuddered at the way he called her baby. It was nothing like the warmth and kindness of Blaze's endearments.

"Then let Rory and Theo go and take me."

She hoped he'd come closer, but he didn't. His eyes narrowed. "You think I don't know you've been taking self-defense classes from that gorilla you've been fucking? Your girlfriend here likes to talk. She told me all about your boyfriend and your classes. So if you're hoping I'm going to move closer so you can stomp my instep or swing that case at my head, you're gonna be disappointed. Drop the case and get on your knees, arms out in front of you, hands together."

"Please, Simon. Please let them go. It can be just you and me."

"Where's the fun in that, Emma? Knees, now. Case over there," he said jerking his head toward the wall.

Emma set the case on the floor and slid it over. Then she dropped to her knees, feeling hopeless and helpless at the same time.

All the training. All the preparing. It was nothing when your assailant had been planning his revenge and used your friends against you. Maybe Blaze could have ended it with a toothpick and a deadly look from twenty paces, but she was powerless to stop this man she'd once thought cared about her.

She held her arms out, hands together. Her eyes pricked with tears.

"Who are you?" she asked. Because there was no sense in pretending he was Simon Marsh any longer.

He arched an eyebrow as he stuffed the gun in his pants and cuffed her. He yanked the cuffs tight enough to make her wince then stepped back again.

"Who am I? I'm the man who's gonna make you bleed for interfering with my plans. It's been three years since I killed Simon Marsh and took his money, and though I couldn't take your identity, I was so close to getting into your accounts and draining you dry before I moved on."

Her throat squeezed. He was psychotic. She'd always thought it was about control and possession, not this. He'd wanted money. All that time, he'd wanted money. It wasn't about romance and jealousy. It never had been.

"Nothing to say, honey?" He came over and gripped her chin in his fingers hard enough to leave a bruise. "I was planning to enjoy watching you overdose on Fentanyl. How sad it would have been when they found you, the poor stressed doctor who couldn't take the pressure of her job anymore."

"Why?" she whispered. "What did I ever do to you?"

He shoved her away from him and she fell, landing on her bad arm and gasping at the pain. He didn't answer her as he went over and put the gun against Theo's head.

Emma's heart climbed into her throat. Rory screamed behind the tape as tears began to streak down her cheeks again.

"I'm trying to imagine the best way to do this," Simon said as Theo glared. "Do I kill all three of you here and make it look like a murder suicide? Or do I draw this out and make you suffer for the extra work you've caused me? If you'd just cooperated, Emma, you'd be the only one dead, and I'd be in a new city, enjoying my life with all that doctor money you have stashed away."

"Let them go and you can have it all. I'll give you the logins to my accounts. You can walk away with everything I have."

His smile was evil. "That's the first sensible thing you've said. But money first, Emma, or I'll splatter his brains all over this wall. Hers too."

She was sensible enough to know he'd kill all of them as soon as he had the money. She had to delay, hope that Blaze got her message soon and came looking for her.

Because he would. She didn't doubt that at all.

"I-I don't have the logins with me. I don't carry them around. I'd need to go to the office. My computer is there."

He seemed to think about it. When he moved away from Theo, she nearly sobbed with relief.

But then he stalked over to Rory, shoved her backward on the couch, and dragged her shirt up to expose her insulin pump.

Emma screamed when he ripped the pump out.

He dropped it and stomped down with his boot. The plastic cracked. Rory looked stunned. Theo was screaming behind the tape, and Emma started to beg.

"Shut up," Simon hissed. Then he laughed. "This is how I was going to get you here in the first place. I knew you'd drop everything to save her if I told you I was going to let her run out of insulin."

Theo was on his knees, moving toward Simon. His hands were tied but he was still a big guy, and he was determined. Simon didn't bother to shoot. He kicked Theo in the face, sending him sprawling backward. Blood poured from his nose and mouth as Theo tried to get up again.

But Simon kicked him in the belly so hard that blood sprayed from his mouth. Emma screamed again and levered herself up to launch at Simon.

Theo tried to rise, but then he just sort of crumpled and didn't move again. Simon went over and grabbed Rory by the arm, dragging her upright as he pointed the gun at Emma.

"Get up. You and Country Barbie are coming with me. If you're lying about the computer, she dies. If not, I'll let you give her a shot."

"Please," Emma said as she levered herself up on legs

that shook. "Theo needs medical attention. Let me tend to him."

"I'll tend to him with a bullet if you don't fucking do what I tell you."

His face was evil. Insane.

Emma swallowed. She wanted to help Theo, stop him from choking on his blood, see if he'd ruptured an organ when Simon kicked him. But if she pushed, he'd die that much quicker because Simon would put a bullet in him.

"I'm sorry. I'll do whatever you want."

"Thank you." As if he wasn't crazy. As if he was thanking her for passing the salt and pepper. "We're walking out the door and getting into my car. Then we're going somewhere safe and waiting until dark."

Emma's heart plummeted to her toes. Safe? There was no such thing as safe so long as they were with him.

But Theo was alive, and so was Rory. The clock was ticking as her body didn't get insulin, but she had a few hours before DKA set in.

"I-I need my medical bag," Emma said as he motioned to the back of the house where the garage was. "I need insulin."

Simon's eyes narrowed. She was positive he was going to tell her to leave it.

Then he shrugged. "Fine. Make it quick."

Emma hurried over and grabbed the bag. It was awkward with her hands cuffed so tightly together, but she managed it. She shot a look at Theo. He was breathing because there were bubbles in the blood coming from his nose.

But she had to turn her back on him, no matter how hard it was to let him suffer, and go with Simon before he did something even worse.

All she could do now was pray that Blaze got her message. Soon.

Chapter Fifty

THE GHOST OPS TEAM HAD A PLAN. IT'D TAKEN THEM A few hours to put it together, but they had clearance from Washington, and they were going in tonight.

But first he was going home to eat and sleep for a couple of hours.

At least he was supposed to sleep, but he'd probably end up balls deep inside Emma first.

It had been hours since he'd spoken to her. He'd left her asleep in his bed when he'd been called in this morning. He hadn't given her an explanation other than he had to go to the range.

He'd think about tonight's excuse later. But at the moment, all he wanted was to get home and make sure everything was good with his girls.

"Damn, dude," Chance said as they went into the range to retrieve their phones from where they'd stashed them while they worked in the secure area. "So you fell for the doc. Never saw that one coming."

Blaze laughed. "Me neither, I promise you."

"Gotta be honest, I thought you had a type. Big tits and ass, lots of curves. That's not Emma."

Blaze's belly tightened. "Emma's gorgeous."

"She is, but she's more the wholesome, nerdy-girl-next-door than the knockout. What I'm saying is I like her, and I think she's good for you."

Blaze stopped to look at his friend. "Good for me? How?"

"You seem less in your head if you know what I'm saying. Like you're looking forward to living instead of thinking about the past."

Blaze felt as if someone had thumped him over the head with a hammer. "You thought I was hung up on the past?"

"Weren't you? We all know what happened in Afghanistan. Your team, your injuries. The road to recovery. Then you didn't want to stay in the farmhouse with us. We all know why."

Blaze's heart was throbbing. "You do?"

Chance put a hand on his shoulder and squeezed. "I've had nightmares about some of the stuff we've seen, but they don't last. Some things circle back sometimes, but it's not consistent. I think yours were pretty consistent."

His mouth was dry. "Ghost knows?"

"Of course he does. We all do."

And Ghost had still wanted him for the team. His friends weren't afraid to operate with him. They didn't think he was a liability or that he'd slip up and get them killed. Even if the stakes were higher in some ways for this mission than for any other.

They trusted him. Believed in him.

So did Emma.

"I didn't know. Thought I was hiding it pretty well."

"You were hiding it. But I think Emma must be helping because, like I said, you seem to look forward to living a lot more than you used to."

Blaze scratched the back of his neck. "I wish I could tell her I'm still working for my country. It doesn't feel right to lie. Especially after the night she fixed you up."

"I know. I get the reason, but it makes it hard. At least when we were HOT operators, we could say we were subject to sudden deployments. Can't say it now, even if it's true."

Blaze pulled open the drawer where the phones were stashed. He found his and picked it up. The screen lit up with three missed calls from Emma and a voice mail. He hit the screen to play the message.

"Hey, Blaze. Theo hasn't heard from Rory and we're afraid she's had an incident. She's diabetic, which you may not know, and this could be an emergency. Theo is headed to her house. I'm right behind him in case she needs help. An ambulance would take too long, and I'm not staying in the apartment and wringing my hands when she could be in trouble. I'm sorry, I hope you understand. I'll call you when I know more, and I won't go anywhere alone, I promise. Theo will be with me at her house, and if we have to go to the hospital, I won't leave until it's safe. I—

There was a hesitation.

"Anyway, I'll see you later. Call me when you can. Bye."

"Did she call back yet? How's Rory?"

Blaze swung his gaze to Chance. He'd forgotten his friend was there when Emma said she was leaving the apartment to meet Theo at Rory's place.

"No, nothing." His voice was hoarse as he checked the calls again. "Just that message at 10:20."

He slid the button to call Emma back. It went to voice mail.

Chance was pale. "That was almost seven hours ago. She'd have told you how Rory was by now. Unless it's bad news…"

"Or she can't call." Blaze's gut churned. "She's not answering her phone. We need to get out to Rory's place."

Seth, Kane, Ethan, and Ghost filed into the room.

"What's wrong?" Ghost asked.

"Emma called about seven hours ago to say she was headed to Rory's place. Thought she might be having a diabetic emergency. She hasn't called again to say what happened or how Rory is, and she's not answering her phone."

"I didn't know she was diabetic," Kane said.

"I don't think any of us did," Chance said. Growled, really. "But something's not right. Emma would have called."

Blaze's blood was ice. "It's Simon. It has to be. Emma said that Theo was worried because he hadn't heard from Rory, which means he expected to hear from her and didn't. If something had happened to her and Emma had to stabilize her, she would have called to let me know. But she hasn't called and she's not picking up. Simon used Rory to lure Emma to him."

He was shaking inside. From fear, from anger. From icy determination to find his woman and put an end to whoever the fuck Simon Marsh really was. Because he knew Simon was involved. Felt it in his gut.

"We have to find them," Chance said. "That was seven fucking hours ago."

"I'm going to Rory's place." Blaze started for the door.

"Hang on a minute," Ghost called.

Blaze stopped in his tracks, resolute in refusing an order if Ghost told him not to go. Didn't matter they weren't technically in the military anymore. They were still operators for the US Government, and an order was an order. He wouldn't get court-martialed, but there would be consequences. He didn't doubt that.

And he was still going after Emma.

"We're all going," Ghost said. "And we need a fucking plan."

Chapter Fifty-One

It was growing dark. And it was cold. The temps dropped as the sun did, and Rory didn't have a coat. Simon had hustled them out of her house and into a small SUV without letting Rory get anything warmer. She was dressed as she must have been dressed this morning, in yoga pants and a sweatshirt with tennis shoes. Her hair was pulled back in a ponytail, and her eyes were red-rimmed.

They'd both been crying over Theo, wondering if he was dead, if someone would come to the house and find him, save him.

Blaze.

He was her hope. But it had been hours now, and she didn't know if he even knew she'd left the apartment.

Simon had taken her phone away. She didn't know if he'd tossed it or simply turned it off.

He'd slapped duct tape over her mouth when he'd put her in the truck. Then he drove them into the woods that bordered the Tennessee River. It was technically a part of the Wheeler National Wildlife Refuge, which meant there were no houses or buildings anywhere.

There was a tent, however. It was off the track, a camouflage structure that Simon had obviously been staying in judging by the number of food wrappers and plastic bottles littering the area. It also explained why they hadn't found him.

He'd shoved them inside, chained their legs together so they couldn't walk, then left again. Because their hands were cuffed in front of them instead of behind, they'd been able to carefully peel the tape off their mouths. They hadn't done it immediately, but the longer Simon stayed away, the braver they got.

Now they huddled together for warmth and talked.

"I'm sorry," Emma said. "So damn sorry. I didn't know he would involve you and Theo. I thought he was after me."

Her voice broke, but she swallowed it back and reached for her friend's hand, squeezing.

"It's not your fault," Rory said. Was she slurring? Fear rolled down Emma's spine. If Rory went into DKA, the window to help her would shrink fast. Simon hadn't brought the medical kit to the tent. It was still in the truck with him, wherever he'd gone.

A sense of helplessness and anger roared through her.

"How do you feel, honey?"

"Tired."

Emma sniffed back tears. "Blaze will come looking for us. We're going to be okay, Ror."

She wished she believed that was true, but she didn't know how Blaze would find them out here. She'd grown up in Sutton's Creek and had a good idea where they were, but he wouldn't know where to look. There were lots of paths into the refuge, lots of unspoiled wetlands. It could take days to find them.

And that would be too late for Rory. She'd be dead by then. Assuming Simon didn't come back and kill them both first.

"I hope he finds Theo first. Do you think he's still alive, Idgy?"

Emma swallowed. If Simon hadn't gone back to finish him, then it was possible. Not that she was saying that to Rory. "He was breathing when I picked up the bag. He could have an internal injury, but if it's a slow bleeder, he'll still be alive. They'll find him, Ror. Blaze will go there first because that's where I told him I was going. Theo might need surgery—probably will—but he's young and strong and tough."

"Casey was so nice to me. He didn't look a thing like you described Simon. And he was shy, too. Sweet. I had no idea."

"What happened?" Her throat ached as she asked the question.

"I was getting ready to go meet Theo. And then he was there, inside my living room. I was surprised, but I still didn't figure it out. He was holding roses."

She'd seen those on the dining room table. They'd still been in the plastic.

"I asked what he was doing there. He said he couldn't wait to see me, that he wanted to surprise me. It was weird, but I didn't listen to the creepy feeling I had. What kind of guy wants to surprise you and then walks into your house like he owns the place? Plus I was sure I locked the door, but he said it wasn't locked. Said he'd knocked and I hadn't answered so he'd come inside. I hadn't even told him where I lived, but I know that kind of thing is easy to find. It felt wrong, but I wasn't sure what to do. I hesitated too long. Then he grabbed me and put the cuffs on. I still didn't know he was Simon then. I started to scream, and he taped my mouth. Then he told me all about you and how he was going to make you pay."

Emma shuddered. "He's a psychopath. I wish I'd realized it before I ever went out with him." She lifted her hands, curled them beneath her chin, and rocked back and forth. "How did I let him kiss me? Touch me? How did I sleep with him and *not know* he'd murdered someone?"

"Not your fault, Idgy. He's very good at being what he wants to be. He had me fooled, too. I thought he was a sweet, shy, engineer type who loved rockets and had a bad breakup."

"How did you meet him?" Because she had to know the approach Simon had taken. She wanted to know.

"He came in the Dawg one night, a bit late, and sat at the bar. He seemed kinda sad, so we talked. He said it was the one-year anniversary of his girlfriend leaving him for another guy. And, you know, since the same thing happened to me, I had a lot of sympathy. I told him about Mark in a vague way, he told me about Grace—" Rory looked horrified. "Oh shit, he said her name was Grace! And I still didn't figure it out."

"There's no reason you should have. There are a lot of women named Grace."

"Maybe not, but I feel like I should have known it was wrong. I should have stopped listening to my head and went with my gut and just grabbed Chance's ass, like you told me to. I can't stand him, but it *would* have been hot for a while. But I was so sure I needed a guy completely opposite of what I usually go for. A nice, quiet guy. Not a loud-mouthed, muscled, irritating, rugged meathead who makes butterflies dance in my belly."

"When we get out of here, you need to stop avoiding Chance and just go for it."

Rory shook her head sadly. "*If* we get out of here."

"Don't talk that way. We're going to get out. Simon wants access to my accounts. Until he gets my laptop, we're safe. And that means Blaze has time to find us."

She didn't really know they were safe until Simon had her laptop and access to her accounts, but she had to believe it for now. Had to have hope to hold onto.

For all she knew, he'd gone to get the computer now. He had her keys. He could figure out which one opened what. He also knew which laptop was hers. The one with the stickers all over the case. He could find it and bring it back. She doubted there was internet access out here, much less phone access, but he could take them somewhere until he had a signal, breach the accounts, and dump their bodies.

Emma shivered.

"I hope you're right." Rory shivered, too. "I don't know how Blaze or his guys can find us, but I hope they do. I'm thirsty, Idgy. And my stomach hurts. It's been hours without insulin."

"A few," Emma said, trying not to let any hint of panic creep into her voice. "But we have time."

"Not as much as I'd like. Trauma can accelerate DKA. I think we've had a bit of that today."

"We have, but it hasn't even been twelve hours. Most signs of DKA occur within twelve to twenty-four hours of your last insulin injection. We have loads of time, Ror."

Rory huddled closer. "You're right. Fuck stress. I need to be okay so I can lay one on Chance the next time I see him."

Emma laughed. It was either that or cry. "Absolutely. Kiss the stuffing out of him."

Rory sighed. The light was almost gone now, and it was hard to see anything in the confines of the tent. Emma tried not to think about crawly things in the swampy wetland nearby.

"Are there things you wish you'd done before, you know, the end?"

Emma thought about deliberately misunderstanding what Rory meant, but she didn't have the energy to pretend. "I wish I'd told Blaze I love him."

"Oh my God, really? You're in love?"

"Yes." Her voice was very small. Not from shame or embarrassment, but from fear.

Fear of all the things she'd never get to say to him if he didn't find them. Even if he didn't return her feelings, it would have been nice to get them out in the open.

"I'm happy for you. Do you think he feels the same?"

"I don't know."

"Then you gotta get out of here so you can find out."

In the distance, she heard an engine. Rory went still, too. Emma willed her heart to stop pounding so hard so the blood wouldn't throb in her ears, but it didn't happen. The vehicle came closer.

"It's him," Rory whispered. "I recognize the sound. Dammit, we should have made a plan for how to jump on him or something. We could strangle him with these chains."

Emma hoped Rory was wrong about the sound, but she didn't think her friend was. If Rory hadn't been tending bar and running the Dawg with Theo, she'd have probably worked on cars. She had an old Chevy truck she'd kept running well past what others had thought was its time.

"We aren't fast enough, Ror. We're too tangled. He thought about that, believe me."

"Where is Blaze? Or Chance? What good are those One Shot guys if all they do is teach classes but can't actually rescue people who need it?"

"A joke? Really?"

Rory nudged her shoulder. "Did it make you laugh?"

Tears filled Emma's eyes as the engine shut off. "You always make me laugh, Aurora Harper. And though I didn't say it enough the past few years, or show it, I love you. I'm so sorry I got you into this."

"Love you, too, Emma Grace Sutton. And you didn't get me into anything. That'd be the sicko psycho out there. I'd love it if a cottonmouth bit him before he reaches the tent. It would be nice to watch him gyrate on the ground as he dies."

"We can hope."

A door slammed. Then Simon whistled a tune as if he had no cares in the world, branches crunching beneath his feet as he walked toward the tent.

Chapter Fifty-Two

A lot had happened since Blaze got Emma's message.
Though he and the guys were on a tight countdown to
infiltrating Royal Shipping later that evening and
destroying the microprocessors, they'd dropped everything
to go find Emma.

When they'd reached Rory's place, the sight of Emma's
car had formed a knot in his gut. Theo's car was there too.
The front door wasn't locked, and he and Chance
breached it with a single nod of understanding and guns
drawn. Kane and Ethan were on the back door. Ghost and
Seth had gone to check the barn and outbuildings just in
case.

What they'd found inside the house dropped Blaze's
heart into the soles of his feet. Theo Harper lay in a pool
of blood, breathing but barely. They'd assessed him for
injuries while Kane dialed 911.

It looked like he'd been kicked in the face with a boot.
There was a print on his cheek, and his nose was broken.
That didn't explain why he was passed out, though.

As soon as the call was made, Chance was on his feet,

running throughout the farmhouse. When he skidded back into the room, his eyes wild, Blaze knew.

Rory was gone, too. He'd known Emma wouldn't be there, because Simon wasn't done with her yet, but the fact he'd taken Rory was chilling.

"What's that?" Blaze asked as Chance bent down to pick something up off the floor and examine it.

"I'm gonna guess it used to be an insulin pump. Jesus, Blaze. He tore her pump off her body. She's not getting insulin."

Blaze's blood chilled. "It's how he's getting Emma to do what he wants."

Or got her to do what he wanted. Emma and Rory could both be dead by now. It had been hours since Emma's message. Hours that Theo had lain there, bleeding and slowly dying.

Ghost and Seth returned. "Rory's truck is still here," Ghost said. "The driveway is gravel and so's the parking pad. No way to tell if any other cars were out there."

Seth was tapping his screen. "Emma had her phone when they left here. It's turned off now, but the last place it pinged a tower was south of town on Church Road."

"What's out there?" Blaze asked.

"Just a second, I'm pulling up a map… A few houses out that way, and a church, but it dead ends before the river. There's a road on here, probably a dirt road, that branches off before that. It goes into the Refuge."

"He could have taken them into the woods." And maybe dumped their bodies. Blaze ground his jaw. No, he refused to believe they were dead. Not until they found bodies would he give up on Emma and Rory being alive. "We need more information. Where does that road go? What's out there?"

"Let me try something," Seth said. He tapped away on his phone, pinching and expanding until Blaze thought he'd lose his mind. Chance paced. Kane sat on the floor beside Theo, and Ghost went out onto the front porch to make a call. Ethan was also at work on his phone, probably looking at Google Maps and getting an idea what lay down that road into the Refuge.

Blaze shoved a hand through his hair and joined Chance in pacing without realizing it. If he lost her now, if he didn't get to tell her how he felt…

If he didn't get to marry her and maybe have that kid with her.

Jesus. It was too much. He'd spent his life not belonging, wanting out, not getting close to anyone except his brothers in this room and on the front porch.

But then Emma came into his life not too long ago and somehow she was it. The one. The person who soothed all those dark spaces in his soul. If he lost her now, he'd lose a piece of himself he'd never get back.

Didn't matter how fast it had happened or how crazy it was to be in love with her so quickly. This thing between them just *was*.

"I think I have something," Seth said, sounding excited. "I checked for any other phones that pinged the tower at the same time Emma's did and how close they were to her phone. I've got one. It's pinged the tower a few times today, though not from the same location as where Emma's phone went dead. It's moved around town, even went across the river to Decatur."

Blaze didn't know how Seth managed to get that kind of information so quickly, and he didn't care. That spark inside him was hope, and he clung to it like a lifeline. "Where is it now?"

"Last ping was south of town on Church Road."

"That's where he's got them. In the woods." Hope rose like a phoenix, swelling and burning inside his belly. "If he's going back out there, he hasn't killed them yet."

Chance started for the door. "Then what are we waiting for? Let's go get Rory and Emma and make Simon Marsh wish he'd never been born."

The sound of an ambulance cut through the night, coming closer.

"That's what we're waiting for," Ghost said, coming back inside. "You think Rory will forgive you if you leave her brother before he's inside that ambulance?"

Chance closed his eyes for a second. Blaze's gut churned. He put a hand on Chance's shoulder and squeezed.

"That's the woman I love out there, but we need to figure this out, brother. We can't just go charging in without a plan. We've got one shot to get them back. Because if we don't do it right, he'll kill them when he hears us coming."

Ethan looked up from his phone and grinned. "Did someone say *plan*?"

Chapter Fifty-Three

SIMON SHONE A BRIGHT LIGHT IN THEIR EYES AS SOON AS he entered the tent. Emma and Rory both turned their heads to shield their vision, but they were going to see spots for a while.

His intent, no doubt.

She heard the clank of the chains as he unlocked them and then felt his hand on her arm, roughly dragging her toward him. "We're going to get that laptop now."

"What about Rory?"

She didn't see the blow coming but she felt it when he slapped her across the face. Hard.

Just like he'd done once before.

Tears sprang up behind her eyes as her cheek throbbed.

"She's staying here."

"You need to let me give her an insulin shot."

"No."

"Simon, please. I know you hate me, but she's innocent. Let me give her a shot before we go."

"You really care about her, don't you?"

Emma sensed danger in his tone. "I'm a doctor. Of course I care," she said, trying to sound neutral.

"I could shoot her, you know. Or strangle her with those chains. Strangulation is always so exciting. Maybe I'll fuck her first and make you watch."

Rory made a sound, but Emma didn't dare turn her head.

"If you kill her now, I won't cooperate. You won't get into my accounts or get any of my money. I have a trust fund, you know. I'll tell you how to access that, too."

She didn't have one, but she was banking on him believing her. Her parents had always done well, and they lived in that big house in the historic district and owned the Sutton Building, but they weren't so wealthy she had a trust fund. Her parents believed in giving back to the community and donating generously to charity, and they believed that Emma would be successful without saving every dime they made to pass on to her someday.

They *believed* in her.

She wished she could tell them how much she loved them one more time.

"You're lying," Simon said after a long hesitation. "You never said anything before."

"Why should I? My salary was enough for a nice apartment, and I had what I needed. And I've always been careful about my family money. It's not the kind of thing you tell people if you want to know if it's *you* they care about. You've seen the house, the prime real estate on a corner lot in downtown. My family founded the town. Do you think they wouldn't have made a lot of money over the past couple of centuries?"

He was still silent, caressing the hunting knife he'd

strapped to his belt, and her pulse ticked away the seconds. Had she pushed too far?

"Okay, I won't kill her yet. But once we get that laptop, if you're lying to me, I'll carve her up and make you watch. Then I'll carve you into pieces and feed you both to the gators."

Emma's heart throbbed as bile rose in her throat. Alligators weren't common in the Refuge, but fifty-six of them had been released into the wild back in 1979 when they were believed to be an endangered species. They'd obviously thrived and multiplied over the years.

Simon laughed. "Gators in this part of Alabama. Who knew? There's a nest of them close by. One of those suckers is at least fifteen feet long. He's gonna be real happy when he tastes you two. Let's go."

He jerked her out the door and yanked her to her feet once they were outside the tent. "You get that laptop, and I'll let you give her a shot. Not before."

Emma's legs tingled as the blood rushed back into them. Her cheek ached and she still saw spots in her vision, but she could also see the path to the green Santa Fe Simon was driving. His grip on her loosened as he shoved her forward. She hadn't seen his gun, but that didn't mean he didn't have it.

She imagined all the scenarios in which she could do something to disable him. Her hands were cuffed tightly in front of her, and her arms ached. The bad one throbbed with pain because she hadn't been able to stretch and move it properly.

She could knee him in the balls. Gouge his eyes out with her thumbs. Stomp his instep.

She could also punch him in the kidney. Once he went down, she could kick him in the head, knock him out. Steal his gun, steal his keys from his pocket and hope the handcuff keys were there too.

Then she'd go free Rory from the cuffs, have Rory free her, and they'd drive out of here.

The vision of doing so was enough to make her want to sob.

Emma stumbled on a root, and Simon kicked her, pushing her forward. She lost her footing, crying out as she fell into the soft dirt of the forest, unable to stop her fall quickly enough with her arms cuffed together.

Emma lay on the ground, breathing in dirt and wet leaves, listening to the deafening sounds of the forest all around, fearful and angry and desperate all at the same time. Her body hurt, her arm most of all, and she thought for the briefest of moments how it would be so nice if she passed out so she wouldn't feel any pain or fear.

"Get the fuck up, bitch," Simon growled. He was standing nearby, not reaching for her. She rolled onto her back and stared up at the tops of the trees. She thought she saw stars peeking through, but maybe not.

A shape moved in the darkness. Or did it? She sucked in her breath, her heart pounding.

Could be a bear. Could be a bobcat. Or just a deer.

Or maybe nothing at all. Green spots still swam in her vision from the bright light he'd shined in her eyes, no matter how much she tried to blink them away. They were improving, but not gone yet.

Anger started to build low in her belly, a fire of injustice and determination not to die this way. She wanted Simon to feel the terror she'd felt, to feel the pain he'd inflicted on Theo.

The pain he'd inflicted on the real Simon Marsh. It was a very un-doctor-like thing to feel, but she didn't care.

Some people were beyond redemption. Beyond kindness.

Simon bent over to grab her arm. Emma knew this was her best chance. Maybe her last chance. He had no intention of returning to let her give Rory insulin. No intention of letting her live beyond the moment he'd gotten access to her accounts. He'd kill her and leave her body in her father's office for him or Brenda to find.

Maybe Simon would force her to take that overdose he'd talked about earlier and make it look like she'd killed herself.

Except for the cuff marks on her wrists and the bruise to her cheek, though he probably had a plan for that, too.

She wasn't going to let him do it. Not without a fight.

He bent closer, reaching for her.

Emma kicked with all her might.

Simon grunted as she landed a hit. But it hadn't landed where she wanted it to, because he was on her in an instant, one hand around her throat, the other balled up into a fist that crashed into her jaw.

Pain exploded. A second later, the forest did too.

Chapter Fifty-Four

Blaze and his team had listened to Ethan's plan then piled into Blaze's truck and headed for Church Road and the Refuge. They'd parked just inside the entry so they could move on foot.

After donning their assault vests and night vision gear, they'd miked up and crept into the forest.

They didn't want Simon to hear them coming, though they'd banked on him not being as quiet as he should be for complete stealth. Not only that, but there was the scent from his car engine so recently driven down the dirt track that didn't belong. They followed that and followed their ears, picking up on sounds that weren't made by the creatures who lived in the forest.

They'd gone about a mile into the Refuge when they got their break. Light flashed in the darkness as someone used it to see where they were going.

The team found Simon's SUV around a bend in the track. Not too far from the road, two shapes moved. Blaze could see Emma with her wrists cuffed together stumbling through the roots and leaves.

And then she tripped and Simon kicked her. Blaze's blood boiled.

They could have shot him from this distance, but they'd agreed it wasn't the smartest choice considering they were supposed to stay under the radar. They would only take the shot if there was no other choice, if Simon was about to shoot his hostages or one of them. Otherwise, they were taking him alive and turning him in.

Not Blaze's first choice but the right one. Simon, whoever he was, would never be free to harass Emma again.

Simon reached for Emma to drag her to her feet, but she kicked out, hitting him in the leg. Blaze's heart was in his throat as Simon grabbed her by the neck and punched her.

He gave the signal to his team.

They erupted, dragging Simon's attention from Emma long enough to distract him. Blaze sprinted toward him, prepared to tackle him to the ground and beat the living shit out of him, when he saw a flash of steel at Simon's waist.

But it wasn't Simon who'd pulled the knife. It was Emma.

Simon turned to grab her, but Emma braced both hands on the hilt and drove the hunting knife into the center of his belly. Simon's eyes went wide as blood poured from the wound. Then he toppled to the side like a house of cards. Emma kicked him away and crawled toward Blaze.

That was the moment he realized he'd called out to her.

He skidded to a halt, dropped to his knees, and dragged her into his arms, his heart pounding like he'd run ten miles instead of a few yards. "I've got you, Sunshine. I've got you."

She fisted his sleeve, her body shaking as if she'd been thrust into a freezer for an hour. But then she pushed back and tried to stand.

"Rory. I have to give her an insulin shot. There's a medical kit in Simon's car."

Chance emerged from the tent, his eyes wild. "Need a fucking key to unchain Rory. Where is it?"

"His pocket," Emma said, nodding toward Simon as Blaze helped her to her feet.

Ghost was the one who retrieved the keys. He unlocked Emma first, then took the keys to Chance, who ducked inside the tent and back out again with Rory in his arms.

Kane brought the medical kit from the Santa Fe. Ethan shone a light on the area and Emma dug into the kit while Kane held it, searching for what she needed. She was splattered with Simon's blood, her split lip was bleeding, and her eye was swelling where he'd punched her.

But damn, she was the most beautiful thing Blaze had ever seen. Emma Grace Sutton had nerves of steel when she needed them. She could have been an operator if she wasn't so dedicated to saving lives.

Chance had carried Rory over, but he didn't put her down as Emma pushed up her sweatshirt and inserted the needle in her belly.

"This will make you feel better," Emma said.

Rory smiled. "I know. You're the best, Idgy."

Blaze thought she slurred a little when she spoke.

"We have to get her to the hospital. She's in the early stages of ketoacidosis, and she'll need to be monitored."

"Theo," Rory rasped.

"He's alive," Chance told her. "We found him and called an ambulance."

"Oh thank God," Emma breathed.

"We should probably get one for that asshole," Seth said, jerking his chin toward where Simon lay.

"He won't be needing it," Emma replied. She looked at her hands as if noticing the blood for the first time. "I drove that knife into his heart."

Blaze tugged her against him as she turned and put her face in his chest. She started to cry as the adrenaline drained away.

"You did what you had to do," Blaze told her, stroking her hair. "You had no choice."

She lifted her head to look at him. Her eyes were watery, her cheeks streaked with tears. "I could have incapacitated him. But he hurt Theo, hurt Rory, and he killed at least one person that we know of. All I wanted was for him to never hurt anyone again."

"Honey, you tried to stop him when you kicked, but you missed. What if you'd aimed that knife somewhere else and missed again? What if it wasn't enough to stop him and he used the opportunity to kill you? You did what you had to do. You didn't do the wrong thing."

She stared at him for a moment. Then she nodded and pressed her face to his chest again. He bent to kiss her head, her temple, squeezing her to him as if he'd never let go.

"Let's get you out of here, get Rory to the hospital."

"Yes, please." She stepped back, intending to walk, but Blaze wasn't having it. He scooped her into his arms and carried her, same as Chance carried Rory.

Rory's head was against Chance's shoulder, her arms

around his neck. She didn't argue with him for once. It made Blaze think she was sicker than she looked.

Emma started groping along Blaze's neck, around to his shoulders, down his chest. Then she felt his face, the helmet, the NVGs.

"What's going on, Blaze? What are you involved in?"

"Nothing but a group of friends with some military training who decided we weren't letting that fucker take you away from me."

It was true, but so much more than that. "You guys just happened to keep all this stuff when you left the military?"

"Nah, we bought our own. We run a range and training facility, babe. Talking about providing some survival training in the future, so we got this stuff to practice."

He thought he heard Ghost snort. Well, sure, it was a bad lie, but what the hell else was he supposed to say?

"Okay, babe," Emma said, laying her head against his shoulder. "Whatever you say. But when I get cleaned up and we're home again, I'm gonna need to hear some more about this new training thing you've got going."

He thought that was it, but she continued.

"Oh, and how you managed to find us in the dark while dressed like commandos and making no sound until you wanted to. Seems like a really interesting story."

"Not that interesting at all," Blaze said lightly.

Ghost snorted again.

"Come on, honey," Blaze said, setting her on her feet beside Simon's car. "Get in so we can take you both to the hospital and check on Theo."

Chance opened the door to put Rory in the back seat. Emma still hadn't moved to climb into the passenger seat. She was so small standing against the side of the car, her body slight compared to his, her limbs delicate. Simon could have snapped her bones if he'd wanted to.

"I want to touch you," she said. "But I've got Simon's blood on me. And I want to say something, but not like this."

"We'll talk, Sunshine. Soon as we get you and Rory seen, okay?"

She nodded. "I knew you'd find me, Blaze. I never doubted you. I-I thought you might not find me in time, but I knew you were looking."

He wanted to kiss her, but he settled for kissing her forehead since her lip was split and she was in pain. "I'll always find you, Emma. Always."

Her breath hitched in. "*Always* sounds like a mighty long time, Blaze."

"Yeah, I know."

"And it's what you meant to say?"

He nodded. "Never been more certain of anything. Now get in the car so we can get on with the rest of our lives."

Chapter Fifty-Five

"How did you find Doctor Sutton out there in the woods, Mr. Connolly?"

The woman questioning them was the same woman Emma had seen in the Dawg. The one that Alex had gone to talk with. She was blond and pretty, but if she had any emotions, Emma hadn't seen evidence of it yet.

The fact she was an FBI agent was a little scary, but then Simon had been wanted for murder in another state. Alex had called Chief Vance to tell him where to find Simon's body. Next thing she knew, the FBI was at the hospital asking questions.

Blaze's expression didn't change as he squeezed her hand. "I tracked her phone, ma'am."

"And you and your coworkers"—she emphasized the word *coworkers*—"basically went out there to find your missing girlfriend and her friend and rescue them. Why didn't you call the police for help?"

"Ma'am, I wasn't thinking clearly. All I knew was that I needed to go get Emma and Rory before Simon Marsh could hurt them. And I was pretty sure I'd get there faster."

"Do you know who he really is?" Emma asked.

Diana Corbin's pen paused on her notebook. "We think he's someone named Kyle Hollis, but we'll have to do DNA testing to be sure. Hollis is wanted for at least three murders we know of, and suspected of two more, but he disappeared before he could be arrested."

"And became Simon Marsh," Emma said.

"Yes. He had a pattern of draining his victims' bank accounts, but Marsh was the first one whose identity he assumed."

"How did he get away with stealing money like that? Wasn't there a digital trail?"

"Offshore accounts, mostly. The FBI was closing in on him when he disappeared three years ago. I have to stress that what I've just told you is sensitive information. It'd be best if it doesn't get out just yet."

"Of course," Emma replied. "Do you think there will be any charges related to his, um, death?"

"It's doubtful. Considering the scene at Aurora Harper's house and her condition, the condition of Theodore Harper, plus your experience in the woods and physical injuries, I think self-defense is an easy call."

Emma didn't want to breathe a sigh of relief, but she felt it deep inside. Yes, she'd been defending herself, but she didn't know how the authorities would view it.

Special Agent Corbin closed the notebook. "I think I have everything I need. Thank you both for your time."

She got up and left them in the small hospital room where Emma had been brought for treatment. Rory had been admitted for observation, and Chance had gone with her. Emma didn't know how that would turn out, but he'd been at her side since the moment he'd carried her out of that tent, and he hadn't left yet.

And Rory wasn't fighting him. A good sign in Emma's opinion.

It was still a long way from grabbing his ass and seeing where things went, but it was a step in the right direction.

Theo was in ICU after surgery, but his prognosis was very good. He'd had internal bleeding, like she'd thought, when his intestines were damaged from Simon's kick. Fortunately, his bowel hadn't been perforated. His nose was also broken, and they'd reset that, too. He was going to look like hell for a while, poor guy. Knowing him, he'd use it to his advantage with the ladies.

"She didn't believe you were telling the complete truth about finding us, did she?" Emma asked after a short interval to be sure they were alone.

The door to the room was closed and she felt safe talking in a low voice. Blaze hadn't let go of her hand.

"No, I don't think she did."

He'd shed the commando gear. They all had. They'd driven to where his truck was parked and he and Chance shed the helmets and goggles, the vests, the weaponry, in record time. They'd put it in the truck and kept on going to the hospital like it was nothing. When the rest of the guys showed up at the hospital, they'd been back to normal as well.

Kinda like superheroes who stepped into phone booths and came out significantly changed.

"Is that a problem?" she asked.

"Could be. But there's no law against what we did. If we'd shot him, it'd be a lot trickier."

"You guys seem a lot like a team of Navy SEALs or something."

Blaze shook his head. "SEALs always get the glory. You realize every branch of the military has special forces, right? The Army has Delta Force, Green Berets, and others you probably haven't heard of. The Air Force has pararescuemen, otherwise known as PJs. The Marines have Force Recon. Yet the SEALs get the glory."

Emma stared. "That's your answer?"

"It is right now."

He leaned forward and kissed her cheek. The one that didn't throb. Emma wanted to kiss him so badly, but that wasn't happening with the way her lip hurt every time she talked. Simon—or Kyle—had gotten in a pretty hard punch before he'd been distracted by Blaze and his guys.

She'd used that distraction to grasp his knife and pull it from the sheath. She hadn't known what she was going to do with it until he turned to attack her again. When she'd been training with Blaze, she'd always wondered what she would really do if she was attacked. If she'd be afraid to act, if she'd hesitate when the moment came.

She hadn't hesitated at all. She'd driven that knife home hard and deep, and she'd known when she did it that Simon wasn't walking away. She'd killed him and hadn't felt remorse.

She felt twinges of it now because she'd once liked the man she'd known as Simon, and she'd thought he cared about her. But the things Blaze had said to her kept going through her head. He'd told her when they were training that you couldn't pull your punches.

You had to act fast and strong, and you had to aim to kill or maim with everything you had. That was how you survived.

It was how *she'd* survived. She'd saved herself, and she'd done it with Blaze's help.

Rory was alive, and Theo was too. That was more important to her than whether or not she could have deflected the blow and injured Kyle enough to stop him.

"I want you to hold me," she said, feeling the need to be in Blaze's arms.

"I'd have to climb into that bed with you. I don't think the nurses will appreciate it."

Emma flipped the blanket back. "Don't care. Please."

Her clothes were gone except her underwear, and they'd given her two cotton hospital gowns for now. One for the front, one for the back. It was more modest than a single one would be, but it wasn't great.

Blaze levered to his feet, all six-foot-two plus of him, and settled beside her on the mattress. He wrapped his arms around her, and Emma turned into his chest, a sob she hadn't expected escaping her.

"Hey, Sunshine, it's okay," he murmured against her hair. "I've got you."

She curled her fingers into his T-shirt. "I know." She hesitated. "Did you mean what you said before?"

She couldn't say the words. Couldn't ask him if he'd really meant to imply he wanted to be with her always. What if he'd said it in the heat of the moment or just because she was hurt and vulnerable?

He tipped her chin up, gently, and forced her to look at him. "Every word. I'm just a boy from Oklahoma with a shitty mother and no roots, a boy who enlisted in the military and did everything I could to make myself better. I'm a man who's made it to thirty-five years of age and never, not once, thought I needed another human being so much I couldn't breathe without her."

Her heart skipped.

"I love you, Emma Grace Sutton. I've never said those

words to a woman before. Never wanted to. When I said I'd always find you, I meant *always*. You're it for me. The woman I want to marry. The woman I want to raise a sassy kitten with, and maybe a kid if life blesses us that way—though I don't care if it doesn't. I want *you*. Just you." He sucked in a breath. "I know I don't have a lot to offer, and there are still things I can't talk about, but damn, Sunshine, I fucking love you so much, and I want to be with you for as long as you'll have me."

Emma couldn't speak. Was she dreaming? Had she taken a blow to the head? Was any of this real?

"It's okay if you don't want those things," Blaze said softly. "I won't be an asshole who refuses to let you go. Told you I wouldn't blow up your phone when you gave me your number, and I still won't. But damn, I'll regret it for the rest of my life that I wasn't enough for you."

Her throat was tight, but his words broke through the barrier. She couldn't stand that he might think he wasn't enough.

"I love you," she said, because it was all she could manage to say. "I love you."

He looked stunned. "You do?"

Emma swallowed the knot in her throat. "Yes," she whispered. And then, stronger, "You're everything I ever wanted. You're tough and sexy and kind to animals, and I'm really sorry for how you grew up, but I don't care about your roots other than how it makes you feel. I want to slap your mother silly, but I also don't want to meet her because I already despise her. And I want you to do what you need to do, because I trust you, and tell me when you can. I've already figured out that the six of you are more than instructors at a range, but that's okay because I know in my bones that you wouldn't do anything terrible or illegal. And it must be important somehow."

He was looking at her like she'd sprouted a second head. Then he laughed. "Damn, Emma, that was a mouthful." He lifted her hand and kissed the back of it. "I love you, and I'm fucking glad you love me. But man, Alex is gonna be pissed."

As if he'd been summoned, the door opened and the man in question strolled in.

"How you feeling, Emma?"

"Like I went three rounds with a gorilla. But also pretty fantastic."

Alex's gaze went to Blaze for a second. "I see that."

Blaze nudged her. "Tell him what you just told me. About the range."

She repeated what she'd said, and Alex sighed. Then he closed the door behind him and walked over to the bed. "I'm gonna tell you something, Doc, but I need you to swear on this man's life that you'll never repeat it outside this room."

Emma bristled. "I'd never do anything to hurt Blaze."

"That's good, because hurting him would hurt all of us. What do you know about Navy SEALs?"

"Really?" Blaze asked. "SEALs again?"

This time Emma grinned. "He's got a thing for SEALs getting all the glory."

Alex shook his head. "It's true, but they seem to be the ones most people have heard of. That's why I asked." He took a breath. "We're like SEALs, but not. What we're doing is important. I can't tell you why, and I can't tell you who we work for, but when I say we report to the highest levels of government, that's who gives us our orders. Nobody knows the truth but the six of us and now you. If you don't keep our secret, it's our lives on the line, and that's not an exaggeration. Blaze loves you. Don't betray his trust in you."

Emma swallowed. "I would never. I won't tell a soul."

"Good." He held out a hand and she took it. "Welcome to the family, Doc."

"Thank you."

The door burst open, and her mother rushed in, followed by her father.

"Emma Grace," her mother cried. "Oh my baby girl!"

Blaze untangled himself from her and stood, kissing her on the forehead. "I've got work to do, babe. I'm gonna leave you to your parents. Let them take you home, and I'll see you later tonight, okay?"

She wanted to beg him not to leave, but she knew that whatever he had to do, it involved his team and that important thing Alex had just told her about.

"Be safe," she told him. "I love you."

He grinned. "Always, Sunshine."

Then he squeezed her hand and walked away to join Alex, leaving her to her gaping parents.

Chapter Fifty-Six

Blaze and the team broke into Royal Shipping, breached the container with the microprocessors again, and placed a charge inside. When they were positive that section of the warehouse was clear of guards or workers, they detonated it, destroying the contents.

Diana Corbin wasn't waiting for them when they cut the fence and went through it. She wasn't waiting back at One Shot, either. She was a little preoccupied with the Simon Marsh/Kyle Hollis case at the moment, which was a good thing for the Ghost Ops team.

When Blaze asked Ghost if he'd had anything to do with that when they were back at the range, he'd grinned before saying, "I made a phone call when we were at Rory's place. Suggested that Special Agent Corbin should head up the Simon Marsh investigation when we caught him."

A stroke of genius, really, because it had gotten her out of the way. Agent Corbin didn't appear to have the weight of the entire FBI behind her when it came to questioning them about Royal Shipping, which seemed to make it more of a personal quest. That was a good thing for their mission, but she could certainly be a problem in the future if she kept at it.

Something to worry about later.

It was nearly dawn when Blaze drove back to town, parked in the lot behind the Sutton building, and climbed wearily from his truck. Chance parked beside him. He didn't need to stay in Emma's apartment now that Kyle Hollis was dead, but he'd be there for another night or two at least. Blaze suspected that had everything to do with Rory, but he hadn't asked.

Blaze hadn't taken three steps when a voice called out, "Melvin is happy again, Mr. Connolly. I thought you should know."

Blaze turned to find Colleen Wright standing behind her building, smoking a cigarette. Damn, she got up early. Or maybe she'd had a séance and never went to bed.

"I'm glad to hear it, ma'am."

"Melvin said that you and Emma Grace should keep the rear apartment. He thinks the sunsets are spectacular from those west facing windows."

She couldn't see his expression, but he was sure she'd have laughed if she did. It was definitely one of surprise. "Thank you, ma'am. I'll take that under advisement."

"You be sure you do."

Chance was waiting for him. "Who's Melvin?"

"You mean you don't know about the Sutton building's ghost?"

Chance snorted. "Nope. There's a ghost?"

"According to Ms. Wright. He wasn't happy for a while but now he is. Which she assures me is a good thing."

"Does he, like, moan and rattle chains and shit?"

"Never heard him. I have no idea how she knows any of this or if she just has a very active imagination."

"Let's go with that one," Chance said with a tired laugh.

"Maybe we should consult her before the next op. Get some paranormal assistance. Or maybe she can hex Diana Corbin for us."

Chance just chuckled.

They reached the back door of the building and unlocked it. Blaze didn't know if Emma would be upstairs in bed or if her parents would have insisted she go home with them for the night. He'd hated to leave her at the hospital, but he'd had to.

It would be that way sometimes, but he knew they'd deal with it.

Emma was his. She loved him, which was a freaking miracle, and he loved her. And he was going to marry her. Maybe not for a few months, but her mother would need that kind of time to plan a wedding anyway.

When they got to the top of the stairs, Emma was standing in the open door. Blaze's heart thumped. He started to tell her she shouldn't be awake, shouldn't be there with the door open, but why not? Kyle Hollis was dead, and Emma was safe. She could open doors and walk outside in the open now without him hovering over her, though he still intended to do that as often as possible.

"Blaze," she said, that one word filled with all the joy he felt in his soul at the sight of her.

He opened his arms and she rushed into them, wrapping hers around him tightly. He bent to inhale the scent of her hair and pressed his lips to her temple. His cock was half hard, but it'd be a while before they did that again. He needed her to heal first.

Chance disappeared without a word, the door to the front apartment closing behind him as Blaze held his woman tight and thanked God she was alive.

He'd been so focused and busy he hadn't given himself a lot of time to process those moments when Kyle had been punching her. How close he'd been to losing her.

"I'm fine," he said. "Perfectly fine."

"Did your thing go the way you wanted it to go?"

He chuckled. "Yeah, textbook."

"Nobody shot or cut? No need for stitches or exams?"

"No, no need."

She stepped back and he got a good look at her face in the light starting to creep through the windows. Her cheek was a little swollen and her eye was black and blue. The cut on her lip was scabbed over.

He reached out and skimmed a finger under her jaw. "If he wasn't dead, I'd kill him for hurting you."

"But he *is* dead, and we aren't." She took his hand, wrapped his fingers in hers, and tugged him inside. "I want you, Blaze. I need you."

He shut the door behind him, his wayward cock swelling again. "I don't think it's a good idea, honey. He hurt you, and you need to rest."

"I have painkillers, and I've been icing my cheek and eye. My arm hurts where I strained the tendon again, but otherwise I'm okay. What I want, more than anything, is to be naked with you. I need to feel you inside me."

"Baby, we've got all the time in the world," he said. "I can wait."

"I want—"

"What?" he asked as she stared at him.

"You're exhausted." She shook her head. "You're right, we can wait. You need to get some sleep."

She pulled him toward the bedroom. Sassy came running from somewhere, and Blaze scooped her up as he followed Emma.

He set the kitten on the bed, shed his clothes, and climbed beneath the covers. Emma joined him, curled her body around his, and sighed as she stroked her fingers through the hair at his nape.

"I love you. Go to sleep."

"I love you, too." He was drifting off when something niggled at his memory. "Sunshine?"

"Mm-hm?"

"Would you go out with me?"

He felt her push up on an elbow. "What?"

"I never asked you out. I promised I wouldn't when you gave me your number in the hall that day."

"I think we've gone beyond a first date, Blaze."

"Doesn't mean I don't want one."

She grinned, then winced as the gesture stretched her lip. "Okay, yes, I'll go out with you."

"Excellent choice, Em. I'll make it worth your while, I promise."

She laughed. "You already have, babe. Oh, and before you fall asleep, my mother congratulated me on being smart enough to land you for a prospective baby daddy and future husband. Not that I encouraged any of that kind of thinking, but apparently telling you I loved you was enough for her."

Blaze squeezed her to him. "If I'm honest here, I think I'm the smart one because I landed you and your family. I never had one of those before, other than my guys."

"You've got us now. All the Suttons in your corner. Always."

He stroked his fingers down the indent of her spine. "Always is a long time, Sunshine."

"It sure is. How fortunate that we get to spend it together."

"Nowhere else I'd rather be."

For the first time in his life, he was home. Really, truly home.

Chapter Fifty-Seven

ONE MONTH LATER...

EMMA DIRECTED the delivery people on where to put the new furniture she'd picked out for their apartment. Blaze's couch and table had been donated to Daphne, who was renting one of the top floor apartments now that she'd been hired at One Shot Tactical, had a steady income, and people to vouch for her.

Emma didn't know Daphne's story, but she thought there was something sad in it. Daphne was friendly, but she didn't share many things about herself. Maybe she would once she'd lived in Sutton's Creek for a while. Most folks warmed up to the small-town environment.

The One Shot guys stayed busy with clients and training, and they sometimes worked odd hours. Emma didn't ask.

Rory had left the hospital after two days and returned to the Salty Dawg, finding a temporary chef to help out, and opening for business after a brief hiatus. Theo had been on bed rest for a couple of weeks, but he was back at the Dawg now too, though he tired out quicker than before. Still, the food at the Dawg was as awesome as always, and they stayed busy.

Rory had hired the guys to put up an alarm system and cameras at her house. Chance had wanted to do it for nothing, but Rory insisted on paying for their labor in addition to the equipment.

Emma sighed. She didn't know what was going on with those two, but they were back to hating each other. Whatever truce they'd had when Chance carried her from the tent had ended.

Emma had harbored such hope for that first week or two when Rory and Chance had seemed to get along so well. Chance was always visiting the Dawg, talking to Rory, and she was talking right back. Then it was over.

Emma never asked if Rory had followed through and gotten that Vitamin D from Chance. She'd been too busy getting her own Vitamin D. Repeatedly. Thoroughly.

Happily.

Emma shifted her thoughts back to Rory as her insides squirmed. Her normally bold friend hadn't said whether or not she and Chance had done the deed. Chance Hughes was not a topic Rory liked to touch on.

Once the delivery people were gone, Emma worked on arranging and rearranging some of the picture frames and artwork she'd bought on the floor. She wanted to make a gallery wall, and she wanted it perfect before they pounded the first nail into the wall.

She looked out the window at the rear parking lot. When Blaze had told her that Colleen said Melvin thought they should stay in the rear apartment for the light, she'd laughed. She'd already decided she liked this apartment better. Yes, there was a parking lot, but it wasn't too big or ugly. There were beautiful buildings all around, and the trees offered shade and greenery to look at. And she could see when Blaze was home, like now.

He parked and opened the door, climbing out onto the pavement. Colleen rushed from the rear of her building to say something to him. They stood there for a few moments, Colleen gesticulating and Blaze nodding.

He made Emma's heart thump every time she looked at him. He was handsome, masculine, and he made her feel both strong and protected at the same time. He held her tenderly, made love to her like a house on fire, and let her know every day how special she was to him.

They would get married next summer. She'd already told her mother, who was both thrilled to plan a wedding and sad it wasn't sooner. But then she'd said that it gave her plenty of time to plan the wedding of the decade in Sutton's Creek.

Blaze finished his conversation with Colleen and headed for the building. Emma scooped Sassy up and went to stand on the landing. When he appeared on the stairs, her heart squeezed.

"Hey you two," he said. "How are my girls?"

"Happy to see you," Emma replied. Sassy merely yawned. Blaze got to the top of the stairs and kissed them both before they went into the apartment and Emma put Sassy on the floor. She shot toward the new couch and jumped on the back of it.

"Looks good," Blaze said. "You were right about the color."

Emma went to the fridge and pulled out two beers. "Thank you. What did Colleen want?"

Blaze laughed as she handed him an icy can of

Monkeynaut. "Aliens. They're hovering over that big field off Church Road before you get to the Refuge."

"Of course they are. What did she want you to do about it?"

Blaze took a drink. "Film them of course. Set up some cameras, show her how to work them."

Emma shook her head. "Are you going to do it?"

"Not if I can help it. Can't your mother get her involved in the town planning committee or the beautification committee or something?"

"I'll ask, but I doubt it. Colleen dances to her own tune."

"At least Melvin is happy."

"He seems to be."

Blaze came over and hooked an arm around her waist, tugging her in close until they were breast to hip. "What about you, Sunshine? Are you happy?"

She set her beer down on the counter and hooked her arms around his neck. Happy? She was ecstatic. She loved Sutton's Creek, loved being home again, even loved working with her dad and getting to know the patients. She'd finally agreed to create her own office instead of using a makeshift one in the stock room.

Patients mostly called her Doctor now, but some slipped up and said her name. She'd come to believe that was part of belonging to a small town. She'd even decided she didn't mind being called Emma Grace by all who'd known her for her whole life. It was slow and Southern and flowed off the tongue when spoken by people whose accents were as thick as the corn in the fields in summer.

She loved it. Loved being home. Loved Blaze Connolly with every atom of her soul.

"Yes," she said, standing on tiptoe to lick his bottom lip. "I am *very* happy."

He set his beer down and hooked an arm behind her legs, swooping her up. "Then I'm about to make you even happier."

Then he carried her to the bedroom and made good on his promise.

———

THANKS FOR READING BLAZE! I hope you loved this start to a new series set in small-town Alabama! As you might imagine, Rory and Chance are NEXT! The question is… did they or didn't they….? Their book is called CHANCE: Ghost Ops.

SCAN THE QR code to join my newsletter list! Get information on sales, new books, and free content.

SCAN ME

Books by Lynn Raye Harris

Ghost Ops

Book 1: BLAZE - Blaze & Emma

Book 2: CHANCE - Chance & Rory

The Hostile Operations Team ® Books
Strike Team 2

Book 1: HOT ANGEL - Cade & Brooke

Book 2: HOT SECRETS - Sky & Bliss

Book 3: HOT JUSTICE - Wolf & Haylee

Book 4: HOT STORM - Mal & Scarlett

Book 5: HOT COURAGE - Noah & Jenna

Book 6: HOT SHADOWS - Gem & Everly

Book 7: HOT LIMIT ~ Ryder & Alaina

Book 8: HOT HONOR ~ Zane & Eden

———

The Hostile Operations Team ® Books
Strike Team 1

Book 0: RECKLESS HEAT

Book 1: HOT PURSUIT - Matt & Evie

Book 2: HOT MESS - Sam & Georgie

Book 3: DANGEROUSLY HOT - Kev & Lucky

Book 4: HOT PACKAGE - Billy & Olivia

Book 5: HOT SHOT - Jack & Gina

Book 6: HOT REBEL - Nick & Victoria

Book 7: HOT ICE - Garrett & Grace

Book 8: HOT & BOTHERED - Ryan & Emily

Book 9: HOT PROTECTOR - Chase & Sophie

Book 10: HOT ADDICTION - Dex & Annabelle

Book 11: HOT VALOR - Mendez & Kat

Book 12: A HOT CHRISTMAS MIRACLE - Mendez & Kat

———

The HOT SEAL Team Books

Book 1: HOT SEAL - Dane & Ivy

Book 2: HOT SEAL Lover - Remy & Christina

Book 3: HOT SEAL Rescue - Cody & Miranda

Book 4: HOT SEAL BRIDE - Cash & Ella

Book 5: HOT SEAL REDEMPTION - Alex & Bailey

Book 6: HOT SEAL TARGET - Blade & Quinn

Book 7: HOT SEAL HERO - Ryan & Chloe

Book 8: HOT SEAL DEVOTION - Zach & Kayla

———

HOT Heroes for Hire: Mercenaries
Black's Bandits

Book 1: BLACK LIST - Jace & Maddy

Book 2: BLACK TIE - Brett & Tallie

Book 3: BLACK OUT - Colt & Angie

Book 4: BLACK KNIGHT - Jared & Libby

Book 5: BLACK HEART - Ian & Natasha

Book 6: BLACK MAIL - Tyler & Cassie

Book 7: BLACK VELVET - Dax & Roberta

———

The HOT Novella in Liliana Hart's MacKenzie Family Series

HOT WITNESS - Jake & Eva

———

7 Brides for 7 Soldiers

WYATT (Book 4) - Wyatt & Paige

7 Brides for 7 Blackthornes

ROSS (Book 3) - Ross & Holly

———

About the Author

Lynn Raye Harris is a Southern girl, military wife, wannabe cat lady, and horse lover. She's also the New York Times and USA Today bestselling author of the HOSTILE OPERATIONS TEAM ® SERIES of military romances, and 20 books about sexy billionaires for Harlequin.

A former finalist for the Romance Writers of America's Golden Heart Award and the National Readers Choice Award, Lynn lives in Alabama with her handsome former-military husband, one fluffy princess of a cat, and a very spoiled American Saddlebred horse who enjoys bucking at random in order to keep Lynn on her toes.

Lynn's books have been called "exceptional and emotional," "intense," and "sizzling" -- and have sold in excess of 4.5 million copies worldwide.

To connect with Lynn online:
www.LynnRayeHarris.com
Lynn@LynnRayeHarris.com